**Also by Peter Lefcourt**

*Nancy Castro*

# The Deal

## A Novel of Hollywood

## PETER LEFCOURT

WASHINGTON SQUARE PRESS

New York   London   Toronto   Sydney   Singapore

ISBN: 0-7434-5644-0

First Washington Square press trade paperback printing January 2003

10  9  8  7  6  5  4  3  2  1

WASHINGTON SQUARE PRESS and colophon are
registered trademarks of Simon & Schuster, Inc.

For information regarding special discounts for bulk purchases,
please contact Simon & Schuster Special Sales at 1-800-456-6798
or business@simonandschuster.com

Printed in the U.S.A.

Politics is not an exact science.
—Benjamin Disraeli

Neither is show business.
—Charles F. Berns

# Preface to This Edition

Hollywood is a grim industrial suburb
populated by gangsters of enormous wealth. . . .
—H. L. Mencken, circa 1933

When I heard that my novel *The Deal*, first published in 1991, was being put back into print, I thought I might update certain contemporary references in order to make the book more resonant to the new reader. After all, it had been twelve years since I'd written it and seven since it had been allowed to drift out of print by another, less tasteful, publisher. Given the speed of social change in the modern world, twelve years is a very long time, and 1991 was, in many respects, another country.

With this concern in mind, I reread the book—an experience for a writer roughly similar to running into an old girlfriend late at night in a badly illuminated supermarket. You may turn and run, or you may discover, as I did, that though she has suffered a little of the inevitable gravitational distension that age brings, she remains a woman you would follow to the yogurt counter.

The other thing I realized in rereading the book was what those cynics, the French, have been telling us for centuries: *Plus ça change, plus c'est la même chose.* That is, with regard to Hollywood at least, only the numbers really change; the truth behind the numbers remains the same. The movie business has always been, and will always be, a crapshoot masquerading as a business masquerading as an art form.

Life during the first Bush administration already seems quaintly distant. Thirty million dollars was serious money for a movie; $500 a night for a hooker in Vegas was top dollar; Sylvester Stallone and Raquel Welch made movies happen; Zagreb was in Yugoslavia.

Today 30 mil is chopped liver for a major studio release; $500 is midmarket for a night with a working girl at the Monte Carlo. Sly and Raquel can't get arrested. And Zagreb has moved to Croatia.

I contemplated making changes: the film could now have a negative cost of $200 million; references could be made to Russell Crowe and Julia Roberts; and we could set the plot in Bulgaria. But I realized that in the ten months or so between the writing of this preface and the book's appearing, $200 million may be the cost of a straight-to-video Chevy Chase movie, Russell and Julia could be doing episodes of *Touched by an Angel*, and Bulgaria might have moved to Romania. *Plus ça change* . . .

So I have decided to offer *The Deal* to you in its original version, with all the names and numbers exactly as they were in 1991. In reading this book you may experience a certain nostalgia for the good old days when you could still get a cashmere sweater dry cleaned for $6.50, a Dolly Parton burger at a studio commissary, a two-bedroom house in Encino for $650,000, and 10,000 Yugoslavian dinars for one U.S. dollar.

But whatever the numbers, the tune remains the same. It's a high-wire act with the band playing "Hooray for Hollywood" on seventy-six out-of-tune bassoons. Bottom feeders like Charlie Berns can still find a brass ring in a banana split. And with respect to Mr. Mencken's observation above, all you have to do is substitute *lawyers* for *gangsters* and you'll be right on the money.

# The Deal

One of the downside risks of producing your own suicide is that you probably won't get the opportunity to reshoot. It's pretty much a one-take business. Barring, of course, a complete disaster, in which case you won't be in any frame of mind to consider the results with any objectivity. You may not, in fact, be in any frame of mind at all. You may be reduced to hanging in there out of pure reflex, your organism metabolizing in spite of your express wishes to the contrary.

This ugly thought occurred to Charlie Berns as he fed a rubber hose through a specially drilled hole in the doggie door that led out to the patio of his 5,400-square-foot house in the Beverly Hills Flats. If push came to shove, he would rather go through with the indignities of his present situation than wind up in veg-etableville. Charlie shuddered at the prospect and resolved to be very careful.

The 560 SEL was parked as close to the house as he could man-age, its rear wheels trampling the flower beds that his vindictive gardener had denuded months ago. José García y García and his brother-in-law Pepe had backed up a truck in broad daylight and gone around the yard uprooting and reclaiming unpaid-for plants. As a parting gesture his gardener had chain-sawed a lemon tree with such precision that it fell squarely into the pool, where it still lay, its dying limbs drooping in the air. Mr. Kim, the pool man, had at first merely cleaned around the tree, fishing out the soggy, overripe lemons and stacking them like cannonballs on the edge of the patio. Then when Charlie failed to remit in the little envelope stuffed under the door every month, he too stopped coming. His parting gesture had been a paroxysm of expletives in Korean, accompanied by spitting and stamping his feet on the deck.

That morning Charlie had gone to Thrifty on Canon and bought seventy-five feet of hose, some putty to fill in the air pockets around the hole in the doggie door, masking tape to seal off any windows that were not airtight, a microwave cherry cheesecake and a half-gallon of Gallo Hearty Burgundy.

In the house a CD of *Eine Kleine Nachtmusik* blared from the player. It had been a choice between Mozart and Mitch Miller, with Mozart winning out in the end because of the class factor. Charlie wanted to go out in a classy manner. At this stage of the game, gestures were important.

After leaving Thrifty, he had dropped two envelopes in the mailbox, one to *Daily Variety* and the other to *The Hollywood Reporter,* containing up-to-date résumés of his credits. Often, in the deadline pressure, they mixed up credits or omitted the most significant ones from the obit. And there wasn't much you could do about asking for a correction.

As he ran the hose along the Spanish-tile patio, he heard the whine of the vacuum machine sucking up leaves down the street in counterpoint to the low-key hum of pool motors. Sounds of a Beverly Hills morning. Empty houses being tended. For months, since Charlie had been evicted from his office at the Burbank Studios, he had been home on this street all day long, and he was familiar with the quiet and the sounds that punctuated it: the pizzicato of lawn mowers, the drone of air conditioners, the whomp of tennis balls, the whoosh of

German-made disk brakes, the demented chirping of overfed birds.

He looked down at his Rolex and saw that it was almost eleven. It was Sunday. No mail. No last-minute reprieve from the governor. His mailbox was filled daily with a collection of letters from lawyers all over Southern California containing threats of varying degrees of explicitness. Before he stopped returning Charlie's calls, his own lawyer, George Melvin, had recommended Chapter 11, after, of course, Charlie took care of *his* legal fees.

"You can't expect me to handle bankruptcy papers for you on a contingency basis, Charlie, can you?"

They were in George Melvin's Century City office with a view clear to Mulholland and back. The lawyer was sitting beside his beveled-glass conference table cracking pistachio nuts. Nobody in town had desks anymore. Desks were out ever since *Los Angeles* magazine ran a feature on the new type of interactive executive.

"Who else is going to do it?"

"I can't do contingency work. It's against the bylaws of the firm."

"George, isn't everything in this town on contingency, one way or another?"

Well, whether George Melvin liked it or not, as executor of his will, he would soon be presiding over the distribution of Charlie's assets, such as they were. It would be a feeding frenzy with meager pickings.

Charlie carefully slit the end of the hose with an X-Acto knife and fit it over the exhaust pipe of the Mercedes. Then he took a large piece of heavy-duty electric tape and bound it around the tail pipe tightly to prevent leaking. When he was finished, he tugged gently on the hose and was pleased when it didn't slip off.

He had considered various ways of pulling the plug. Completely hopeless with firearms, he immediately eliminated blowing his brains out. Charlie had never handled a gun in his life and didn't see why he should start now. He ruled out pills as well. You never knew exactly what the right dosage was, or whether you'd throw up first and just get very sick. In any case he would have been reduced to an over-the-counter product. His Valium prescription had been shut off months ago. His doctor wasn't returning his calls either. And hanging was just too technically complex, requiring a strong-enough rope, a strong-enough place to hang the rope, the proper noose. If you didn't do it right, it could be a terrible mess.

Asphyxiation by Mercedes exhaust seemed the best way of going about it. Nothing jarring, nothing overly technical or unpleasant. He would just drift across the border without any formalities, transported by the efficiency of German engineering. *Auf wiedersehen* . . . Have a nice day. . . .

It was while imagining the purring pistons of the engine of the 560 SEL that he suddenly realized the gas tank was low. Typical of all the decisions he had made lately, he hadn't filled up the car, figuring there was no point in checking out with a full tank. He had no idea how much exhaust it took to do the job. This was one time he didn't want to be caught short.

He tried to remember where he had left the keys after coming back from Thrifty that morning. He put away the X-Acto knife and walked back through the bleeding flower beds to the patio, looking around on the rusting deck furniture for his keys, which were nowhere to be found.

He retraced his steps, starting from the back door to the kitchen where he had entered earlier. While in the kitchen he absently opened the refrigerator and found nothing but a bottle of flat Perrier. On the counter, however, was the rapidly defrosting cherry cheesecake. He sliced off a small piece to tide him over, eating it right off the knife. He decided to put what was left in the freezer. Opening the freezer door, he discovered a microwave pizza that he thought he'd already eaten. The last pizza. There was no point leaving any assets unamortized. He took it out, popped it into the microwave, then resumed looking for his car keys.

They turned out to be in his jacket pocket, draped over the banister in the hallway, where he had left them when he had gone upstairs to tape the windows shut. Charlie went back out the patio door to the Mercedes, turned the key in the ignition and watched the gas needle barely budge off the empty mark.

Back inside the house, he grabbed his $1,900 French leather jacket and then couldn't remember where he had left his wallet. The microwave beeped. He opened the door, looked at the bubbling cheese strands running off the edge, and decided to pass.

It required all his concentration to remember that his wallet was in the back pocket of a pair of dirty jeans lying in a heap upstairs in the bathroom. His cleaning lady had volunteered to go on the cuff when he explained to her about his cash-flow problem, but Charlie hadn't wanted anybody around these last few weeks as he sank into the mire of genteel poverty. Since he rarely went out, he didn't need much in the way of clean clothes. Frozen pizzas were basically maintenance-free. So he wound up living off the fat of the land, a Bedouin in his own house.

Actually he had been doing quite well in this scaled-down existence until they disconnected the TV cable. The sons of bitches came right in the middle of *Donahue* and pulled the plug. Charlie lay there on the couch and watched three transvestites and their mothers dissolve into snow. Sometimes, late at night, he could get a decent signal off the rusted 1950s roof antenna. That was the point at which he started sleeping during the day.

There was no one to disturb Charlie during the day because his phone was cut right after they clipped the cable. Not that anybody would have called him. Certainly not Brad Emprin. When his agent of twenty years, Jerry Belcher, bought the ranch after a triple bypass, the agency had tossed him around to various people until he finally landed on the desk of a twenty-eight-year-old ex-network development director.

They had their first and last lunch at a trendy pasta place on Melrose. They sat uncomfortably on minimalist Italian furniture, amid a cacophony of conversation from tables too close to one another, as his new agent put away a skimpy pasta primavera without cheese.

Brad Emprin was concerned about cholesterol. He ate a low-fat, high-fiber breakfast every morning, then ran three-point-five miles, showered and got into the office by eight so that he could read scripts before the phones started ringing.

"You know how many scripts I take home on an average weekend?"

Charlie shook his head.

"Twelve, maybe fifteen. They're piled up next to my bed. Sometimes on a Friday night, I just grab something to eat and get right into bed, knock off a half a dozen before falling out."

"That's great, Brad."

"You got to keep up with the material. That's the name of the game—material."

Charlie nodded again. There was an extended silence as Brad attacked lunch. Finally, Charlie looked at him and asked the inevitable question, "So what's going on?"

Brad took a sip of his San Pellegrino water and cleared his throat. He flexed his jaw muscles trying to dislodge a pasta strand from his teeth.

"Things are a little slow at the moment, Charlie, but I've got feelers out all over town. In fact just yesterday I was talking about you to someone."

"Who's that?"

"Deidre Hearn."

"Who?"

"She's a very bright lady. Started out as a reader for Mike Corvene a couple of years ago. Now she's at a major studio."

"She's a reader?"

Brad drained the Pellegrino, looked off for a moment at an anorexic woman talking like a machine gun at the next table.

"She's this close to Norman." He indicated by placing his thumb and forefinger a fraction of an inch apart.

"Brad, she can't say yes. What's the point of talking to someone about me doing a picture if that person can't say yes?"

"I think she's having sex with Norman. Maybe not. Someone told me he thought she was having sex with Norman. . . . Look, Charlie, the point is that this lady is going to be running a studio someday. She's hot. I know it. And she's aware of you."

"Aware of me?"

"Name of the game. Client awareness. We talk about it in the staff meeting all the time."

"Great."

"She's a pistol. I'm telling you. . . ."

Charlie closed his eyes for a moment, rubbed them gingerly. Often this was an effective means of dissipating anger. When he opened them, however, Brad Emprin was still sitting across from him talking about client awareness. Charlie put his finger to his lips to indicate that his agent should be quiet.

"Brad, I want you to watch my lips carefully, okay?"

Brad nodded dutifully.

"I don't need any more people aware of me. There are a number of lawyers and collection agencies around town that are already aware of me."

"I understand what you're saying, Charlie."

"Do you?"

"Absolutely . . ."

Brad Emprin sat across from him nodding for a long time, then excused himself to use the phone. When he got back, the check had arrived.

"I'm afraid we're going to have to split this, Charlie," he said, shaking his head sadly. "It's the new agency policy. No more client lunches."

He stared at the check for a minute, then: "Thirty bucks'll cover you. You got a parking ticket you need validated?"

The phone calls that followed were punctuated by long beats of silence interspersed with Brad's list of people who were aware of Charlie Berns. Then Brad was in meetings when he called and took a day or so to get back. Eventually, when Brad returned one call six days later Charlie hung up on him. And when the phone company yanked the line, he wasn't bothered anymore by Brad Emprin.

As he drove south on Beverly Drive Charlie wondered what the reaction to his suicide would be at the Monday-morning staff meeting where they sat around and discussed client awareness. Whatever else Brad Emprin and his colleagues would say, they wouldn't be able to say that people weren't aware of him that particular morning. They all would have read the trades on their Exercycles before the staff meeting and they would be aware that Charlie Berns, fifty-two, producer of such films as et cetera, sucked a Mercedes tail pipe that morning in his Beverly Hills home.

He pulled into the gas station on Little Santa Monica and went directly to the full-service pump. The short Iranian with the KLOS T-shirt handed him the clipboard. Charlie signed on a Union 76 credit card that had been cut off two months ago. It gave him some satisfaction to stiff the Iranians. They were taking over the goddamn town. They could have it, as far as he was concerned. He was out of here. Let the Iranians line up behind the rest of them.

Charlie left the gas station and headed back across Beverly Hills. He drove up Canyon Drive for the last time, dry-eyed, without regrets. Turning the corner at Elevado, he passed a mini-van full of tourists with their maps to the stars' homes. There were no stars anymore on Charlie's block; the houses were all owned by Arabs, Iranians, Koreans and people like Charlie, who had bought in the sixties and couldn't afford to pay their gardeners anymore.

Charlie pulled to the end of the driveway, then put it in reverse and backed carefully over the vacant flower beds, getting as close to the patio as possible and out of view from the street.

Leaving the engine on, he got out, crouched over the tail pipe and started to reattach the hose. The door chimes rang. Charlie ignored them. When they persisted, he got up, went back inside, cranked Mozart up louder on the CD player.

Back outside, he returned to the task of reattaching the hose with a leakproof fit. Humming along with *Eine Kleine Nachtmusik*, working intensely, Charlie did not notice the figure approaching him from the end of the driveway.

"Hello?" the figure called.

Charlie didn't hear. Mozart was at a crescendo. The figure was practically on top of him before Charlie turned around and looked up at a tall skinny kid standing over him with a knapsack.

"I think your bell's out of order."

Charlie stared at this young man, drawing a blank.

"I tried calling you lots of times, but your phone's out of order. The phone company said it's been disconnected. . . . When I decided to come out here, you were the first person I called. When I couldn't get you on the phone I decided to come out anyway. Nobody knows where you are. My mother's kind of worried. . . . What are you doing anyway? You left your motor running. . . ."

He was shouting to be heard over the *Nachtmusik*. Charlie scratched his head. Recognition flooded through a moment before the kid said, "You okay, Uncle Charlie?"

His sister Janice's youngest kid Lionel. Several years ago at a funeral in New Jersey Lionel had gotten him in a corner and bent his ear about wanting to write for the movies. Charlie had mumbled some vague encouragement, promised to help him when he was ready to come out to Hollywood and try to break into the business.

Charlie hadn't expected him to show up. Certainly not on the day of his suicide.

"I would have called if your phone wasn't on the blink. But you said that whenever I got out here, I should get in touch. So here I am."

"How long are you out here for?"

"For as long as it takes."

"It takes to do what?"

"Make it. I got a script with me. I want you to read it."

"Uh-huh . . ."

"It's based on the life of Disraeli."

Suicide requires a fair amount of concentration. You don't want to get interrupted when you're in the middle. It opens the flood-gates to all sorts of equivocations and doubts. Lionel's arrival on Charlie's patio at that moment did precisely that. It threw Charlie off. He had been cruising along, dealing with the preparations in an orderly fashion. Now, instead, he found himself in his kitchen splitting the microwave pizza with his nephew.

They were sitting across from each other at the bar as Lionel described his odyssey across the country in a Trailways bus, gathering material, as he put it. It was all grist for the mill, life real and raw out there west of New Jersey.

"My next script's going to be about Nebraska. The story of a modern-day cowboy, except this guy's a crop duster, but you intercut his story, see, with his alter ego a hundred years ago. Kind of a parallel structure . . ."

Charlie nodded, poured himself a glass of Hearty Burgundy.

"What are you working on now, Uncle Charlie?"

"I'm sort of between pictures."

"I saw *Jailbreak* the other night on TV. They cut the hell out of it."

"Yeah, they do that."

"Can't show tits on TV, huh?"

Charlie shook his head solemnly.

"They show almost everything else. They got people with their tongues down each other's throats on the soaps in the after-noon. That's why I wanted to do this picture on Disraeli. There were standards back then. People just didn't whip their clothes off. They didn't even sleep in the same bedroom. . . ."

"Lionel," Charlie interrupted, "how'd you get here?"

"I took the bus, I told you. A hundred and twenty-nine dollars. From Newark."

"No. I mean to my house. You don't have a car. The bus station's downtown."

"I have a map."

"I see. . . ." Then a moment of hesitation before asking, "Where are you staying?"

His nephew smiled a half-baked little grin, shrugged and said, "I was kind of hoping . . . here."

"Here?"

"You said that I could stay with you when I came out here."

"I did?"

"Uh-huh. I'm kind of short on money."

A silence of some duration followed. Lionel dove into the cherry cheesecake and Charlie poured himself another glass of Hearty Burgundy. Finally:

"How short of money are you?"

"I got a couple of hundred."

"*Two* hundred dollars?"

"A hundred eighty actually."

"That's not going to go too far in this town."

"I figure I'll sell my script."

"I don't know how hot Disraeli is right now."

"Would you read it? I really want to know what you think about it." And he was off the bar stool and into his knapsack. He dug out a thick bound manuscript, handed it to Charlie.

The title page read *Bill and Ben.* Charlie stared at it for several seconds. "William Gladstone and Benjamin Disraeli," Lionel explained. "They were kind of like Jules and Jim. I was thinking about Tom Cruise as Disraeli."

At three o'clock in the morning Charlie, not yet dead, lay awake in his upstairs bedroom, his mind spinning at high rpm. He wasn't thinking, as might be expected, about the fortuitous arrival of his nephew shortly before he was planning to pollute his brain with carbon monoxide. Nor was he thinking about Benjamin Disraeli, though Lionel had stood over him until he

had read all two hundred pages of his screenplay. He was thinking about Bobby Mason.

One of the qualities that had helped Charlie Berns survive in
Hollywood as long he did was a nearly photographic memory
for details. Every morning he read the trade papers, culling a collection of seemingly trivial facts about the shifting tides around
him. It was for Charlie a sort of ritual recitation, like the daily
reading of the Koran. It gave him solace to know that the show
went inexorably on in spite of earthquakes, assassinations and
wars. Somewhere in town at every moment a deal was being cut.
He slept better knowing that.

But he wasn't sleeping at the moment. He was remembering a
filler item in the gossip column of *The Reporter* that mentioned
that Bobby Mason, the biggest black box-office attraction in the
world, was considering a conversion to Judaism following an
emotional location scout of the Holy Land for his current picture.
Bobby's manager had said that his client was interested in scripts
with a Jewish theme.

One of the early scenes in Lionel's script depicted the baptism
of the young Benjamin Disraeli into the bosom of Christ, renounc-
ing his Judaism. It was an easy lift, as far as Charlie was concerned.

Downstairs in the guest room his nephew Lionel was presumably asleep. Charlie would have to explain some things to him in
the morning.

A few hours ago Charlie Berns was a man at the end of his
rope, or, more accurately, his tail pipe. But that was before Lionel
showed up with a script. A producer was someone who had a
property. And Charlie now had a property. Or would in the
morning when he optioned the rights to *Bill and Ben.*

It was overly warm in his bedroom. And then he remembered
why. He got out of bed, stripped off the perspiration-drenched
pajama shirt and started carefully to peel the masking tape off his
sealed windows.

# 2

"Galump."

"Glump?"

"No, galump. Like a shoe dropping on the ceiling over your head."

Gunter Greisler, the service manager of the BMW dealership, raised a Teutonic eyebrow dubiously. "We've taken the automobile apart and put it back together again. We find nothing to cause that sound."

"It's under the driver's seat when you make a right turn and brake at the same time."

"I drove the automobile. Personally. I turned right and applied the brake. Just as you said. Nothing. I'm sorry."

Brad Emprin was getting annoyed. This was the third time he'd had the 325i in the shop with the same complaint, and they still couldn't find the problem. At 120-an-hour labor, the tab was mounting, and still his car persisted in making the galump sound every time he made a right turn while he was braking.

"The suspension under the driver's seat is hydraulically lubricated. . . ."

Brad got in the car and drove away. Two lights from the shop, he braked sharply and pulled the wheel to the right.

*Galump.*

The first wave of gas tickled the wall of his stomach. Nine-fifteen on a Monday morning and it was beginning already. In spite of the jog and the hot shower he'd had at six-thirty, he felt the stress gathering in the east.

The week stretched out in front of him in menacing fashion, a series of hurdles and challenges that at the moment he felt inadequate to face. The sludge pile of scripts he had taken home that weekend had been particularly dreary. In forty-five minutes they'd be gathered in the glass conference room, and he hadn't a legitimate idea in his head.

Instinctively he reached for the car phone, got the office. Tanya told him that there were no calls but that Charlie Berns was waiting for him in his office.

"Charlie Berns? In my office?"

"Yop."

"What's he want?"

"I don't know."

"Did you tell him I had a staff meeting as soon as I got in?"

"Yop."

"Jesus . . ."

Brad Emprin considered the emptiness in his brain—the lack of anything, no matter how remote or inconsequential, resembling a legitimate idea to help him shine during the fast-approaching show-'n'-tell period at the agency. Anxiety gripped him squarely by the shoulders and whispered sweet menaces into his ear.

As he double-clutched to avoid braking and turned right onto Santa Monica Boulevard, he wondered whether it was too early to drop his first Valium of the week.

"This has got to be quick, Charlie, because I've got a staff meeting in six minutes."

"Okay."

As Brad Emprin sat in his tiny windowless office opposite Charlie Berns, his eyes scanned the first page of the trades. He continued to browse, trying to catch up on the morning's news, as he listened to his client.

"I got a script."

"A script?"

"I've optioned it. Exclusive."

"What's the script?"

"It's about Disraeli."

Brad took his eyes off *Variety* and looked at his client squarely. He seemed a little demented this morning, or at least more demented than usual. He wondered whether Charlie Berns was on drugs.

"Israel?"

"No. Disraeli. Benjamin Disraeli, the English prime minister."

"What happened to Thatcher?"

"Brad. This is a hundred years ago. During Queen Victoria's reign."

Charlie reached down to a battered briefcase, took a thick-bound script out.

"It's for Bobby Mason."

Brad looked at him more carefully, searching for the punch line. Charlie didn't crack a smile.

"You putting me on?"

Charlie shook his head slowly.

"Bobby Mason does black karate movies."

"He's looking for scripts about Jews, Brad. It was in the trades. Disraeli was a Jew."

Brad's eyes panned right beyond Charlie's shoulder, through the glass partition to the conference room, where the agents were already starting to gather.

"Well, look, get me a copy of it and I'll work up some coverage on it."

"I want you to read it. This morning."

"I've got a staff meeting."

"Bring it up in the staff meeting. See who's got the best approach to Mason's people."

"Charlie, do you know the number of people trying to get scripts to Bobby Mason?"

"That's why I'm with this agency, Brad. You people are supposed to be able to get this type of thing done."

"Yeah. Okay. Sure. . . . Now, I got to run. Leave the script. I'll call you as soon as I have a reaction."

Once again, Charlie's head shook slowly from side to side, like a recalcitrant Indian chief.

"I'm going to stay here. We'll talk after your staff meeting."

Brad Emprin abandoned his office to the mad Indian chief and sought refuge among his colleagues.

Though they had pretensions of informality, staff meetings at GTA were highly ritualized affairs. Sy Green, the head of the agency, presided over two-dozen agents and subagents in the large fishbowl conference room on the twenty-fourth floor of the Century City high-rise. The dress code was tie without jacket, making the point that even though it may only be 10:00 A.M. Monday morning, people had already worked up a sweat.

The idea was to brainstorm projects, put together packages, run down the catalog of available slots for the clients, in order to maximize deal volume. In practice, however, these sessions often degenerated into highly inaccurate gossip sessions. The staff meeting that Monday morning was no exception. It started off with good intentions, the attempt to shoehorn an extra picture into a top client's already heavy schedule.

"What about Paul? What do you think, Sy?" Jeff Yankow shot across the table.

Sy Green digested this notion for a moment, taking a pensive bite of his poppy-seed bagel, then slowly shook his head.

"Why not? He's got an eleven-week hiatus before he does the

thing in Munich. The picture starts up the ninth. We can get him boarded to be in and out before the first."

"It won't make." Sy Green pronounced this judgment with oracular gravity. A pause as he swallowed the last of the bagel, rubbed his hands together to shed the poppy seeds. "Someone want to tell me why this deal won't make?"

The agents looked at one another, wondering if there was some clue to this question in the weekend script packet. Nobody knew. Taking a toothpick out of his shirt pocket, Sy Green nodded and went to work on the upper incisors. The tension mounted in the room.

"Nobody in this whole goddamn agency knows why we can't put Paul in this picture. . . ."

He shook his head again, ruefully. "You know what the sign of a good agent is?" Sy Green tapped his head with his knuckle. "He keeps it all up here—everything that happens in this town gets registered up here."

Tap tap on the noggin again. "It's your own personal computer you carry around with you, you take home with you. You take it to bed with you. . . . Harry Gorlich, who founded this agency, could tell you who the second-unit cameraman was on a picture. Harry had it all up here. . . . He didn't have to carry lists around. Now everyone's got lists instead of brains. A lists, B lists, shit lists. We might as well all go home. Someone calls, we'll send him a list."

Sy Green stopped talking. It was more than anyone had heard him say in a long time. He sat there and quietly cleaned his teeth. More silence. Everyone waited for a shoe to drop. Finally, Jeff Yankow said, "Why can't Paul do the picture, Sy?"

"He won't work with Grey."

This pronouncement floated over the room causing more consternation until Cissy Fuchs piped up. "They . . . never worked together."

Sy Green shook his head again, allowing a little smile of triumph to float across the conference table. "*Canary Yellow.*

Nineteen eighty-three. Paul is set to do the picture in Seattle with Ivan Grey directing. Three weeks into prep he walks. Can't stand the director. He actually threw a punch at him. Or maybe it was the other way around. They wind up doing the picture with Hackman."

"*Canary Yellow?*" Scott Nemith muttered.

"It was so bad they never released it," Sy Green explained. "Not to mention two point five over."

"Listen," Jeff Yankow persisted, "why don't we try to roll over Grey's deal. If he goes, then Paul'll probably do it."

"It's play or pay."

"So we buy him out."

"They're already eight-fifty into the script on this picture. They're not buying anybody out."

Everyone tried to think of ways to get Ivan Grey off the picture. The entire agency noodled the problem, an obstacle in the way of a deal.

Then John DeMarco happened to mention that Ivan Grey had bought a house in Benedict Canyon and was now spending more time here than in London.

"How much did he pay?" Cissy Fuchs asked.

"One point eight."

"How far up?"

"Between San Yisidro and Clear View."

"That's a terrific price. . . ."

"I looked at a two-bedroom in Sherman Oaks yesterday. Six-fifty. For *two* bedrooms. In fucking *Sherman Oaks*. Can you believe that?"

"That's nothing. Doug Henry paid seven in *Mar Vista*."

That one stopped traffic for a while. No one could top it.

Sy Green called the meeting back to order. "Does anybody have a decent idea about *anything* this morning?"

It was a slow morning. Collectively torpid biorhythms plagued the agency. Nobody had an idea worthy of being laid out on the glass conference table, among the bagels and doughnuts.

It seemed like the propitious moment for Brad Emprin to send up a trial balloon.

"What about Bobby Mason in the life of Disraeli?"

Though he couldn't hear anything, Charlie Berns observed this moment through several barriers of glass. It stopped the meeting cold. It may have been Brad Emprin's delivery, but nobody laughed. The suggestion merely floated around like room freshener. He was not known for one-liners. Nobody even smiled. Nobody touched the remark with a ten-foot pole. Nobody even used it as a segue. It was merely ignored.

Brad Emprin had the good sense to let it die right there. He sat there for the rest of the meeting listening to his intestines gurgle and contemplating the damage done to his career. He figured he had set himself back a good six months.

When the meeting finally ended, he slouched out of the conference room and returned to his office, where he found Charlie Berns still waiting for him.

"What'd they say?"

Brad Emprin sank down into his orthopedic chair and shook his head. "Sy thinks it's a stretch."

"Of course it's a stretch. So what? If Olivier can do Othello, why can't Bobby Mason do Disraeli?"

For a long moment Brad Emprin stared at Charlie, as if he were invisible. It had been a long morning. He suddenly felt exhausted. He wished it were Friday and he could go home and get into bed with his scripts.

"Charlie, listen, I got a sinus headache. Can we talk about this some other time?"

"I don't think so, Brad." Charlie was on his feet, heading for the door. "See you."

"Leave the script. I'll look at it. . . ."

Charlie didn't leave the script. He walked briskly through the soft gurgling of the Monday-morning phones until he got to the elevator, neglecting to get his parking ticket stamped.

Which, for a man in his financial straits, was imprudent.

It wasn't until he was driving north on Century Park East that he refocused his energy away from being angry at the twenty-eight-year-old insect that represented him. He turned it back constructively to the problem—getting the script to Bobby Mason.

In his salad days Charlie Berns had a catalog of methods to get scripts past agents and managers. This one, though, was going to be difficult. Bobby Mason was a paranoid hermit, who lived in an armed camp in Holmby Hills rumored to be patrolled by the most venal attack dogs in town. He rarely went out. And he was supposedly on his way to Israel to make a picture.

These obstacles, however, merely inspired Charlie. In fact he hadn't felt this inspired since the day he had decided to kill himself. He drove west on Santa Monica, the morning sun at his back, his future in front of him.

Another meeting took place that Monday morning which would have repercussions on Charlie Berns's recently resurrected life. Charlie wasn't even aware that this meeting was taking place, nor, for that matter, were any of the participants in that meeting aware of Charlie Berns, Brad Emprin's assurances notwithstanding. Deidre Hearn had apparently failed to make her boss, Norman Hudris, aware of Charlie Berns, if she herself was even aware of him.

In many respects the meeting was not unlike the GTA staff meeting. It began with lofty purposes and degenerated ineluctably into gossip, innuendo and character assassination. Though this meeting also took place first thing Monday morning, nobody took off a coat, and the chair didn't lick poppy seeds off his lip.

In any event, Deidre Hearn was not invited to the monthly studio-production status meeting. The meeting was on a vice-presidential level, and she was merely a director of creative affairs, reporting to the vice president of production, West Coast, Norman Hudris. All the production vice presidents reported to the president of the production arm of the studio, Howard Draper, who reported to Frederick D. Weston, the CEO of Allied Continental Industries, the conglomerate that owned the studio. Frederick D. Weston, aka Frederick the Great, reported to the bank.

Howard Draper was referred to around town as the demi-WASP. A part of him reflected the influence of Andover, Yale, Wharton and the New York Athletic Club. The other half was nurtured in the completion-bond business for action/adventure and soft-R sex pictures, which gave Howard Draper a seat-of-the-pants feel for the lower part of the spectrum of public taste. It was undoubtedly this training which attracted ACI when they were looking for someone to run production after they bought the studio.

It hadn't worked. The other half of Howard Draper's con-flicted soul took temporary control of him, and he went inexpli-cably soft, greenlighting a series of murky and ambitious flops with the hopes of winning creative respectability. The studio was floundering through six consecutive quarters of red ink, due, as Sidney Auger, the vice president of business affairs put it, to Howard Draper's forgetting how to think with his dick. Frederick the Great had decreed from his throne in New York that unless the feature-film division began to generate a profit for ACI, he wanted the entire production staff out the door. With Howard Draper leading the way.

The meeting opened with a status report on films presently in production. Norman Hudris generally dozed through this por-tion of the meeting, a dry recitation of budgets, schedules, good dailies, bad dailies. There wasn't much to be done once the train was out of the station. All you could do was worry or threaten the director, and neither did much good.

When they got around to development, Norman scanned the notes he had made that morning, which his girl had typed up neatly for him. There was a list of scripts to recommend, properties to pursue, writers, stars, directors he wanted to attract to the studio. Norman kicked off his report with a top priority—getting *Shopping Mall Terror* off the ground.

"*What's* it called?" Barney Sedlow, West Coast distribution v.p., asked.

"It's just a working title," Norman reassured them. "But I think we ought to make a bid on this script. And fast."

"Why is that, Norman?" Howard Draper emerged from his terminally bored-looking trance.

"For one thing, it's a terrific story. Relevant, contemporary, exciting. It's got terrorism, sci-fi, sex, everything. Secondly, it belongs to Karen Kolodny and Bruce Spears, and I think we should get into business with them."

"Who's it being offered to?"

"Everyone. The agent's asking for sealed bids submitted by the close of business Wednesday."

"Is there coverage available?"

"I'm having Deidre cover it right now. You'll have it on your desk after lunch."

"Who's it for?"

"I think we could go A list on the girl. Maybe Raquel."

"Boobies?" Sidney Auger's high-pitched voice emerged from the other end of the table.

"Huh?"

"Are we talking boobies here? If we are, you might as well forget Raquel. She won't do boobies."

"Anyone'll do boobies if the price is right. Even Meryl'll do boobies."

"Meryl'll do boobies if you let her play Mother Teresa in her native language."

"What language is that?"

"The fuck do I know."

"Who wants Meryl to flash boobies anyway? You interested in Meryl's boobies? Is *anybody* interested?"

"They're not that bad. . . ."

"How do you know? You never see them."

"Never see what?"

"Her boobies. Name a picture where she showed boobies."

"Some picture she made a long time ago with what's-his-name . . ."

"With who?"

"I can't remember."

"She showed boobies?"

"Uh-huh . . ."

"How were they?"

"I can't remember. It was a long time ago."

Norman Hudris finally managed to steer the conversation back to *Shopping Mall Terror*. Howard rubbed his temples with the tips of his fingers, a gesture he adopted whenever he was asked to authorize a major expenditure. He liked to think himself above the mundane considerations of dollars and cents, and it upset him to be reminded that he was, in fact, the checkbook when it came to six-figure acquisitions.

"How much do you think it's going to cost?" he hedged.

"I doubt it'll go out at much less than four, four-fifty."

Howard nodded, rubbed his temples again. "Offer three-fifty. Maybe we'll get lucky." Then quickly, to get off the subject, "What's happening with Bobby Mason?"

"He's making a picture in Israel."

"Why isn't this studio making that picture?"

"We only have a first-look deal with him."

"Norman, that was a rhetorical question. I know why we're not making *that* picture. What I want to know is why we're not developing the next one."

"We haven't found anything right for him."

Howard Draper sighed deeply. It was a sigh with venom in it, and everyone at that meeting, especially Norman Hudris, felt it.

"What *isn't* right for Bobby Mason?"

"He's a limited actor, Howard. . . ."

"Find a script. Steal a script. Type up the phone book. If there are enough karate scenes and eight million dollars on the table, he'll do it."

"Howard, he saying he's tired of just doing karate movies. He's looking for substance."

Howard Draper raised his eyes to the ceiling and murmured, "God help us."

"When are you getting your phone fixed?" Charlie's nephew, Lionel Travitz, asked him.

"What?" Charlie replied absently. He was going through a stack of back issues of *The Hollywood Reporter.*

"How can you live without a phone?"

"I'm getting it taken care of."

"And you know what else? All the windows are taped up. It's hot in the house."

"That's for the fumigation."

"What fumigation?"

"For termites. They come and spray shit in the house. You have to seal up the windows."

"When are they going to do this?"

"I don't know. I have to call them."

Charlie found the filler item he was looking for in the gossip column of the February eighteenth edition.

. . . news from the Holy Land where Bobby Mason is scouting locations for *Desert Commando,* his action pic to unspool in the Negev in March, is that BM is wild about Israel. Not only is he interested in doing more pics in that country, but he's actively looking for properties to do with Jewish themes, according to Rabbi Seth Gutterman, the star's spiritual adviser on things Jewish. . . . Don't call us, call Norman Hudris, whose studio has a four-pic first-look deal with Bobby M. . . .

Charlie got up, went to the refrigerator, his mind starting to turn over. Opening the freezer compartment, he scoured inside for something to eat.

"There's nothing in there," Lionel said.

Charlie looked over at his nephew, who was sitting on a stool with a yellow pad making a list.

"What do you eat anyway?"

"I eat out a lot."

"I'm making a shopping list. I mean, you need things like dish detergent."

"That's great, Lionel."

"If you have the time, we can go to the store this afternoon."

"I have a meeting this afternoon."

"I can't go shopping without a car."

"There are buses. . . ."

And Charlie was gone, out the kitchen door before his nephew could reply. Lionel put down his list for a moment and thought about his good luck. His uncle had optioned his screenplay for five thousand dollars. Five thousand *dollars*. In one lump sum. In New Jersey people got weekly salaries and didn't get paid for just the *possibility* of using something, which is how Charlie explained option agreements. His uncle had assured him that he had to run the option agreement by his attorneys before money could change hands. But not to worry. It was pay or play. Pay or play. Lionel liked the sound of it.

Charlie Berns had long ago mastered the trick of getting into a studio without an appointment. The old agents, the ones who still worked the lot, had taught him how. You approached the guard gate, slowed down but didn't come to a complete halt and rolled through the gate with a wave at the guard and your eyes straight ahead, masked behind dark sunglasses.

Charlie sailed through the gate without incident and parked his car in somebody's spot. What were they going to do to him? There was already an updated obituary on file for him. Finding

Deidre Hearn's office turned out to be relatively simple. Since, according to Brad Emprin, she was screwing Norman Hudris, her office couldn't be that far away from his in the producers' building. Charlie found it three doors down from the vice president of production's second-floor suite of offices.

Deidre Hearn, 206. Charlie entered without knocking. The waiting room was tiny and dark. A young male secretary was on the phone.

"Noooo . . . that's fucking unreal," he said, then, seeing Charlie, he whispered quietly into the receiver, "Just a moment, Brian . . ."

He swiveled to Charlie. "Yes?"

"I'm here for Deidre Hearn. Charlie Berns."

"She's in a meeting." Then the secretary's eyes scanned the appointment book on the desk. "Do you have an appointment?"

"Eleven o'clock. I'm early."

The young man's eyes returned to the book, then looked up at Charlie. "I don't show anything here."

Charlie nodded, shook his head sadly. "My girl's out sick. I have this temp they gave me, who assured me she made this meeting. I bet you she crossed it with Dawn. I have a meeting with Dawn tomorrow. . . ."

The two of them stood their ground for a long moment, each one entrenched in a position already stated. They were clearly at an impasse.

The impasse was interrupted by the door to the inner office being opened and the emergence of a tall woman in a short leather skirt, boots and a pencil stuck in a bob of dark hair. She took Charlie in with a quick pan down to his aged Italian loafers and registered a blank.

Though he had been assured by Brad Emprin that Deidre Hearn was aware of him, she didn't give that impression. When the secretary began to explain that *he* was not responsible for this man's presence in her office, Charlie said, "Hi. I'm Charlie Berns."

She turned back toward him for another look, came up blank again.

"Brad Emprin's spoken to you about me."

A spark of recognition appeared in her eyes at the mention of the GTA tyro. But not much of a spark. One recognition circuit in her brain seemed to flicker dimly and was about to expire.

"He said you were aware of me. Apparently, you're not. I guess I have to fire him. You just can't get good help these days. . . ."

Charlie smiled, trying to sell the line. She allowed her mouth to curl ever so slightly. He took this as an opening, certainly the best he was going to get. He started in. Tappety-tap. Shuffle ball change . . .

Minutes later he was sitting on an uncomfortable leather couch in her minimalist office, a degree less small and dark than her secretary's. Staring at him was a shelf full of scripts, the title and author written across the ends of the pages in red Magic Marker. The blood of a hundred writers was coagulating on Deidre Hearn's shelf.

Alan, the secretary, petulantly brought coffee, and when the small-talk phase of the meeting drew to a close, Charlie rubbed the back of his neck, a nervous habit he had when he was tense, and plunged in.

"I have a script for Bobby Mason."

"Who doesn't?" She leaned back in the leather cushions, her skirt riding up a little higher.

"This is something he's going to want to do."

"Really?" She tried unsuccessfully to keep the ennui out of her voice.

"You must hear that a lot, right?"

She nodded, smiled. "Three times a day."

"When you're hot you're hot."

"If I told you the number of scripts I send over there every week. . . . He doesn't even read them. His manager and six agents read the material for him. Then they pitch it to Bobby. If he likes the idea, it goes in development. The floor for a deal with Bobby Mason is eight million plus a gross position on the back end. Pay or play. You still want to tell me your idea?"

"It's about Benjamin Disraeli."

Charlie delivered the line without irony, just as Brad Emprin had at the GTA staff meeting that morning. But Charlie must have had better timing because it broke Deidre Hearn up. She exploded like a woman who hadn't had a good laugh in a long time.

"I love it. Bobby Mason as Disraeli. Put him in one of those long Victorian frock coats . . . karate-chopping Bismarck. It's brilliant. . . ."

Charlie took the tap shoes off and headed for the door.

"Please," she said, forcing herself to stop laughing. "I'm sorry. I didn't mean to insult you. You got to admit it's a wild idea."

He turned around, saw that she was sincerely trying to apologize.

"It just got to me. I've been in here reading awful scripts since eight-thirty this morning."

She got up, tugging her skirt down, and approached him.

"Listen, Charlie, it's a pass, but I really appreciate your bringing it to me. Maybe we can hook up on something else."

"Maybe."

"Bobby Mason doesn't even know who Disraeli was."

"Probably not."

"This Jewish stuff'll blow over. He was going to become a Black Muslim after Kareem converted. He did the whole number, changed his name, wore a dashiki, and then he started going out with Miss Finland. Five foot ten, blond from head to toe and Lutheran. Bye-bye Muslims."

Charlie smiled. They were standing there at the door, the meeting already ended. Though her eyes were still moist from laughing, she was doing her best to redeem herself. She stuck her hand out and said, "Thanks for stopping by, Charlie. I'm certainly aware of you now if I wasn't before."

"Right," said Charlie, shaking her hand, which was unexpectedly soft and warm. And in addition to being more intelligent than your average young barracuda, she had terrific thighs.

Just to set the record straight, Brad Emprin's skinny on Deidre Hearn was incorrect. She hadn't slept with Norman Hudris to get the job as his executive assistant. Her best friend, Cissy Fuchs, was the one who had slept with the vice president of worldwide production, and it is probable that Brad Emprin merely misunderstood a tidbit that had drifted out of the ladies' room at GTA and made its way circuitously to his cubicle.

In certain respects Deidre Hearn was an old-fashioned girl. At thirty-eight she hadn't abandoned hope that there was a guy out there with her name on him. Unfortunately, the hours she worked were hardly conducive to meeting men. The business seemed full of either married or gay men, and the occasional unmarried, heterosexual guy in her age range was generally a divorcé on the rebound, interested in younger and firmer stuff.

She worked till nine or later practically every night, got home to her one-bedroom condo in West Hollywood, stuck something in the microwave and turned on the TV. One glass of wine, and she was comatose on the couch.

On Thursdays she left work early to keep a seven o'clock appointment with Ellen, her nondirective therapist in Studio City. She and Ellen often discussed the paradox on Deidre's life: The higher up she moved in the uncharted free-for-all of show business, the more limited her prospects became. As a reader, she came in contact with lower-level executives, agents, writers. But as a director of creative affairs she came in contact almost exclusively with Norman Hudris, who, as already noted, was engaged extracurricularly with her best friend and, as far as she was concerned, was not in the running for any nonprofessional role in her life. He was soft in all respects. And he was paranoid. Norman Hudris knew that she and Cissy were tight, and he

knew that she knew and that she knew he knew and that Cissy
knew she knew and knew that he knew she knew.

After Charlie Berns left her office that morning, she tried
unsuccessfully to wade back into a script about suburban werewolves that Norman had been pressing her to read. She tossed it
into the pile to be returned by Alan with a note from her
attached, and stretched out on the floor to do her back exercises.
This entailed grabbing each leg at the knee and pulling it up into
her chest fifteen times. In order to accomplish this in a tight skirt,
she had to hike it up above her waist.

In the middle of the exercise the door opened and Norman
Hudris entered unannounced. Deidre's mail-order bikini panties
were doing only a token job of covering her, and Norman Hudris
did a double take before muttering, "Jesus, Deidre, you ought to
lock your door, for chrissakes."

"If you'd knock, I wouldn't have to."

"Where's the faggot?"

"Alan?"

"Yeah. He's not at his desk."

"I don't know. Maybe he's in the men's room."

"Probably thinks he'll get lucky. In this studio you take your
chances in the men's room. I need your coverage on the werewolf
script."

Norman Hudris often made segues without any discernible
pause. Deidre was used to his fragmented attention span and
splattering, whiny speech.

"I haven't written it yet."

"What? Deidre, I told you I needed it ASAP."

"I couldn't get through it."

"You didn't *read* it?"

"I read twenty pages."

"Deidre, I pitched it in the production meeting. I promised
them coverage by noon."

"Here's the coverage. D-R-E-C-K."

"How do you know? You didn't finish it."

"Norman, it's dreadful. The characters are all clichés. The premise is ridiculous—werewolves taking over a shopping mall. . . . Extraterrestrial werewolves, no less. Werewolves from Neptune. I mean, come on, Norman, this is truly dreck."

"Howard wants us to make an offer."

"Offer a hundred bucks. See what happens."

He glared at her sitting smugly at her desk, playing with a paper clip. She infuriated him with her Bryn Mawr attitude.

"If you're wrong on this, I'm going to be very pissed."

"Norman, the extraterrestrial werewolves are trained in Iraq."

The Synagogue for a Humanistic World was set in a cul-de-sac in the hills above Encino. You had to drive up a narrow road lined with cypresses until you emerged into a clearing, face-to-face with the sanctuary.

Rabbi Gutterman had the architect design it in the shape of the holy ark, two glassed-in sections bisected by a central gallery. The stained-glass windows looking out on the Valley depicted scenes from the Holocaust done by a survivor of Dachau in a whimsical Hasidic style reminiscent of Chagall. The roof was Mediterranean tile with skylights. There was a lightly chlorinated reflecting pool; jade and forsythia climbed the stucco walls. On the hill behind the building a satellite dish kept the rabbi in touch with world events. From a distance the synagogue resembled a Mexican spaceship that had landed on a hilltop in Encino.

Charlie parked his car in the nearly empty lot. There was a Coupe de Ville with the plate SHALOM 19 in a space marked RESERVED FOR RABBI GUTTERMAN. Charlie crossed the gravel drive-way and entered the building by way of a sculpted portal with gilt-bronze bas-relief.

The offices were off to the right, the chapel straight ahead. He had been here years ago on the occasion of the bat mitzvah of a studio executive's daughter, where he had gotten exceedingly drunk and burned his bridges at that studio for years.

Charlie walked straight ahead and entered the chapel. He

went down the central aisle, flooded in diffused sunlight from
the tinted skylights, to the first row and sat down in a pew. He
needed to gather his strength before he pitched the rabbi.

He suddenly felt woozy. He had barely slept last night, over-
stimulated by the events of the day. Now the energy devoted to
the planning and execution of his suicide was beginning to dissi-
pate, replaced by a manic new energy. In between, however, was
the nagging realization that he was on very thin ice. He had actually had the hose threaded through the doggie door when Lionel
turned up.

It hadn't been the debts and the failure so much as the
inevitable accommodation with the uselessness of the next twenty,
thirty years. They stretched out in front of him endlessly, and he
had seen himself marking time and waiting for it to be over. Like
a ball team hopelessly mired in last place in September playing out
the string.

It had started out almost as a dare to himself. Would he really
do it? Could he pull it off? As he made the preparations, he was
conscious of playing a game, seeing how far he could get to the
edge without falling over. And it was surprisingly easy. It had
actually cheered him up, given him a sense of purpose.

The fact that he had no children and an ex-wife whom he
hadn't seen or spoken to in ten years made it even simpler. No
farewells, no remorse. A clean getaway. Slip away quietly in the
night.

Charlie looked up at the chrome-and-glass ark with the silk-
screened curtains that contained the holy scrolls. There were no
answers there. He began to nod. . . .

He was still sitting there, his lidded eyes staring straight ahead
at the ark, half-asleep, when a resonant voice called from the
back of the chapel. "Hello there."

Rabbi Seth Gutterman walked down the aisle to Charlie's pew,
sat down beside him.

"Can I help you?"

Charlie looked at him—a large bearded man in a pale-blue

velour jogging suit and a black silk yarmulke stuck on the top of a nearly bald head—and rubbed his eyes. Then he stuck out his hand. "Charlie Berns," he said.

"Seth Gutterman."

"Pleased to meet you."

"We don't see too many people in the sanctuary at this hour."

"Actually, Rabbi, I came here to discuss business."

"Business? What kind of business?"

"Show business."

The rabbi stared at him for a moment, then, "I don't discuss show business in front of God. We'll go to my office."

Rabbi Gutterman's office had been done by a Sephardic Moroccan designer in earth tones, accented by touches of ebony and marble. Plaques from civic organizations and Israel Bond fund-raising drives shared the wall with framed glossies of the rabbi with various Hollywood personalities. There were prints, lithographs and an oil painting, the rabbi informed Charlie, that had been done by Martin Buber's grandson, which he had picked up at auction for a song. Light streamed in through the Dachau stained-glass windows, making irregular patterns on the flokati rug.

"So, Charlie Berns, what brings you to talk to a man of God about show business?"

Charlie looked over the rabbi's shoulder to the picture of him with George Burns and Milton Berle. Beside it there was one of him kissing Liza Minnelli. He had come to the right place.

"I'm making a movie about Judaism."

"What kind of movie?"

"It's based on the life of Benjamin Disraeli."

"Disraeli? He converted. He was an apostate."

"We're going to do some work on that in the rewrite."

"In fact, he was worse than an apostate. During his term as prime minister Jews weren't allowed to sit in the House of Commons. Did you know that?"

"No. You see, that's why I wanted to get someone like you involved. As a kind of technical adviser."

"Technical adviser?"

"Associate producer would be the actual title."

Rabbi Gutterman leaned back in his desk chair, scratched his beard.

"I'm a pretty busy man. Besides the congregation, I'm on the mayor's youth council, I'm chairman of the West Coast Symposium on Humanistic Revisionism. . . . I'm writing a book. . . . Are we talking above-the-line here?"

"Absolutely," Charlie replied.

"Where are you shooting?"

"Probably in Israel. Interiors in Rome, post in London."

"Who's directing?"

"We haven't set a director yet. We'll probably go for one of the top. I think this is Milos's type of picture."

"Milos? Terrific idea. I love Milos. He's fabulous. Did you see *Gandhi?*"

"Yes."

"I couldn't stay for the whole shoot, of course."

"I wouldn't expect you to. Just work with us on the script and the casting."

"So, who do you have in mind for the lead?"

"Actually, I was thinking of going against type. . . ."

# 3

*Whomp* . . . Bobby Mason catapulted into the padded wall, hit the floor, came up fighting, hands flexed in front, muscles tensed for a counterattack.

Terry, all six-foot-three blond inches glistening with a fine sweat, moved in for the kill.

"Just try it, motherfucker," Bobby hissed.

Terry smiled, looked off to the left and up a fraction of an inch. When Bobby took the bait, allowing his concentration to wander a few degrees off target, it was all the space Terry needed. *Thump.* He hit him low, knocking his legs back out from under him and landing him on the floor.

Terry gave him a moment's respite, then grabbed him by the shoulders, yanked him up, and threw him back across the room into the other wall.

*Crunch.* Bobby went flying into the pads and back off again, tumbling over and skidding to a stop halfway back across the room. *Thud.*

He got up unsteadily, tried to flex. But Terry was on him before he could regain his balance, leg-whipping Bobby and putting him back on the floor in a split second.

The law of diminishing returns kicked in. Bobby didn't get up for at least five seconds. Terry reached into his repertoire and came up with a stunning coup de grace. He grabbed him by the ankles, stood him on his head, then kicked his arms out from under him and let him topple over backward in a heap. *Splosh.*

Bobby lay there panting. Terry looked down at him, preparing to go after the rib cage with his Reeboks, but Bobby put up his hand and muttered, "Okay."

"You sure?"

Bobby nodded, continued lying there catching his breath, as Terry took a towel out of his gym bag, mopped the sweat off his face.

"You want to get me a Perrier, man?" Bobby managed.

Terry got a bottle of mineral water out of the small fridge in the corner, brought it over. He sat down on the specially designed beige exercise carpet in the guest house of Bobby Mason's Holmby Hills estate and shook his head.

"You took the feint."

"Yeah. Right."

"Got to be careful about the eyes. Once you follow the eyes, you're dead."

A phone gurgled in the corner of the room. Terry answered it.

"Yeah . . . Uh-huh . . . just a second." He turned to Bobby. "Your ten o'clock's here."

Bobby nodded, got up.

"He'll be right there." Terry hung up the phone as Bobby walked over to his weights, grabbed a sweatshirt, threw it over his shoulders, grimaced.

"Too rough on you today?"

"I told you, man, I want you to beat the shit out of me. Keep coming at me, try to kill me."

They walked together through the formal garden toward the main house. A platoon of short yellow men were trimming the hedges.

"See this garden?" Bobby motioned. "The guy who designed it for me was an art director for Luke Godard."

"No shit."

"It's a scale model of Louis XIV's garden at Versailles."

"Far out . . ."

They entered the house through the billiards room.

"Thanks, man. Barry'll write you a check."

Bobby dismissed him in the main hall of the mansion. Terry walked out past a bearded man dressed in a black cashmere jacket and a silk scarf.

Rabbi Seth Gutterman got up from the Edwardian love seat that graced the entry. Under his arm, beneath his suede tallith bag, was an illustrated edition of *The Talmud Made Simple*. Beneath that was a copy of *Bill and Ben*.

"Shalom," he said.

"Shloom, man."

Bobby Mason and his spiritual adviser repaired to the deck chairs around the pool. Bobby ordered a Dr. Brown's Cel-Ray tonic. The rabbi took tea. As they sat under the large Côte d'Azur sun umbrella, Bobby casually tossed chocolate-covered marshmallows to his Dobermans, who snapped them up like storm troopers.

"Some dogs you have there," the rabbi remarked with attempted casualness.

"Let me tell you something, Rabbi. You don't want to piss those dogs off, you know what I mean?"

The rabbi nodded nervously.

"I give the command, you're chopped meat."

"I don't doubt it."

"Watch this. . . ." Bobby took a whistle from a chain around his neck, blew it once. A high-pitched squeal froze the dogs in their tracks. They stopped devouring the marshmallows, looked straight at Bobby, who explained to the rabbi, "See, that's the command sound. They're ready for orders. There are two dozen different orders I could give them. *Kill* and *maim* are two entirely different commands. You would only use *kill* if the dude had a gun. *Maim*, they stay away from the vital organs, work on your legs. . . ."

"How interesting."

"Swim," Bobby commanded.

Without hesitation, the dogs dove lemminglike into Bobby Mason's Olympic-size swimming pool. Then, treading water, they turned and faced their master, waiting for the next command.

"Very impressive," the rabbi murmured.

"You want them to swim laps, dive to the bottom?"

"No thanks. Perhaps we should get on with our lesson."

Bobby dismissed the dogs with the *out* and then the *home* commands, and they slunk off to patrol the perimeter of the property. The rabbi took a sip of his chamomile tea, smiled at Bobby. "I thought we might talk today about the commitment of becoming a Jew," he began.

Bobby leaned back in his chair flexing his shoulder and leg muscles alternately to let them cool down from the workout without cramping.

"Your decision to become a Jew is a very serious step. Judaism, Bobby, is not a coat that you can put on and take off when it gets too warm or uncomfortable or out of fashion. It's not something we add to or subtract from our being. It becomes a part of us, an integral part of us. It stays with us, night and day, and travels with us, and eats and sleeps with us. It even goes on location with us."

Bobby nodded, started massaging his upper thigh muscles with the tips of his fingers.

"Now just as there are people like you who come to the Torah after wandering in the wilderness, there are people who turn away from the laws of Moses after having been born into the covenant, who try to take off that garment once they put it on. And do you know what they find? They find that they can't

escape their birthright. You remember we talked last time about
Esau, who sold his birthright to his brother Jacob for a mess of
porridge?"

"Right."

"Well, a birthright is also a birth obligation. You have to take
the good with the bad, the light with the heavy. . . . "

"Gotcha."

"Now today I want to tell you about a famous man who was
born wearing that coat and tried to shed it. He was a man who
reached great prominence in his life, who became the head of a
government, mingled with kings and queens, made decisions
about war and peace. . . ."

Somewhere in the house, phones continued to gurgle softly.
Lines lit up on the extension console within Bobby Mason's reach
on the table, but Bobby had left instructions that he was not to be
disturbed during his spiritual instruction.

The rabbi warmed to his lesson. "At the age of twelve, this
man's father had him baptized in the Christian religion in order
to try to facilitate his movement in the polite society of the time,
which, of course, did not accept Jews. Nothing new there. Been
going on since the days of the Romans. But can we hold a twelve-
year-old responsible for his father's actions?"

The rabbi shook his head rhetorically. Bobby Mason followed
suit.

"As you know, Bobby, we Jews recognize thirteen as the age of
responsibility, the age at which a young person takes on the
covenant with the bar mitzvah ceremony. So this conversion that
the father forced on the son was not to be charged against the
son's account with God. God would forgive him. But he spent his
entire life with an aching gap in his soul. He was an incomplete
man. Despite all the worldly honors he received, despite being
knighted by the queen, despite having a requiem mass per-
formed at Westminster Abbey upon his death, this man lived a
hollow life. This man walked in weariness wherever he went."

"Yeah."

"You see, Bobby, he tried to take the coat off. It doesn't work. Judaism, Bobby, is strictly pay or play. You don't settle out on it once you sign on. There is no out deal. . . ."

At nine that night Howard Draper was sitting with his wife, Winnie, and his accountant, Yale Canoff, at the Bellagio Gardens about to order dessert. The rack of lamb *forestier* was not overly tender, and he was thinking of something soothing to chase it with.

"What are you going to have, Winnie?"

His wife, petite and lean, blessed with a digestion that could compact anything without serious consequences, replied, "I don't know. Maybe the *îles flottantes* . . . what do you think?"

Howard Draper shrugged. He had no opinion at all about what his wife should have for dessert. He wanted her opinion on what *he* should have. All day long he was required to have opinions. At night he would like others to have opinions for him.

"I had *îles flottantes* once at this little château in Normandy. To die from." Yale Canoff flushed with pleasure at the memory. By all indications this large florid man should have been dead a long time ago, judging by his total disregard for calories and cholesterol. Howard Draper, who was told by the doctor at his last checkup to eat more prudently, resented the fact that his accountant not only gallivanted around France on his clients' money but ate potentially lethal items without keeling over.

"Christ, it's been so long since we've been abroad I can hardly remember," Winnie announced with a martyred expression. "Howard has to work all the time."

"If I didn't work, Winnie, Yale wouldn't be able to eat *îles flottantes* in little châteaux in Normandy."

"I'd settle for a long weekend in Santa Ana. . . ."

"If I were you, Winnie, I'd go with the assorted sorbets. They're very good here," Yale Canoff volunteered, trying to sidetrack the conversation from its potentially inflammatory course.

Howard Draper was tempted to announce to his wife, right in the middle of the Bellagio Gardens and her agony over dessert options, that if he didn't somehow manage to turn things around at the studio by that summer the options for dessert would become considerably more limited. He hadn't even confided in his own accountant that Frederick the Great had issued a fiat about profitability in the entertainment division. There was no point in telling Winnie. Nothing would slow her down. She would have sailed right through the Depression without missing a beat. She would have sold the plumbing before she gave up her *îles flottantes.* . . .

So immersed was he in these unpleasant thoughts that he didn't notice a short chubby man in a Stetson hat, who walked up to the table and stuck out his hand.

"Howard."

Howard Draper did a momentary take before he recognized Bobby Mason's manager. Bert Sully was a soft-spoken, vapid Texan, who affected a genteel politeness to camouflage the talons—a barracuda with soft gums. He had gotten his hooks into Bobby Mason a few years ago and had taken him to the bank and back many times. He wore string ties and called women ma'am.

Howard Draper recovered with his best demi-WASP smile. "Bert. How are you?"

"Just dandy."

"Say hello to my wife, Winnie, Yale Canoff . . . Bert Sully."

"Howdy do." Bert nodded, tipped the Stetson imperceptibly. "See here, Howard, I don't mean to bother you over your dinner, but I need to have a dozen or so words with you."

"Certainly, Bert. Have a seat."

"No reason to bother your pretty little woman's head on that account, Howard. You come take a stroll to the conveniences with me, and I'll have you back here in no time."

"Would you excuse me," Howard said, as he got up, untucking his napkin.

"He'll be back for dessert, ma'am. You have my word. It was indeed a pleasure." He bowed to Winnie, then nodded at Yale. "Mr. Granoff."

After Howard Draper followed Bert Sully toward the men's room, Winnie piped up, "Christ, only in this town do you do business in the crapper. Who is that guy anyway?"

"Bobby Mason's manager."

"He looks like Jack Ruby."

Meanwhile, in the art deco men's room of the Bellagio Gardens, Bert Sully moseyed over to the urinal and unzipped.

"You don't mind if I have a whizz, do you, Howard? I talk business better on an empty bladder."

"Not at all," Howard Draper assured him, the WASP side of his split personality cringing.

"How would you people like to make Bobby's next picture?"

Howard Draper replied with as much poise as he could muster under the circumstances. "You know we want to be in business with Bobby."

"I'm glad you feel that way, Howard. Now I'm going to tell you something. Probably shouldn't tell you this because you don't tell a fella you're about to make a deal with how much your boy wants to make this deal. Kinda like letting a steer in on the fact that you're about to put a branding iron up his ass, if you follow me."

Howard Draper smiled, nodded vacuously.

"See, my boy Bobby's got a picture he wants to make."

"What's that, Bert?"

Bert Sully shook himself off slowly, deposited a lungful of phlegm in the urinal, zipped up. He walked over to the pale pink sink, started to wash his hands.

"There's a script he's in love with. Wants to put it in the works. And he wants to put it in the works at your shop, Howard. What do you say?"

"Great . . . what's it called?"

"*Bill and Bob.*"

*"Bill and Bob* . . . who owns it?"

"If you move fast, Howard, you will."

Norman Hudris's voice kept fading on the car phone as he drove through Beverly Glen at nine-thirty the next morning, trying to have a conversation with Howard Draper on *his* car phone as he drove in from the beach on Sunset. Every time Norman went around a steep curve his voice evaporated into the foggy morning air.

Howard Draper was already furious that Norman had not been home when he called him immediately upon returning from the Bellagio Gardens last night. The vice president for production, West Coast, had spent the night with Cissy Fuchs at the latter's house in Toluca Lake. And when Norman called his service in the morning and got Howard's urgent message, his boss had already left for the studio.

He dressed hurriedly and got in his car, finally managing to get patched through to Howard Draper's car phone through Howard's secretary.

"Where *were* you, Norman? I kept calling until midnight."

"I've been having trouble with my phone. . . ."

"What?"

"My phone. It's been acting weird lately."

"Well, get the phone company to fix it."

"They're supposed to be . . ."

"What? I can't hear you."

"I said they're supposed to be out this week. . . . Hello, can you hear me?"

"Norman, you keep fading on me. Where are you?"

"I'm having trouble with my car phone too. . . ."

"What?"

"The car phone . . ."

"Norman, can you hear me?"

"What?"

"Can you hear what I'm saying?"

"I can hear you fine. Can you hear me?"

"Just listen, Norman. I want you to buy a script."

"What script?"

As his Corniche passed over the San Diego Freeway, traffic noise rose to provide further interference. Howard yelled into the phone, "Buy a script called *Bob and Bill*."

"*Bob and* who?"

"*Bob and Bill*."

"*Bob and Bill*?"

"Right. Buy it."

"From who?"

"What?"

"Who do I buy it from?"

"Call Bert Sully."

"*Bob and Bill*?"

"No . . . *Bob and Ben* . . ."

"You said *Bob and Bill*. . . ."

"I meant *Bob and Ben*. Maybe it's *Ben and Bob*. . . ."

Deidre Hearn was having a Cobb salad in the commissary when she got paged by Norman Hudris. She disliked being interrupted during lunch, the only time of the day that she theoretically wasn't at the beck and call of her boss. There was a waspish tone in her voice when she picked up the phone.

"What?"

"I want you to put a deal memo through on a script."

"Don't tell me Howard bought the werewolf story."

"No. This is another script. It's Bobby Mason's next picture. Call Bert Sully. He'll give you the details."

"All right . . . can I go back to my lunch now, Norman?"

"After you call Bert."

"It's one o'clock. People are at lunch."

"Deidre, this is important. Howard wants us to close on this before the end of the day."

"You're kidding. . . ."

"As soon as you close with Bert Sully, have Business Affairs lock up the writer."

"Norman, what is the project?"

"Something called *Ben and Bill.* Or *Bill and Ben* or *Bob and . . .* the fuck do I know. Sounds like some sort of buddy picture. Get me coverage on it as soon as you can."

"Did anybody read the script?"

"Deidre, we're talking about a Bobby Mason picture. Call Bert Sully now."

He hung up. She stood there for a moment, holding the phone, as Norman Hudris's voice dissolved into the ether. Across the room the abandoned Cobb salad looked back at her forlornly. Jesus, she swore under her breath. Didn't anybody ever shut down for a minute? She managed a caked smile at an agent she knew, started to try to find a waitress to wrap up the remainder of her lunch, decided she was no longer hungry, put a ten on the table and left the commissary.

Back in her office, she went to the big Rolodex on her secretary's desk for Bert Sully's number. Alan was having lunch at Pesto, the nouvelle Italian place in Brentwood. One of these days she'd get around to firing him, but for the moment she didn't have the patience to break in someone new.

"Well, howdy do," Bert Sully said to her when she'd gotten him on the phone. She couldn't stand the man. He made her Cobb salad start to churn.

"Hello, Bert. How are you?"

"Just dandy."

"Norman tells me Bobby wants to put a script in development."

"Yes, ma'am."

"That's terrific. . . ." She tried to keep the vinegar out of her voice.

"It's a heck of a notion."

"So I hear."

"You happen to have a gander at the Korean grosses on *Vigilante Destroyer,* by the way?"

"Not yet."

"Broke the house record in every theater in Seoul. And those little yellow fellas know a thing or two about martial arts, now, don't they?"

"Yes, they do. . . ."

"Course, this new thing's a little different cup of tea, but I said to Bobby, 'Bobby, you can't keep doing the same old thing, now, can you? Got to keep stretching. You're a star, Bobby, and your fans'll follow you from here to eternity.' . . ."

"What's the name of the script?"

*"Ben and Bob."*

*"Ben and Bob?* Norman said it was *Bill and Bob."*

"Could be. I haven't finished reading it yet. It's about this Jewish fella over in England who fights injustice."

"What?"

"Some fella name of Disraeli. Israeli fella . . ."

Deidre dug her heels into the carpet to keep from sliding off the desk she was leaning on. It took every bit of strength to keep from losing it, as Bert Sully went on about Bobby Mason's commitment to playing Benjamin Disraeli.

". . . wins out against tremendous odds. David and Goliath. *Death Wish. High Noon.* But, you see, this Jew fella is in the government. Fighting injustice from within. Helluva story. He's crazy about the area. . . ."

When Deidre finally recovered, she muttered in a barely audible whisper, "Bert?"

"Yes, ma'am."

"Who controls the property?"

"Producer by the name of Charlie Berns. With an E. Jewish fella, I reckon . . ."

While this conversation was taking place, Brad Emprin was having lunch at Pesto with a hot young director he was trying to sign. They were commiserating over problems with their BMWs in a window banquette diagonally across from where

Deidre Hearn's secretary, Alan, was sitting with his friend Brian.

"I've had it in three times. They've ripped it apart, top to bottom, can't find a thing. As soon as I get two blocks from the place—*galump.*"

The hot young director nodded supportively over his angel-hair pasta. "I've had three complete brake jobs in twenty-five thousand miles. Seven hundred bucks a throw. I'm seriously thinking of trading it in for a Honda."

"You can trade it in for three Hondas."

"Tell me about it."

Brad Emprin took a sip of his San Pellegrino with a twist and sighed, *"C'est la vie."*

The director had just made a picture in Paris, and this was Brad Emprin's attempt at a segue.

"I hear," he said, following up, "the picture you just did is fabulous."

The hot young director looked dubiously across at the agent and said, "No one's seen it."

"I mean, from dailies . . ."

"Dailies have been closed. I haven't even shown it to the studio yet."

Fortunately, Brad Emprin was interrupted by a phone page at that moment. Excusing himself hastily, he got up and crossed to the telephone, heard the voice of Deidre Hearn on the other end.

"Sorry to bother you at lunch, Brad, but I'm getting heat to close this deal fast."

"What deal?"

"We want to buy *Bob and Ben.*"

"What?"

*"Bob and Ben,* the Disraeli project."

It took Brad Emprin several moments to remember the events of yesterday. Charlie Berns. The staff meeting. The sinus headache . . .

"Right," he said. "Fabulous script, isn't it?"

"I wouldn't know. I haven't even seen coverage on it. Howard wants to buy it, so I'm buying it. And I'd like to buy it before the close of business today. Do you represent the writer as well as the producer?"

"Uh-huh," he lied again. "One-stop shopping."

"Brad, this is just one of a shitload of scripts in development for Bobby Mason. So don't back up a truck, all right?"

"Deidre, have I ever backed up a truck?"

Deidre was tempted to tell him that he'd never had the opportunity to, but she knew, with her instinctual sense of jungle survival, that small animals were the most vicious. She remained businesslike.

"I just checked Charlie Berns's credits out. He hasn't worked in three years."

"His wife's been terribly ill . . . some sort of inoperable thing. . . ."

"I'm sorry to hear that. Look, we're taking a big chance here giving him control of this picture."

"Uh-huh," Brad Emprin said, noncommittally, keeping the ball in her court, as he tried to remember if Charlie Berns even had a wife.

"We'll come in with a respectable figure, but don't expect a piece of the studio on this one, all right?"

"Uh-huh."

"I'll have my Business Affairs person call you in thirty minutes with a firm offer."

"Sounds good to me."

"By the way, Brad, how is that restaurant? My secretary loves it."

"It's fabulous. . . ."

He apologized to the hot young director, who told him he was due in the cutting room in five minutes and offered to split the check.

"Please," Brad Emprin insisted, "this is on us. We never let a client, or a potential client, pay for his own lunch."

Driving back to the agency, he felt the little trickle of panic sweat under the armpits, the first sign of an anxiety attack. How the fuck was he going to negotiate a deal for a writer he didn't represent on a script that he hadn't read for a client he wasn't even sure was still with the agency? And what if Charlie Berns's wife was in perfect health and happened to be a close friend of Deidre Hearn's?

He reached into the glove compartment, took out the car tranks and popped a five-milligram tab.

At three forty-five that afternoon the author of *Bill and Ben*, Lionel B. Traven, né Travitz, was sitting on a bus surrounded by three bags of melting groceries. Traven was the pseudonym he adopted in honor of the famous B. Traven, the rumored author of *The Treasure of the Sierra Madre*, a film that Lionel Travitz had seen thirty-one times before deciding to adopt the nom de plume of his alter ego.

Though he didn't know it yet, Lionel was on the wrong bus, destined to make a left instead of a right on Beverly Drive and begin its descent into the bowels of Los Angeles. He was thinking of other things, his mind spinning with the possibilities of his new career as a Hollywood screenwriter. His uncle had said there would be rewrites to do on the script, but not to worry about them at the moment. The first step was to package the material, as he referred to it, and get a studio interested in the story. Then they'd take care of fixing the script.

Meanwhile, Lionel had settled into the back downstairs bedroom of his uncle's house. He was going to start his new screenplay about the existential Nebraska crop duster as soon as he got a typewriter. With the $5,000 he'd be getting for the option of *Bill and Ben*, Lionel would be in good shape for the immediate future. His needs were small, and with his map and his growing knowledge of the bus system, he'd get along fine.

He looked out the bus window through the hazy glare of the afternoon sun. The sky was neither blue nor gray, but a neutral color that defied description. Almost nobody was on the side-walks. All you could hear was the constant hum of car engines and air conditioners. The street corners had pastel minimalls with take-out taco places and suntanning solariums. If you lived in a place where the sun allegedly shone all the time, why would you want to go inside to get a suntan? There were no bars or pool halls or dogs on the street. There were no fire escapes. People sat in convertibles listening to Walkmen with earplugs. The traffic lights changed every thirty seconds. Los Angeles was the most peculiar place that Lionel had ever been to.

Things had been chaotic when Brad Emprin got back to his office and tried to contact Charlie Berns. Tanya, of course, was nowhere to be found, and, to make matters worse, she apparently had the wrong number for Charlie Berns in the Rolodex. He paced the floor of the outside office, trying to structure a deal in his head, feeling the Valium cloud disintegrating, until his secretary returned from her noon yoga class.

"It's about time you got back," he snapped.

She barely blinked. Yoga made her placid. He wasn't entirely convinced she wasn't on some sort of downers as well.

"You got the wrong number for Charlie Berns in the Rolodex. And I need to talk to him right away."

Flipping expertly through the Rolodex, she came up with the number, dialed it as Brad Emprin insisted, "It's no use. I tried it half a dozen times. You get a recording that the line is out of order. He must have changed his number. The least he could've done was told us."

She flipped the interrupter, dialed the phone company's busi-ness office, found out that it was indeed Charlie Berns's phone number, but that it had been disconnected and that there was no new listing.

"How can he have his phone disconnected? How can you live in this town and not have a phone that works?"

The other line lit up. Tanya answered it in her narcose voice. "Brad Emprin's office."

It was the Business Affairs person.

"I'll see if he's back from lunch," Tanya said into the phone, then, hitting the "hold" button, "You want to talk to Pat Caroway?"

How could he talk to her when he didn't even know the name of the writer he was supposed to represent? His sinus headache was returning. He couldn't do a Sinutab if he was going to do another Valium. He'd have to choose one or the other. He shook his head. Tanya released the "hold" button and said, "He's away from his desk at the moment. Can I have him get back?"

She scribbled a name and number as Brad Emprin retreated into his office, opened the desk drawer, looked at the drugstore he kept in there. Beside the office tranks and the Sinutabs, there was Gelusil, vitamin C, zinc, Rolaids, Bufferin, Excedrin, Bronkaid, Robitussin and Metamucil in tablet form. He went for the Sinutab. The antihistamine gave him a little speed buzz, which he would need if he were to get through this afternoon.

Back in the outer office, he had Tanya write down Charlie Berns's address. He grabbed it and headed for the door, passing John DeMarco coming in from lunch.

"Tough hours you keep."

Brad Emprin did not even attempt to explain. He took the elevator down to the garage, got in the car, started it up, felt the vapor lock smother the ignition of the still-warm engine. He babied the 325i out of the garage, and as he sped down Santa Monica Boulevard, the antihistamine kicked in.

Charlie Berns sat on a peeling rattan deck chair beside the ravaged flower beds of his patio, reading a biography of Benjamin Disraeli. It was slow going, a laborious journey through the labyrinthine parliamentary sparring of mid-nineteenth-century English politics. After a somewhat colorful youth as an adventurer and novelist, a parvenu from a middle-class Jewish literary family trying to penetrate the privileged circles of power, he became a bastion of conservative politics, trumpeting the glory of the empire and the queen until he quietly expired from gout in 1881. Apart from a few interesting financial peccadillos in his youth and a trip through the Mediterranean whoring with the British garrison at Malta, the majority of his life was spent shuffling between the government and opposition benches of Parliament, riding the thrust and parry of Whig and Tory infighting.

Lionel's screenplay was a faithful recounting of Disraeli's political vicissitudes, focusing on his lifelong duel with his Liberal opponent, William Gladstone. There were eloquent speeches from the government bench in the House of Commons, a witty voice-over narration from Disraeli's letters to his sister, Sarah, and a Wagnerian deathbed scene. It was literate, poetic, well crafted and entirely uncommercial. There wasn't a studio executive in town who would get past page twenty.

Bobby Mason wouldn't get past page one—a narration of Disraeli's speech in defense of protective tariffs over a tight shot of his tombstone at his country house in Hughenden. At no point in the script did Benjamin Disraeli resort to martial arts to resolve his problems. He never took his shirt off. And the only woman in his life, besides his sister and Queen Victoria, was a frumpy widow of a wealthy textile manufacturer whom he married late in life for financial reasons.

Of course, ever since Charlie had first read the script the night of Lionel's fortuitous arrival, he knew there was no way it would ever go before a camera in Hollywood in remotely the same fashion as his nephew had written it. He was counting on the fact that Bobby Mason wouldn't read a script until it was ready to shoot, and by that time Ben Disraeli would kick enough ass to keep him interested. . . .

Immersed in thought, Charlie didn't hear the doorbell ring. It rang several times to no response. Brad Emprin stood at the front

door, riding an antihistamine buzz, impatiently pushing the
doorbell button. Eventually, he gave up and, pissed, was returning maniacally to the 325i to consider his next move when he
noticed the carnage along the side of the house. He had never
seen anything like the ravaged condition of the flowerbeds. It
was as if some antishrubbery bomb had torn through Charlie
Berns's yard, leaving destruction in its path.

Who the fuck napalmed Charlie Berns's house? Brad Emprin
walked up the driveway on the side of the house to get a better
look. That's when he saw the carcass of the lemon tree protrud-
ing from the pool. He kept walking until he reached the rear of
the house and saw his client stretched out on a deck chair in
Bermuda shorts.

"Charlie?"

Charlie looked up and saw his agent standing on the patio in
a Bullocks Men's Shop Giorgio Armani suit, carrying a Hermès
attaché case.

"I didn't know you made house calls, Brad."

"I had no choice. Your phone's out of order."

Charlie nodded, finished up the note he was making.

"Charlie, how can you do business in this town if you can't be
reached?"

"That's what I have you for."

"I need to talk to you."

Charlie put his pad down. Brad Emprin looked around for
some place to sit, but there was nothing on the patio besides
Charlie's deck chair. So he stood, uncomfortably shifting his
weight in his new Bally loafers, trying to ignore the fact that there
was a tree sticking out of his client's swimming pool.

"Deidre Hearn. Remember, I told you I had made her aware
of you? I pitched her the Disraeli script and she got real interested."

"No kidding?"

"Uh-huh. I told her about the Bobby Mason casting idea and
she flipped."

"Really?"

"In fact, I got her so hot she made an offer on the script, without even reading it. Can you believe that?"

Charlie shook his head with mock incredulity "That's terrific, Brad. That's real good work."

"The thing is, Charlie, I need to close on the writer too if I'm going to make a deal for you. Who is he, anyway?"

There was no transition between these two sentences. Though Charlie Berns may have been unemployed and suicidal, he was not dumb. On the contrary. If there was one thing he understood it was leverage. And for the first time in a very long time Charlie Berns had some.

"I own the script, Brad. The deal's going to be with me."

"With you?"

"Actually, with Charles Berns Productions, Inc."

"Charlie, it's not going to fly."

"How's that?"

"The studio's going to want to control the development of the script. They're not going to do a coproduction with you and give you creative control."

"Well, then, we'll have to find another studio, won't we?"

The Sinutab was starting to break down. He felt the dreaded tightening around the eyes and the slow infiltration of the sinus cavities.

"You're not going to hold a gun to the head of a major motion-picture studio."

"They can pass. It's a free country."

Brad Emprin was having trouble following this conversation. Though paranoid and a hypochondriac, he was not dumb either. Taking a deep, cleansing breath, a yoga technique that Tanya had taught him for stressful moments, he decided to talk man-to-man to his client.

"Charlie, can I tell you something straight? Just between us?"

"Sure."

"Don't take this personally, but I got to level with you. Deals are not piling up on my desk for Charlie Berns."

"That so?"

Brad Emprin nodded. "To be perfectly honest with you, I consider us lucky to have an offer for any picture on the table. This is no time for you to get difficult."

"Well, that's your opinion, Brad. You're entitled to it. I guess I ought to look for other representation."

"Charlie, that's not what I'm saying. I believe in you. The whole agency does. I mean, we've been knocking on this door for a long time. Now the door's opened. Don't walk away."

Charlie got up from the deck chair, scratched the back of his neck.

"Sit down, Brad." He indicated the vacated deck chair.

"That's all right."

"Sit down. You look like your loafers are bothering you."

They were. They were a half-size too small. Brad Emprin went over and sat uncomfortably on the edge of the rattan deck chair. Charlie paced the patio for a moment.

"Okay, Brad, let me explain to you what we're talking about here. Just so we're straight. Bobby Mason has a first-look deal with Deidre Hearn's studio, right? Bobby Mason wants to do a script called *Bill and Ben*. I have an option deal signed by the author controlling the worldwide rights in all media to *Bill and Ben*. For eighteen months, renewable to thirty-six. You following me so far?"

Brad Emprin nodded.

"Good. Now if Deidre Hearn's studio is not happy with a coproduction with Charles Berns Productions, then they have a perfect right to pass. No hard feelings. I will go elsewhere. *Someone* in this town will be interested in this deal, Brad. Take my word for it. . . ."

"Charlie . . ."

"Shhh. Here's where you come in. Listen carefully. If you and your agency are interested in negotiating this deal for me, you're in for ten percent of everything that accrues to me on this project. If not . . ."

"Of course we're interested, Charlie. That's not the point."

"Tell me what the point is."

"I don't think they're going to buy it."

"Let's put it on the freeway, Brad. See if it gets run over."

For the first time in his short career, Brad Emprin made a deal from his car phone. He drove around the quiet, tree-lined streets of the Beverly Hills Flats negotiating deal points. Charlie sat beside him with the yellow pad writing everything down. Every time the Business Affairs woman had to go check a point with her superior, Brad Emprin had to call Tanya and have her get ready to patch the call back through to the car phone.

It was a long and arduous process. They reached a fairly serious obstacle when Charlie demanded a small gross position on foreign markets. The Business Affairs woman said there was no way it would ever fly. When she went off to discuss the point with Norman Hudris and Howard Draper, who was now involved, as was Bert Sully from his office in Bobby Mason's house in Holmby Hills, Charlie listened carefully as Brad Emprin braked the 325i hard and turned the wheel to the right. He swore to his agent that he could actually hear the *galump* whose existence the BMW service manager denied.

The deal was closed at six-thirty, as the sun was disappearing over the maples of Beverly Hills. In return for giving the studio a three-year option to make the movie, Charlie Berns had a development fund of $250,000 for the script, creative control over the script process, subject only to a good-faith agreement to accept input on the part of the studio, consultation with regard to casting, two gross-profit points in Europe, one point five in Asia and Australia, sequel and remake rights in perpetuity, including television series and novelization, an office suite and a secretary in the producers' building, and a parking space in the A lot.

When Brad Emprin hung up the car phone, he was a virtual

puddle. He shook his head, muttering, "They gave you everything. Can you believe it?"

"When you're hot, you're hot, Brad."

That evening Charlie took his nephew out to celebrate the sale of
*Bill and Ben*. They sat in a booth in a Thai restaurant on Sunset
and drank Thai beer and ate things that Lionel had never heard
of before.

"Fifty-two *grand* . . . ?"

Charlie nodded, working his chopsticks through a plate of
lamb curry.

"Boy, I never thought they'd pay anything like that. I mean,
that's more money than my old man makes in a whole year. . . .
Do I have to wait till they make the movie?"

"The money's yours whether they make the movie or not."

"No kidding?"

"No kidding."

Charlie did not bother to inform his nephew that the money
he was receiving for his script, $52,500, was Writers Guild mini-
mum for a high-budget feature film, as this picture most certainly was going to turn out once Bobby Mason's involvement
inflated the above-the-line costs. It was also the minimum per-
missible to pay for the acquisition of the script. But, besides the
rewrite expenses, the rest of the money wasn't payable by the
studio unless they greenlighted the picture.

"If they buy the script, why wouldn't they make the movie?"
Lionel asked.

At the moment Charlie didn't want to confuse his nephew
with too much insight into the abstruse practices of the movie
business. He tried to keep it as simple as he could.

"You see, Lionel," he explained, "this movie's now what's
called 'in development,' which means, basically, that the script
has to get rewritten while the studio thinks about whether or not
it wants to make the picture."

"I don't get it. Why do you have to rewrite it if you like it enough to spend fifty-two thousand bucks to buy it in the first place?"

"Nobody really likes a script unless they've had a rewrite or two done on it."

He shook his head, muttered, "That's very weird."

"You get used to it. Like religion. It doesn't make a lot of sense, but you learn to work with it."

Lionel ate pensively for a moment, chasing the curry with liberal splashes of Chardonnay.

"So what happens now?"

"Well, first we get rewrite notes from the studio. Then we get a writer to rewrite the script."

"What do you mean, 'get a writer'? *I'm* the writer."

"Absolutely, Lionel. You're the writer—"

"So what's this about getting a writer?"

"Lionel, listen. You're *the* writer. We wouldn't be making the movie if it wasn't for you. You're the main guy."

"*Main* guy? Why are there other writers? I don't understand."

Charlie put down his chopsticks. This was going to be delicate. He searched for the right analogy to explain how things worked. He couldn't simply tell him the truth—that very little, if anything, of the screenplay he had written would appear on the screen. Sooner or later he would have to break the news to him, but not now.

"Let me put it to you this way, Lionel. Think of yourself as the architect of a cathedral. You're the one that figures out where the nave and the transept are going to be, where the choir loft is, you design the size and placement of the windows. . . . But you don't actually paint the stained-glass windows, now do you?"

Lionel shook his head.

"You delegate the little tasks to craftsmen so that you can keep your mind on the whole. You're the creator. It's your baby. Your name's going to be up there on that screen. . . . 'Written by . . . Lionel . . .' What's your last name again?"

"Traven is my screen name. I'm very confused."

"Don't be. It's just pictures. That's the way they work. How do you like the curry?"

Lionel nodded absently, wondering whether someone else had painted B. Traven's stained-glass windows.

They sat there eating in silence for a long moment until Lionel asked, "Uh . . . what if I don't like the stained-glass windows?"

"You'll like them."

"Really?"

"Trust me."

"Sure."

"Lionel, try to understand one thing."

"What's that?"

"No windows, no cathedral."

# 4

When Charlie drove on the lot in the morning, he didn't breeze through the gate as he usually did, waving perfunctorily and avoiding eye contact. Today he stopped and announced himself.

"Charles Berns, producer of *Bill and Ben*."

The guard shuffled through his pass list and found Charlie's drive-on, handed it to him. "Put this on your windshield, Mr. Berns. Do you know where the producers' building is?"

"Sure do."

"Park in a visitor's spot until your sticker comes through. Just leave the pass on your dash."

"Thanks." Charlie gave him a friendly salute and drove on. Noblesse oblige.

The producers' building was long and low, a sleek ocean liner with a Spanish-tile roof. A gardener was manicuring the jade and rose shrubs that bordered it. A small birdbath trickled water listlessly, but no birds were taking advantage of a free drink. There was something about the bearing of the building that discouraged casual drinking. All was deathly quiet except for the low hum of air conditioning, punctuated by the desultory cadence of the trimming shears.

The gamut of cars parked in front started at a Rolls-Royce Corniche for Howard Draper and moved down incrementally to Deidre Hearn's Acura Legend. He parked beside the Acura, not bothering to read the name on the space. Anyone parked to the right of Deidre Hearn, Charlie figured, couldn't possibly outrank him.

He entered the building, carrying his beat-up briefcase and a large Rolodex containing the names and addresses of friends and associates, the home phone numbers of actors, directors, writers and agents, and a cross section of the best restaurants in town. Or, at least, what used to be the best restaurants in town. It had been a while since Charlie had dined out well.

Number 309, indicated on his drive-on pass, turned out to be a large, nearly empty suite of offices on the top floor. There were a few pieces of mismatched furniture scattered about, but it was otherwise empty except for the phones, two to an office. Nobody of any importance in Hollywood had fewer than two telephones in his or her office, no matter how small the space was.

Settling into a new office was not an unfamiliar experience for him. Like most independent producers, he had spent his career moving from picture to picture, from studio to studio, occupying offices very much like the one he was in at the moment. Empty, they always looked like hotel rooms, temporary and vulgar, neuter, waiting to adopt the character of the next occupant.

He sat down at the large ugly desk, swiveled and looked out the window in back of him. It was a familiar street scene. Lawn sprinklers discharged spray indifferently into the hazy mid-morning air; a mail cart made its rounds; a prop-rental truck drove slowly toward the gate; a security guard pedaled a bicycle toward the soundstages . . . the flora and fauna of a studio lot. They all looked the same to Charlie. You seen one, you seen them all. . . .

His back to the door, he didn't notice a young woman standing in the doorway to the outer office. She stood there for a moment and then cleared her throat. "Mr. Berns?"

Charlie swiveled around and faced a thin thing with dark hair and a pale Modigliani face.

"I'm Enid Schonblum," she said.

"Hi."

"I've been assigned to you. Temporarily. From the studio. Until you get your own secretary."

She spoke in short, aspirated bursts, each one dying on her tongue as if she were mortified at having spoken at all.

Charlie nodded, rubbed the back of his neck.

"If that's all right. With you."

"Sure."

"You had a call. From Deidre Hearn. She wants to talk to you. As soon as you're in."

"Thanks."

They stared at each other for a moment, trying to figure out where to go from there. Eventually Enid Schonblum looked away, melting under Charlie's glare. Her eyes on the carpet, she murmured, "Should I try her for you? Now?"

"What about this office?"

"This office?"

"Furnishings."

"Oh. You want to furnish? The office?"

"I think it would be nice."

"I see. Furnishings. I suppose that's Office Maintenance. I'll see if I can get them. For you. Now."

And she stole away to her desk in the inner office. Charlie took a deep breath. He didn't know whether he would be able to survive Enid Schonblum. Producing a picture was difficult enough without having a secretary who sounded as if each word she uttered were the last word she would ever say on this earth.

The furnishing was a diversionary tactic to get this woman out of his office. She made him terribly uncomfortable. He needed to think. Now that he had a foothold into the system the trick was to keep afloat and not get sidetracked by, among other things, office furnishings.

Deidre Hearn was going to be a problem. Right away he had spotted intelligence behind her facility with the argot of the business. By now she had undoubtedly read *Bill and Ben* and was trying to figure out how in God's name her studio had shelled out a quarter of a million bucks for it.

Charlie wasn't prepared to reassure her yet. And he wasn't going to be able to get by Deidre Hearn with analogies to cathedral architecture. Eventually he would have to deal with her. But in the meantime he needed to get the script into presentable shape before the entire house came crumbling down on him.

When he had read *Bill and Ben* for the very first time, the day of Lionel's arrival, one name had immediately sprung to mind as the person to fix the script. Charlie's years of working in movies had taught him the unenviable habit of being incapable of reading anything without simultaneously thinking about having it rewritten. Lying on his bed that fateful night, sweltering from the taped-up windows, he had projected the arc, figured out the rough schedule he'd have to follow to pull it off. The linchpin was having a new script in time to get the green light right after Bobby Mason's Israel picture. There was a small window of opportunity that he could exploit if he moved fast.

Madison Kearney's name was in the Rolodex under W, for writers. There were half a dozen crossed-out phone numbers after his name. This was not an easy man to find. One of the reasons that Madison Kearney remained a largely undiscovered secret, besides the fact that he was a drunk and a madman, was that he was almost impossible to contact. In a town where people were as eager as possible to be found, where they hired publicists and took out ads with phone numbers prominently displayed, where they had agents and managers bandying their names about, Madison Kearney was essentially incognito. The only listing for him was a P.O. Box registered with the Writers Guild.

Charlie dialed the last, uncrossed-out number on the card. He got the recording he usually got whenever he tried to find the writer. This number is no longer in service and there is no new number.

He would have to spend the morning, or what was left of it, combing the bars of Eagle Rock. Grabbing his briefcase containing a copy of Lionel's draft and the biography of Disraeli, he started for the door when his secretary emerged, effectively blocking his exit.

Charlie skidded to a halt. She looked immediately down to her yellow pad and uttered, "I called Office Maintenance. They're sending someone up. With requisition forms. You can choose from various styles. Danish modern. Antique. Early American. You can request repainting. Too. If you want it. It takes five days. They do two coats."

She ran out of gas abruptly. If she hadn't, Charlie was considering going right through her. He didn't have time to listen to her struggle to get a thought out. She seemed incapable of uttering more than a syllable or two without stopping for a new breath of air. He had never in his life met anybody who spoke as slowly as this woman did. You could die waiting for the next sentence.

"That's great," he said.

She nodded, looked down at her shoes, which, Charlie noticed, were excessively sensible.

"Look," he said, "I have to go off the lot. I'll be back later."

He started to walk toward the door, but she held her ground, occupying the narrow doorway with her ethereal presence. Charlie halted once more.

"What do you want me to do? About Office Maintenance?"

"Listen, why don't you handle it."

"Me?"

"Uh-huh."

"You want *me?* To choose the furniture? For your office?"

"Why not? You look like you have good taste."

He made another go at the door, and this time she gave ground, stepping aside. As he headed for the hallway he heard her ask, "What about Deidre? Hearn? Her phone call?"

"I'll get back. To her. Later."

Avoiding the elevator, Charlie went down the stairs and slipped out the door minutes before Deidre Hearn headed up the same stairs to his office. She found Enid Schonblum aspirating into the phone about paint colors.

"Excuse me," Enid said into the phone and looked up at her. "May I help you?"

"Is Mr. Berns in?"

"He was. In. He's off the lot. Now."

Deidre glanced at her watch. She had telephoned barely half an hour ago.

"Did you tell him I wanted to talk to him?"

"Yes. I did. He said he would get back to you. Later."

"Do you know where he is? Is he reachable? Does he have a phone in his car?"

This was a great deal to respond to at one time. Enid struggled to phrase an answer that would do justice to each of the three questions. Meanwhile, Office Maintenance wanted to know if they had been cut off. She was unable to handle the overload. She went off-line, blinking frantically at Deidre and holding Office Maintenance closer to her ear, as if that gesture alone would respond to their question.

Deidre Hearn did not deal well with slow-moving people. She stood there, idling roughly, glaring at the catatonic secretary, who finally managed to shake her head, as an all-purpose answer.

"Well, if you *do* hear from him. Tell him to call me. Please."

"Yes. I will. Certainly."

Deidre whirled around, exited the office, headed back downstairs to Norman Hudris's office. Norman's secretary said he was on the phone with Howard Draper. Deidre entered anyway. If he could walk into her office without knocking, she could walk into his while he was on the phone.

"Jesus . . . No kidding . . . ?"

Norman waved her to one of his Mies van der Rohe knockoffs. She sat down in the uncomfortable chair and watched him pacing with the phone at his ear.

"Thirty-five and an eighth? That's down two and a half since Monday. . . . What'd he say?"

His indelible suntan seemed to fade a few shades. "Who? Really . . . ? How come nobody on Wall Street knows about this?"

Deidre got up, unable to sit still at the moment. She wandered over to the coffee table, which held this morning's copy of *Variety*.

"Howard, tell me something," Norman whined on. "Shouldn't ACI's stock be going *up* if the Japs are waving a lot of cash around?"

A first-page box caught Deidre's eye: MASON LINES UP NEXT PROJECT. She read on with interest:

Bert Sully, Bobby Mason's manager, has announced the actor's next project after finishing *Desert Commando* in Israel, a buddy movie called *Bill and Ben*. "This is not your ordinary Bobby Mason movie," Sully was quick to point out. "This picture has a whole other level to it that will surprise people who think that Bobby is only interested in action." Asked who they were considering for the colead, Sully replied, "We're going to go after a world-class name. . . ." Answer your phone, Sly. . . .

She put the paper down, sank back into the couch, incredulous, muttering to herself until Norman got off the phone, exclaiming, "This studio is so badly in the toilet that the ACI stock won't go up even with a takeover rumor. Can you believe it?"

Deidre wasn't concerned about the stock price. At her level, she didn't have stock options.

"Howard says that Katsubishi is thinking about a tender offer, not even being *discreet* about it, and Wall Street doesn't give a shit. The stock is going *down*. . . ."

Deidre handed the paper to him. "Did you read this?"

He looked at the box and nodded.

"It's on the first page."

"So that's good, no? Publicity . . ."

"Norman, did you read my coverage?"

"Not yet."

"I put it in your 'in' box at nine o'clock last night. When I finished reading *Bill and Ben*."

"I'll read it tonight."

"Don't bother. Let me tell you what we just bought for a quarter of a million dollars. We just bought the story of Benjamin Disraeli."

"Who?"

"Benjamin Disraeli, prime minister of England under Queen Victoria."

"We did?"

She nodded. "We bought a slow, talky, English period piece for a man who can barely get two sentences out without having to be looped."

Norman sat down opposite her on the modular couch, staring blankly off into the distance as his assistant elaborated: "We have a twenty-five-year-old functionally illiterate black karate champ playing a middle-aged, nineteenth-century British writer and politician, known for his articulateness and wit."

"What . . . what about Bill? The buddy?"

"Bill is William Gladstone, the leader of the Liberal party in Parliament. The script is mostly about their rivalry over hot issues like protective tariffs in England in the eighteen seventies."

Norman sat there for a moment, rubbing his chin, massaging his neck muscles to get the kinks out. He'd pulled something playing tennis that morning. He'd have to see if he could get in to see the chiropractor on the way home.

"Protective *tariffs?*" he murmured weakly.

"Uh-huh."

"Well," he said after a long moment, exhaling deeply, "I suppose we'll just have to fix it in the rewrite."

Charlie cruised East Sunset in the 560 SEL, checking the bars on either side of the street. It was slow going. Each time he saw a possibility, he had to park the car, get out, enter, talk to the bartender. At eleven o'clock in the morning, they all looked pretty much the same inside—dark, drafty, nearly deserted, with one or two hard-core rummies sitting silently at the bar gazing off into space with the beatific look of drunks.

The Mexican bartenders were not helpful. When Charlie described Madison Kearney to them, they merely shook their heads with Aztec stoicism.

He had worked his way east as far as Alvarado when he parked in front of the El Caballero Lounge, a pastel-blue stucco tavern on the south side of the street. Locking the car, he entered the bar and was greeted by "Besame Mucho" blaring from the jukebox. He looked around, his eyes adjusting to the darkness.

The place resembled a cantina in a B western—with a kind of dark lethargy and the smell of beer and incipient violence. Seeing no one at the bar, Charlie was about to turn around and exit when the door to the men's room opened and a man staggered out. Six-foot-three, slouching, long blond-gray hair over his eyes, Madison Kearney made his way carefully to the closest booth, collapsed onto the scarred leather seat.

Charlie walked over and sat down in the booth opposite Madison Kearney, who looked up from his tequila and blinked several times, trying to focus.

"How you doing, Madison?" Charlie said.

The man nodded, went back to his tequila, his head sinking lower on his chest.

"I got a job for you."

"What's that?"

"A job. A rewrite."

"Call my . . . agent. . . . He knows where to find me. . . ."

"You're here, Madison. I found you."

"Yes, he generally knows where I am. . . . Call him. William Fucking Morris . . . "

"Madison, you don't have an agent. You haven't had one for a long time."

"You go over to that phone over there and you dial the William Fucking Morris office, 555–7451, and you ask to talk to them. They know where I am. . . . And I'll tell you something else. I'll tell you something else. . . ."

He drifted off, the thought, whatever it was, slipping from the shaky toehold it had established in his booze-sodden brain. Charlie took a deep breath. This was going to be tough. Getting Madison Kearney out of this bar, getting him relatively sober, getting him in some sort of shape to work out a new story and write a draft of the script seemed, at the moment, to be nearly insurmountable.

Somehow, however, he was going to have to do it. The future prospects of *Bill and Ben* were sloshing around in the pickled brain of Madison Kearney, slouching into his tequila in the El Caballero Lounge on East Sunset.

"All right, Madison, let's go to work," Charlie said cheerfully.

"The William Fucking Morris Agency. One fifty-one El Camino Drive. Beverly Fucking Hills, California."

Madison Kearney delivered the line with as much dignity as he could muster before throwing up in his own lap.

By mid-afternoon Deidre Hearn realized she was in trouble. The symptoms were familiar—the vague sense of disorientation, the drifting away from the moorings as an unpredictable giddiness and the concomitant danger of exploding into fits of uncontrollable laughter at any moment came over her. Like migraine headaches, these attacks came upon her without warning, and she needed to anchor herself quickly and securely to something solid.

The only thing that effectively dissipated the fluttery sense of hysteria was to sit on her therapist Ellen's sun porch in Studio City, curled up on her wicker couch, an afghan around her knees, sipping a cup of peppermint tea.

At three-thirty that afternoon, after not having heard from Charlie Berns all day and after having been told by his agent that Charlie Berns did not have a functioning home telephone, Deidre dialed Ellen and asked for an unscheduled appointment.

"It's Alice-in-Wonderland time again. Can you squeeze me in?"

Alice-in-Wonderland time was code between them to indicate the onset of one of these attacks of acute unreality. She described them as the feeling of being at the Mad Hatter's tea party, the feeling that everyone around her was intently going about some perfectly sincere exercise in madness and didn't realize it.

At six that evening she found herself sitting on Ellen's couch, trying to explain the latest round of madness that was overtaking the studio.

". . . I mean, I realize that there's a crude logic to it. Box office is box office. The man sells tickets. But Bobby Mason as Benjamin *Disraeli*. Please. Not in a million years. And Norman doesn't seem to be upset; neither is Howard Draper. These guys spend all their time hyperventilating about the stock . . . which seems to be the object of the exercise . . . drive the stock up higher and higher. . . . I mean, I thought we were all there to make movies and exercise a reasonable degree of intelligence in our choices— but this cockamamie idea. . . . Listen, there's a scene in this script where Disraeli meets Bismarck in the Radziwill Palace in Berlin to negotiate an end to the Russo-Turkish War and they sit there eating herring, smoked salmon, caviar, speaking this awful French to each other . . . you know, like Sid Caesar, neither of them can really speak French . . . I mean, it's very funny, it's hysterical, in fact . . . that's when I started losing it. . . . I mean, every time I think about Bobby Mason eating herring and speaking French to Sylvester Stallone . . ."

That was it. Deidre went off the edge again. She laughed so hard that the peppermint tea spilled all over the afghan.

"I'm sorry. The afghan's washable, right?"

"Don't worry about the afghan. . . ."

"Anyway, we bought this script for two hundred fifty thousand from some fly-by-night producer who doesn't even have a home phone. I can't reach this guy. His agent doesn't even know where to reach him. . . . What kind of a producer can't be reached? I mean, what's the point of my doing my job and reading this material if no one listens to what I'm saying? Norman just shrugs and says we'll fix it in the rewrite. Rewrite? How can you rewrite this? I mean, Bobby Mason negotiating the end of the Russo-Turkish War . . ." She stopped herself abruptly before she went over the edge again.

Ellen sat in her bentwood rocker, swaying slowly back and forth, nodding contrapuntally. When she spoke, it was in a soft, caressing monotone. "Use it," she pronounced, with a small, self-satisfied smile.

"What do you mean?"

"Exactly what I said. Use the absurdity of the situation to define your own clearness of purpose."

"That's just the problem. I don't have a clear purpose there. Nobody listens to me."

"So what?"

"Huh?"

"Just stay focused."

"It's really difficult to stay focused on anything when what you do every day is totally ignored."

Ellen sighed deeply, maternally, shook her head. "Deidre, I thought we resolved this conflict a long time ago. You're thirty-eight years old. You shouldn't be expecting people to conform to your idealistic preconceptions any longer."

"I just expect people to make some sense. . . ."

"Forget about other people. You have no control over them. Stay within yourself. Stay focused. Carve out areas of sanity within the absurdity. Use your focus as a machete to chop away the undergrowth so that you can see the trees."

In the middle of this extended metaphor, Deidre started to drift. Staying focused was fine if you knew what to focus on. But what was the point of chopping away the underbrush if you didn't particularly know where the path was leading?

And yet Ellen's voice soothed her. She sank into the handwoven throw pillows and relaxed for the first time since she had opened her eyes that morning. If it was only a $100 massage, so what? It worked.

Somehow she had to develop the ability to sit at the Mad Hatter's tea party without losing it. It was just a technique, after all, like meditation. It could be mastered if she applied herself diligently.

If the Mad Hatter wanted Bobby Mason to eat herring and speak French, then that's what would happen. And when the Queen of Hearts said, "Off with their heads," she would sit there quietly with the others and nod her approval.

Madison Kearney awoke on the couch to the odor of spaghetti sauce simmering in what passed for the kitchen of his one-bedroom stucco bungalow in Silver Lake. Ordinarily, the odor of food upon waking from a binge would have been enough to send him into the bathroom retching. He looked down at the caked front of his pants and realized that he already had. That was good. That meant that the hangover would be tolerable. But who the fuck was cooking spaghetti sauce in his kitchen?

He rolled his legs off the couch, got up with some difficulty, walked into the kitchen and discovered a man standing there at the counter, grating cheese into a bowl. The man looked vaguely familiar, but shit if he knew who he was or why he was in his kitchen.

"Who the fuck are you?"

"Charlie Berns."

When that didn't register in Madison Kearney's feverish eyes,

Charlie named the last picture he rewrote for him. *"Vengeance Is Mine."*

The writer blinked, scratched his head, unable to place it. Charlie gave him a hint.

"The independent drug lord who tries to muscle in on the Mafia trade in Brooklyn. Gil Warner and Joanne Hall. Filmed for three point eight. Went in the toilet. . . ."

It was certainly not the fault of Madison Kearney's taut, violent script that the picture never opened. The director tried to remake *The Godfather,* and they wound up with kitsch Italian neorealism.

Recognition began to slip through the alcohol haze. He stared at Charlie for a moment, then blurted out, "Fight under the Brooklyn Bridge with AK47's. Oil drums get blown up . . . the hero commandeers a caterpillar rig and uses it as a tank . . . ?"

"You wrote it. I produced it. You like Parmesan cheese on your spaghetti?"

"What are you doing in my kitchen making spaghetti?"

"You have to eat something, Madison."

"Why is that?"

"Because you need your strength for the rewrite."

"Rewrite? What rewrite?"

*"Bill and Ben.* It needs a lot of work."

"Oh yeah?"

"It's a page-one rewrite, Madison. And you're the guy to do it."

"Do we got a deal?"

"Not yet."

"You got to call the Morris office."

Charlie put the cheese down and reached for the corkscrew. He poured out two small glasses of Chianti, handed one to the writer, who dove into it. When he came up for air, Charlie recorked the bottle and said gently, "Madison, your guy at the Morris office's no longer there. He retired. Besides, you don't need them to make a deal with me. I've always been straight with you, haven't I?"

He nodded, eyeing the Chianti bottle.

"Might as well save yourself the ten percent. This is going to be down and dirty. Twenty-five grand. Out the door."

"I don't know. . . ."

"Tell you what, let's have one more drink before dinner, then talk about it over the spaghetti, see how you feel then. Okay?"

As soon as he saw Charlie take hold of the Chianti cork, he nodded his agreement. A couple of glasses were going to be necessary to prime the pump anyway. Madison Kearney would be worthless completely dry.

Norman Hudris disentangled himself gingerly from the moist embrace of Cissy Fuchs and rolled over to his side of the bed. He lay there, breathing evenly, staring up at the acoustical ceiling in Cissy's three-bedroom split-level in Toluca Lake, the major spoil of her divorce settlement. Norman was hoping to get a few hours' sleep before the onset of his nightly bout of insomnia.

For months now he had been waking at 4:00 A.M. and lying there till dawn as an army of anxieties paraded in front of him. Things were not going well in his life. The pressure at work was becoming so intense that he dreaded showing up at the studio every morning. He spent hours in his office staring at the phone, simultaneously hoping it would ring and praying that it wouldn't.

There was little doubt in Norman's mind that Howard had lost confidence in him and was looking for a replacement. The signs were clear—the little slights and dismissive gestures that Howard now adopted in his presence, the cold shoulder he got in dailies when he entered the screening room and sat alone in the second row, in front of the editors, the fact that he wasn't invited to the New York preview of the studio's latest release.

This growing disdain was so evident to Norman that he had asked a friend at ICM to send some discreet feelers around town.

So far the only bite they'd gotten was some vague interest at NBC
in their Standards and Practices department. Hardly a step in the
right direction, as far as he was concerned. He toyed with independent production, but he had an innate fear of being out there
without a net. Indie Prod was like Dodge City in the 1890s. To
survive, you had to carry a gun and shoot fast. There were bodies scattered all over town of guys who tried to make it out there
on their own.

There was the slow erosion of the stock, from fifty-nine and a
half to below forty and falling steadily. Maybe he should get out
now, put the equity into a medical building in the Valley or one
of those windmills up north that his accountant was always talking about. As a renter with no family deductions he was getting
killed on his taxes every year. He had to do something about that
too.

And the chest pains were coming back, the vague feelings of
distress on his left side. Recently he'd had an echocardiogram
and a treadmill. The doctor told him there was nothing wrong,
but Norman wasn't entirely convinced. His uncle Phil had
recently had a bypass. Last month a vice president at Disney,
who had just had a clean EKG, keeled over while jogging.

In a larger sense Norman felt he was losing control over his
entire life. The days drifted smoggily into one another; pictures
got made or didn't get made; the stock price slowly slipped
another notch as he grew older. He was forty-one, no longer in
his prime for a production vice president. He was approaching
the older limit for a Young Turk. He didn't want to become an
Old Turk. Not in this town . . .

"Norman?"

Cissy Fuchs's voice penetrated the queasy fog that had
wrapped itself around him.

"You awake?" she whispered.

"Yeah."

She put a hand on his chest, played with the sparse strands of
hair.

"How much did you pay for the Bobby Mason script?"

"Didn't Brad Emprin tell you?"

"He said three-fifty, but I think he's lying."

What a bullshit artist Brad Emprin was. Two-fifty was bad enough. Norman only went that high because Howard had insisted on closing the deal that day.

"Brad's bullshitting."

"Three?"

"Not even . . ."

"What's it about?"

"What's what about?"

"The script. For Bobby Mason."

"It's a buddy picture. Couple of guys called Bill and Ben. Anyway, it needs a lot of work."

Cissy continued to tease the wiry chest hairs with the tips of her painted nails.

"How about Cal Tremont?" she offered.

"Who?"

"Cal Tremont. For the rewrite . . . he's terrific and he's fast. . . ."

"I'll talk to Deidre about it," he murmured and turned over, away from her. Good old Cissy. She never stopped working.

This picture could be a breakthrough for the studio. They needed a hundred-million-dollar grosser in the worst way. It would get the accountants in New York off their backs and give him some credibility with the distribution and sales guys, who seemed to be looking directly at him whenever they reported the difficulty in booking pictures these days. Maybe it would even get the stock moving in the right direction and fend off the Japanese, who were hovering around the studio like vultures waiting to descend and pick apart the carcass.

Jesus Christ, what if they *could* get Sly to play opposite Bobby Mason? Think about *that*. Bobby and Sly in the same picture. Fuck, they could gross over two hundred with that marquee. Maybe even two fifty . . .

\* \* \*

"Think Israel. Think commando. Think desert warfare. Think hand-to-hand combat. Think lean, tough sabra, maybe Sephardic Jew from North Africa, black even, maverick enforcer, anti-terrorist . . . has a pal named Gladstone, English, MI6 maybe, intelligence, doped out the Falklands, kind of a 007 type, he's the costar . . . they're pals. . . . Think of a girl, English also, upper class, name of Victoria. . . . Maybe our guys are both *schtupping* her. . . ."

Charlie paced the living room as his host lay on the couch smoking and blinking his rheumy eyes. He didn't know how much was getting through to Madison Kearney, but he needed to keep bombarding the man with scattershot notions. Sooner or later one might penetrate and set off a chain reaction in his febrile imagination.

"What if the black guy, call him Lev Disraeli, had recently converted to the faith. Maybe he grew up in Tunisia or Saint Louis. You know what I'm saying?"

Madison Kearney nodded. The pump was still sucking air. It was making loud descents into the well and coming up dry.

"The guy's a street fighter. The other guy, the limey's kind of worldly, you know, been around, maybe he went to Oxford, but they're tight. They met . . . where did they meet? Let's not worry about the backstory right now. We'll fill that in later. . . . Say Lev's on to a PLO terrorist plot to blow up an Israeli nuclear plant. But he can't go to Jerusalem because that'll compromise some deal that Bill has going down. . . . So what does he do . . . ?"

Madison Kearney didn't move a muscle. For a moment Charlie thought he had nodded out until the writer got up from the couch and started pacing in the opposite direction. He hummed to himself, nodding furiously as if he were having some sort of conversation with himself. After several minutes of this activity, Madison Kearney whirled around and faced Charlie. He rocked back and forth several times on the balls of his feet, like a dervish. Then he started to talk, beginning in a small, quiet voice and gathering volume and pace as he went along.

"The coon's a weapons expert, bounced off the Special Forces for going off the deep end in Nam. He emigrates to Israel, the last just war, right? This is his type of country. Six Day War. Entebbe. He can relate to this scene. . . . He meets the chick, falls for her—nude swimming scene in the Negev—but she doesn't trust his commitment to the cause. To prove it he tries to join up with Israeli Intelligence, volunteers himself for a suicide mission in Lebanon, but they're leery. So they get Bill, who's a control agent with an English passport, and get him to tail Lev to see if he's a counterespionage agent. . . . The kicker is that both these guys are working for Langley, but neither one knows the other one is. See? They're both in deep cover. . . . The chick's a Mossad operative . . . grew up on a kibbutz, can drive a tank and go down on a guy at the same time. . . . *She* doesn't trust either of them, even though she's yanking both their cords. You following me?"

Charlie nodded quickly. "Keep going."

"Open the picture in Beirut. We're in the bazaar at night. Someone heaves a grenade into a melon truck. . . ."

Charlie grabbed a yellow pad from his briefcase and started writing as fast as he could.

Deidre Hearn insisted on being patched through to Brad Emprin's car phone at nine-thirty the next morning. The agent was coming over Beverly Glen, the sunroof open, licking his lips. He had applied Chap Stick up at Ventura and Coldwater, but as he hit Mulholland he could still feel the dryness.

Reception was crystal clear on the top of the mountain. Deidre Hearn came through without interference.

"Where is he?"

"Who?"

"Charlie Berns."

"Did you try his office?"

"I've been up there a dozen times. His secretary keeps saying he's off the lot. She doesn't know where he is. Either she's a complete ditz or deserves an Academy Award."

"You try him at home?"

"He doesn't have a home phone, remember? You told me that yesterday. There are painters in his office. He's getting his office *painted*, Brad, instead of talking to us about the rewrite."

"He's just probably looking for a writer."

"We're the ones paying for the rewrite. He's supposed to consult with us."

"It's a helluva script, isn't it?"

"Yeah. It's great. . . ."

Brad Emprin still hadn't read the script that he sold on Monday. Deidre Hearn's next allusion, therefore, escaped him.

"I think we ought to beef up the part about the repeal of the Corn Laws. What do you think?"

"Sounds good to me. . . ."

Deidre took the phone away from her ear for a moment. *Use it. Stay focused.* She picked up the machete and started hacking away at the underbrush.

"Would you mind giving me his home address?"

"We're really not supposed to do that, Deidre."

"I understand, but in this particular case there doesn't seem to be any other way of contacting the man."

"Look, I'll swing by, tell him to call you."

"Brad, we just wrote your client a big check. He's got a deal that could make him a very rich man if this picture does well. I'd like to talk to him. This morning. Is that too much to ask?"

"Well, yeah, I don't know. . . ."

"Brad, just give me the address, will you? I promise you I will not take advantage of your client. Honest."

"Okay, yeah, all right. I'll have my girl call you with it."

"Thank you."

"Listen, Deidre, I just had a thought."

"What's that, Brad?"

"For the rewrite? You need someone who's good and fast, right?"

"Uh-huh."

"How about Paul Dubin?"

It took two more phone calls back and forth between Brad
Emprin, his secretary and Deidre's office before she had the
address. There was interference between the GTA office and the
BMW on Beverly Glen, or so his secretary said. The secretary
made sure to get *her* mailing address at the studio so that she
could send her Paul Dubin's résumé.

As Deidre was leaving the office Alan swiveled around on his
chair and announced, "I may not be back from lunch until
around three."

Deidre didn't say a word. What was the point? She nodded
perfunctorily and exited. Next Monday she'd start interviewing
for a new secretary.

The address was in the Beverly Hills Flats, between Sunset
and Santa Monica, an area full of enormous old houses in a
hodgepodge of architectural styles. She had read that these
houses now started at two million. People would buy them and
tear them down to build new, more ostentatious ones.

Charlie Berns must have bought his house a long time ago,
when they were still affordable. From what she could learn, his
career had been declining for some time. In fact, it had never
really taken off. He had produced a bunch of B movies, putting
together financing in various creative ways, getting the picture
shot one way or another. People like Charlie Berns hovered
around the periphery of the business. They were like gypsies,
hustling, keeping the balls in the air, surviving against the long
odds of staying alive in the jungle.

There was something about the man that had struck her during their brief meeting in her office. A certain quiet aloofness, if
not indifference. In his own way, he seemed somehow . . . *focused*.
He tap-danced without losing the tempo of the music. And when
she turned him down, his eyes remained calm. He seemed to be
amused inside, as if he had half expected the turndown.

Whatever gave him the notion in the first place of peddling a script about Benjamin Disraeli to Bobby Mason? The idea was completely loony. But Bobby Mason had saluted it and somebody at the Mad Hatter's tea party had put it in the works because Charlie Berns was now in development. And whatever she happened to think of him, they were in business together— that is, *if* she could find him.

As she pulled up to the address Brad Emprin's secretary had given her, she saw a forlorn, neglected-looking house, a house that had not been cared for in some time. The lawn was parched from lack of water, brown and dying; the flower beds looked as if they had been violated by some vindictive animal. There were eucalyptus nuts scattered promiscuously across the lawn and sidewalk.

She walked up to the front door, crunching the eucalyptus nuts under her heels, inhaling their acrid odor. The doorbell looked rusted and unreliable. She pressed it, heard nothing. She knocked on the door. Then, after a moment, she knocked again, louder.

Digging a notepad out of her Vuitton shoulder bag, she began to scribble a note to Charlie Berns. As she was searching for the right tone, a tone that would get results without sounding stern and humorless, the door opened. A young man stood in the doorway, half a sandwich in one hand.

"Hi," he said.

"Hello . . . sorry to bother you, but does Charlie Berns live here?"

"Yop."

"Is he in?"

"Nope."

"Can I ask when you expect him?"

The young man shrugged, took a bite of his sandwich. "Your guess is as good as mine. You a friend of his?"

"Actually, I'm a business acquaintance. It's kind of important that I talk to him."

"He's my uncle."

Transferring the sandwich to his left hand, Lionel thrust out his right hand. "Lionel Travitz," he announced.

"Deidre Hearn," she replied, shaking his hand.

"Tell you the truth, I haven't the slightest idea where he is. You see, I don't really know him that well. I just came out from New Jersey and I'm staying with him until I get my own place."

"I see. . . ."

"I figure the beach'd be nice. Maybe Malibu. Do they got buses that go out there—to Malibu?"

"Yes, they do. Listen, can I leave a message for him?"

"Sure."

"Just ask him to please call Deidre Hearn as soon as he gets in. Here's my office and home numbers. . . . He can call me any-time."

"The phone's out of order here."

"Yes, I know," she smiled. "That's why I drove over here."

"Right. Well, nice meeting you."

"Good-bye," she said, turning around and walking away.

Lionel stood in the doorway as Deidre Hearn retreated down the front walk in her short tight skirt. Not bad, he thought. A little chunky in the hips, but definitely above average. He watched her get into an Acura Legend and drive away.

Lionel closed the front door and walked through the living room to the sun porch, where he had started working on his crop-duster movie. Uncle Charlie had told him that his money was still tied up in paperwork, but that he could charge a typewriter in his name at a stationery store in Beverly Hills. Lionel had bought an IBM Selectric and two reams of paper and was trying to rough out some scenes for *Dust in the Heart*.

He was searching for the central metaphor. Just as protective tariffs dominated *Bill and Ben*, he wanted an image to run through this screenplay like the nave of the cathedral he was going to design. So far he had sketched an opening scene.

\* \* \*

MEDIUM LONG SHOT of a barren Nebraska cornfield—
DAWN. All is deathly quiet except the CLATTER of locusts.
Suddenly in the east, the MOTOR of a single-engine plane
can be heard, faintly at first, then gathering volume as it
rises in the east like Christ on Easter morning. . . .

Maybe the Christ image was too much. He meant it to set the
tone. It was only a working metaphor, a brushstroke, a stained-
glass window. He remembered what his uncle had told him.
Keep your eye on the nave and don't sweat the stained-glass
windows.

He sat down at the IBM, took a moment to get his subcon-
scious untracked and began to let her rip.

# 5

Deidre Hearn's secretary Alan's friend Brian had a small cluttered cubicle at one of Hollywood's trade papers. As assistant obituary editor, he was responsible for keeping an up-to-date credit résumé on the town's leading personal ties so as to be ready to go immediately to press when someone kicked. As soon as he got the word that some industry-related person had bought the ranch, he had to assemble pertinent biographical information to run in the next day's edition.

What had been puzzling Brian recently was a list of credits that had arrived at the paper for a producer who, as far as anyone could ascertain, had not died. Not yet, at least. In addition to information off the AP and UP wires, Brian's boss, Sara Donleavy, had contacts at local hospitals and police precincts to keep her informed of any newsworthy DOAs. And Charles F. Berns, producer of *Killer on the Lam, Bulletproof Battalion, Vengeance Is Mine* and *Suburban Hussies,* among others, was not listed anywhere as officially dead.

He wasn't listed anywhere as officially alive either. Nobody at the paper had heard anything about him in years. None of the three talent guilds had a listing for him. His agent of record was dead, and the few people Brian could unearth who had worked with the man within the last ten years disclaimed any knowledge of his fortunes or whereabouts.

Brian couldn't understand who had sent him the updated list of credits that had resurfaced from the pile of memos, phone messages and clippings on his desk. Brian's boss had told him to forget it. Better not to publish an obit for a guy whose death was not confirmed than to run one for a guy who was still alive, she said. And this guy was not a hot ticket anyway. He was definitely in the walking-dead category.

The walking-dead category described people who were unfortunate enough not to realize they were no longer alive. In spite of the death sentence that had been pronounced upon them in absentia and universally recognized, they persisted in walking around, going shopping, driving their cars and generally acting as if they were not dead. They did all these things, in a sense, posthumously, stubbornly flaunting their continued existence in the face of generally accepted rumor and reliable innuendo.

It was Alan who would inform Brian over lunch at Chez Takasushi, a new Franco-Japanese hybrid in Century City, that Charles F. Berns was not only not dead but the producer of the next Bobby Mason movie.

"You're kidding," Brian intoned.

Alan shook his head as he speared a small slice of raw abalone with his chopsticks.

"Somebody sent me an updated list of credits. They usually don't do that unless they're about to croak or just did."

"Well this guy hasn't croaked as of last Monday."

"Really?"

"He waltzes into Deidre's office without an appointment and manages to get fifteen minutes with her. Tête-à-tête. And guess who's doing Bobby Mason's next movie?"

"Lucky him."

"Lucky us. We haven't had a hit in a year and a half."

"How does a man who hasn't produced anything in years get

to do a hot box-office star's next movie? He's not sleeping with Deidre, is he?"

"Oh please . . . give me a break," Alan moaned.

"Well, how else do you explain it?"

"I haven't the slightest idea."

"I wouldn't discount the possibility that he's having sex with her."

"Deidre's not having sex with anyone, believe me. I mean, do you know how she *dresses?* Butch leather skirts up to her belly button and these flimsy tops that look like they're right out of the wardrobe trailer for *Irma la Douce* . . . and she prances around in these three-inch heels that you wouldn't put on Dolly Parton. I mean, *really.* . . ."

Meanwhile, at a more desirable table, closer to the sushi chef, Norman Hudris sat with Andre Blue, a production vice president at a rival studio. They were not discussing Deidre Hearn's wardrobe. They were discussing Norman Hudris's future.

Andre Blue—a tall, thin, fastidious man with a nasty streak in him—had risen to a level that Norman felt was wildly beyond his competence. He oversaw production of a slate of fifteen movies every year, and, at the moment, he was on a roll, with a couple of nine-figure grossers in the past year. Purely accidents of time and place, Norman was convinced, but there was no denying that his luncheon companion was a hot ticket around town.

Norman and Andre had started out together as junior agents and had kept in touch over the years, meeting periodically to exchange information and gossip. When his career first started going south, Norman had confided in Andre Blue. He told him that he was convinced that Howard Draper was combing the woods for a replacement and that he, Norman, would like to beat his boss to the punch. He was on the lookout for something else. It didn't even have to be a promotion. He would consider a lateral move or even, under the right circumstances, a slight demotion.

"It's not very live out there, Norman," Andre Blue announced with his air of imperious authority.

"Tell me about it."

"A lot of people are sitting around waiting for the phone to ring. Consider yourself fortunate that you have a job at the moment."

"Yeah, but for how long?"

"Aren't you being a little paranoid?"

"Andre, the studio's in the toilet. Someone's going to come in and clean house. And all of Howard's people are going to be on the street. I mean, the thing is that even though Howard has no confidence in me, I'm still his production vice president. I'm going to go down with him. I'm in a no-win situation, don't you see? Howard wants me out, and I'm going to get blamed when they get rid of him. I'm basically fucked. One way or the other."

"What about Universal?"

"Are you serious?" Norman looked as if his stomach had just turned.

"Why not?"

"I know people who went to work out there and haven't been heard from since. It's like a black hole. . . ."

Andre deftly picked a fleck of basil off his tuna sashimi. He ate for a while in silence, demurely taking small bites of his lunch with the attitude of a fussy and highly critical man. The word around town was that Andre Blue had to wash his hands immediately after shaking hands with anyone. Agents told their clients only to shake hands upon leaving the office.

"Maybe this Bobby Mason picture'll take off," Andre said.

"You heard?"

"It's all over town."

"Yeah, well, we got to make the picture first."

"It's pretty hard to fuck up a Bobby Mason picture. You get a hundred million just by putting his name up on the marquee."

Norman sighed, shook his head sadly. What difference would it make if the Bobby Mason picture went through the roof? He wouldn't get the credit for it anyway.

"So, you're off to Tel Aviv. . . ."

"Huh?"

"Isn't that where you're shooting the picture?"

"We *are?*"

"Bobby Mason's becoming a Black Zionist."

Norman looked up from his squid. He expected to see Andre Blue's dryly insinuating smile leaking sarcasm. Instead he looked directly back at Norman and said, "That's what I hear."

"Jesus . . . why doesn't anybody tell *me* these things?"

"He's taking lessons from a rabbi. He wants to shoot everything in Israel now. That's where you're going to be shooting the picture, Norman. Wherever Bobby wants to shoot, you shoot."

"Israel?"

Andre Blue nodded, took a sip of his Chassagne-Montrachet '73. "The food's awful. And they've got Palestinians taking shots at you. If I were you, Norman, I'd tell them just to shoot it and ship the negative when they're finished."

Enid Schonblum had opted for a light beige with tan trim. In the absence of specific input from her boss, she selected what she considered the most neutral shade on the color chart that Office Maintenance had given her. The painters had to leave a day between coats, and so today she sat alone at her post, fighting off the mild nausea she felt from inhaling paint fumes.

Besides a number of calls from Deidre Hearn and a call from Parking to assign him a permanent spot, nobody had tried to reach Mr. Berns at his new office. Which was rather peculiar, Enid thought, for a movie producer who had just been given a large office in the producers' building. The fact that he had been off the lot and unreachable for days was even more peculiar. She had never worked for anyone who didn't call in for their messages every few hours when they were away from their office.

So Enid Schonblum sat guard steadfastly at her desk hour after hour waiting for a phone which didn't ring to ring. That's how Norman Hudris found her when he walked into the office after his lunch with Andre Blue.

"Is he still at lunch?"

"No. I don't think so."

"Where is he?"

"He's off. The lot."

"Do you expect to hear from him?"

Enid looked painfully to the off-beige rug, did not immediately reply. Norman thought she hadn't heard, and repeated the question.

"I wouldn't know," she managed at last.

Norman wondered if he was speaking the same language as this reedy broad with the strange aspirated voice. The office reeked of paint.

"When is the last time you've heard from him?"

"I haven't. Heard from him."

"Beg your pardon?"

"Not since the first day."

"You haven't spoken to him at *all* since last Tuesday?"

"Yes. I mean no. That is. I haven't spoken to him. At all."

"May I have his home phone number, please."

"I don't have. His home phone number."

He did his best to keep his impatience under control. It was fairly obvious to him by now that this strange girl in Charlie Berns's office was on drugs. The studios were full of them now, menials who took a variety of exotic pharmaceuticals on the job.

"You don't have his home phone number?" He spoke as slowly and as distinctly as he could. It didn't seem to do any good, however, because the druggie just looked back at him and shook her head. Then, as if he were talking to a three-year-old, he said, "No . . . home . . . phone . . . number?" He made large charadelike gestures, the way he sometimes did to make himself understood to his Salvadoran cleaning lady.

"Yes. I mean no. No home phone number."

Norman did an abrupt about-face and headed downstairs to Deidre's office. Her secretary, as usual, was not at his desk. He entered her office and found Deidre lying on the couch with a script.

"You know what I just heard at Takasushi?" he said, without introduction. "Apparently, we're making the Bobby Mason picture in Israel. I mean, don't you think something's wrong when the head of production, West Coast, has to find out in a sushi restaurant where his studio is shooting a picture?"

"You should read the trades. That's where Bobby Mason wants to shoot all his pictures now."

"I thought this picture was about protective tariffs in England."

"It's about Benjamin Disraeli, a famous ex-Jew and soon-to-be martial-arts expert. . . . Norman, how do you think this studio got to do this picture anyway?"

Norman sat down at Deidre's desk and started mangling her paper clips.

"Where the fuck is he?"

"He?"

"Charlie Berns. The guy we just hired to make this movie."

"Nobody knows where he is, Norman."

"You don't know where he is?"

Deidre put down the script, swung her legs over the couch, stood up, smoothing down her skirt. "I don't know where he is. I swear to you I don't know where he is. I've been trying to reach him for days now. I even went to his house. He's not there, and his nephew, who lives there, doesn't know where he is either. Even his agent doesn't know where he is."

"How could a producer with a development deal just vanish?"

"Maybe he just took the money and went to Rio."

"Deidre . . ."

"Look, you told me to make this deal. I made the deal. You told me to read the script. I read the script. You told me to write coverage. I wrote coverage. The coverage said, don't buy this script. You bought the script. Fine. But I'm not responsible for keeping tabs on the whereabouts of producers who don't have a home phone and don't go near their office."

"What about the rewrite? What are we going to do?"

"What do I know, Norman? I just work here."

Norman picked up Deidre's phone, dialed an extension. "Is he in, please? It's Norman Hudris . . ."

He waited for several seconds, then: "Don, have we issued any money yet on the Charlie Berns deal?"

Norman began to pace with the phone, nearly dragging it off Deidre's coffee table. "When? Jesus . . ."

He hung up, turned to Deidre. "They sent the check. Should we stop payment?"

"I'm not sure that's a very good way of beginning a relationship with a producer."

"Yeah, but what if he *did* go somewhere?"

"As long as it's not to another studio."

"That's not funny, Deidre. That's not the slightest bit funny." Norman leaned back in the chair, rubbed his eyes. He began to feel pains on his left side again. Shit, not here. He didn't want to buy it in Deidre Hearn's office. Maybe it was just stomach gas from the sushi.

This movie was turning into a nightmare already. They were barely in development and he felt like he had been on the picture for years. The producer had taken a powder. The star was a Black Zionist who got eight million plus a piece. They were going to be shooting in Israel. Shells were coming over the border daily from Lebanon. Palestinian terrorists put bombs in buses and airport lockers. . . .

He felt another chest pain and started calculating how long it would take the paramedics to get him to Cedars in rush-hour traffic.

Lev Disraeli was in a tight spot. Pinned down on the near shore of the Litani River behind the carcass of his overturned Land-Rover, running out of clips for his AK47, low on water, he absently flicked his tongue against the cyanide capsule wedged against a molar and considered his options. He had one grenade of dubious manufacture and a radio with a bad cell. Who would he call anyway? The Mossad had a price on his head, convinced he was a double agent. MI6 had told his contact in Beirut that they would deny any knowledge of him. And Langley had kissed him off a long time ago. There was only one person he could turn to. And that person wasn't even in Lebanon at the moment. . . .

Bill Gladstone was sitting at a café in Nicosia sipping Metaxa and eyeing a small blue Fiat parked suspiciously close to the date stand he knew was a letter drop for Syrian intelligence. Embedded in one of the mother-of-pearl rims of his Italian sunglasses was a minuscule camera capable of photographing clear images at fifty yards.

A woman gets out of the blue Fiat. Tall, graceful, a walk that he would recognize anywhere. Click. Click. Click. He continues to snap pictures of Victoria Albert, the woman with whom he has just spent the night at the Hotel du Levant, her snatch dripping with his seed. . . .

Charlie stopped writing, looked over at Madison Kearney, who was lying on the couch devouring pretzels and thinking out loud.

"I think that's a bit much," Charlie said.

"What?"

"That line about her snatch. There are a lot of women executives in the studios these days."

"Forget it. It's not going to work anyway. If he thinks she's going two ways now we blow the fuck scene on the sailboat. The fuck scene on the sailboat is what's going to send this picture through the roof. You see it? Water coming over the gunnels, the boom swinging back and forth above them, *whomp*, soundtrack of African drumbeats mixed with electronic synthesizers . . . there's not going to be a limp pecker in the house, believe me."

"So who's in the blue Fiat?"

"Anybody. Doesn't matter. It's just a cutaway from Disraeli pinned down in his jeep."

Charlie pulled gently at his fingers to relieve the cramp in his right hand. On the floor was a pile of yellow legal pages filled with Charlie's sprawling handwriting.

They had been at it for days now, maybe longer. Charlie had lost track of time. They slept like cats for a couple of hours, with Charlie going out periodically to bring back frozen pizzas, cigarettes and a tightly rationed supply of Hearty Burgundy. He was afraid that if he went away for more than half an hour, if he abandoned Madison Kearney too long, the writer would lose the thread and they'd have to start all over again. His attention span was fragile, his connective synapses frayed by years of bathing in alcohol.

Nonetheless, they were making slow, steady progress. Bill and Lev were up to their ears in trouble and bullets. Disraeli had already kicked a great deal of ass without having opened his mouth for more than a few tough laconic bursts of dialogue along the way. The plot was impossibly complicated but he wasn't concerned. They'd throw in a Morris-the-Explainer scene somewhere at the end to tie it all together. At the moment, the trick was to keep the balls in the air.

To show that Lev Disraeli was not a man entirely without spiritual dimension, Charlie had managed to get Madison Kearney to insert a little Judaism between the bullets. There was a scene in a synagogue in the old section of Jerusalem, where Disraeli slips into the shell-scarred building to elude his Syrian tail and winds up lingering as a group of devout old men pray. He watches them, moved by their piety, overcome by thoughts of his tenuous connection with the faith. Madison Kearney had wanted one of the Syrians to take out the ark with a flamethrower, but Charlie vetoed it for the moment. Bobby Mason wanted Jewish. They'd give him Jewish. They could always cut it out in editing.

"Take five," Charlie said, getting up and going into the kitchen to check out the supplies. There was less than a finger left in the Hearty Burgundy jug, not enough to get Madison Kearney seriously derailed. Charlie had discovered that the man was useless when totally dry. You had to keep him lightly lubricated in order to prevent his mind from slipping into one of his recurring paranoid fantasies. Once, late at night, when they had run out of wine, an ambulance siren down the hill on Sunset had sent the writer scurrying under the kitchen table, clutching a baseball bat as if it were an AK47, convinced they were about to be invaded by storm troopers. Charlie had to make an emergency run to an all-night Ralphs to restock.

He slipped outside, closing the broken screen door behind him, and got into his car. As he backed out of the driveway onto the narrow, hilly street, he realized not only that he had no idea what day it was but that he had no idea what time it was either. The clock on the Mercedes had been out for years, and Charlie never wore a watch.

He gazed through the dirty windshield and tried to make out whether the sun was coming up or going down. It was one of those gauzy gray-white days when you couldn't see the sun. You had to take someone's word that it was up there behind the cloud cover. The street was full of small sagging stucco houses, looking dark and forlorn inside. There were patches of unruly vegetation alternating with fallow stretches lying neglected. It was no longer a neighborhood. It was just a spot on the map above the Golden State Freeway.

He rolled down the hill to Sunset, cruised east looking for a phone, found one in a Chevron station. He got out of the car, put a quarter in the phone, dialed the studio switchboard.

"Charlie Berns please."

After a moment that breathless, overaspirated voice that he had nearly forgotten came across the wire.

"Charles Berns's office . . ."

Charlie rubbed the back of his neck. He suddenly remembered the wilting flower who had been assigned to him from the secretarial pool. But he couldn't remember her name, so he said, "Hi. What's going on?"

There was a silence on the other end. Then she repeated, "Charles Berns's office. May I help you?"

"Hi. It's me. Charlie. Any calls?"

A longer silence this time. Finally: "Mister? Berns?" That was her all right. Two separate sentences of one word each.

"Yeah. How you doing?"

"Oh, Mr. Berns. A lot of people. Want to know. Where you are."

"Who?"

"Well. The studio. Deidre Hearn has called. Every day. Several times. Norman Hudris came by. Wednesday. Your nephew. Lionel Travitz. He's worried about you. Where are you? Mr. Berns?"

"Excuse me, what's your name again?"

"Enid."

"Enid, listen, I'm doing research on the script. I'll be back in Monday. Maybe Tuesday. Okay?"

"What should I say? When they ask me? Where you are?"

"Tell them . . . I'm in Lebanon."

"I beg. Your pardon."

"Beirut."

"Mr. Berns?"

"Yeah . . ."

"You're really not. In Lebanon. Are you?"

Charlie looked around at the graffiti-scarred landscape of East Sunset and figured he might as well be.

"No, I'm not."

Another long silence on the line. Then she said, "About the painting . . ."

"Huh?"

"The office. Painting. It's beige."

"Beige?"

"With cocoa-brown trimming."

"Excuse me?"

"I thought it was. Preferable. Restful. On the eyes."

"Sure."

"What about furniture? Danish modern? Country French?"

"Sounds good to me."

"You're supposed. To choose."

"Got to run. I'll see you soon."

He hung up before she spoke again. Would he ever be able to have a normal conversation with that woman without feeling like he was sinking slowly into quicksand? As he walked back to the car he had a brainstorm. They needed someone to walk out of the blue Fiat and get mowed down by machine-gun fire from the date stand, right? She'd be perfect.

At about the same time that Charlie Berns left the phone booth on East Sunset, Bobby Mason was in the VIP Lounge of Lod Airport in Tel Aviv giving an impromptu press conference upon his arrival in Israel for six weeks of location shooting on his film *Desert Commando*. Beside him stood Rabbi Seth Gutterman, who had taken advantage of the opportunity of traveling in the pre-empted first-class section of the 747, along with Bobby's body-guards, to coordinate Israel Bond fund-raising with the home office.

Bobby fielded questions put to him by the world press concerning his decision to shoot his pictures in Israel and his interest in becoming a Jew. Security was tight. Israeli personnel, along with Bobby's private muscle, watched for a telltale gesture, their eyes scanning the room like gun turrets.

After being welcomed to Israel and given a plaque by the Tel Aviv Chamber of Commerce, Bobby was asked why he had decided to shoot this picture in Israel.

"The people, man. They're hospitable. They're solid. Down home."

He was asked what it was that appealed to him about Judaism.

"It's a bottom-line kind of deal, you know what I mean? You have a pretty good idea where you stand with the Big Guy all along. He doesn't fade in and out on you. In return you got to commit to Him. It's like this coat, you see, once you put it on, you got to keep it on through all kinds of weather."

Rabbi Gutterman looked over at his disciple, smiled with pride.

He was asked if he was learning Hebrew.

"Working on it. *Shloom, haverim.*" Smiles alternated with looks of total consternation. Nobody was exactly sure what he said. Bobby's phrase was translated in a number of totally different ways. *Der Spiegel* thought he said, "*Sie haben . . .*" and construed it to be an attempt, albeit inaccurate, to respond to the question in German. The reporter compared it to Kennedy's famous "*Ich bin ein Berliner.*"

He was asked if Clint Eastwood was going to be in the picture.

"Clint who?" Big smile. They ate it up.

He was asked if he thought that all the violence in his movies was not a bad image for world Judaism. Bobby looked sincerely wounded for a moment before he recovered.

"There isn't a guy in any of my movies gets his ass kicked that isn't some major slimebag, dope dealer, terrorist, Vietcong, that kind of degenerate. Anybody who's against freedom, you know what I mean?"

The London *Times* correspondent asked him if he was in sympathy with Israel's foreign policy.

"Yeah. Absolutely."

Then the Mideast correspondent of France's left-leaning *Le Monde* asked if he didn't see any parallels between the plight of American blacks and that of the Palestinians.

Rabbi Gutterman chose this moment to wrap things up by thanking the assembled reporters for their warm welcome to Israel. They made their way through the crush of photographers out to the waiting car.

In the limo on the way to the Hilton, Bobby relaxed with a

Pepsi and looked out the window at the arid countryside. Orange trees and condos. Just like Anaheim.

When they reached the outskirts of the city, Bobby turned to his head bodyguard.

"What paper was the Frog with?"

"What's that?"

"The Frog, asked me about blacks and Palestinians."

"I don't know."

"Find out."

"Right."

"He shows his ass on my set, kick it the fuck off."

# 6

The Disraeli deal, as it was referred to at GTA, gained Brad Emprin a new respect from his colleagues. Packaging a Bobby Mason picture was major league, and Brad Emprin dined out on it. The agency was abuzz with misinformation surrounding the genesis of the deal. Some of the younger agents had never even heard of Charlie Berns.

The identity of the writer of the script that had attracted Bobby M. was a subject of intense speculation. Names as diverse as Gore Vidal, Arthur Miller, Tennessee Williams (posthumously) and, inevitably, B. Traven, still alive and eluding publicity in Mexico, were bandied about.

Brad Emprin reported the deal at the weekly staff meeting. When he outlined the main points—a floor of two-fifty with escalators going to a potential telephone number, and more, if worldwide grosses approached the level of Bobby Mason's recent pictures—there was a respectful, almost awestruck silence in the glass conference room. You could hear the sound of Sy Green's molars mashing the poppy seeds of his bagel.

"One point five in Asia?" Jeff Yankow articulated.

"That's right," replied Brad Emprin. "Two in Europe."

"Jesus," Bill Browner said, "after Mason takes his bite up front there's not going to be anything left for the studio."

"Don't worry about the studio," Sy Green said. "They'll be crying all the way to the bank."

"Who's the writer?" Cissy Fuchs piped up.

"Somebody Charlie found. Some kid in film school or something."

"We ought to go after him," Jeff Yankow suggested.

"Sounds good to me," Brad Emprin nodded.

Cissy Fuchs's interest in the name of the writer had been titillated by Norman Hudris's coyness on the subject. When she had asked Norman who it was, he claimed he had forgotten the name. She sensed that something unorthodox was going down. But it wasn't until she met her friend Deidre Hearn for dinner one night, at a retro fifties diner on Melrose, that she learned that Brad Emprin had indeed been sitting with his head up his ass when the golden apple fell on him.

"You're kidding," she intoned.

"Afraid not," Deidre Hearn responded with a sardonic smile. "Not only don't we know who the writer is, but we don't even know who's doing the rewrite."

"Don't you have input on the rewrite?"

"Of course we do. The problem is we can't find the producer."

"Charlie Berns?"

"Uh-huh."

"Doesn't he live in town?"

"In a house in the Flats with defoliated shrubbery. The problem is he's not there. And nobody knows where he is."

"Really?"

"Really."

"Doesn't he have an office on the lot?"

"Yes. Except he's not in it. There's nobody in it but painters. This is the screwiest deal I've ever been around. We buy a property without reading the script, from an anonymous writer, put together by a semidefunct producer. And what's it about? Benjamin

Disraeli. Benjamin Disraeli is not exactly a hot property. . . ."

She began to describe the herring-eating scene in the Radziwill Palace and stopped just in time. Just before the hysteria descended upon her. She didn't want to lose it in a restaurant on Melrose with Cissy Fuchs.

She took a large slurp from her strawberry milk shake and shifted gears. "So how's Norman?"

Cissy Fuchs shrugged.

"That good, huh?"

"I don't know, Deidre. I'm beginning to think there's no future in this relationship."

"I could have told you that."

"What?"

"It's not going to happen with Norman Hudris."

"How can you say that?"

"Cissy, Norman Hudris is forty-one years old and never been married. What does that tell you?"

"He's not gay, Deidre. Take my word for it."

"I'm not saying he's gay. I'm saying he's a write-off."

Though Cissy Fuchs was perfectly prepared to bemoan her problems with Norman Hudris, she wasn't necessarily willing to listen to someone else criticize him. She looked up aggressively from her guacamole burger and said, "What are you talking about?"

"A forty-one-year-old single man is single for a reason. I mean, it's not like he hasn't had opportunities. Norman's a decent-looking guy, he's got a good job."

"He just hasn't connected with the right person yet."

"Norman doesn't want to connect with anybody but himself. He spends most of his day in his office with the door closed worrying about the ACI stock going down. He doesn't even read scripts anymore. And every time Howard calls him into his office, he stops by my office to tell me that this is it, that Howard's going to can him. Now how can a guy like this give anything to a relationship?"

"Deidre, why are you saying this?"

"I'm just trying to be a friend."

"No you're not. You're just being a bitch."

"Cissy . . ."

"Just because *you* don't have anybody in *your* life doesn't mean that everyone else's relationships are screwed up."

"Come on, Cissy. . . ."

"You know, maybe if you got laid now and then, you wouldn't be so bitchy."

For a moment neither woman spoke as the charged air settled in around the table. Cissy Fuchs hadn't allowed herself an outburst like this for a long time. When she spoke again, her voice was softer. "I'm sorry. I didn't mean it that way exactly. . . ."

"It's okay."

Driving home, Deidre could still feel the sting of Cissy's words. And she had only herself to blame. She had no business attacking Norman.

Deidre could barely remember the last time she had slept with a man. It was going on a year. At least. So memorable was that event that she couldn't recall what he looked like, where she met him, or any of the other details of the evening. All that was left was the memory of asking him to leave when she woke up in the middle of the night and found him still there.

She had managed to accommodate herself to abstinence. She didn't even fantasize about sex anymore. Work tended to expand and overflow the borders of her life, filling up all the available space. She no longer felt sexual, in any sense, and in not feeling sexual, she had no desire for men.

When she brought the subject up in therapy, Ellen explained that her lack of sex drive was merely symptomatic of a deeper loss of life force inside. She was allowing herself to grow fallow through neglect and lack of self-esteem. Ellen began talking about Jung and anima and animus and Deidre pulled the plug and drifted in the fumes of her peppermint tea. The last thing she needed in her life right now was Carl Jung. It was bad enough she had Benjamin Disraeli to contend with.

That night she got into bed with volume one of Moneypenny and Buckle's *The Life of Benjamin Disraeli, Earl of Beaconsfield*, which Alan had gotten for her, with some difficulty, from the UCLA library. Lying on her king-size Pier 1 bed, made up with Snoopy sheets, wearing a Victoria's Secret silk nightshirt and sweat socks, Deidre drifted off to sleep on the undulant waves of Ben Disraeli's parliamentary vicissitudes.

Lionel Travitz-Traven wondered what he should do about the disappearance of Charlie Berns. It was over a week since Lionel had seen or heard from his uncle, and he was beginning to fear that something may have happened to him. Lionel rattled around the big empty house, trying to make progress on his screenplay, but as the days went by and there was no word from Uncle Charlie, he became increasingly distracted.

The big house, drafty and sparsely furnished, began to oppress him, especially during the day when there was an unnatural quiet. The street, the entire neighborhood, resembled an opulent ghost town, abandoned by its population at the height of affluence. Lionel wondered whether anybody actually *lived* in Beverly Hills.

Unable to work, Lionel took to spending the long afternoons prowling on buses, exploring the flat, endless grid of the city. His map in his lap, he verified the existence of suburbs and districts with evocative Spanish names like Pico Rivera and Costa Mesa. He visited gigantic shopping malls that loomed like science-fiction fantasies come to life, browsed aimlessly in their air-conditioned chain stores. He went out to Malibu and couldn't find it.

As the days went by he felt more and more disoriented. He felt like he was living in suspended animation. He spoke to no one; no one spoke to him. He debated going to the Beverly Hills Police Station and filing a missing-persons report. Finally, one day, he telephoned Charlie's ex-wife, who lived in Palm Springs, and explained the situation. Standing at an outdoor phone on Sunset Boulevard, he had a long chat with his Aunt Jan.

"Don't worry about him, Lionel. He tends to disappear from time to time. He always comes back."

"His phone's been disconnected."

"I'm not surprised. He forgets to pay bills. They used to turn the phone off periodically until I started paying the bills. . . . Are you all right?"

"Yeah. I guess so."

"Do you have money?"

"I have a hundred and twelve dollars."

"That's not very much, Lionel."

"Yeah, but I just sold a screenplay for fifty-two thousand dollars."

"What?"

"Uncle Charlie's optioned it. As soon as the paperwork's done, I'm going to get a check."

"Lionel . . . may I suggest something?"

"Sure."

"Get yourself an agent."

"An agent?"

"While you're at it, get a lawyer."

After hanging up, Lionel opened the Beverly Hills Yellow Pages and found, between Tailors—Wholesale and Tank Testing and Inspection, a listing for Talent Management. There were sixty-one of them. Then he turned to Investigators—Private and found listings for 127 detective agencies, specializing in areas as diverse as surveillance/husband/wife and location of hidden assets. He wondered whether he could option a detective to find Uncle Charlie.

Not knowing who else to call, Lionel tried the woman in the tight skirt who had come to the house. He dialed the number she gave him and was asked by a male secretary if Ms. Hearn would know what the call was regarding. Lionel said he didn't know.

Alan swiveled impatiently in his chair. Besides having Brian on hold, there was another call coming in.

"Just a moment," he said and hit the "hold" button.

Lionel might have died on hold if Deidre Hearn had not at that moment picked up the wrong line to make a call from her office and found Charlie Berns's nephew on the other end.

"Who's this?" she asked.

"Lionel Travitz."

Deidre blanked on the name. "Are you holding for someone?"

"Yeah. You."

"Me?"

"You told me to call you anytime. Night or day. I'm calling."

"Who is this?"

A phalanx of motorcycles was passing by at that moment. Lionel stuck his hand over one ear, pushed the receiver tightly against his other ear and shouted, "Lionel Travitz. Charlie Berns's nephew."

"Oh hi. Have you heard from your uncle?"

"No. That's why I'm calling. I wanted to know if you heard anything."

"Nothing."

"I'm starting to get worried," Lionel shouted, as the motorcycles downshifted for a light. "Do you think I should call the police?"

"The police?"

"File a missing-persons report?"

"I wouldn't do that just yet."

"I spoke to his ex-wife. She said he used to disappear a lot."

"I see. . . . Well, I suppose he'll turn up."

"Yeah."

"I'll call you if I hear from him."

"I don't have a phone."

"I forgot. Well, I'll ask him to drop by and see you."

"He lives here."

"Try not to worry too much, Lionel. I'm sure he's all right."

"Probably."

"Good-bye."

Deidre hung up the phone and leaned back in her desk chair. Jesus! A missing-persons report for a producer. . . . She got up, went out to the reception area.

"Alan," she said.

Alan put Brian back on hold, swiveled around to face his boss.

"Doesn't your friend Brian work for the obit editor on one of the trades?"

"Uh-huh."

"Would you check with him and see if anything's come through on Charlie Berns?"

"Just a second." Alan hit the "hold" button, got Brian back. "Brian, you remember Charlie Berns? The guy you got the pre-mature obit for . . . ? Right . . . is he still not dead?"

Ordinarily, lunch at "21" was an event to which Howard Draper looked forward. Sitting in the subdued elegance of the restaurant, surrounded by powerful men in sober suits, gave him the feeling of being at the hub of the universe, the refectory of the gods. Since its renovation, the restaurant seemed even more conservative, even more stately, even more like an old-fashioned London men's club.

Today, however, Howard Draper was not relishing the thought of his lunch with Frederick Weston. He had been summoned to New York by Frederick the Great on very short notice, and, besides having to cancel a tennis date for Friday morning and a weekend at La Costa that Winnie had terrorized him into booking, he'd had to take the red eye in on Thursday night so that he could attend a preview of the studio's next release earlier that evening before flying out.

All during the flight, he shuffled and reshuffled the preview cards, trying to find a bright side to the lukewarm response to the picture, but no matter how he manipulated the cards, their verdict remained unequivocal: They were sitting on a turkey.

Another one. He had been hoping to announce that good news was just around the corner. Now he was going to have to bob and weave under the withering interrogation of the chairman of Allied Continental Industries.

He had landed at Kennedy in a spiteful, cold drizzle that made the city seem more inhospitable than usual. The cabdriver offered to let him out on the side of the Long Island Expressway when Howard asked him to put out the cigarette he was smoking. They stood in traffic before the Midtown Tunnel, the cabdriver lighting one cigarette after another, as a radio jabbered loudly in Spanish and taxi horns screamed at one another like hostile lunatics. He closed his eyes and tried unsuccessfully to tune it out.

Howard Draper had lost his New York survival mechanism. Fifteen years in the laid-back passive-aggressive vacuum of Southern California had stripped him of his protective reflexes. After finishing Wharton he had spent two years with an investment-banking firm on Wall Street. Armed with the noblesse oblige of Andover and Yale, he was able to roll with what punches the city threw at him. But he was twenty-five then, and he had not yet had his nervous system dry-cleaned by the California sun.

Now he could no longer cope with the violent assault on his senses. He had no illusions of being able to cut it in the Apple anymore. The decibels alone would defeat him.

His room at the Sherry was small and overheated. Two hundred thirty-five dollars a night for a room overlooking an air shaft. He got undressed, took a shower and tried to grab a few hours' sleep before lunch, but he lay there listening to the stray sounds of the city floating up at him from sixteen floors below, as his mind idled roughly.

In his attaché case was a development report prepared for him by Norman Hudris, a list of pictures in various stages of preparation with prospective casting elements attached. Though Frederick Weston knew next to nothing about the movie business, he had definite opinions about it. Periodically Howard would receive a curt note on the gold-embossed stationery of the chairman of the board remarking about some detail in a film that had offended him. He would scribble a line at the bottom saying, "Do we really want people to think that ACI supports this?"

Who was supporting what? ACI was a monolith of subsidiaries, interlocking directorates and holding companies, the extent of whose tentacles nobody, not even the lawyers, fully understood. How could this financial and legal abstraction ever have a consistent point of view on anything? Even Frederick the Great could not claim to speak absolutely for Allied Continental Industries. Nobody could. It reported to God and the New York Stock Exchange.

He drifted into a stuporous sleep five minutes before the phone rang with his wake-up call. Howard struggled back into the shower, shaved, brushed his teeth with the portable Interplak toothbrush he never went anywhere without. Putting on his dark-gray wool suit and a silk tie that Winnie assured him was sufficiently sober, he went downstairs to walk the eight blocks to the restaurant.

The rain was coming down harder. Walking without an umbrella was out of the question. When he asked the doorman to get him a cab, the eyebrow went up with that martyred expression that New York doormen use to deflect any request made of them. "Do you have to be someplace in the next hour, sir?"

"Yes. I have lunch at '21' in fifteen minutes."

"You're not going to make it in a cab."

"I beg your pardon?"

"There are no cabs when it rains."

Of course. Howard had forgotten another of the axioms of life in the Big Apple. He looked around him searching for a solution. The doorman immediately grasped the problem.

"You've got Bloomingdale's on Fifty-ninth. You've got Bergdorf's on Fifth and Bendel's on Fifty-seventh. . . ."

Dodging puddles, Howard made it to Bergdorf's on the run

and purchased an Yves Saint Laurent umbrella for $99.50. Then he had to run the rest of the way to avoid being more than a few minutes late for his twelve-thirty lunch appointment.

Frederick Weston sat at a choice corner table, glaring over a martini with the air of a man who is not used to being kept waiting for an appointment. He nodded imperceptibly when Howard offered the traditional couldn't-get-a-cab disclaimer, motioned for him to sit down, as if the restaurant were merely an extension of his office.

"Have a martini, Howard. The olives are flown in from Sicily."

Without waiting for a reply, he motioned with a finger to the waiter, pointed to his glass, then turned back to Howard and said, "You're looking fit, Howard. Playing a lot of tennis?"

Howard Draper smiled perfunctorily. It was always in the innocuous-sounding small talk that Frederick the Great established the hidden agenda of the confrontation. The implication was perfectly clear: Howard, and by extension the whole goddamn studio, was cavorting in the sybaritic pleasures of the California sun instead of toiling to keep up their end of the ACI balance sheet.

"Still don't have a backhand."

His demi-WASP training enabled Howard to field these types of veiled accusations gracefully. He was adept at the art of small talk, more adept than this imperious, cranky autocrat with whom he was having lunch. Howard felt completely at ease floating in the gentle waters of nonsubstantive conversations. He could stay afloat for hours, bobbing and weaving languidly.

Frederick Weston, on the other hand, disliked this aspect of the lunch ritual. He sat there glumly sipping his martini as Howard chatted amiably about last night's preview, mentioning this star and that celebrity and carefully avoiding any references to the preview cards.

It wasn't until the *croquettes de saumon cru* that the chairman of the board raised the inevitable subject of production deficits and sluggish third-quarter earnings. By that time Howard had drunk a second martini and a glass of the Pouilly Fumé and felt equal to the task of defending the studio's upside potential.

Howard Draper had an ace in his attaché case, the one real potential breakout project on the slate. Norman Hudris had assured him that the script rewrite was proceeding expeditiously and that they were slotting it for production as soon as possible. In the face of the downbeat bottom line of the balance sheet, Howard had a legitimate response. He took it out and presented it, hoping it would keep him afloat through dessert.

When Howard had finished, Frederick the Great sat pensively for a long moment and then said, "How much are we going to pay this karate star to do a picture for us?"

"Eight million dollars."

"Eight million dollars." Frederick the Great repeated the phrase as if it were oral copulation. "When does he get it?"

"He gets it up front."

"I see. Is that . . . *all?*"

Howard shook his head. "He gets a piece. . . ."

"Gross or net?"

"Dollar one."

"Let me ask you something, Howard. How do you make money paying someone eight million dollars up front plus a gross-profit piece?"

"His last picture grossed one hundred thirty-five million domestic, over two worldwide."

Frederick the Great shook his head, wiped a trace of errant *sauce pêcheur* from his chin. "The lunatics are taking over the asylum."

"That's the picture business."

"I don't get it. We're in business with *him*. He's not in business with us. We're lending him eight million plus the cost of the picture, interest-free, so that he can sit there and siphon off the gravy while you, me and the banks are sitting downstream watching with our thumbs up our ass. What kind of business is this?"

"Show business."

"It's not a business, it's a goddamn roulette wheel. I'm going to level with you, Howard. I didn't want to acquire the studio. I was one vote short on the board from blocking it. Did you know that?"

Howard attempted to shake his head rhetorically, in the same tone as the question, but Frederick the Great wasn't taking no for an answer. He went on, expanding on his theme. "This is extortion."

"We could pass. . . ."

"Howard, you just sat there and told me that the studio needs this picture. You don't make the picture, you die. Isn't that what you just said?"

"Not exactly."

"Would you care to rephrase it?"

"I think it's a good investment."

"A man puts a gun to your head and you call it a goddamn investment! Some fucking investment!"

With that, Frederick the Great turned his attention to his *ris de veau provençale*, polishing it off with a vengeance. Howard ate what his dwindling appetite permitted of his *truite amandine* and avoided eye contact with his luncheon companion.

"You like sushi, Howard?" This apparent non sequitur came after the waiter removed their plates and brushed the bread crumbs off the table.

"Not very much."

"Develop a taste for it."

That was it. Frederick the Great offered no further explanation. He was not a man known for speaking in parables. His sense of metaphor was largely limited to the adjectives *goddamn* and *fucking*. But that was the extent of the sushi talk at lunch.

In fact, there was very little talk of any kind whatsoever for the remainder of the meal, and Howard was obliged to keep up a desultory, one-way conversation, in the manner of a man hitting a tennis ball to himself against a wall.

As he got up to leave, Frederick the Great looked at him from beneath his bushy eyebrows and said, "Let me see if I have this straight, Howard. I'm going to have to report to the board that the whole ball game is in the hands of some black-belt jungle bunny who's going to be walking around with eight million dollars of our money. Is that it?"

"In a manner of speaking . . ."

When Charlie Berns finally left Madison Kearney's house late one night, he had with him several hundred pages of scribbling on a yellow legal pad. As a reward for having finished a first draft, Charlie left the writer a gallon jug of Hearty Burgundy on the kitchen counter and a note promising to be in touch.

The heavy night air of Silver Lake, redolent of false spring and the cloying sweetness of jade and forsythia, made him mildly dizzy. Charlie drove slowly down the hill toward Sunset with the weary exhilaration of having midwifed a difficult birth. Keeping the writer lightly lubricated, loose enough to dredge into the lurid depths of his imagination, was a tricky balancing act, and Charlie was exhausted from the effort.

A script worthy of the unique talents of Bobby Mason was buried somewhere within those scribbled pages. The story dripped violence from beginning to end. It chopped, slashed, crunched and pulverized the enemies of the Free World. At Fade-out there was a long trail of dead bodies. As closing credits rolled across the screen—over a helicopter tracking shot of Lev Disraeli driving a jeep with a rear-mounted machine gun into the Negev sunset—there was no doubt who won the war.

Charlie had arrived at the critical phase of the operation. He had a script, the sine qua non of the producing business. Now he had to move from development to production, a deceptively small step that reached across a gaping chasm of corpses. The town was littered with unconsummated films, projects perishing from neglect, deals dying on the vine. Development was an enormous purgatory, populated by producers wandering around with their scripts and packages waiting to be summoned into the

Promised Land. Many are called and few are chosen. Charlie, however, had reason to believe that he would be among the chosen. He had what is referred to as an *element* attached, a *major element.*

His major element was going to read Madison Kearney's work, as soon as Charlie got it cleaned up and typed, and the studio put a little package on top of it, a package with a pretty pink bow on the outside and eight million dollars inside. The major element would find, moreover, that the script contained a feature that would distinguish this particular pink package from other pink packages containing the same eight million dollars.

Besides the synagogue scene with the old men praying, Charlie had gotten Madison Kearney to throw in a scene where Lev Disraeli leads the inhabitants of an embattled kibbutz in a hand-to-hand defense of its apple orchards against invading terrorists. In the penultimate sequence, a reenactment of the Judas Maccabeus story, Lev Disraeli rescues a besieged temple, emerging victoriously through the dying fires of the battle carrying the Torah.

Lev Disraeli was one tough Jew. He spoke with lethal hands and feet. It was a role made in heaven for Bobby Mason. He had little doubt that once Bobby Mason read it, once he tasted the sharp, clean vengeance of Lev Disraeli, they'd have a Go picture.

Driving west through the empty city, Charlie felt a sense of satisfaction. Even though his back ached from Madison Kearney's lumpy couch, even though he had no phone and no gardener, even though there was an updated obituary for him on file in the trades, he felt like the worst was over. He felt like he had hit bottom and bounced up ever so slightly. He was off the floor. People were *aware* of Charlie Berns once more.

If he was ever again tempted to run the hose through the doggie door, he would remember the infinite possibilities of regeneration in this business. You were never quite as dead as people gave you credit for.

*    *    *

At nine that morning Lionel found Charlie sitting at the counter in the kitchen. Barely awake, he did a double take, as if his uncle were the last person he expected to see in the kitchen of his own house, sitting calmly eating a frozen taco.

"Uncle Charlie . . ."

Charlie looked up from the accumulation of handouts he had found in his mailbox, mumbled a hello.

"You're back!" Lionel exclaimed.

Charlie nodded, took a sip of instant coffee. "How are you doing, Lionel?"

"I was worried about you."

"How come?"

"Well, I mean you just disappeared. For a long time. You didn't even call."

"No phone," Charlie said.

"Are you okay?"

"Uh-huh."

Lionel sat down on the stool opposite his uncle, waited a moment, then, "They've been looking for you."

"Who?"

"The studio. A girl came by last week. She told me to call her as soon as I heard from you."

"Tall, dark hair, tight skirt?"

"Yeah."

"I'll call her later. Thanks."

Charlie went back to his mail. Mixed in with the junk was an envelope with a Century City return address. Charlie opened it up, examined the contents, then said, "Lionel, we're going to the bank this morning."

"The bank?"

"Uh-huh. You just won the lottery."

Lionel sat in the cavernous lobby of a bank on Wilshire Boulevard shivering in the arctic chill of the air conditioning. As he waited for his uncle to conclude his business, he looked around the nearly empty lobby and marveled at its dimensions. You could fit a used-car lot in here.

On the way to the bank Charlie had offered no further explanation of his absence except to say that they were proceeding nicely with the picture and that Lionel was about to get a check for $15,000, representing start-up and story money for his screenplay. More would be forthcoming as soon as the rewrite was submitted.

Lionel had been trying to figure out what to do with all this money. It was inconceivable to him that this much cash was paid to anyone in one lump sum. He could buy an entire car and have money left over for gas.

Better to be frugal with it. You never knew where your next job was coming from. He'd put it in the bank and withdraw money as needed. With fifteen grand in the bank, Lionel calculated he could live modestly for a long time and finish his screenplay about the crop duster.

Charlie helped him fill out the forms. In the blank space for occupation Lionel proudly wrote *screenwriter*. When they were through, the clerk handed him a passbook with $14,900 and five crisp twenty-dollar bills. Lionel walked out of the bank a man of means.

On the way back home, Lionel said, "I guess I ought to get my own place now, huh?"

"If you want."

"You mean, I'm not bothering you?"

"Nah."

"Really?"

"I don't intend to be around much once the picture goes."

They drove for a while in silence. Then Lionel said, "You know, it's real easy to get to the bus from your house."

"Sure."

"I don't know how to drive. I never got around to learning. . . ."

"Stay as long as you want, Lionel."

And that was the extent of the discussion.

Charlie ran the light on Santa Monica and headed north past the eclectic rows of Taj Mahals on either side of the wide street. A 450 SL pulled up beside them at a stop sign. A woman in tennis whites was at the wheel, her hair tied back fashionably, her long tanned fingers absently drumming a rhythm on the wheel. In her lap, an immaculately groomed poodle sat contentedly. On the woman's face was a trace of supreme ennui, matched perfectly by the poodle. The Ennui Sisters.

Lionel stared at her. She dismissed him with a perfect economy of gesture, her face barely even recognizing the presence of someone in her line of sight. Then her foot eased down on the accelerator and she was gone. Out of his life forever.

More and more he felt like an invisible man in this city. Nobody seemed to notice you at all. Nobody talked to you. Nobody even made eye contact with you.

He felt blown around like a leaf in a dry wind. He felt as if his senses were anesthetized. He felt cut off from the rest of the world. He wondered if anybody was out there.

"Uncle Charlie?" he said.

"Yeah . . ."

"Maybe we should get the phone reconnected."

The Louis XV armoire barely made it through the door. Enid Schonblum watched as the moving men grunted and groaned and eventually got it into the office with inches to spare. The armoire was the pièce de résistance of the decor of Charlie Berns's new office. One of the other secretaries had told her how to requisition furniture from the Prop Department by writing it against the picture she was working on.

Enid didn't know what picture she was working on, but the same secretary who told her about the Prop Department told her that she was working on a picture called Bill and Ben. It was, the secretary said, a vehicle for Bobby Mason and a very hot project. Enid didn't follow the movie business very closely and didn't know what a vehicle was or who Bobby Mason was or why he was so hot. She had tried to educate herself by reading the trade papers every day but found the diction to be indigestible.

She had the moving men put the armoire up against the wall, between the Early *Empire* sconces. The *Directoire* settee against the opposite wall needed a low table to go in front of it, and she made a mental note to return to the Prop Department and see if she could get one of those old country *pétrains* she had seen there.

"We're going to need. More electrical outlets," she said to the moving men.

"Wrong department," one of them answered on the way out the door. "You want Electrical."

She sat down at her desk to call Electrical. As she was dialing the extension, Charlie Berns walked in the door. Enid did not immediately recognize him. After all, she had only seen him for a few minutes, and that was some time ago. Her ear to the phone waiting for Electrical to pick up, she started to ask him if she could help him, but he merely smiled vaguely and went into the inner office.

Just as Electrical picked up she realized that the man who had entered the inner office was Charlie Berns, the man she was working for. She put Electrical on hold, got up and stood rooted at her desk trying to decide how to handle this situation. She hadn't been prepared for his arrival. The decorating was incomplete. There were still a few odds and ends she wanted to get from the Prop Department. And there was the major question of curtains or Levolors.

She was standing at her desk compulsively smoothing her skirt when Charlie Berns appeared in the open doorway and motioned for her to enter.

She took her phone log and steno pad and entered his office. He was sitting at his Regency desk, a pile of yellow pages in front of him.

"Excuse me," he said, "what's your name again?"

"Enid."

"Right . . . Enid, can you type?"

Enid, nodded, then started to qualify her answer. "Not perfectly. I make mistakes."

"Are you ready to start?"

"Start?"

"Typing."

"Typing. What?"

"The script."

"Pardon me. What script?"

*"Bill and Ben."*

"Oh, *that* script."

"That's the name of the picture. That's why we're all here."

"Of course . . . excuse me. Mr. Berns. You need to make a decision. About Levolors."

"Huh?"

"You have a choice between Levolors. Or curtains. Unless you want to pay. Yourself."

"Ellen . . ."

"Enid."

"Enid, I thought we decided that was your department."

"You want me. To decide?"

Charlie nodded, turned his attention back to the stack of yellow pages. "I'm going to have to dictate this to you. It's pretty illegible."

Enid stood in front of his desk for several moments nodding gently. Then she said, "Mr. Berns?"

"Yes."

"I have Electrical. On hold."

# 7

Deidre Hearn read the last page of *Bill and Ben* and laid it down gently on the pile on her desk. She leaned back in her chair, closed her eyes and tried to find a quiet spot within herself to get centered. It was a stress-control technique recommended by Ellen for dealing with incipient hyperventilation. When Deidre felt at peace and relatively centered, she got up and screamed.

Alan dropped the phone and came running in. He found his boss standing in the middle of her office, her hands folded in front of her, staring at the floor.

"Did you just scream?" he asked.

She looked at him askance, as if the question had no basis in reality. Why would she scream at ten-thirty in the morning in her own office? Things were normal enough. There was the usual pile of scripts on her desk, phone calls to return, Styrofoam coffee cups scattered about. Outside, the morning cloud cover was burning off on schedule.

"Are you all right?" Alan persisted.

"Why shouldn't I be all right?" she said, recovering.

"You just screamed."

"I screamed?"

"Uh-huh."

"Me?"

"I think it was you. I mean, there's no one else around."

"How do you know?"

Alan looked around for a moment, then back at Deidre. He wondered if this wasn't a case of Tourette's syndrome. Last week he had watched a rerun of *Quincy* about an old lady who uncontrollably screamed out obscenities.

"Maybe you should lie down."

"That's not a bad idea."

She went over to her couch, stretched out, took a few more cleansing breaths. Alan continued to stand in the doorway watching her.

"You want something, Alan?"

He shook his head and withdrew. She would fire him this week, for sure. As soon as she felt a little more centered. For the moment she had to pull herself together; she couldn't go on screaming in her office. Directors of creative affairs didn't spontaneously lose it like that.

They weren't in Kansas anymore. No doubt about it. Maybe it was time to have Ellen refer her to the heavy-duty guy in Westwood with the couch. He'd written books on personality disorders. He prescribed drugs. Five days a week for a year or two. Get it all taken care of. Once and for all . . .

Her thoughts were interrupted by the buzz of the intercom. She reached over for the extension phone, picked up, heard Alan's nasal voice, "Norman's on two eight."

Shit. She might as well get it over with. She swiveled her feet around, hit the two-eight line, took a deep breath and said, "It's the most violent script I've ever read, Norman."

"When's the coverage going to be ready?"

"Did you hear what I just said? It makes Rambo look like Snow White."

"What?"

"It's crass, vulgar, silly, badly constructed . . . not to mention right-wing, sexist and anti-Semitic."

There was a long pause on Norman's end of the line. Then . . . "Bert Sully loves it."

"Bert Sully? Who the hell sent *him* a copy?"

"The producer."

"He's not supposed to release a script until we okay it."

"You know what that means?"

She said in as controlled a voice as she could muster, "Norman, we can't make this picture."

Another long pause on the other end. Then Norman said, "Bert says he thinks Bobby's going to be crazy about it. Can you have the coverage by three?"

Charlie Berns was sitting at his desk, reading glasses perched on the end of his nose, scanning the trade papers and trying to digest a god-awful patty melt that he had made the mistake of ordering from the commissary, when Deidre Hearn walked into his office. They hadn't seen each other since that very first day when he had walked in without an appointment and tap-danced. She sat down opposite him without being invited.

"Charlie, can we talk?"

"Sure."

He looked at her over his half-moon glasses, trying to decipher the expression on her face. She was a hard read. Obviously very smart, but not necessarily running on all cylinders.

Without any prelude she launched into, "I think you and I can cut through the bullshit and get right to it. Okay?"

"Okay."

"I hate the script. I hate it a lot."

"I appreciate your candor."

"It's awful. And you know it, don't you?"

"No, I don't know it."

She tilted her head the way one does to a child who has just told a fib. "Are you going to sit there and tell me you think it's a good script?"

"What's a good script?"

"Come on, Charlie, we're not going to talk Screenwriting 101 here, are we?"

"A good script is one that gets made. . . ."

"That's very cynical. . . . How'd you get to Bert Sully? That's what I want to know."

Charlie removed his glasses, leaned back in the chair, rubbed his eyes while she plowed on.

"Do you realize that you're already seriously in breach of contract? You remained incommunicado, with no way for the studio to contact you. You went ahead and hired someone to do the rewrite without clearing it with us. You sent the script to an actor's representative without our approval. I get the impression that you think you can go ahead and make this picture without us. . . ."

"You have any ideas for a director?" he asked, interrupting her recitation of his sins.

"What?"

"I was just wondering if you had anybody in mind to shoot the picture."

"Charlie, did you hear what I just said?"

He nodded, then said without acrimony, as a simple statement of fact, "It seems to me that's all pretty much academic at this point, isn't it?"

"I don't think the decision of this studio to commit thirty million dollars to a movie is *academic*. . . ."

"What I mean is it has very little to do with what you or I might think of the script. Bobby Mason's going to do it or he's not going to do it. Either we have a picture or we don't have a picture. I just thought we ought to find out as soon as possible. Save everybody a lot of trouble."

He sat there calmly rubbing his eyes. "Listen . . ." she started up again, but shut down again immediately. His impassiveness disarmed her. He turned his tired eyes toward her, and she avoided them.

She sat there listening to the asthmatic wheeze of the air conditioning as he spoke in his soft, almost detached voice. "We ought to be careful casting Gladstone. Too strong an actor'll blow Bobby off the screen. What do you think?"

"Charlie, do you really think you can pull this off?"

He held her look for a long moment, testing her sincerity. "Maybe," he said finally.

"You know, you're starting to remind me of old Ben Disraeli himself. He was quite a tap dancer too. I mean, when you think about it . . . this relatively unknown, broke Jew manages to get elected to Parliament. . . ."

"He wasn't that unknown. He had published books, he had influential friends."

"Yeah, but he didn't ride around in a jeep with a machine gun mounted on its rear."

"That's Lev Disraeli. A totally other guy."

"No kidding."

"Lev Disraeli's a movie. Benjamin Disraeli's a dead English prime minister."

"Whom you've managed to parlay into a development deal and maybe even a picture. Congratulations, Charlie."

She got up, started for the door.

"Deidre . . ."

She turned around, faced him, one hand on her hip, a look of impatience on her face.

"You're not going to recommend this picture, are you?"

She shook her head.

"I'm sorry to hear that."

"Don't worry, Charlie, nobody listens to me anyway."

Norman Hudris walked down the hallway to Howard Draper's office reviewing his out deal. Every time he took this long walk down the quiet, carpeted hallway of the first floor, past the framed photos of bygone stars, he reformulated the independent production deal he would try to make before leaving his post as vice president of production, West Coast.

It was pretty much standard procedure. The studio and he would issue a joint statement that he was stepping down to pursue opportunities as an independent producer. He would be set up with an office, secretary and a small development fund. The quid pro quo would be to give the studio first look at any project he was developing. Basically, it amounted to room and board.

Indy Prod, as it was referred to in the argot of the trade papers, was a vast, uncharted and overpopulated purgatory that allowed you to tread water and maintain a vaguely comfortable standard of living while you were waiting for the next turn at the crap table. But to everyone out there listening to the tribal tom-tom it was clear that you had been fired. And you had to walk around with the stigma of failure carved into your forehead. At least until you produced a hit, or you managed to get people to think you produced a hit, or the people who originally fired you went down themselves or retired to Palm Springs.

Norman had gone over and over the numbers in his mind until he could tell you down to the dollar just what he would need. During his 4:00 A.M. bouts of insomnia he had pared his nut down to the bare minimum that would enable him to stay afloat. There was the rent on the house off Coldwater, the balloon payment on the car lease, the two spec houses in Santa Barbara that his accountant told him he couldn't afford not to get into, the time-share on the apartment in Mazatlán. . . . It added up.

There were certain things, after all, that were necessities of his station in life. He thought of them, essentially, as the cost of doing business. In the circles he moved in one couldn't operate out of an apartment in Van Nuys.

As he pushed open the door to Howard Draper's office, Norman squared his shoulders, prepared once again for the worst. How many times could he be summoned down here and emerge without being fired?

Howard's girl smiled noncommittally at him and held up five fingers to indicate that Howard would be a moment.

"He's on with New York."

Norman sat down on the leather couch and picked up a copy of *Variety*. Skimming through it absently, he came across a filler item:

. . . the search has begun for a major star from Blighty to play opposite Bobby Mason in his next actioner, *Bill and Ben*, set to unspool shortly in the Holy Land after BM wraps *Desert Commando* at the end of the month. Only stiff upper lips need apply. . . .

Somebody had one hell of a press agent. The goddamn script hadn't even been approved yet. In any event, the publicity couldn't hurt. Even if the picture eventually fell through, having the studio associated with a major production was good press. It would send the signal out to the community and to Wall Street that they were getting back on their feet. And maybe the fucking stock would start moving in the right direction. ACI had closed at thirty-four and three-eighths Friday, down another five-eighths.

Howard Draper opened the door to his office and beckoned for Norman to come in. He looked cool and composed as always in his Cardin gray suit and Paulo Pescinni shoes. The office was an archetype of understated elegance. English walnut furniture, beige deep-pile carpeting, Currier and Ives prints on the wall. His desk was barren except for a copy of Deidre's coverage on *Bill and Ben*.

"Coffee, Norman?" he offered.

"No thanks."

Howard sank into the recesses of his leather chair and pointed to the report on his desk.

"I assume you've read this."

Norman nodded, shifted uncomfortably in his chair. He began

to see what this meeting was going to be about. Before Howard
fired him, he was going to drag him over the coals.

"According to your director of creative affairs, we shouldn't
shoot this picture."

"I think that Deidre tends to get a little too cerebral from time
to time."

"What does that mean exactly?"

"She forgets we're in the business of making mass entertainment."

"What do *you* think of the script?"

"Well . . . it's a first draft . . . it's a little rough but I don't see
anything that can't be fixed. . . ."

Howard picked up the coverage and read in a matter-of-fact
voice, " 'This script is a cynical attempt to cheat an audience. It is
basically a series of bloody action sequences, sprinkled with
heavy-handed stabs at religious and political moralizing, poured
like so much Parmesan cheese on overcooked pasta. Its message
is violent, reactionary and bigoted. It is devoid of any redeeming
social value. We are exposing the studio to ridicule and attack
from Jews, blacks, Muslims, Palestinians, Israelis and women, to
name just a few of the groups that it manages to insult. If we have
any pretense at all of moral responsibility as film producers, then
we ought to burn this script.' "

Howard put the report back down, folded his hands, leaned
his chin on them and looked directly at him, eyebrows raised in
that interrogative expression that meant that the ball was in
Norman's court.

"I think she got a little carried away there," Norman said, after
a moment. "The thing about Deidre is she still thinks she's in
English Lit at Bryn Mawr. But she's very good. She knows what
she's doing."

"If she knows what she's doing, Norman, then we're in big
trouble."

Howard took a sip of Earl Grey tea from the Sèvres cup beside
him, leaned back for a moment in his chair. "I had lunch with

Frederick the Great at '21' last week. You know what he asked me?"

Norman shook his head rhetorically.

"He asked me if I liked sushi."

"Sushi? They serve sushi at '21'?"

Howard looked at him with forbearance, then shook his head slowly. "No, Norman, there are, thankfully, still restaurants that do not serve sushi. . . . Tell me, why do you think the chairman of the board of Allied Continental Industries has sushi on his mind?"

"I don't know. . . ."

"Think hard."

"Katsubishi?"

Howard gave one of his barely perceptible, noncommittal nods, more a subliminal blinking of the eye than a nod.

"An acquisition?"

"That's right. Frankly, it smells to me like a shotgun wedding. Given the grosses we've been generating, I wouldn't be surprised if they haven't been quietly looking for a buyer for a while now."

"Jesus, they're going to throw us to the Japanese."

The digits started to click again in Norman's mind. He had been counting on cashing out his stock at a floor of thirty-four in order to leverage the Santa Barbara houses. . . . Now if the Japanese were really moving in on the studio, that could push the stock back over forty, maybe even to forty-five or fifty. . . .

"You realize, of course, what all this means?"

Norman was way ahead of him. Howard Draper's stock holdings had to be considerably more extensive than his own.

"Bobby Mason has the attention span of a three-year-old. It's conceivable that next week or next month he'll develop a passion for Mormonism or Hare Krishna or whatever. . . ."

Norman sat there nodding for several moments before murmuring, "I see what you're getting at."

Howard smiled his charming, creased-eyelid smile, the work of a Bedford Drive plastic surgeon. "How soon can we shoot?"

"According to Bert Sully, Bobby Mason has a window of availability of ten weeks following the wrap on the picture he's doing now."

"It looks to me," said Howard, "like we're in preproduction."

Whatever Charlie Berns may have said to Rabbi Gutterman at the time, the picture was not offered to Milos. It was thought that this was not quite Milos's type of material. All over town speculation raged about who was going to direct *Bill and Ben,* which was advertised as the turning-point picture in Bobby Mason's career.

The great majority of A-list directors declined interest in the project, some expressing privately their doubts that Bobby Mason's career had anyplace to turn *to,* except perhaps to a larger bank. In spite of the general skepticism regarding the martial-arts star's latent talents, however, there was no shortage of B-list directors interested in the job. It was a high-profile project with a definite back-end potential that would enable a profit participant to ride to the bank along with Bobby, albeit with a considerably smaller satchel in hand.

The script was kept under wraps to enhance the mystique of the project. Every agency in town that handled directors scoured their lists for a candidate. GTA was no exception. Already representing the producer, Brad Emprin smelled a potential package and an opportunity to increase the agency's commission on profit points considerably.

Sitting in his office were Cissy Fuchs, Jeff Yankow and Bob Browner. Ever since the Disraeli deal was consummated, Brad Emprin's small office had become a gathering place for informal conclaves.

"You'd think," said Bob Browner, "he'd at least return his own agent's phone calls."

"He's busy," Brad Emprin maintained, defending his client, whom he hadn't seen or spoken to since the day they made the deal on his car phone on Rodeo Drive. "The guy's got a picture to shoot."

"I've never seen a studio push the button so fast on a script," said Jeff Yankow. "It must have been rewritten overnight."

Bob Browner turned to Cissy Fuchs. "Did you find out who the writer is yet?"

Because of her liaison with Norman Hudris she was supposed to have inside information on this picture, but either Norman wasn't talking or he had sworn her to secrecy because she was extremely tight-lipped about *Bill and Ben*.

She shook her head. Norman wasn't talking much about anything to do with the picture. In fact, Norman wasn't talking much about anything at all. For the last week she had only spoken to him briefly on the phone. They hadn't had dinner, or even lunch, or gone to a screening. He hadn't spent the night. He said he was up to his ears at work.

Leslie Moran stuck his head in the office. "There's an offer out to Caine for Bill."

"Did Connery pass?"

"Must have."

"How could you pass on two million and a piece?"

"What about Conrad McBain?"

"For Bill?"

"No . . . to direct."

"Do we still represent him?"

"Shit if I know. Anybody got a client list?"

"Whatever happened to Conrad McBain?"

"I heard he was doing episodes of *Knots Landing*."

"Let's pitch him. Why not? Call Charlie, Brad, and run the name by him."

Brad Emprin nodded. The fact that Charlie Berns was not returning his phone calls had not prevented him from being the repository of suggestions from just about everybody regarding booking the picture, to the extent of having people from other agencies call him to ask if he could help them get through to the producer.

That all this activity was going on without a formal deal in

place was a tribute to Bobby Mason's viability. The announcement of interest in the script from his manager was sufficient to
launch an abundance of trial balloons, filling the smoggy skies
above Sunset Boulevard with low-flying craft of every color. The
discussion that morning in Brad Emprin's office was just one of
a great many similar discussions going on in every agency and
casting office in town.

Meanwhile, in his air-conditioned trailer in the Negev, the
linchpin behind all this frantic activity was slowly turning the
pages of Madison Kearney's draft of *Bill and Ben*. Wearing nothing but a pair of khaki army fatigues, Bobby Mason lay on the
built-in couch and sipped a Pepsi as he followed Lev Disraeli's
war against terrorism.

The script had arrived by messenger from Tel Aviv that morning, rushed down to the location in the desert for Bobby to read
between setups for the day's work. The little box with the pink
ribbon that had to accompany the script had been transmitted by
a simple phone call from Howard Draper to Bert Sully in which
no figures were actually mentioned but no room was created for
doubt about how much was going to be in the little box with the
pink ribbon when it arrived on Bobby Mason's doorstep.

The second assistant director knocked on Bobby's trailer door.
"They're ready for you, Mr. Mason," he said.

"Right . . ." Bobby answered. He was wrapped up in the
sequence where Lev takes the Torah out through the flaming
temple. It would be one hell of a shot. Bring the fucking house
down. He wouldn't use a double either. Shit, man, this was the
*Torah*. The Lord's word. The genuine article. Transmitted directly
to Moses on Mount Sinai. Everything in this next picture was
going to be authentic. He wanted to use a real Torah and made a
note to talk to the propman as soon as they put one on.

Marking his place in the script, he got up, wrapped the
ammo clip around his bare chest, grabbed the AK47 prop gun
and headed for makeup.

*   *   *

"Pushing the button" is not unlike a declaration of war. In officially marking the moment when a film moves from development to preproduction, it mobilizes a great deal of potential energy that has been lying in wait to go to battle. It is a sort of frontier, a point of no return, marching orders that, once issued, are difficult to rescind.

A great deal of money suddenly becomes available. Funds are unfrozen and begin to flow freely. Along with the benefit of access to this newborn liquidity, the producer enjoys an entirely new sense of leverage. Heretofore he was merely one of many dogs barking to be fed. Now he has the can opener; he has a new legitimacy that elevates him to another echelon in the Byzantine pecking order of the movie business. He has the power of the purse, the ability to spend money. Dogs begin to bark at him now. Loudly.

Preoccupied with her remodeling, Enid Schonblum was not in the least prepared for the deluge of phone calls that descended upon Charlie Berns's office the morning after Bert Sully called Howard Draper to tell him that Bobby had officially approved the script and the button that had been unofficially pushed days ago was now officially pushed. The word spread around town, borne by swarms of agents who had infiltrated like a Fifth Column days before war was declared. Enid was nailed to her desk taking phone messages, unable even to go over the carpet samples that had arrived that morning.

By the time Charlie got in at ten-thirty, Enid's phone log was on its third page. She looked up at him, exasperated, shook her head. "It's been crazy. All morning. The phone hasn't stopped. Ringing."

Charlie glanced down at the list of names, didn't recognize most of them. In the three years that he had been sinking into the marshes, the players had recycled, and there was a whole new cadre of agents out there. He did, however, recognize the names of the vice president of production and the director of creative affairs, who had called at 9:05 and 9:06, respectively.

He decided to call Deidre first. She picked up immediately and said, "Congratulations."

"Do you really mean that?"

"No."

"That's what I thought."

"Since the studio has decided to be insane enough to make your picture, however, I'll try not to be a bad loser, okay?"

"Okay."

"But promise me one thing."

"What's that?"

"You'll take some of my notes on the script."

"I welcome your notes on the script."

"Even though Bobby loves it?"

"I hadn't heard yet."

"Didn't you get a call from Bert Sully?"

Charlie scanned the list, found the name, which Enid had written as Bert Sullen.

"Apparently I did."

"Listen, there's this scene where Lev takes out the cave full of terrorists with the bazooka. . . . ?"

"We'll talk."

"Sooner than you think. There's a meeting in Norman's office at three this afternoon."

"I got a call from him."

"That's what it's about. That and the welcome-aboard speech."

"What's the welcome-aboard speech?"

"It's basically how thrilled the studio is to have you doing this picture, how high they are on it, and how confident they are you can bring in a fabulous picture for no money. You know, sort of like the manager going out to the mound to talk to the pitcher and tell him to get it over the plate but keep it low. . . . Charlie, show up. Okay?"

"Sure."

"And be on time. He's the head of production of the studio."

"I'll be there."

He hung up and dialed the extension for Norman Hudris, who said, "Welcome aboard."

"Thank you."

"Charlie, I can't tell you how high we are on this picture. . . ."

Present at the meeting that afternoon in Norman Hudris's office were, in addition to Norman and Deidre, the vice president of casting, the vice president of business affairs, the vice president of publicity and their various assistants. Everyone sat on Norman's leather couches and chairs brought in for the occasion, legal pads on their knees, waiting for marching orders.

Charlie was given the seat of honor, between Norman and Deidre, facing the gathering. After five minutes of banter, in which the vice president of business affairs, Sidney Auger, told a Polish joke and a teamster joke, Norman brought the meeting to order by introducing Charlie and reiterating how thrilled he was that Charlie was aboard. He then reminded everyone of the importance of this picture to the studio and of the fact that they had only ten weeks' lead time to prep it.

Norman then asked Sidney Auger what his eyeball budget was. The vice president of business affairs had the reputation of being able to come within a million of the final budget based on a simple reading of the script.

"All in Israel?"

Norman nodded.

"How much are you willing to go on Bill?"

"Two."

"The director?"

"Seven-fifty, one if we have to."

Sidney Auger closed his eyes and, clicking figures in his head like a silent adding machine, opened them up ten seconds later. "Thirty-one, three," he pronounced.

Norman winced. Sidney Auger shrugged. "Well, what do you

expect? You're giving away half the store up front to the help."

"That, as you know, is the cost of doing business," Norman said.

Sidney Auger shrugged, as if to say it wasn't *his* fault that budgets had gotten out of hand.

Candace De Salvio, the head of casting, a woman with long purple fingernails and outlandish Navaho jewelry, piped up, "What about Victoria? Are you going to give me some money to get someone decent?"

"Do you think you can *get* somebody decent?" Norman looked at Charlie and said, "No offense, Charlie, but getting a decent actress to play opposite Bobby isn't going to be easy."

"I understand," Charlie said.

"Candace, can I cut right through this and tell you what we need for Victoria?" Norman said.

Before he could answer his own rhetorical question, Sidney Auger answered it for him. "Boobies," he articulated with perfect gravity.

Norman nodded. "I'm afraid Sidney's right. She spends half the script without her clothes on."

"Frankly, Norman, even getting a bimbo to play those scenes isn't going to be easy. It's pretty exploitive." Candace De Salvio, too, looked at Charlie and apologized. "No offense, Charlie."

Charlie waved indulgently.

"There's going to be some rewrites," Deidre volunteered.

"Oh Christ, don't turn her into a nun," Sidney pleaded.

"We're going to tone down the violence," Deidre explained.

"Well, that's good," said the vice president of publicity. "Maybe we can get a PG-13."

"Don't count on it," said Norman. "Unless you want to lose the boobies."

"No way I want to lose the boobies."

It was after the boobies discussion that Sidney Auger brought up the matter of the blocked Yugoslavian funds. The studio had over $5 million in distribution revenues stuck in Belgrade that could be cashed in to lower the nut of the picture. *If* they shot it in Yugoslavia.

Norman looked at Sidney with a tired smile. "Sidney, you read the script. It's about an Israeli anti-terrorist fighter defending his homeland. How do you shoot that in Yugoslavia?"

"What does Israel look like?"

"I don't know."

"It looks like San Bernardino. It's hot and they grow melons. There are places in Yugoslavia which are hot and where they grow melons too."

"Sidney, there's a political problem. As you may know, our star is very anxious to shoot in Israel."

"I'm talking just the interiors. You do the postcard stuff with Bobby and a small crew, get the look, you know, grab Mount Sinai, the Wailing Wall, that shit, in Israel, then for all the inside stuff, like the hotel sequences, the CIA stuff, the fuck scenes, we're on soundstages in Belgrade."

Norman looked over at Charlie. "What do you think?"

"It's not a bad idea."

"Do you think Bobby'll buy it?"

"I don't know."

"It'll take five right off the top," Sidney went on. "Easy. We got a lot of dinars lying around there growing old and moldy."

Deidre felt the perspiration forming in the palms of her hands. She was starting to lose her center. The Mad Hatter was at it again. A movie about an Israeli with the last name of a famous British prime minister played by a black American and shot in Yugoslavia. Nobody blinked an eyelash.

Hey, what the fuck . . . sounds good to me. . . .

When Charlie got back to his office he found another three pages of phone calls. Among them Rabbi Seth Gutterman. He decided to talk to his technical adviser before calling back Bert Sully, even though Deidre Hearn had made him promise to call back Bobby Mason's manager without delay.

The rabbi got on the phone, sounding cheerful. "So, Berns, what am I, a stranger?"

"I've been a little busy, Rabbi."

"That's what I figured. I read in the trades we got a Go picture."

"Yeah."

"*Mazel tov.*"

"Thank you."

"So when are you sending me the shooting script?"

"Well . . . there've been some conceptual changes."

"Conceptual changes? What kind of conceptual changes?"

"Nothing drastic."

"It's still about a Jew, isn't it?"

"Absolutely."

"So you need some technical advice, right?"

"Right."

"So what about Milos?"

"Milos?"

"To direct."

"I don't think we're going with Milos on this."

"Too bad. I was looking forward to working with him. . . . Listen, Berns, you don't mind if my press guy puts something in the paper about my being executive producer on this picture, do you?"

"Actually, Rabbi, it was associate producer."

"Same thing, no? Actually he already did it. You know how these press people are. You can't hold them down. . . . So, Berns, you'll send me the script? We'll talk?"

"Absolutely." Charlie hung up the phone, walked into Enid's office.

"Enid . . ." Immersed in her carpet samples, Enid hadn't seen him coming, and she started. "Oh. Mr. Berns. I didn't see you. There."

"Enid, I have a job for you."

"Of course. Mr. Berns."

"I want you to track someone down for me." He put in front of her a piece of paper with the name Dinak Hrossovic written on it. She looked at it, then, "Who is he?"

"He's a director. I want to talk to him."

"Should I call? Information?"

He shook his head. "You have to call Belgrade. In Yugoslavia. . . . The Yugoslav Ministry of Film. And you find someone there who knows how to get in contact with this man. And you get me the number. Okay?"

Enid sat there nodding for a moment. Then, "Do I dial nine? To get Yugoslavia?"

# 8

Charlie Berns sat in the first-class section of the KLM 747, his eyelids heavy from the double scotch he ordered after dinner to help him sleep, listening to the hum of the engines. They were somewhere over Greenland. Presumably. He would have to take their word for it. As far as he was concerned, it was anybody's ball game up here in the ether.

His nephew Lionel sat beside him, already asleep. Charlie had decided to take the kid with him on this trip to Amsterdam and Israel as a kind of recompense for the butchery he had committed on his script. When Lionel had finally read Madison Kearney's desecration of his masterpiece, he had broken down and cried. It had taken a long, avuncular, heart-to-heart talk, in which Charlie explained the facts of life in the picture business, to convince Lionel not to pack up and go back to New Jersey.

Eventually Lionel came around to accepting the notion that his cathedral had become an armored bunker, without nave, apse or stained-glass windows. He consoled himself with the promise of someday having the clout to bring the life of Lev Disraeli's distinguished ancestor Benjamin to the screen. He even accompanied Charlie to Madison Kearney's house in Silver Lake to help them accommodate the studio's notes and made a significant contribution to the next draft. And now he was thrilled to be going on his first trip to Europe to meet a big-time director and a real movie star.

The big-time director had been noncommittal on the phone when Enid finally tracked him down in Amsterdam, where he was shooting low-budget skin movies. It was Sidney Auger's idea of using the blocked Yugoslavian funds that had got Charlie thinking about Dinak Hrossovic. It was one of those random, almost gratuitous associations that can make or destroy careers in the movie business. The name popped into his head in the middle of the meeting in Norman Hudris's office. Charlie Berns had not thought about Dinak Hrossovic in a long time. Nor had anybody else in Hollywood, for that matter.

Dinak Hrossovic's career had taken a meteoric plunge in 1969 when, as a twenty-eight-year-old wunderkind, fresh from a Cannes Film Festival *Palme d'Or*, he had told the head of a major Hollywood studio to get his fat ass the fuck off his set and not to bring it back. Hrossovic became unemployable in the States after that.

Charlie used him on a quickie western he threw together in Spain in the early seventies. He discovered then that Dinak Hrossovic was a marvelous action director. When it came to movement, to bullets, to blood and gore on a grand scale, nobody put it in the can better than this irascible Yugoslav. He had a positive genius for photographing carnage, for getting the bloodletting and death throes from every conceivable angle, and doing it on schedule.

Convincing the studio to trust a $31.3 million movie to a director who hadn't worked in the States in more than twenty years required more than a little tap-dancing. He pitched Hrossovic as a maker of schedules and a respecter of budgets, qualities much admired by studios. He pitched Hrossovic's familiarity with his native country, which would facilitate the Belgrade work and perhaps result in an even greater savings to the studio. He dug up his award-winning Cannes film, an extravaganza about the Crimean War, and Charlie, Norman and Deidre sat in a dark screening room in the basement of the producers' building watching regiments of Hussars being impaled graphically on Tatar swords.

Eventually Norman agreed that if Charlie could get Hrossovic to go to Israel to meet Bobby and if Bobby approved him, then they could go with him. Which was the purpose of this trip. They were to meet with Hrossovic in Amsterdam, show him the script, get him to go to Israel with them to meet Bobby. If it all worked out, the director would stay in Israel and begin scouting locations.

The scotch sloshed around in his brain, but Charlie was unable to drift off to sleep, kept awake by something that Deidre Hearn had said to him just before he left. They were having lunch in a Mexican restaurant on Pico. She had gradually become less disagreeable with him as the days had passed and Charlie had removed some of the more egregious gore from the script. But she retained, nonetheless, a vaguely disapproving attitude toward him and the picture.

"You're walking around with a live grenade in your back pocket, Charlie. Don't sit down on it."

What Deidre Hearn didn't know was that he had some experience with live grenades. She didn't know about the hose and the doggie door and the masking tape on the windows. She didn't realize that for some time now Charlie Berns had been juggling grenades. As far as he was concerned, things were going splendidly.

They sat in the bar of the Holiday Inn in Amsterdam drinking watered-down mai tais and trying to have a conversation over the ear-splitting rock music. Dinak Hrossovic had suggested they meet there, for reasons that eluded Charlie, but given the language barriers among them, it didn't seem to make much difference that they could barely hear one another.

At best, Dinak Hrossovic spoke approximate English. The first assistant director would often have to translate his instructions to the crew, and, as far as the actors were concerned, it didn't matter much because Dinak didn't talk to them at all when he could avoid it. He disliked actors. If it was possible to make movies without them, he would do it.

The Yugoslav had shown up at the bar an hour and a half late with a tall thin woman of indeterminate nationality, half his age, whom he introduced as Wilna, his assistant. She kept one hand firmly on Dinak's thigh, the other wrapped around a dark, smelly cigarette. Periodically he would turn to her and say something in what sounded like Russian but could have been Swahili, for all Charlie knew.

Drifting in and out on waves of jet lag, Charlie did his best to explain what *Bill and Ben* was about. He might have saved himself the trouble. Dinak Hrossovic was not overly concerned with The Big Picture. He was happy with a script he could break down to a shot list, plenty of extras and stuntmen, and all the gadgets you could give him—long lenses, cranes, dollies, helicopters, Steadycams, Ritters, the whole toy box.

When Charlie was finished, Dinak drained his mai tai, turned to Wilna, said something to her. She nodded. Then he turned back to Charlie.

"He gonna do his own stunts, the karate *shvartzer?*"

"I don't think you want an eight-million-dollar star running around dodging squibs, Dinak."

"Steve McQueen does own stunts for me."

"Well . . ."

"Maybe Steve play the other lead? What you think, huh, Charlie?"

At this point Lionel, who was trying to keep his eyes off Wilna's thigh-stroking, piped up: "Steve McQueen's dead."

"No kidding?"

Charlie nodded. Wilna exhaled loudly. Dinak crossed himself, muttered: "Son of a bitch owe me two hundred dollars. . . . What you think of Bronson, huh?"

"Bill's supposed to be British."

"Bronson don't have to talk. I do a whole picture with him he don't talk once."

"Actually, Bronson's getting a little old for the part, don't you think?"

Dinak took a large handful of cocktail peanuts, put them in his mouth, chewed them.

"This karate *shvartzer*, he gonna be a pain in the ass?"

"From what I hear he's no problem. Likes to get it in the can and get on with it."

The waitress brought them another round. The music got worse—some hybrid form of Eurorock, loud and throbbing with lyrics in no recognizable language. Charlie plowed on over the noise. "Anyway, like I told you on the phone, the studio wants to do the interiors in Belgrade. Save them a lot of money."

Dinak nodded, took more peanuts. "Crews in Belgrade. Very lazy. You got to light fire under their ass, keep them moving. . . . You got camels in the picture, Charlie?"

"None."

"I don't work with no camels. Camels can kill you."

"What's wrong with camels?" Lionel asked, curious.

"They shit. You say *action*, they shit. Like on cue. You do a picture about shitting camels, that's okay."

"No camels," Charlie reassured him. "So, what do you say, Dinak? You going to shoot this sucker for me?"

Dinak shrugged, took the smelly cigarette out of Wilna's hand, took a puff, put it back. "No studio assholes on set, yes?"

"I promise. They're going to be back in L.A. We're not even going to send them dailies."

"Asshole come on my set, I throw him the fuck off, Charlie."

"Absolutely."

Another conversation in machine-gun Swahili transpired. This one went on for a while, with Wilna doing most of the talking and Dinak nodding, eventually petering out into a few desultory phrases and nods. Dinak turned back to Charlie.

"You got tanks, Charlie?"

"I got tanks, I got armored cars, I got AK47s, bazookas and Uzis."

"Okay, Charlie, I do the picture for you."

"You'll want to read the script, of course."

"Plenty time to read the script. We drink to the picture."

Dinak raised his mai-tai glass. Charlie smiled, said, "To *Bill and Ben.*"

Everybody drank to the health of the picture. Then Dinak Hrossovic and Wilna left to go back to the set to wrap Dinak's current production. He promised to be at the airport at eight o'clock the next morning.

Fortunately, KLM Flight 921 was delayed, because so was Dinak Hrossovic. He showed up at the airport fifteen minutes late with a light meter around his neck and Wilna. This was the first indication that Charlie had that Wilna was on the picture. Charlie took Dinak aside to explain that the studio had only authorized this trip for three people. Dinak shrugged, said he couldn't go anywhere without her. If he wanted him to go to Israel, then Wilna would have to go too. That was the way it was. Plain and simple.

So Charlie had to buy a fourth first-class ticket for the director's assistant, as she would be referred to in the budget and on future expense vouchers. She was now officially on the crew of *Bill and Ben,* written off as an above-the-line item.

It was on landing in Tel Aviv that Charlie learned that Wilna traveled on a Polish passport. It was Polish and not Swahili that Wilna and Dinak had been speaking to each other. Charlie could only wonder what conceivable value a Polish-speaking assistant would be with an Israeli or Yugoslavian film crew. But, nonetheless, she was on the picture. Irrevocably. To be written against his profits. Though not against the dollar-one profits of Bobby Mason, of course. Wilna wouldn't cost Bobby Mason a penny.

Walking through Lod Airport, they were surrounded by automatic weapons. Soldiers were everywhere, their eyes scouring the crowd for the errant gesture of the terrorist. It wouldn't have fazed Lev Disraeli. He would have taken out the whole airport in one bloodcurdling attack.

Already Charlie could see the built-in camera inside Dinak's head working, studying the light, framing shots. The director walked with his hooded eyes straight ahead, like a subjective tracking shot. He didn't miss a thing.

"Charlie, you see what they got?"

"Who?"

"The Yids. Thompson SA automatics. They shoot your dick off at two hundred yards."

"No kidding?"

"You get me some for picture, right?"

"Do my best . . ."

When they arrived at the baggage carousel, there was a tall heavy-set man with a hand-lettered sign that said BURNS. Charlie identified himself.

"*Shalom,*" the man said. "Eliezer Gurion, manager, location."

"Pleased to meet you," said Charlie, shaking hands. He introduced Lionel, Dinak and Wilna to the Israeli location manager. While waiting for the bags to arrive, Eliezer explained that their trip out to the location to see Bobby would take longer because one of the roads leading there had just been closed due to a bomb threat.

Eliezer reassured them by saying that bomb threats happened every day in Israel, that he himself was a trained army officer, as was the driver, who had commanded a tank battalion during the Six Day War. Wilna disappeared to the ladies' room, emerging forty minutes later, their luggage having arrived long ago, without a word of explanation, not even to Dinak.

They got into the air-conditioned van and headed south toward the Negev. In addition to being an ex-tank commander, the driver turned out to be a Polish immigrant, and he drove with his head turning constantly toward Wilna, beside him in the front seat, gesticulating and talking in Polish, and no doubt appreciating her taut thighs exposed in a short skirt, all the while keeping the van well over one hundred mph. Charlie looked out the window at the flat white light of Israel. Sidney Auger was right. It did look like San Bernardino.

It was late afternoon before they reached the location of *Desert Commando*, a desolate section of the southern Negev. They arrived as the crew was just about to film the day's big production shot. A small army of extras was milling around waiting to make war, while the assistant directors bellowed into bullhorns in Hebrew, Arabic and English, and propmen rigged trip wires and squibs.

Charlie and Dinak stood and watched the scene with professional interest, declining Eliezer's invitation to wait in the production trailer until Bobby finished the shot. They watched the cameraman stop down the aperture to accommodate the lower light level, watched the director, impassive in the middle of the chaos, his eyes silently imploring the sun to slow its descent. The extras were in place; the effects men were ready. All that was missing was the star.

Dinak squinted into the sun, turned to Charlie and said, "If he don't get shot five minutes, he gonna be in deep shit."

Charlie nodded, watched, caught up in the tension, as one of the a.d.'s ran over to the makeup trailer, disappeared inside. The director looked back up at the sun, then at his watch, trying to decide, no doubt, if he should go to the makeup trailer himself to get the star out.

The door to the trailer opened a few moments later, and the a.d. emerged, followed by a man, bare to the waist, a machine-gun belt strapped across his black chest, glistening with artificial sweat that had been applied in the makeup trailer.

Lionel was struck at how short Bobby Mason actually was. He seemed to be of only average height, a fairly unremarkable-looking man in the center of all this activity. While a woman ran alongside him daubing his face, a propman ran up and handed him a gun.

"A Schneider semiautomatic," Dinak observed.

Charlie nodded. He would take Dinak's word for it. Bobby approached his mark, and the operator up on the crane checked his focus, shouted something down to the first a.d., who shouted something to one of the propmen, who shouted something to an assistant, who ran as fast as he could to the prop wagon. All this transpired in a matter of seconds; languages changed back and forth as orders were transmitted down the line of command. And all the time the director kept looking up at the sinking sun.

They managed to get it in three takes before the cameraman pointed to the light meter and shook his head. It was an inexorable judgment. Nobody quarreled with the light meter. The a.d. called a wrap. The tension dissolved from the scene in a matter of moments. Cigarettes were lit, body language relaxed, the director and the star retired to their trailers.

Another day in the can. A few thousand feet of film exposed. Twelve hours' work for a minute and a half of usable film. It was almost like medieval tapestry-making in its painstaking inefficiency.

They were asked to wait a few minutes while Bobby showered before being ushered into the enormous Winnebago flown over especially for him. It dwarfed the other trailers. Its air-conditioning unit alone looked like it could handle a good chunk of the Negev.

Bobby Mason received them in a purple velour jumpsuit and white Nikes. Everybody shook hands. They sat on built-in couches in the spacious living room of the trailer while an assistant served Pepsis.

Conversation was sparse in the beginning, neither Bobby nor Dinak being great talkers. Charlie tried his best to keep things flowing, with the help of Lionel, but it wasn't until Dinak asked Bobby about the Schneider semiautomatic that the ice got broken. The two of them went on for some time comparing the advantages of various assault weapons.

Charlie eventually managed to bring up the question of the script.

"It's all right," Bobby said when asked how he liked the latest rewrite.

"Do you have any notes you want to give us?"

Bobby thought for a while, finally nodded and said, "I think it should be a little more Jewish, you know what I mean?"

Charlie looked at Dinak for help, hoping that the director would do a little tap-dancing for Bobby. Directors were supposed to be able to communicate with actors. But not this one. As far as this director was concerned, the film could have been about a Seventh-Day Adventist. He had no idea what Bobby was talking about. There was a long, awkward moment, filled with the sound of slurping Pepsis.

"Are there any specific scenes that you think we can make more . . . Jewish, Bobby?" Charlie asked.

"I'm talking in general, man."

"Right."

More silence, more slurping.

It was Lionel, finally, who stepped in and filled the vacuum. "I think I understand what you mean," he said. "We need to put a spiritual dimension in Lev's motivation."

"That's it, man. A spiritual dimension. Exactly."

Everybody nodded. A spiritual dimension seemed to be just what was needed. They'd get right to work putting one in. Sure. Right.

It wasn't until they were in the van on the way back to Tel Aviv that Charlie asked Lionel what in God's name he meant by a spiritual dimension. Lionel looked at him and shrugged.

"It sounded like a good thing to say," he explained.

Charlie stared at him for a moment, searching for a trace of sarcasm before realizing that his nephew was perfectly sincere. He smiled to himself. Maybe Lionel was better suited for the business than he had thought. Second only to the principle of leverage, one needed to understand the device of the smoke screen, the art of responding to inane questions with the illusion of substance.

They would, indeed, add a spiritual dimension to the screenplay. The next copy of the script that Bobby Mason would receive would be printed in paper of a different color.

With all his other problems, the last thing Norman Hudris needed was to start having hallucinations. He needed a grip on reality, however murky that reality might be, in order to function in the treacherous terrain of studio politics. But there he was, eating his avocado and shrimp salad at the commissary, and having a very sharply focused vision of a group of Japanese having lunch at a table across the room.

There were at least ten of them, all in dark suits, silently nibbling on the Dolly Parton Burger Plate and drinking Diet Cokes. Norman looked around him to see if anyone else was aware that there were ten Japanese eating cheeseburgers in the commissary, but no one else seemed the least bit concerned.

So this was it, the classic Fifth Column—yellow Quislings in business suits come to reconnoiter the terrain. Beside each chair was a thin attaché case containing, no doubt, the latest profit-and-loss statement, a miniature calculator and a yardstick to measure the real estate. After lunch they would walk the soundstages, total up the square footage, divide it into potential revenue to compute the yield per square foot.

This was obviously it. Pearl Harbor would be any day now. Norman pushed away the avocado and shrimp salad, got up and went toward the exit farthest away from the Japanese. Outside in the bleak midday sunshine, he felt dizzy. He put his finger against the carotid artery to check his pulse, tried to calm himself as he hurried to his office. His Rolex said 12:22. The Big Board would be closing down in a little more than half an hour.

Since his talk with Howard, Norman had been tracking ACI

stock several times a day, following the minuscule twitches in either direction, trying to discern a trend one way or the other. But the stock had been circling thirty-four dollars a share for two weeks now.

Not anymore. It was going to move now. He needed to tell Grant about the Japanese in the commissary before the news was all over the street.

Grant McKelwayne, his broker in New York, was getting used to these phone calls every afternoon during the last half-hour of trading. So much so that when he picked up his phone at 3:29 and heard a voice ask, "What's it doing?" he knew immediately not only whose voice it was but what it wanted to know.

"Thirty-three and seven-eighths," he answered, having anticipated the call and checked the stock a few minutes before the phone rang.

"Yeah, well, this is it. It's going to move now," Norman said.

"What makes you say that?" Grant inquired matter-of-factly.

"They're here. They're actually checking the place out."

"Who?"

"The Japanese. Katsubishi. Ten of them."

"Listen, Norm, I'm not showing anything on the computer."

"That's because the computer doesn't know yet."

"Doesn't know what?"

"That they're taking over the studio."

"Are you sure about that?"

"Jesus, Grant, I just saw them with my own eyes. Ten Japanese eating cheeseburgers in the commissary. They have attaché cases with them."

"Norm, let me tell you something. Even if ACI dumps you, there's no telling how the street is going to react to that information. You're just a small part of ACI's balance sheet. It might have no effect on the stock."

"You bullshitting me?"

"Norm, do you pay me to bullshit you? Listen, the Katsubishi rumors have been around for a while. If the market was going to react to them, it probably already has."

"So what should I do?"

"About what?"

"My shares. Should I dump them now or wait?"

There was a moment of silence over the line. Norman waited to hear the voice of the oracle from New York telling him what to do. Finally, in a tired voice: "Norm, it all pretty much depends on what the upside potential of the studio is at the moment."

"Uh-huh . . ."

"Norm, you're running the studio, aren't you? *You* tell *me*."

# 9

Dinak Hrossovic was officially approved by the star the day after their meeting in the desert. Anybody who knew his way around an AK47 was okay by Bobby Mason. Charlie promised to get his writers working immediately on giving the script a spiritual dimension and to have new pages out as quickly as possible.

Leaving Dinak and Wilna in the Hilton in Tel Aviv, from where they would scout locations for a week, Charlie and Lionel got on a plane back to California to work on the rewrite and see if they could settle the major casting. The minor roles they would cast out of London, but Bill and Victoria would have to be chosen with the advice and consent of the studio.

Back in his office in the producers' building, Charlie found Enid buried in submissions from agents. Her desk was piled with stacks of glossies and résumés of actors eager to be considered for roles in the picture. Enid was very put out by the deluge of unsolicited deliveries that arrived every time the mail cart passed. There were so many envelopes that she started having to pile them on the Regency settee, which entirely ruined its graceful lines.

In an attempt to be useful, she had opened them, removing each glossy from the envelope and paper-clipping the attached note to it. In the process she couldn't help noticing how many of the notes began with a reference to Brad Emprin: "Dear Charlie . . . in speaking to Brad yesterday, he mentioned that you were looking for someone for your next picture for the role of . . ."

Deidre Hearn called to welcome him back.

"How were things in the Holy Land?"

"It looks like San Bernardino. Just like Sidney said."

"I hear you're adding a *spiritual dimension* to the script."

"Right."

"Whose idea was that?"

"Bobby's."

"Really? I wouldn't have imagined that he knew what a dimension is, let alone a spiritual one. . . . Is he going to say a prayer over the bazooka?"

"Deidre . . ."

"Charlie, who's Seth Gutterman?"

"Who?"

"*Rabbi* Seth Gutterman."

"Why?"

"There was a piece in *The Reporter* calling him the executive producer. You don't have the contractual right to give out that credit. Bert Sully takes it on all Bobby Mason's pictures."

"He's sort of a technical adviser."

"For what? The guy's a rabbi. This movie's not about Jews, it's about automatic weapons."

"When I was still making a movie about Benjamin Disraeli, I thought we could use a Jewish tech adviser."

"Charlie, were you ever really making a movie about Benjamin Disraeli?"

"I thought you were going to be nice."

"I'm trying. I really am."

After he got off with Deidre, Charlie finally took a call from Brad Emprin, who, Enid claimed, had been calling several times a day while he was away.

"So how's the guy?"

"Fine, Brad. What's up?"

"Hey, you know, I just wanted to make sure they were treating you all right. Office okay?"

"No problem."

"Sounds good to me. So, listen, I've got some ideas on directors for you."

"I've got a director."

"No shit. Who's that?"

"Dinak Hrossovic."

"Who?"

"Dinak Hrossovic. He's a Yugoslav. You probably haven't heard of him."

"Hey, as long as he's your guy, right? So who are you going with for Bill?"

"We haven't set Bill yet."

"I hear Caine passed."

"We haven't offered the part to anyone yet."

"No shit . . ."

"Listen, I've got to run, Brad."

"Yeah, right. Where *were* you anyway?"

"Tel Aviv."

"No shit. Yeah . . . well, sounds good to me. . . ."

A major casting strategy meeting took place in Candace De Salvio's office late that afternoon. Still on Tel Aviv time, Charlie floated through the meeting in a fog, doing his best not to fade out and pitch forward onto the Turkish rug that graced Candace De Salvio's office.

Candace proceeded with the reading of the A list, big-money English actors. After each name, the comment was the same: "He'll never do it." Followed by, "Offer him a million five and see what happens."

When it came to Victoria, the list was longer. Since she was no longer the Queen of England but a nymphomaniacal Mossad operative, it had been decided that boobies were more important than an English accent. Another boobies conversation ensued, with various opinions being offered as to who would and who wouldn't show boobies.

Charlie sat there trying to keep from nodding off. It was similar to every casting meeting he had ever attended. Names were brought up and either immediately discarded or put on one of the lists that Candace De Salvio's assistant kept, hundreds of names thrown out in a sort of anarchic chorus of free association. Characters were assassinated, careers maligned without the slightest attempt at due process. It was the classic lowering of expectations, the moving from the realm of the ideal to the realm of the possible.

Two days later, after the A- and B-list names had been checked out and all of them had either passed or been unavailable, they moved from "She'd be terrific" to "She won't hurt us" to "We can live with her" to "Oh, Jesus, *her?*"

Along with the casting meetings there was a series of marketing meetings that Charlie had to attend. Before the ink was even dry on the Bobby Mason deal, the sales guys were on the blower selling the picture to every market in the world. While Charlie was in the air to Amsterdam, deals were already being struck to distribute *Lev Disraeli: Freedom Fighter,* the new working title of the picture, in Sri Lanka, Swaziland and Senegal.

According to the distribution guys, the picture was pre-selling so well that they were already in profit. Charlie found this out from Deidre. He wasn't supposed to know. Nobody wanted to tell a producer that a picture was anything but severely over budget lest he go out and spend more money, or, as Deidre put it, he got it over the plate but high.

Charlie had avoided sending a copy of the revised script to Seth Gutterman, the official rabbi on the picture. Now that they needed a spiritual dimension, however, there might be a way for the rabbi to be useful in return for the executive-producer credit he wasn't going to get. So Charlie got on the phone and called him.

"So, Berns, you go to Israel and you don't take me?"

"Sorry, Rabbi. It was just a quick run to scout locations."

"You don't think I know from locations?"

"Listen, Rabbi, I'm really sorry but I just found out my girl forgot to send a copy of the new script to you."

"Tell me about it."

"I'm going to messenger one over to you right away. Then I'll get your notes and put you with the writer."

"Sure. . . . Listen, Berns, what about Meryl for Queen Victoria?"

"We wrote Queen Victoria out of the picture."

"How can you do a picture about Disraeli without Queen Victoria?"

"Well, like I said, we had a little concept change. Look, read the script. Then we'll talk."

"Berns, any chance of getting me a point or two on the back end?"

"I'll work on it."

In order to implement the star's notes Lionel became the official writer on the picture. Again. There was no point in getting Madison Kearney's input on ways to make the script more Jewish. Besides being an anti-Semite, when he was lucid enough to be anti-anything, Madison Kearney did not relate well to general notes. You had to be very specific with him. You had to say things like, change the dog to a cat, or, more appropriately in his case, change the luger to a derringer.

Charlie went by the house in Silver Lake, found the writer sleeping it off on the couch, the same couch that Charlie had used during the writing of the first draft. He didn't bother waking him up. Charlie left a check on the kitchen counter.

Lionel threw himself into the rewriting work with great energy. He went with Charlie to see Rabbi Gutterman and get his input at the synagogue up in the hills above Encino. It was one of those rare clear days when you could see to the other end of the San Fernando Valley.

"Not bad, huh?" the rabbi said, pointing out of the window of his office.

Charlie and Lionel nodded in unison.

"A day like today, you can see to Cucamonga and back."

"Anyway, Rabbi, what do you think we can do to make the script more Jewish?" Charlie asked.

"This script? You could circumcise it, you could put tefillin on it, it wouldn't be Jewish."

"Yeah, well, you know how it is. The studio gives its notes and you start rewriting and pretty soon you have a whole new script."

The rabbi looked at Charlie gravely and said, "Berns, I don't know if I can put my name on this picture. It's profane. It's— you'll pardon the expression—*goyish*. This picture, Berns, not only has nothing Jewish about it, but worse than that, it's sacrilege."

"Well, you see, that's why we need you, Rabbi. We need to add a spiritual dimension."

"Spiritual dimension? What are you talking about? Let me ask you something, Berns, would you put a pickle on a banana split?"

Charlie and Lionel shook their heads in unison.

"You've got a two-hundred-million-worldwide-gross picture here. You put a pickle on it, what're you going to have?"

Charlie began to lose the thread of the conversation. He couldn't tell which way the rabbi was moving in his argument. It was like some abstruse Talmudic debate.

"You have *dreck*. That's what you have."

"Well, if you feel that way, Rabbi . . ." Charlie got up, motioned to Lionel that they were leaving.

"Where you going?" the rabbi asked.

"It seems obvious to me that you don't want to work on the picture."

"Did I say that? Did those words ever leave my mouth?"

"I know what *dreck* means."

"I should hope so. A Jewish boy like you should have some connection to his heritage. Sit down, Berns, we'll talk."

Charlie sat back down again. The rabbi lit a menthol cigarette in a mother-of-pearl holder, sat back in his chair for a moment.

"You know what the trouble with the world is," he expostulated. "Everyone wants a spiritual dimension. Pick up a spiritual dimension in ten easy lessons, just send nine ninety-five, money-back guarantee, dial-a-spiritual-dimension . . ."

"Rabbi, we're here because the star, Bobby Mason, has requested that we give the script a spiritual dimension. We thought that maybe you . . ."

"You want a spiritual dimension? Sure, why not?"

"I thought you didn't want to be associated with the picture. . . ."

"Did I say that?" He shook his head rhetorically, answering his own question. "What I said, Berns, was I didn't know if I could put my name on this picture as executive producer . . . not that I wouldn't work on it. Isn't that what I said?"

There is a term in engineering called "an elegant solution." It is used when an unforeseen problem is revealed requiring a new solution, and the solution to that problem results in the system ending up working better than it had before the discovery of the problem. It seemed to Charlie Berns that the rabbi's distaste for the script became, in a sense, an elegant solution to the problem of adding a spiritual dimension to the picture without having to add, at the same time, another executive producer.

The Sunday-morning tennis brunch at Jay Kessler's Malibu house was an A-list event. Studio heads, major stars and heavyweight agents in La Costa tennis whites mingled following some ruthlessly amicable tennis. A great deal of both business and gossip transpired there. It helped to be there to defend your reputation, even if being there required having to let Jay Kessler beat you in tennis and then facing a cornucopia of unappetizing food.

To paraphrase Oscar Wilde, the only thing worse than being invited was *not* being invited.

Howard Draper found himself, this Sunday morning, standing on Jay Kessler's Mexican-tile patio overlooking the Pacific, a watered-down Bloody Mary in his hand. Beside him was Flo Gamish, personal manager to some of the biggest names in town, devouring an enormous plate of lox, eggs and onions between puffs from her filtered Gitane. Howard did his best to keep upwind of the lox, eggs and onions, which, at this delicate hour of the morning, threatened the tranquillity of his demi-WASP stomach.

"I have to tell you, Howard, when your Disraeli picture was announced, I had Jeremy on the phone from London *begging* me to call you."

"Really?"

"Apparently he's some sort of amateur historian or something. He's always dreamed about playing Disraeli. The problem with Disraeli, apparently, is he's just very dull. Nobody's ever written a script about him."

"So I hear."

"Anyway, when I told him that it wasn't about *that* Disraeli and that it was going to be played by Bobby Mason, we had a good laugh. Do you know what Jeremy called him?"

Flo looked around her, double-checking, before saying to Howard, sotto voce, "Sugar Ray Disraeli."

Howard smiled benignly, drained the Blood Mary, hoping to discover a little vodka at the bottom of the cup.

"You know, we're getting between four and five for Jeremy now," Flo went on.

Howard blinked. He didn't think that Jeremy Ikon, best-actor Oscar or not, was worth four million dollars. But he wasn't going to tell Flo Gamish that.

"Of course, he's always wanting to run off to play Richard the Third at some tiny little theater off-Broadway for two hundred fifty bucks a week. Don't repeat this, Howard, but he would pay *you* to play Benjamin Disraeli."

This conversation was interrupted by the host himself, Jay Kessler, who put his large hairy arm around Howard Draper's shoulder and said, "Well, Howard, how does it feel to be working for Bobby Mason?"

Howard creased his eyes slightly in the perfect demi-smile. Let them mock. It was all right with him. For once *he* was going to laugh all the way to the bank.

"I hear he's getting twelve up front and a piece."

"Not true, Jay."

"Ten?" Flo tried.

"No . . ."

"He's being coy, Flo. Howard's being coy. All I have to do is call Bert Sully to find out. . . . So is it true you're going to be commuting to Tokyo pretty soon?"

Howard shrugged. "You know how it is, Jay, we're always the last to know."

"Just like my ex-wife," Jay said, exploding into a loud, phlegmy laugh. "Listen, she's got nothing to complain about. She actually owns this house. Do you know she rents it to me? For an arm and a leg . . ."

Gradually Howard managed to disentangle himself and edge toward the door, trying to make his escape as unobtrusively as possible. He was stopped dead in his tracks by a pair of pale-blue eyes. They belonged to Jacqueline Fortier, an actress of French-English origin, who had the exquisite manners of a woman of fine breeding to go with a body that didn't quit. Howard knew her vaguely from a dinner party years ago when he had sat next to her and been mesmerized by her beauty and charm. In the car on the way home Winnie had practically accused him of having an erection at the dinner table. How the hell would she have known, sitting on the other side of the table putting away the chicken marengo like it was her last meal on earth?

Howard inclined his head, his eyes traveling across the patio toward Jacqueline Fortier. They exchanged the smile of two people who weren't sure whether they actually knew each other but

suspected they may, before Jacqueline was swept away by
Nikolai Fenderakov, her latest flame, a Russian gymnast who
was launching a career as an actor. Or trying to.

As the Corniche effortlessly negotiated the Sunday traffic along
the Coast Highway, Howard found his mind turning back toward
Jacqueline Fortier. She was so exquisitely lovely, so quiet, so
refined. She represented for him some sort of antipode to the daily
business of fighting a losing war. He was at the wheel of a ship that
was seriously listing. They were taking water at an alarming rate.
How nice it would be to abandon ship, simply requisition a lifeboat
and paddle off to the coast of England where Jacqueline Fortier
would be waiting for him in a Georgian country house with stables
and hunting dogs. They would live there quietly, nobly, unhur-
riedly. . . . They would sip Château d'Yquem and converse in their
perfect diction, their well-bred sense of understatement, their conversation witty and restrained, without being pestered, nudged or
bottom-lined by the likes of Jay Kessler or Flo Gamish. . . .

The reverie was abruptly shattered by the buzz of the car
phone. It was Norman.

"What do you think about Nigel Bland for Bill?"

"I don't know, Norman. What's he want?"

"One point two."

"That's a lot of money for an aging limey."

"He still means something in Europe."

"Listen, Norman, you know who'll do the picture for two hundred and fifty a week? Jeremy Ikon."

"Really?"

"Uh-huh. All we have to do is go back to the script about the
prime minister."

There was a long silence on the other end of the line. Finally,
Norman said, "Are you . . . serious?"

"Sure. Why not? We'll get Jacqueline Fortier to play Victoria.
Get an Academy Award while we're at it."

"Howard . . . we have a pay-or-play contract with Bobby
Mason."

There didn't seem to be any sense at this point in mentioning to Norman that he was joking. Besides having no sense of humor, Norman tended to brood when he thought someone was making fun of him. So Howard just merely plowed over the remark and went on steering the ship.

"See if you can get Bland down to a million flat," he said.

"He already turned down a million one."

"All right. Give him a million two," he said and hung up. He switched off the incoming call button and swung the Corniche to the inside lane to catch the light at Sunset and turn east toward town.

A million one, a million two, a million three . . . what did it matter? It was only a Monopoly game. You either landed on Boardwalk or you didn't. He slipped on his Porsche Carrera sunglasses against the mid-morning glare and did his best to return to Cornwall.

They closed Nigel Bland at a million three, the agent managing to extort another hundred grand at the end with the story of a competing offer which was, no doubt, apocryphal. But Norman didn't care. He wanted to get on with it. Howard authorized the final step on Sunday afternoon at four, and by Monday morning they had the aging English matinee idol locked in.

As Candace De Salvio had predicted, however, finding someone to play Victoria was difficult. The role had been turned down by so many actresses that Jay Kessler told Sy Green, over lunch at the Polo Lounge, that they were so desperate they were ready to settle for a white girl with two tits. The joke went out the door, up Sunset and over Laurel Canyon like a brushfire. By two-thirty, it was going around the Universal mailroom.

In an attempt to make the role more attractive, Charlie had Lionel remove some of the nudity, but that didn't have much of an effect. Nobody, it seemed, was eager to help Bobby Mason spray Beirut with machine-gun bullets, even in clothes.

The price inched up. At a million, they began to get some

interest from semirespectable actresses. But they all wound up demanding even less nudity than was in the present script. Norman dug in and refused further nudity cuts. He knew who the ticket-buyers were for *Lev Disraeli: Freedom Fighter*.

What was left, then, were starlets, models, waitresses with some acting ability. In any case, nobody pretended that it would take a great deal of acting ability to play the role of the nubile Mossad agent. They would have to "discover" Victoria.

Dinak was back from Israel, and every afternoon he and Charlie and Wilna and Deidre and Candace De Salvio sat in Charlie's office and saw possible Victorias. A nonstop parade of beauties were in and out of the office in tight shorts, halter tops, bathing suits, lingerie. Enid sat cringing at her desk as the candidates sat around in her Louis XV chairs, making up, smoking, putting their Sprite cans directly down on the Second Empire end tables without using the coasters she had put out there especially for that purpose.

The search dragged on. They were four weeks from D day, and no Victoria yet. Panic began to circulate in the halls of the producers' building. Norman had a gastrointestinal attack that was so severe he had to be taken to the Cedars-Sinai ER, where he was told to exercise more and not eat lunch at his desk. There was no question of pushing back the picture. Bobby Mason's stop date was written in cement.

There is no telling what might have happened had Tricia Jacobi not appeared at this point. As soon as she walked into the office, Charlie knew the search was over. She wafted in on a refreshing scent of bubble bath, wearing a baby-blue jogging outfit and three-inch heels, her strawberry-blond hair streaming down over her shoulders. There was something overwhelmingly fresh about her, inviolate. Charlie could see her slipping her perfect white teeth around the pin of a grenade, pulling it and tossing it into a passing jeep without losing the audience's sympathy.

She sat down, casually removed her jogging-suit top to reveal two perfect breasts outlined under a tight white T-shirt that said,

KISS ME I'M JEWISH. Her agent had apparently done his homework because she led with what she considered her strength. "I know you might find this hard to believe, but I'm actually one-eighth Jewish."

There was dead silence in the room. Nobody knew what to say.

"I know I don't look Jewish, but my father's grandfather was named Meyer Jacobi. He came to Duluth from Smyrna in Turkey. He was a Sephardic Jew. He was in the clothing business and he married my great-grandmother, who was Swedish. . . ."

She went on telling her life story to the stunned silence of the people in the room. But Charlie wasn't listening. He was already picturing her in scenes from the script, wardrobing her, cutting her, looping her, as he would inevitably have to in order to lose the midwestern accent. He would probably have to dub her entire performance. But so what? The camera would love her. And so would the audience.

She had "likability," a quality that is a sine qua non for success in the picture business. The audience rooted for her. You wanted her to succeed, to be happy, to kill the terrorists. And no matter how violent or seamy the picture was, no matter how brutal or naked she was made to be, she remained innocent, the girl next door, the Delta stewardess who leans over your seat and asks if you wouldn't like her to freshen up your coffee.

When she finally left the room, after bringing her family tree up-to-date and recounting a summer working on a kibbutz in Israel, Deidre let out a large sigh and said, "Do you *believe* her? A cross between Barbi Benton and Golda Meir."

"She's it," Charlie said.

Dinak nodded. Wilna nodded in Polish. Candace De Salvio shrugged and said, "She won't hurt us."

Deidre looked cautiously around to see if there was a smile on anybody's face. There wasn't. Then, softly, tentatively, "Charlie, are you putting me on?"

"No. She's Victoria."

"Tricia Jacobi! The one that just walked out of here?"

"She's perfect."

Deidre grabbed her glossy from the coffee table, turned it over and read the credits listed on the reverse. " 'Miss Duluth, 1984 . . . *Where's Charley?* Northern Minnesota Community Theater, 1985 . . . *Miss Julie,* La Placenta Civic Theater . . . *Riptide,* 1987 . . . *Sorority House Stakeout* . . .' Should I go on?"

"Deidre, we don't need an actress. We need a look."

"Yeah, but she doesn't *look* like an Israeli agent. She looks like a dental hygienist. I mean, she's got blond hair. . . ."

"Have you ever heard of hair dye?"

"You make them red-brown," Dinak said suddenly.

"Dinak, you need to play against the blue eyes. Israeli women have black hair. . . ."

"I'm not talking hair."

"What are you talking about?"

"Nipples. You make them the color of Burgundy wine. I back-light them. Beautiful . . . You see. . . ."


Late one afternoon Charlie and Deidre were walking through the back lot. The fading sun cast long shadows between the sound-stages, giving their sharp angular geometry the feeling of a surreal industrial city.

Inside the enormous hulking shells, cameras were rolling, footage was being shot. Crews moved in and out of the sound-stages and trailers in desultory fashion. They were on the clock. Thousands of dollars ticked away minute by minute, hour by hour. The army had to be fed.

Charlie and Deidre walked along in silence, feeling the peculiar nostalgia movie people feel on the back lot of a studio. They stopped to let a platoon of red-coated British colonial soldiers move by, their swords glinting in the last rays of the sun. On a soundstage somewhere, the Battle of Yorktown was going to be replayed. The extras talked idly among themselves, gossiping, comparing agents, fussing with their wigs, smoking a final cigarette before being asked to lay down their lives for Cornwallis.

Charlie stared at them for a moment, almost trancelike, then murmured, "It's amazing, isn't it?"

Deidre turned to him, not sure she had heard what he said. He had spoken very softly. "It's amazing that it ever gets done. It's amazing that anybody ever shoots a foot of film, isn't it?"

She looked at him, astonished. She had been thinking exactly the same thing.

Deidre Hearn would remember this shared moment as marking the beginning of something. Just what it was, she wasn't sure. But later that night, sitting on the wicker couch in Studio City, she told Ellen that something had definitely happened. Ellen looked up from her knitting with that peculiar creasing of the eyebrows that indicated that Deidre needed to explain what she had just said.

"I don't know exactly what happened. I mean, we were just walking on the back lot. Whenever I walk on the back lot I get this strange feeling, you know, like the ghosts of all the old actors and directors and writers, all those words from old movies are stored up in the soundstages, in the walls, collecting there like layers of wallpaper or rust or something. And like I'm a part of this continuum. . . . You understand what I mean?"

Ellen hadn't the slightest idea what Deidre Hearn meant but she didn't want to discourage what could be a very cathartic outpouring. And so she nodded rhetorically, giving Deidre permission to keep going.

"Instead of just making movies everyone's trying to fuck everyone else. We spend the day making phone calls, avoiding phone calls, waiting for phone calls. It's a power game. What we're supposed to be doing is making films. That's what it's all about, right? Sooner or later film has to roll through the camera. But nobody cares about making films anymore. We might as well be making lawn mowers or harpoons or ice-cube trays. What difference would it make? Nobody gives a shit. They're too busy making deals. . . ."

Deidre stopped to catch her breath for a moment. It was perfectly quiet on the sun porch except for the faint squeaking of Ellen's rocking chair.

"So anyway, there we were, Charlie Berns and I, standing there watching these extras in costume. The sun was setting and it was sort of surreal, kind of like Salvador Dalí. I mean, the whole thing about making movies is surreal enough, but sometimes you get surreal on surreal, and it's like whipped cream on ice cream . . . it's overwhelming. The British colonial army marching through the back lot with eighteenth-century wigs and Reeboks, and you say to yourself, 'Am I dreaming this?' But you're not dreaming. That's the point. This is it. This is what it all boils down to. There's nothing else that matters at this point. Whatever the deal was, if it was one point two million or two point one million, who cares? It's time to roll the cameras. A handful of sixty-buck-a-day extras in red coats are going to get shot twenty-five times and bleed ketchup into the Astroturf. . . . So he turns to me and says, 'It's amazing it ever gets done, isn't it?' What's amazing is that that's *exactly* what I'm thinking at that moment. It was like he was inside my head reading my thoughts. Isn't that weird?"

Ellen rocked placidly for a long moment before asking, in her quiet, nonconfrontational voice: "*Who* is this man, Deidre?"

"Well, that's just it. He's a very hard read. I don't really know. . . ."

"Because it sounds to me like you're trying to tell me you may be getting involved."

"Jesus, I hope not. This is not a guy you want to get involved with. This guy's a walking minefield. He's in his fifties, probably has at least two ex-wives. . . . His career's in the toilet. . . . I mean, nobody knew who he was before this picture. He lives in a white elephant in the Flats with ripped-out shrubbery and no telephone. . . . He's kind of funny-looking, sort of rumpled and out to lunch. He looks like he just woke up half the time. . . . But there's something about him. . . ."

"What?"

"I don't know. That's what I'm trying to tell you. He doesn't buy into the bullshit. It's like his ego isn't involved in the process. He doesn't make any excuses. He just does it. He floats through it all with a kind of Zen-like calm. You know what I mean?"

Ellen finished a row of stitches for the new afghan she was making before replying.

"It sounds to me, Deidre, like you *are* getting involved with this man. Am I right?"

"I don't know, goddamnit!" Deidre was surprised by the emotion of her own outburst. She had practically shouted.

Ellen allowed the moment to dissolve quietly into the therapeutic calm of the sun porch.

"I mean," she said, her voice subdued once more, "it's been so long I forgot what it feels like."

"Deidre, do you remember the talks we had about how you make choices? We talked about appropriate and inappropriate choices. We talked about a propensity to choose men who were inappropriate as a way of avoiding involvement. didn't we?"

"Uh-huh."

"It sounds to me like we have a case study in inappropriateness here. This man gets a ten on the inappropriateness scale. Are we going to be sitting here three months from now with you in tears wondering why it didn't work? Are we going to be having to pick up the pieces again?"

Deidre sat there assailed by the truth of Ellen's words. It was undeniably inappropriate to have anything to do with Charlie Berns. The man was an accident waiting to happen, a clearly advertised disaster area.

Anyway, he would soon be off to Belgrade to make this ridiculous picture and she wouldn't see him for months. In fact, she might never see him again. She would soon be off on other pictures, mercifully finished with *Lev Disraeli: Freedom Fighter.*

Driving home from Ellen's, Deidre felt the little cold sadness that often overcame her following their sessions. She felt as if her insides had been vacuumed. She felt as if she were drowning in appropriateness. Suddenly she thought about the original Disraeli script and how refreshingly absurd it was, how wonderfully inappropriate.

She started to giggle again over the herring-eating scene with Bismarck in the Radziwill Palace. She had to pull over and wait for the fit to pass. She sat in the parking lot of a 7-Eleven on Coldwater and roared her guts out until she was able to regain enough composure to drive back over the hill.

# 10

With less than two weeks before the cameras were set to roll on *Lev Disraeli: Freedom Fighter*, Charlie, Dinak, Wilna and Lionel were en route to Belgrade via London. The ten-week shooting schedule called for principal photography to begin in Yugoslavia and then move to Israel, a reversal of the usual procedure of shooting the exteriors first, to guard against weather problems. For a multitude of reasons, however, ranging from the availability of some key crew members to the rate of exchange of the dollar vis-à-vis the Israeli shekel, the decision had been made to spend the first four weeks on soundstages in Belgrade before going out and blowing up the Negev.

The blocked dinars, fortunately, were immune to the vagaries of exchange rates, and with the substantial sum locked away in their Yugoslavian distributor's coffers they were able to buy the best production talent the country had to offer. A crew was busily at work building the sets they would need to double for the King David Hotel, the American embassy and the hotel rooms for what Sidney Auger referred to during production meetings as "the fuck scenes."

Rabbi Gutterman and Lionel's work on adding a spiritual

dimension to the script had been well received by the star, who was going to try, for the first time in his film career, to deliver a soliloquy to the camera. It was Lionel's idea, a sort of stream-of-consciousness interior monologue delivered from the top of Mount Zion as Lev Disraeli reflects on the continuum of Jewish history since Moses led his people out of Egypt. They'd lay it in over a helicopter shot of Bobby Mason alone against a setting sun.

The star had wrapped *Desert Commando* and was presently on his way to Palm Springs, via Las Vegas, to rest up for his next picture. Tricia Jacobi was busy shedding a few excess pounds while studying the Torah to get into character for her portrayal of Victoria Halevi, the sabra intelligence officer. And Nigel Bland, according to his agent, was "firming up a bit" as well in order to be able to play the love scenes with Victoria without a stunt double.

They would be in London for two days to clean up some minor casting and to meet Nigel Bland for a drink. They checked into suites at the Dorchester and went to work immediately.

The script called for a number of characters of indeterminate origin and race—freelance terrorists of no precise national allegiance. The studio was concerned about offending any of the actual Palestinian, Iranian or Libyan terrorist organizations and risking reprisals during production. Care was taken, therefore, to create what is called in the movie business "n.d." terrorists, i.e., "nondescript" terrorists, terrorists without any specific characteristics that could link them to an identifiable group or nationality. Nowhere in the script was a terrorist described physically. In order to avoid reference to a specific language, they never spoke. They were silent and multicolored. Lionel suggested they make one blond and blue-eyed, just to balance out the spectrum, but Norman Hudris said he had never heard of a blond, blue-eyed terrorist.

Their London casting director had arranged a schedule of interviews with Sudanese, Saudi, Somali, Bengali and Pakistani actors. They sat in the suite at the Dorchester and saw a collection of off-white, nondescript actors. Since the actors didn't speak in the movie, there was no point in having them read, and they were reduced to sitting in the stuffed Edwardian armchairs sipping tea and making small talk.

The following afternoon, after they had hired their cast of n.d. hit men, they went downstairs to meet Nigel Bland in the bar. They found him sitting at a corner table, away from the light, already into a brandy. Nigel Bland was probably pushing sixty, though his agent listed him as forty-three. He had a florid, boozy face redeemed by remarkably clear blue eyes and a strong chin. Well over six feet, he uncoiled with some difficulty from his chair and greeted them, shaking hands and muttering, "Good of you to come."

After pleasantries and a second round of drinks, Nigel Bland turned to Dinak and said, "Tell me, Dino, what the devil do *you* make of this chap Bill?"

Dinak blinked several times, rubbed his forehead, was about to issue one of his classic shrugs, when Charlie came to the rescue: "Well, Bill is a basically sympathetic character. Though he competes with Lev in the love story, they wind up being on the same side."

The actor nodded furiously at this information, took a long sip of his brandy, nodded some more. "Aha," he uttered, as if what Charlie had said was a revelation to him, then, "Actually, he's a bit of a double-dealer though, isn't he?"

"How's that, Nigel?"

"Well, you see, after having a diddle with the girl in the King David, he goes through her purse and takes out the roll of film, now doesn't he?"

"Well, yes, but he does that to protect her from Mordecai, who he knows is going to search her later."

"I see. . . . So when they first meet in the bar in Beirut, Bill thinks she's working for the terrorists? Is that it?"

"Not exactly . . ."

Nigel began to nod furiously again. Charlie and Lionel exchanged a look. It was disconcerting to discover at this late date that one of the lead characters had entirely misunderstood the story.

"Well, it'll all work out, I suppose," Nigel said. "Shall we have another round?"

Several rounds later everyone was on excellent terms. Charlie decided not to bother explaining the intricacies of the plot to the man who was to play Bill Gladstone. Nigel Bland was apparently the type of actor who had difficulty keeping a lot of variables in his head at one time. You needed to explain things to actors like that scene by scene, preferably just before they went on camera. You didn't want to belabor them with too much information too soon.

By the time they separated later that evening, after dinner at the Savoy Grill accompanied by several bottles of Château Pétrus, they were all dear friends. Outside the restaurant, they hugged and kissed like they were saying good-bye at a wrap party.

"See you in Belgrade," Nigel waved, as he got into a cab and drove off.

Charlie stood there waving back and watching the cab disappear into the London drizzle. Seven hundred eighteen pounds of hard currency had just been charged to the picture. The auditors back at the studio would blanch at this one, but by then the train would be well out of the station and chugging along quite nicely.

Belgrade. No other city in the world can claim to have been totally destroyed at least a dozen times in its history. From the first sack by the barbarians in the fourth century B.C., through the Romans and the Turks, to Hitler's systematic saturation bombing, its ravishers have always been thorough, if nothing else. The city has risen repeatedly in its ashes, like a stubborn phoenix, continuing to rebuild itself.

As their JAT flight descended into Surčin Airport, overflying the sprawling, somewhat charmless city below, Dinak explained this Yugoslavian propensity for self-immolation. "God don't like you, he makes you a Serb," he said, looking dourly out the window as if he were less than thrilled to be back home. His compatriots seemed to be no more thrilled to see *him*. As they went through passport control, Dinak got into a loud argument with an immigration official. It started with a series of low, breathy, gesticulated sentences and degenerated into a high-pitched screaming match, accompanied by Dinak banging his fist on the counter.

The official stamped his passport so hard that it fell on the floor. Dinak kicked it across the room, to indicate, perhaps, how he felt about his nationality. Riding into town in the taxi, Charlie asked him what the problem was.

Dinak scratched his forehead, shrugged. "Son of a bitch don't like me."

"You know him?"

Dinak shook his head. "He's a fucking Slovene." As if that explained the ferocious argument that had just taken place.

"Are all . . . Slovenes like that?" Lionel asked.

"Fucking Slovenes. Slovenes and Serbs argue all the time. It's nothing. Worse with Macedonians. Real assholes, Macedonians. You scream at Macedonian he don't even know you screaming at him. You have to scream at him in Macedonian."

They checked into the Hotel Balkanska on Ulica Maršala Tita. It was a large hotel across from the Tito Mausoleum, with poorly soundproofed rooms looking out on the noisy thoroughfare. It was Dinak who had suggested the hotel, once again for reasons that escaped Charlie. It had the virtue, however, of being large enough and vacant enough at this time of year to accommodate the entire cast and crew. Everyone, that is, except Bobby Mason. Bobby's contract called for certain amenities that were not available in the Hotel Balkanska. Their local production manager had to have a suite in the Intercontinental Hotel specially refurbished with Jacuzzi, VCR, vibrating bed and a refrigerator full of Pepsi soft drinks.

Tabor Gubca, the production manager, was to become a very important member of the crew of *Lev Disraeli: Freedom Fighter*. In Yugoslavia he was the man with the can opener. Though Charlie was the producer and the ranking officer on the picture, he was entirely dependent upon Gubca because Gubca knew how to get to the dinars. Neither Charlie nor Dinak had the slightest idea where the blocked dinars were actually coming from.

When Charlie asked for something, Gubca had one of two basic responses: "Can do," or "No way." It was either feast or famine with him, and he never qualified or explained any of his decisions. It didn't help, of course, that he was a Bosnian from Sarajevo and, as such, not overly sympathetic toward Serbian directors, but he did his best to hide his feelings and do his job. He did better than Dinak, who referred to him simply as "the fucking Bosnian."

The fucking Bosnian took them out to the studio to inspect the work that had been done on the soundstages. The Novi Beograd Studios, across the Sava River in Novi Grad, was a sprawling complex of buildings with high walls resembling a prison. The art director, a tall thin esthetic-looking man named Marka Mladosi, had done an excellent job designing the sets. Working from photographs, he had duplicated the interiors for the scenes they would shoot later in Israel. While Dinak walked the sets, grunting, inspecting the gaffing, checking the wild walls, Charlie and Lionel stood in the middle of the entrance foyer of the U.S. embassy in Jerusalem marveling at the precision of Marka Mladosi's work.

"Terrific work, Marka," Charlie commented to the man standing beside him puffing on a *niska drina*, the smelly local cigarette whose acrid odor Charlie would learn to hate.

The art director shrugged modestly and said, "No problem."

"It's really great. I mean, it's like you're actually there," Lionel enthused.

"Piece cake," Marka Mladosi explained. "You have enough dinars, I do anything. You want Sistine Chapel, I give you Sistine Chapel. Piece cake . . . you know big producer Ed Mutnik?" he asked.

Charlie shook his head.

"He come here last year to do picture. I design him a fountain for swimming pool in L.A. I make him miniature Trevi Fountain in Rome."

"Uh-huh . . ."

"I make it for house in Holmby Hill. You know Holmby Hill?"

"Sure do."

"You give me photo. I do it. Piece cake."

When they got back to the hotel that evening there was a message to call Norman Hudris at the studio. Charlie looked at his watch, calculated that with the nine-hour difference it was only 8:00 A.M. in Los Angeles, and wondered what Norman Hudris was doing in his office so early.

Norman had actually been in his office since seven that morning. He had wanted to get New York early and see what was happening with the stock. He took the call from Charlie in Belgrade on his Exercycle, between the fifth and sixth mile.

"How's it going?" Norman asked, panting.

"Fine," said Charlie.

"That's good. . . . Listen, I got a call from Bert Sully last night. . . ."

Charlie felt himself tighten up. A call from the star's manager to the head of the studio on the eve of production was never good news. Norman paused, letting his words hang for a moment, then, "Anyway, it seems he's got a little problem with the script."

"I thought Bobby loved the rewrites."

"He does. He's crazy about the Jewish stuff. The monologue on the mountain, he adores it. Listen, before I forget, we can always lose the monologue in post, right?"

"Right."

"You know, in case it doesn't work."

"No problem. We can lift it right out. . . . What does Bert Sully want?"

"It's about the fuck scenes."

"Which ones?"

"The ones with Bobby."

"What's wrong with them?"

"He doesn't want to do them."

"Why not?"

"As near as I can figure from Bert Sully, Bobby doesn't like playing love scenes. He figures it's not his strong suit."

"Yeah, but why does he wait till we're just about to shoot to tell us that? He's had the script for months."

"Who knows?"

"It's not that easy a fix. The whole love triangle is based on those scenes. We can't just lift them out of the script like they were never there."

"You're going to have to figure out something, Charlie."

"It's going to throw the whole production board out of kilter. . . ." Charlie heard himself objecting, listening to the words come out of his mouth, knowing all the time that it was pointless. If Bobby Mason didn't want to do the fuck scenes, then he wasn't going to do them. It was as simple as that.

"Tell you the truth, Charlie, it may be a blessing in disguise."

"How do you figure?"

"Marketingwise . . . lot of people aren't comfortable watching fuck scenes between people of different colors. Like in Natchez, Mississippi, not to mention Johannesburg . . ."

"Right."

"Don't get me wrong, Charlie. I'm not prejudiced. But with the cost of making pictures these days, you can't overlook a single market."

"I suppose not. . . ."

There was a long moment of silence. Static crackled over the ten thousand miles separating them.

"Listen, is it all right if they ride in the same jeep together?" Charlie asked, deadpan.

"As long as she doesn't go down on him."

Norman hung up, checked the odometer. He had just passed mile six. He stepped up the pace. He wanted to get ten miles in before the morning staff meeting.

Actually, the suggestion that they lose the fuck scenes between Lev Disraeli and Victoria Halevi had not come from Bobby Mason. It had come from Frederick the Great via Howard Draper. Someone had made the mistake of sending the chairman of the board a copy of the script. According to his secretary he stormed into his office at 9:00 A.M. sharp, demanded that she get Howard Draper on the line in Los Angeles. Howard was woken up at six to be told that ACI did not want its name on any motion picture that "promoted irresponsible miscegenation."

Howard hung up the phone and lay there for a long while wondering if there was a difference between responsible and irresponsible miscegenation. Then he called his vice president of production, West Coast, and told him to lose the fuck scenes.

Meanwhile, in the Bobby Vinton Suite at the Riviera Club in Vegas, Bobby Mason had just finished miscegenating with two showgirls from the road company of *Oh! Calcutta!* Viki and Pam were both five ten and slim, the way Bobby liked them, one blonde and one redhead. Whenever he indulged in one of his sporadic constitutional ménages à trois, he liked to have girls with different-colored hair but always the same color skin. White. Preferably very white. When it came to miscegenation Bobby Mason was a purist.

He gave each of them a $500 chip to play with and dismissed them. He took a long hot shower, then stretched out on the bed to catch a little Talmud before going out and doing his five miles of road work.

He opened the thick black volume, *The Talmud Made Easy*, and started the chapter called "Isaiah." The book had large print and was annotated and illustrated to make it easier to follow. He read for a while, quickly starting to glaze over. Between the miscegenation and the hot shower he was fading.

The phone rang. Bobby ignored it. His security people in the next room were supposed to screen his calls. It kept ringing until he finally picked up. "Yo . . ."

The call seemed to be coming from another planet, so faint was the connection.

"Who is it?" Bobby repeated.

"Jew bastard," a gravelly voice spit out.

"Huh?"

"Nigger Jew bastard," the voice amplified and then hung up.

"Fuck you too, buddy," Bobby muttered, slamming down the phone. Pissed, he got up and went over to the connecting door, opened it and looked into the adjoining room. One of his security guards was fast asleep. The other was emerging from the bathroom with a newspaper.

"Didn't you hear the fucking phone?" Bobby snapped.

"Sorry, Bobby, I was in the can. . . ."

"I just got a hate call."

"From who?"

"They didn't leave their name."

"You want me to call the cops, get it traced?"

"Jesus. Forget it."

He closed the door, crossed to the closet, hesitated between his blue and his pink Nike sneakers. Decided on the blue. They were less conspicuous.

As he laced up his Nike sneakers he wondered whether it was foolish to jog in Vegas in broad daylight. There could be some crazy guy with a scope rifle in a window. Like the guy who got Kennedy. And it was coming out of both barrels now. He had both the Jew and the nigger haters on his ass. He wondered whether Sammy Davis had had to put up with this kind of shit.

* * *

When Tricia Jacobi made her entrance into Tascorama, the new punk Mexican place on Robertson, wearing a gold lamé blouse and ruby-studded toreador pants, her hair up in an Ingrid Bergman bun, two large tortoiseshell earrings dangling beneath, she stopped traffic. Every eye in the place followed her as the mâitre d' led her across to Brad Emprin's table.

He got up, took both her hands in his and raised them to his lips, a maneuver he had seen Charles Boyer pull off in a movie on cable. Tricia Jacobi blushed delightfully and sat down. He suggested an aperitif. She said she had a wardrobe fitting to go to that afternoon. Brad Emprin told her that was no excuse not to have a drink at lunch. He ordered two strawberry margaritas, in spite of the fact that he had popped a couple of Sinutabs in the car on the way over. If worse came to worst, this wouldn't be a bad way to o.d.—having lunch with a soon-to-be major new star at a conspicuous table in a trendy restaurant.

"So, you excited about going to Belgrade?"

"You bet," she replied, flashing a potent smile. It was the kind of smile that people who have learned to smile for a living threw at you. Brad Emprin found it a little overpowering at close range. Unconsciously, he moved his chair a few inches back from the table.

"Sounds good to me," he offered and turned the conversation to the pleasures of shooting in Yugoslavia, where, he explained, he often went to meet with his clients who were shooting there.

"Do you have a lot of big clients?"

Brad Emprin nodded casually, took a sip of the strawberry margarita. "A few," he admitted. "Well, I mean Jack's been with me for years . . . but, you know, it's not how big a star they are. It's the relationship that's important."

"I know what you mean," she agreed. "I've been with Herbert Cain for just ever and ever. He's like a father to me."

"Herbert who?"

"Cain. He has a little agency in the Valley. . . . He used to represent Paul Anka."

He smiled vaguely and said, "It's good to start out with a ma-and-pa shop. It helps in the beginning," then added, as an afterthought, "at least until you start getting hot. Then you're in a different ballpark. . . ."

Their appetizers were served. She took a bite of her tamales Benedict, stopped, looked across at him.

"Uhh . . . what do you mean . . . in a different ballpark?"

"You're on a whole different level of the business. you're not in Kansas anymore, if you know what I mean. If you're not careful you start feeling the altitude. . . ."

"Really?"

He worked over his *taco mondo carne* without looking back up at her.

"You're up there in the stratosphere and suddenly you start to get a little dizzy. Lack of oxygen . . ."

"Lack of oxygen?"

"Strangulation at the source. Happens all the time. Talented actress gets the one big break she's been waiting for. The picture gets made. It gets released. A little bit of flutter and then it kind of dies down for a while. . . . The phone stops ringing. Suddenly nothing's happening. Boom. Six months later she's back going out on cattle calls for laundry detergent."

"You really think it can happen that fast?"

"Without follow-up? Absolutely. Follow-up's the name of the game. Follow-up and foresight . . . you see who Richard Farley is having lunch with over there?"

He indicated a Paramount vice president and a major movie star, who were involved in an intense conversation in the corner. She shook her head.

"He's having lunch with Mitch Terrazzo. You know who Mitch Terrazzo is?"

"No."

"A vice president at Paramount. What do you think they're talking about?"

She shook her head again. "They're talking about the picture Richard Farley's going to make after he finishes shooting the next three pictures on his schedule."

"Really?"

"You better believe it. You've got to move before the picture is in production, let alone released. Let me ask you something, your guy, what's his name . . . Hank?"

"Herbert. Herbert Cain."

"Herbert. What's he doing for you right now while you're sitting here having lunch with me?"

"He's probably having his lunch."

"With who?"

"Herb usually grabs a sandwich at the deli on Ventura. . . ."

"He should be following up. . . ."

"Following up . . ."

"Do you know why Richard Farley and Mitch Terrazzo are having this conversation today?"

She shook her head once more on cue, getting used to the Socratic rhythms of the dialogue. "Because somebody followed up. Somebody had the foresight to get Mitch Terrazzo on the phone and set this lunch up. You follow me?"

"Uh-huh . . ."

"The thing about the ma-and-pa shops is they can't get it done. They don't have the manpower to follow up. They don't have the connections. They can't pick up the phone and get, say, Charlie Berns on the line. Charlie Berns doesn't know who they are. . . ."

Tricia Jacobi sat there, no longer interested in her lunch. She was wondering if it wasn't all slipping away already. Right then and there, while she was having lunch at Tascorama with the man who represented Jack . . .

Last week she was just another aspiring actress taking lessons, refining her instrument, selling a little real estate on the side.

Suddenly, the door had been opened. Miraculously. She was able to glance inside, see down to the end of the corridor where a crowd of admirers was standing and applauding. It looked magnificent to her. But she was already losing oxygen. Slow strangulation was setting in. The door was already starting to inch closed again.

Herb was a sweetheart. He'd gotten her a guest star on *Spenser: For Hire*. She had played a bulimic junkie and received mention in one of the reviews. And it was Herb who had read in the trades that Bobby Mason was thinking of converting to Judaism, who had come up with the idea of the T-shirt. But it had taken two weeks to get the audition. They had to go through the casting director. The truth was that Herb couldn't just pick up the phone and get Charlie Berns on the line.

The waiter brought her *ropa vieja turtare,* but she no longer had any appetite. Actually, she wasn't feeling very well. The image of an oxygen shortage had made her feel faint. She ran her hand over her forehead, massaged her temples. A cool sweat had broken out under her armpits, threatening to stain the gold lamé blouse. She began to hyperventilate ever so slightly.

"Mr. Emprin," she managed, in a soft, underaspirated voice, "this is embarrassing but . . . do you happen to have . . . any Valium?"

"No problem. I've got some in the car." As he got up to go get them, he asked, "Five milligrams or ten?"

"I think I'm going to need a ten. . . ."


Deidre Hearn sat on the Italian leather couch in Norman Hudris's office playing idly with an ugly jade paperweight that Norman had bought in Ensenada. They were in the middle of a meeting, another long, boring, inconsequential meeting that would drag on most of the afternoon and keep her from attacking the ever-growing pile of scripts on her desk.

The subject of this meeting was the marketing of *Lev Disraeli: Freedom Fighter*. The studio had run a series of concept tests to see if there was any inherent consumer resistance to overcome in marketing the picture. They had shown a synopsis of the story and a list of alternate titles to a group of demographically selected subjects. Barry Cornwall, the v.p. for marketing, a thirty-five-year-old refugee from Madison Avenue, was reporting the results.

"We're through the roof, of course, on eighteen to twenty-five black males . . . though some of them had trouble with the title. A couple of them thought Disraeli was Italian, and it was a Mafia picture."

Sidney Auger began humming the theme music from *The Godfather*.

Barry Cornwall forged ahead. "Anyway, not to worry. As long as Bobby Mason's name is above titles, they're going to buy tickets."

"We're going to need repeat business from that group," Norman said.

"We ought to get it, as long as we don't get too Jewish."

Norman turned to Deidre with a pained expression. "I'm telling you, that Mount Zion monologue is going to kill us. It's going to bury us."

"We can always cut it, Norman."

"I don't even think we should shoot it. You know, word can get out from the set. . . ."

"From Belgrade?"

"They're shooting that in Israel," Sidney Auger corrected.

Barry Cornwall cleared his throat, to indicate that he had not finished with his test results. He summed up his report by saying, "Guys, I think we've got to stop jerking ourselves around on the title."

"What's wrong with the title?"

"First of all, you're looking at only a thirty-one percent approval factor with women. More than two thirds of women twenty-one to forty-five won't go see this picture based on the title alone. That's disastrous."

"What about Nigel Bland? Women like him."

"Nobody under fifty, Norman. That's a hard figure."

Barry Cornwall's words hung heavily in the air for a long moment. Norman got up, walked over to his desk, sat down, played with a paper clip. Then: "So what are you saying, Barry?"

"I think we need a title change."

"You got any ideas?"

"First of all, I think we need to lose the name Disraeli. You've got two negatives. You've got Jewish and you've got Italian."

"Barry, the star of this picture, without whom we wouldn't even be discussing it, wants to do a picture about a Jew," Deidre said. "That's why it's getting made."

He looked back at her condescendingly. "I'm aware of that, Deidre. Let me ask you something . . . does he have anything in his deal to say he has title approval?"

"No, but we'll have a major attitude problem on our hands."

"So, don't announce it until after you're in the can and you have all the loops you need. What's he going to do then? Sue us?"

"What are you suggesting we change it *to*, Barry?"

"Well, first of all, I think we need a name. A tough, macho, sexy name. Like Kojak or Rambo . . . that kind of thing. So maybe in deference to Bobby we keep it starting with the letter D. . . . What do you think of Decker?"

There was no response. Barry Cornwall took this as a cue to run more names by them. "Darrow. Drake. Diamond . . . Lev Diamond . . ."

"I don't know, Barry . . ." Norman's voice sounded a little manic.

"You don't like Lev Diamond?"

Norman shook his head.

"I really think Decker's the best. It's a swing name. You can tell Bobby it's Jewish and still get the women twenty-one to forty-five into the theater. Listen, I've come up with a tag line, you want to hear it?"

Norman exhaled, shrugged. He was almost beyond caring.

Barry turned pages of his legal pad, found what he was looking for. "Listen to this," he announced. " 'Decker: When It Hits the Fan You Want Him on Your Side' . . ."

At this point, Deidre Hearn excused herself from the meeting. She exited Norman's office, walked to the ladies' room at the end of the hall. She went in, looked around, made sure it was deserted. She entered a stall, closed and locked the door carefully, sat down on the toilet seat. And screamed.

# 11

Principal photography on *Decker* (When It Hits the Fan You Want Him on Your Side) began on Stage 9 of the Novi Beograd Studios on a hot, cloudy Monday morning. If getting a green light was tantamount to a declaration of war, then starting to shoot was the invasion of Poland. Except that it usually didn't go as smoothly.

In order to get over their jet lag and rest up, Nigel Bland and Tricia Jacobi had arrived a week ago. Bobby Mason, however, did not deplane from the private jet loaned him by a multimillionaire from Rancho Mirage—with whom he was partnered in a business venture, selling sweat socks, called Jock Socks—until the Friday night before the first day of production. The late arrival did not leave the men's wardrober a great deal of time to fit the star. Fortunately BM's wardrobe was largely limited to mixing and matching a selection of designer combat ensembles.

Charlie had gone out to the airport with Gubca in the limo to meet him. The paparazzi were there in full force, a few having driven all the way from Italy to get a picture of the American superstar. Bobby walked down the ramp of the Learjet, wearing lollypop dark glasses, a Lakers jacket and his yellow-and-green Nikes.

"How you doin'?" he waved to the assembled press. Flashbulbs went off as reporters shouted questions in a Babel of languages.

"Hey, pretty good" was Bobby's basic answer to the torrent of words coming at him, summing up with a gracious "Catch you later" as they slipped into the limo.

All the way in from the airport they were followed by speeding Fiats full of reporters leaning out of windows trying to shoot pictures through the darkened limo glass. Inside the air-conditioned Lincoln, Bobby sipped Pepsi and listened as Gubca outlined the first week's shoot. The production manager spoke in his calm monotone, going over the details as if he were talking to a kid on his first day of school. Gubca was a completely unflappable man. He hadn't batted an eyelash when Charlie asked him to switch around the entire shooting schedule to accommodate the rewrites entailed by losing Bobby's love scenes. And he didn't react visibly when Bobby said, almost casually, "By the way, what happened to my fuck scenes?"

Gubca looked at Charlie, who blinked just once, to get his balance. He had been sandbagged by Norman Hudris. Royally. That was for sure. But there was little he could do about it at the moment.

"We gave the love scenes a lot of thought, Bobby. Let me tell you where we came out on that. . . ." Charlie carefully slipped on the Capezios.

"When you asked us to put a spiritual dimension in the script, we realized part of that dimension involved keeping Lev above the everyday concerns of ordinary people. He has a mission—to obliterate terrorists. That's his raison d'être. He's not interested in getting rich or famous or making it with women. He's acting out of the devotion he has for the Jewish people. Remember the monologue on Mount Zion? What does he say again? 'These are my people, from Moses to Moshe Dayan. . . .'"

Nevertheless, Charlie got a phone call in his room at the Balkanska at 3:00 A.M. that night. It was Deidre this time. She had just gotten a call from Bert Sully.

Charlie woke Gubca up and told him to rearrange the board to go back to the previous draft. Gubca muttered, "Can do," and the fuck scenes were back in the movie. They were going to miscegenate after all.

There were other last-minute glitches before the cameras rolled. One of the n.d. terrorists, scheduled to work on the first day, was detained trying to board his plane at Heathrow. He fit the international terrorist profile to a tee. Moreover, when the police searched his baggage they found a propaganda pamphlet put out by a Palestinian group. The actor explained that he was trying to get into character for his role. He had never even been to the Middle East. He didn't speak Arabic. He was Pakistani, born in North London.

Then the sheer body stocking they had gotten for Tricia to play her nude scenes in turned out to be too big. It bunched up in places, revealing that she was really not naked. Charlie faced the alternatives of waiting for another one to be ordered from L.A., juggling the shooting schedule and giving the actress a few days to put back on the five pounds she had shed with her crash diet or simply asking her to play the scenes actually nude.

He talked Stanislavski and Method; he told her about Hedy Lamarr in *Ecstasy*; he talked Art with a capital A. He promised her artistic lighting and judicious editing. He told her that the great actresses didn't even *see* the camera. They worked in a purely abstract dimension, a sort of spiritual dimension. . . .

Several hours later he got a call from none other than Brad Emprin, who, apparently, now represented Tricia Jacobi.

"Sorry, Charlie, there's no way I can let her do it without the stocking."

"Brad, don't forget you're also supposed to be representing my interests. If I have to push back the start date because of a body stocking, I could be in trouble. . . ."

"I hear you, Charlie. I really do. The thing is, if I let her do it for you, I'm going to have to let her do it for everyone, right?"

Tricia was immediately put on a diet of pasta and *ražnići*, a starchy local specialty, and given milk shakes a half dozen times a day. Unfortunately, this high-calorie diet didn't agree with her. She spent the first few days on the set running back and forth to the bathroom, effectively neutralizing the calories from the *ražnići*.

Nigel Bland, for his part, arrived overweight, as if he had somehow demonically acquired the five pounds that Tricia had shed. He told Charlie not to be concerned. He'd sweat them off in twenty-four hours. However, when Nigel discovered that there was not only no sauna in his room but none in the Hotel Balkanska or, to Tabor Gubca's knowledge, in the entire city of Belgrade, Charlie had his agent on the phone. Nigel always had a sauna in his room on every picture. It was practically boiler-plate in his deals. He thought *everyone* knew. . . .

Charlie navigated this chaos without flinching. Though it had been a number of years since he had produced a picture, he discovered that his reflexes were still there. He hadn't entirely lost the knack of captaining the ship through the shoals.

Dinak, the mad technocrat, was ready to roll. He had done his homework, preparing a complete shot list for the first week's work. The battle plans, at least, were clearly drawn. But like all battle plans, they needed to be constantly modified to fit the actual terrain. The director spent a great deal of time with Lionel, who had become a kind of assistant director-associate producer-screenwriter on the picture. The kid was learning quickly how to roll with the punches, tirelessly pounding out revision pages till all hours of the night. When Charlie informed him that the fuck scenes were back in, after Lionel had been up for two nights straight trying to give the story coherence without them, he just nodded and went back up to his room to rework the script.

The night before the first day of shooting, as Charlie lay in the bathtub at midnight trying to recover from the inevitable series of last-minute catastrophes, and to calm down enough to get some sleep before the 7:00 call in the morning, the phone rang. He reached a soapy hand across the tub and picked up the receiver.

"Yeah . . ." he muttered, expecting to hear the even-toned Gubca announcing yet some new disaster. Instead he heard the far-off voice of Deidre Hearn.

"Charlie?"

"Hi."

"How are you doing?"

"Okay."

"I hope I didn't wake you. I figured . . . the night before the first day of shooting you'd be up late."

"Right . . ."

"Last-minute emergencies . . ."

He wondered what last-minute monkey wrench *she* was about to throw into the gear works. He lay there in the tepid bathwater and waited for the other shoe to drop. There was a long moment of staticky silence on the line before she said, "Anyway, I just called to wish you good luck tomorrow."

Charlie didn't know what to say. He was completely disarmed. Studio executives did not generally call the night before a shoot to wish you good luck without a hidden agenda. He recovered just before she was about to hang up.

"Thanks," he said.

"You're welcome."

"Keep the ball low, huh?"

"No, Charlie. Just get it over the plate."

He hung up, lay back in the bathwater and thought about Deidre Hearn. She was smart, she was attractive, she had taste and judgment, yet she seemed to be strangely absent at certain moments, almost as if she were hearing voices. Occasionally, during a meeting, Charlie had observed a distracted, nearly demented look on her face. He had the strange impression that she was on the verge of breaking out in laughter.

Unlike most of the Young Turks he had run across in the business, she acted as if she suspected there was another dimension
to the world having nothing to do with making pictures. With an
attitude like that she wouldn't go very far. Charlie hoped that
Deidre Hearn had made alternate career plans. He wouldn't
want to see her out on the street.

He dragged himself out of the tub, dried off with the minuscule towel provided by the hotel, fell on his bed and conked out.

A little after 7:00 the following morning Charlie sat on Stage 9 in
a chair marked PRODUTTORE, amortized by the propman from the
last shoot he had done for an Italian company, holding a cup of
very strong coffee. In the DIRETTORE chair Wilna sat with Dinak's
copy of the script, smoking and doodling in the margins. The
*direttore* himself was in conversation with his cameraman, a fellow Serb, fortunately, about the lighting of the first shot of the
day, a simple dolly shot that was to take Bill Gladstone, MI6
agent, down a hallway in the King David Hotel to enter the
room where he would eventually have a diddle with Victoria
Halevi.

Marka Mladosi had built the hallway with doors to match the
actual doors of the King David. He stood there, *niska drina* burning down to his knuckles, supervising his workers. It was a simple shot. One actor, no dialogue, simple set. They should be lit
and shooting within an hour. The first shot was important. It set
the pace, the tone for the rest of the picture. He and Dinak had
chosen to start with a simple shot to demonstrate to the actors
and the crew that this was an efficient operation.

The second assistant director approached Charlie to tell him
that Nigel Bland wanted to see him in his dressing room. Charlie
went over to one of the two smaller trailers flanking the mono-
lithic custom-made Airstream they had imported for Bobby
Mason, who was back at the Intercontinental sleeping, his call
not being until noon. Charlie knocked on the door, was asked to
come in.

Nigel Bland sat in a brocade dressing gown, his large hands around a cup of tea laced with brandy, staring at his script as Charlie entered.

"Good of you to come. Cup of tea?"

"No thanks. Something wrong, Nigel?"

"I've been looking over this first scene, and I'm not entirely clear on it, I'm afraid."

"You mean Scene 71A?"

"Precisely."

Charlie opened his copy of the script, turned to Scene 71A. Under the heading INTERIOR HALLWAY - KING DAVID HOTEL - DAY there was only one sentence: "Bill walks down the hallway, enters Victoria's room."

"What's the problem?"

"You see, I'm not sure exactly how to play it."

Charlie looked back down at the script page, reread the simple declarative sentence, looked back up and said, "You just walk down the hallway and enter the room."

Nigel nodded with that furious rapid nod of his, then said, "Of course. But I'm a little in the dark as to just *how* he should walk down the hall."

"I don't think there's anything subtextual here, Nigel. I mean, you walk down the hall, open the door."

Nigel nodded some more. Charlie could see the redness in his eyes. The man had obviously been up very late with his brandy bottle. The makeup man would have to camouflage the hangover as best he could.

"Here's what I'm thinking, Charlie, and correct me if I'm off the mark here. Bill has just come from meeting with his contact at MI6. I would imagine he's a bit testy at having to get orders from Whitehall. He's rather the independent one, isn't he now? In any event, he goes to the King David to meet with the girl, whom he has a bit of a rod for. Perhaps he's even thinking that he'll have it on with her that afternoon. You follow me?"

Charlie nodded.

"So I should think that when he comes down that hallway he's rather a bit chewed off at the MI6 people as well as being randy, isn't he now? Could we not have both these attitudes playing in the way he *approaches* her door?"

"Sure . . ."

"I'd like to try a sort of walk that *reflects* the contradiction in his feelings. Do you see what I mean?"

"Sounds good to me," said Charlie.

"Of course, I wouldn't want to *over*play it. . . ."

"I wouldn't worry about that."

"Do you suppose you could have a word with Dino and have him print several takes? I could play it different ways then, you see."

"Certainly, Nigel."

Charlie found Dinak studying the light bouncing off one of Marka Mladosi's period light sconces. He explained the situation to him, and they devised the first of many duplicities they would engage in with Nigel Bland. Dinak would call *print* after each take, then add a phrase in Serbian to indicate whether the operator should actually mark the take for printing.

They did thirteen takes that morning of Bill Gladstone walking down the hallway of the King David Hotel for his assignation with Victoria Halevi. The subtlety of Nigel Bland's performance was largely wasted on everyone but Charlie. He sat in his PRO-DUTTORE chair and marveled at the modulations of facial expression and gait that the actor adopted. To those who were unaware of the subtext, however, they all pretty much played the same way: a man with a hangover walking down a hallway.

Howard Draper sat over his high-fiber breakfast with *The Wall Street Journal*. He read it every morning before opening the trades, a carryover from his days on the street, cursorily glancing at the major stories, absently checking the various markets, the way people tend to check the batting averages of players on teams they no longer have any real rooting interest in.

Winnie was still in bed. She rarely rose before ten. They hadn't had breakfast together for years. The house was quiet, delightfully so. The live-in housekeeper was off in her cubicle on the other side of the house watching *Wheel of Fortune*. She wouldn't emerge until she heard the door between the kitchen and the garage close, indicating that the master of the house was gone for the day. Howard very rarely saw the Guatemalan woman who lived under his roof, which was just as well with him. He was finicky about his privacy, especially, in the morning. Breakfast, to the demi-WASP, was not a meal to be taken in public.

Outside, the automatic sprinklers were quietly spraying the bougainvillea. A little man in a straw hat leaned over the flower beds aerating the soil. The two-horsepower pool motor turned on, stirring the perfectly chlorinated pool water, whose alkaline level was checked twice weekly.

The temperature inside the house was precisely seventy degrees, monitored by thermostats that regulated the twin six-ton Carrier heating and air-conditioning units on the roof. In addition there was a Honeywell air-purifying system that constantly cleaned and recirculated the air. The doors and windows were all discreetly wired by Westec, and infrared light beams and carpet sensors provided around-the-clock security.

In the middle of this perfect universe, Howard Draper sat with his breakfast. Life was soft and kind here in this optimum environment. There was a sense of quiet well-being that glowed inside him, the feeling that there was nothing loud or harsh or evil in his immediate vicinity. Life was indeed lovely this morning. . . .

Until the phone rang. Howard looked at his watch and felt the perfection of the moment disintegrate. It was seven forty-five. The studio would not call him at that hour. Which meant only one thing.

He rose, carefully wiping his chin with the linen napkin, and went over to the breakfast-nook phone.

"Yes?"

Howard Draper heard the familiar voice of Frederick the Great's secretary saying, "Would you hold please for Mr. Weston."

He stood there and felt a small knot in his lower intestine. His morning had begun to go downhill, and it wasn't even eight yet. It seemed to take forever before he heard the rumpled baritone of the chairman of the board of Allied Continental Industries.

"Howard?"

"Good morning."

"Banzai . . ."

Norman Hudris got the news of the Katsubishi acquisition on the car phone coming down Sepulveda. His broker called to tell him that the ACI stock had opened at thirty-four that morning and had been rising steadily as the details of the deal were made public. It was at thirty-five and an eighth by 11:00 A.M. New York time.

"It's lock, stock and barrel, Norman. Right down to the paper clips."

Norman downshifted the Porsche harshly, forgetting to double-clutch. "Jesus, Grant. They really did it?"

"The whole nine yards. Real estate, film library, distribution apparatus . . ."

"No kidding . . ." Norman felt the strange, lightheaded calm that came over him in situations when something he had been fearing actually occurred. "So what do you think?"

"I think it's going to top out at thirty-six, then slip back down to about thirty-five and a half," Grant McKelwayne said.

"Jesus . . ." Norman muttered, not thinking about the stock for the moment. He was way ahead of his broker. Norman was thinking about the unthinkable. Norman was thinking about being unemployed.

A 735i suddenly braked in front of him, and Norman nearly

rear-ended him. Jesus. Get it together. Don't wipe out now. Not at least until you put the sell order in.

"So what do you think?"

"I think thirty-six's safe, anything higher's dicey."

"Yeah, but what if it keeps going up?"

"That's a possibility."

"When should I get out?"

"It's your call."

"So what do you think?" Norman repeated, stalling for time.

"I just told you. You can get out now or take a chance on riding the elevator."

"Yeah . . . right . . . Listen, Grant, what do you hear about personnel?"

"What's that, Norman?"

"Any word on the street whether they're going to clean house?"

"I haven't heard anything."

"Nothing at all?"

"The Japanese are pretty tight-lipped about that kind of thing. . . . So what do you want to do?"

"About what?"

"The stock."

"I don't know. What do you think?"

They eventually settled on a sell order at thirty-five. As soon as Norman hung up with Grant McKelwayne in New York he dialed Burbank to talk to his friend at NBC and find out if the job in Standards and Practices was still open.

Not having a car phone, Deidre Hearn's drive to the studio was uneventful. She drove through the early-morning low fog listening to Sinatra on the cassette player. She knew all the words to *Songs for Swingin' Lovers,* and she sang along with The Man as she swung the Acura onto the lot. Her first indication that something big had gone down was that the guard at the gate, Shorty, didn't wave at her as he usually did. He had his nose in the want ads.

Another thing. It was only nine o'clock and Howard Draper's Rolls was in its spot.

As she entered the producers' building and walked down the long hallway toward her office, she began to sense that something was indeed afoot. She could almost smell the pervasive aroma of collective anxiety. Through the open doorways to the various executive offices she could overhear bits and pieces of intense personal conversations that secretaries were having, and she could see that the doors to their bosses' offices were tightly closed, which meant that they, too, were having intense personal conversations.

It had all the appearances of a full-blown bank panic. People were heading for the lifeboats. When a particular picture flopped or a deal collapsed, you would see the executive in charge and his entourage abandon ship together, but it seemed this morning as if the entire first floor of the producers' building was heading for the lifeboats. Not to mention the guard at the gate.

Her own office was no exception. Alan had been on the phone with Brian for half an hour, discussing his future. He whispered that he'd be right back to him, hung up, turned to Deidre as she walked in the door.

"Did you hear?"

"What?"

"The studio."

"What about the studio?"

"They sold it. To the Japanese."

Deidre sighed and nodded. Unlike others, she did not find the news that earth-shattering.

"They've been talking about selling the studio for a long time."

"Two hundred seventy-five million."

She nodded again, and as she started to enter her office, Alan said, "I'm going to take a long lunch hour today, if it's all right with you."

Deidre turned back to him and said, "Alan, I don't give a fuck when you come back from lunch. I'm giving you two weeks' notice. As of right now."

And without waiting to see the reaction on his face, she turned and entered her office. She crossed to her desk, sat down in the uncomfortable swivel chair. She removed her shoes, hiked up her skirt, took a script off the top of the shit pile and went to work.

There was one other person at the studio who wasn't overly concerned about the Katsubishi deal. Who wasn't, for that matter, even aware of it. Upstairs in Charlie Berns's office Enid Schonblum was supervising the installation of a discreet off-white woolen carpet that would tastefully underscore the tones of the Louis XVI armoire and sideboard. The furniture was all out in the hallway to facilitate the carpet layers, along with the phone, which was sitting on the cheap industrial-wear hall carpet gurgling quietly.

This was no time to be distracted by the telephone, however. The installation of woolen carpet was a particularly delicate business, requiring great care to prevent bunching the fabric and causing little air pockets that could lead to the premature aging of the carpet. And Enid did not have complete confidence in the two Office Maintenance workers they had sent over to do the job. She literally stood over them to make sure they kept the carpet taut.

That afternoon she would go through the set dressing department to pick out the artwork for the walls. She had in mind the group of Turner landscapes she had seen during her scouting trip last week. They would be restful to the eye without being frivolous.

People moved back and forth through the hallway, past Enid's ringing phone, sharing rumors from the outside. Some started packing up their desks. Others eyed the desks of their superiors. Spouses, boyfriends, agents, shrinks were called. . . .

Through all this turmoil Enid remained at her post, looking down over the carpet-layers' shoulders, correcting errors as she observed them as the rest of the studio hurried toward the lifeboats. It was every man for himself and damn the torpedoes. Except Enid Schonblum. She wasn't going anywhere.

When the advance guard of Katsubishi troops eventually arrived, they might very well find an abandoned garrison with only one worried-looking woman kneeling down over her carpet checking for air pockets.

# 12

News of the Katsubishi deal spread quickly from Burbank to Tokyo, to Paris, London and Singapore. Word didn't, however, get immediately to Stage 9 at Novi Beograd Studios outside of Belgrade. There they were moving forward with the production of a movie without much concern for the fact that the ownership of the negative had changed hands. In a sense, the name of the company for whom they were ultimately working was pretty irrelevant to the cast and crew of *Decker*. For them the only name they cared about was Tabor Gubca's, whose signature was on their paychecks every week.

Bobby Mason wasn't concerned either. His money was pay or play even if they sold the studio to the Martians. There was no way they were going to stiff *him*. BM sat in his room at the Intercontinental watching a videocassette of *To Hell and Back*, one of his top-ten movies. The production manager was only able to find a copy dubbed in Italian, but Bobby knew every line of the movie by heart anyway.

Next door his security guys were playing Hearts and waiting to find out if they were going to shoot Scene 127B that evening or if they were going to wrap and carry the scene till tomorrow.

Bobby had been on a standby call all day due to problems with the body stocking in one of the fuck scenes. During rehearsal Nigel Bland's fingernail had gone through the fabric causing an extended tear, which had to be carefully resewn with flesh-colored thread. Then Tricia Jacobi had been indisposed for another hour with digestive problems. They were over two hours behind, and it was looking doubtful that they would get to Bobby's scene this evening.

Bobby had the guys call down for pizza. He heard the knock on the door in the adjoining room, heard Sal open it, take the pizza, sign for it.

Moments later Sal knocked on his door.

"Yo," Bobby called. The door opened and Sal entered with Bobby's pizza and two Pepsi soft drinks. Sal lifted the ornate silver service to expose a small square pizza with a piece of salami lying on top.

Bobby frowned. "Jesus. It looks like someone puked on it."

"We're not in New Jersey, Bobby."

"Tell me about it. Will you look at this shit? They throw a slice of salami on it and call it a sausage pizza."

Sal put the pizza and the Pepsi sodas down on the chintz antimacassar, checked his watch and said, "Doesn't look like they're going to get to you tonight."

Bobby nodded, gingerly cut himself a slice of the pizza.

"You want to play some hearts?" Sal said.

"Maybe later, after I eat."

Sal nodded, withdrew to the adjoining room, closed the door behind him. Bobby opened one of the Pepsi cans, took a long swig. At least they couldn't fuck with Pepsi.

He ate the pizza without looking at it, figuring it would go easier that way. On the screen Audie Murphy was blowing away an entire platoon of Krauts with a bazooka. As Bobby watched the extras in German uniforms crumble and die, the screen began to fog on him.

Jesus. Didn't *anything* work in this fucking country? He got up to check the controls and suddenly felt very dizzy. He sat back down again on the edge of the bed, rubbed his temples. He reached for the Pepsi can and missed, knocking it over. Pepsi spilled out all over the handwoven Turkish carpet.

Next door Sal had already gone down, clutching a piece of pizza in one hand and the queen of spades in the other. The two goons watched him in consternation before they, too, fell over unconscious, victims of Yugoslavian pizza.

It wasn't until Bobby's driver knocked on the door to the security suite at 6:30 the next morning to take him to the set for a 7:00 A.M. call that anyone knew there was something wrong. The three security men from New Jersey were still out cold and had to be virtually pounded awake by the driver. They got up unsteadily, looked around at the remains of the salami pizza, then at the unslept-in beds and scratched their heads.

Then Sal went next door and found Bobby Mason's room deserted. They all stood around Bobby's room staring at one another. Nobody knew where he was. Nobody in the lobby or at the front desk had seen Bobby Mason leave. While Sal sat down to try and clear his head, the driver telephoned the set to inform them that the star would not be in makeup on time.

Charlie was informed of the disappearance of his star by a telephone call from the phlegmatic Tabor Gubca.

"What do you mean, he's *absent?*" Charlie almost bellowed into the phone.

"No sign of him. Not in his room, nobody see him leave. Look like bad pizza."

"Bad pizza? Gubca, what are you talking about?"

"They order pizza last night. Everybody . . . puff, out like light bulbs. So we shoot around him, no?"

Charlie heard the rustle of the call sheet as Gubca was already putting together an alternate day's work.

"We pull 83, 84 and 85 inside, lose the car . . . can do. You like that?"

"Gubca, what do you mean *bad pizza?*"

"Drugged maybe. They all gone to sleep. Nobody knows, Charlie . . . I got idea . . . We go with 85 first without Bobby, then do wardrobe change on Tricia for 83, 84 while we light for 23B . . . then if he show up, we can pull 17 back and blow off 23B. . . ."

Charlie threw some clothes on, didn't bother to shave. By the time he arrived at the Intercontinental, there was a policeman on duty outside Bobby's suite. He refused to let Charlie in until Charlie's driver identified him in Serbian as the producer of the movie. Inside the room were the three goons from New Jersey, the head of hotel security, and Lieutenant Ljabovic of the Belgrade Police Department, an unkempt man in a worn Burberry.

Lieutenant Ljabovic took Charlie aside, offered him a *niska drina.*

"No thank you."

He lit one himself, inhaled, allowed the smoke to exit between a row of badly stained teeth. "Do you know what I think, Mr. Berns?"

Charlie shook his head.

"I think we cannot rule out foul playing here."

"Really?"

Lieutenant Ljabovic nodded. "Drug in pizza. I have sent remains to the laboratory for tests. We see." He took out a small notebook, as he had no doubt seen Columbo do, and asked Charlie, "Does Mr. Mason have enemies?"

"Look, to be honest with you I really don't know him that well. . . . Do you think he was kidnapped?"

The lieutenant shrugged, then wrote something, presumably in Serbian, in the notebook.

"When was he last seen?"

"I don't know. I saw him on the set yesterday for a wardrobe fitting. . . . Why would anybody want to kidnap a movie star?"

Lieutenant Ljabovic smiled indulgently, as if he were dealing with a child. "Mr. Berns, perhaps you are upset. Maybe you lie down for a while. We wait for laboratory tests on pizza. Then we know."

Charlie was summoned to the phone. It was Dinak from the set.

"The fucking Bosnian wants to do 85 first. I tell him we got big lighting job, we go with 17-A. He tell me you agree to 85."

"Dinak, Bobby may have been kidnapped."

"Yeah. That's what the fucking Bosnian saying. We shoot around him, Charlie. But not 85 first, okay?"

It was well after nine in the evening in Los Angeles when Charlie finally got through to someone at the studio. Howard Draper was long gone, sitting on his sun porch in the Colony, already into his third Tanqueray rocks. Norman Hudris was traveling north on the San Diego Freeway through the Sepulveda Pass, top down, doing ninety. He had just hung up the car phone with Cissy Fuchs, breaking their first date in nearly a month in order to have dinner with the head of NBC's Department of Standards and Practices. The only person Charlie could rouse was Deidre Hearn, who was just about to fling the final script of the day into the shit pile when the phone rang.

She picked it up herself, Alan having stalked off petulantly at lunch and not come back.

"Hello . . ."

"Deidre, it's Charlie."

"Hey, how's it going?"

"Not so hot. Somebody drugged Bobby Mason's pizza and abducted him. . . ."

One thing about Charlie Berns. He got fairly quickly to the point and didn't embellish it. Deidre didn't even bother to ask him to repeat this astonishing sentence. She instinctively knew that what he had said was true and that she had understood what had to be understood. She said nothing.

It was Charlie who said, "Deidre, you there?"

"Holy shit."

"I thought someone there ought to know."

"Who did it?"

"We don't know."

"Holy shit," she repeated.

"I tried calling Norman, but he was gone."

"Norman's meeting with people at NBC. He's bailing out. Vice president of Standards and Practices."

"What about Howard?"

"He's leaving for Oahu tomorrow. He figured it's a good time to take a vacation. The studio's been sold to the Japanese."

"What?"

"ACI unloaded us. Everyone's heading for the lifeboats."

"Who's running the show?"

"Beats me."

"Congratulations."

"Don't be funny, Charlie. . . . What are you going to do about Bobby?"

"We'll shoot around him."

"How long can you do that for?"

"Couple of days maybe."

Neither of them said anything for a long moment, then it was Deidre who said, "Crazy day, huh? The studio gets sold and the star of its big picture gets kidnapped. On the same day. In what other business could this have happened?"

"Maybe the Japanese took Bobby . . . you know, get them out of paying the eight mil and the piece."

"They drugged his *pizza?*"

"Yeah . . ."

She broke out laughing. So did he. They sat there on either end of a ten-thousand-mile telephone connection laughing uproariously. Under the circumstances it seemed as appropriate a response as any.

In spite of his efforts to keep the news from the company, word of Bobby Mason's disappearance had reached the set long before

Charlie arrived on Stage 9 that morning. He discovered that work had ground to a virtual standstill. The crew was gathered in clusters listening to portable radios. News bulletins of the kidnapping were interrupting regularly scheduled programming. Though details were still sketchy, speculation was rampant.

The leading suspects were the Palestinians, who, in spite of the fact that the terrorists in the script were painstakingly nondescript, may very well have taken umbrage with the vigilante Zionism of *Decker*. But nothing so far had come out of PLO headquarters or that of any other Palestinian group. The Iranians, as well, were keeping a low profile. So were the IRA and the Red Brigade. One local news commentator mentioned the racial aspect of the abduction, suggesting a possible international action on behalf of the Ku Klux Klan.

Meanwhile, no film was being shot. In addition to the turmoil among the crew, Tricia Jacobi had locked herself in her trailer, refusing to open the door until she was assigned a twenty-four-hour security detail.

Neither Dinak nor Lionel had been able to convince her to let them come in to talk to her. Charlie knocked on the door softly, waited, then said through the closed trailer door, "Tricia, it's Charlie."

No answer.

"Listen to me, Tricia. I know you're upset. It's understandable. We're all a little upset. But we have to keep on working. You're a professional, Tricia, and professionals don't allow upsets to keep them from working. . . . Do you understand what I'm saying?"

Still no response from inside. "We'll work out better security arrangements for you. I promise. Why don't you open the door and we'll talk about it."

The door remained closed. Charlie quietly slipped on the Capezios.

"Tricia, you ever hear the story about Joan Crawford in Mexico?"

Shuffle, ball change . . .

"She was making a picture way down south someplace, where there were banditos. Real nasty guys. All they had were a couple of rent-a-cops to protect the company. One day the banditos ride right onto the set in the middle of shooting, firing their guns in the air. The rent-a-cops disappear. The banditos demand the money and jewels. The production manager gives them the petty cash and the costume jewelry. Then they want the women turned over. There was Joan Crawford, her secretary and her wardrober. The banditos say that unless they turn over the women, they're going to shoot everybody on the location. Joan overhears this in her trailer and comes out wearing nothing but her slip, walks right over to the head bandito, tells him to get down off his horse and take his clothes off. Right here. Let's see how big his cojones are. . . . She's ready if he is. . . . The guy takes off like a bat out of hell. Incredible, huh? Now *there* was a professional. . . ."

Tricia Jacobi opened her trailer door and invited Charlie inside to discuss beefed-up security measures. Within an hour she was back in her body stocking ready to work.

Dinak got the crew away from their radios long enough to finish lighting the hotel room, while one of the a.d.'s was dispatched to get Nigel Bland out of the jerry-built sauna that Marka Mladosi had made for him using an old closet and a kerosene heater.

The scene was one of the restored Bobby Mason fuck scenes that Lionel had suggested could be adapted to be played with Nigel. All they really had to do, he pointed out, was cross out Decker in the script and put Gladstone in its place. The scene played equally well with Bill, further evidence of Madison Kearney's tight story construction. The script supervisor was instructed to make the change; new pages were hastily run off.

Tricia insisted that they clear the set for her nude scenes even though she was wearing a body stocking. Everyone but the director, the first a.d., the operator, one grip, the script supervisor and the d.p. were banished to an area behind a wild wall as Dinak directed Nigel, his nails clipped, and Tricia, in her resewn body stocking.

Charlie and Lionel sat behind the wall and listened to the rustling of Tricia's body stocking, Nigel's heavy breathing, punctuated by Dinak's periodically calling *action* and *cut*. They counted fourteen takes before they heard Dinak call *cut* prematurely. Soon everyone on the set was talking rapidly in Serbian.

Charlie and Lionel went around to the other side of the wall to find out what was going on.

Dinak looked at Charlie and nodded. "I knew it, Charlie."

"What's going on?"

"Fucking Macedonians."

Charlie looked at him, completely confused.

"Sons of bitches!"

"What?"

The operator motioned for everyone to be quiet as he listened to more of the news bulletin through the earphones. Then he said a bunch of things to Dinak in Serbian. Dinak turned to Charlie. "You know who take Bobby?" Dinak verified the name with the operator.

"Commando for Free Macedonia."

"Who are they?"

"Sons of fucking Macedonian bitches, that's who they are." And Dinak spit copiously on the floor, right beside the camera dolly. The operator and the d.p. spit as well. The key grip, an Albanian, and the script supervisor, a Croat, withheld comment.

"Macedonian *separatists*? Who the fuck are *they*?"

Sidney Auger's voice was tinged with exhaustion. For the past two days it had been virtual chaos at the studio. Howard had taken off to Oahu and was returning only his lawyer's phone calls. Norman was staying home, ostensibly flu-ridden, as he negotiated terms on his NBC deal. As ranking vice president, Sidney Auger had become the acting head of the studio.

It was a job he didn't want. The phone was ringing off the hook with reporters wanting to find out what was happening, with lawyers trying to establish an insurance claim, with producers worried about the continuity of their deals, with agents trying to ride the wave of the new regime and sell pictures. What new regime? There were no instructions out of either New York or Tokyo. . . . And now, as if all that weren't enough, the goddamn star of a $32 million-dollar picture gets kidnapped in Yugoslavia.

Sitting on the functional Naugahyde couch in Sidney's office, Deidre explained, "They want Macedonia to be independent from Yugoslavia."

"So they grab Bobby Mason?"

"Apparently."

Sidney Auger took off his glasses and rubbed his eyes. He looked down at a half-eaten *tostada grande* without interest, then back up at Deidre. "He couldn't at least get taken by the Palestinians or the Iranians? These guys are strictly minor league. I mean, nobody knows who they are . . . ."

"I think that was the point, Sidney. They want publicity."

"Well, they certainly got it."

Sidney got up, started to pace, thinking out loud. "They probably don't know the difference between up-front and back-end money, right? What if we offer them a fat piece on the back end? We'll juggle the books. They'll never see a dime. . . ."

"Sidney, they didn't grab Bobby because they wanted to get into the movie business. Take my word for it. And if they want to negotiate, it won't be with us."

"Who with?"

"The government in Belgrade."

"The government in Belgrade," he repeated, shaking his head. "So we sit here with our thumbs up our asses waiting for Belgrade to make them independent?"

"I think once they've gotten all the publicity they want, they'll let him go."

"Right. And meanwhile, we're in the toilet. You realize we have a firm stop date with Bobby?"

"What about the insurance claim?"

"Force majeure. They're calling it an act of civil disorder and anarchy. We'll be in court for five years. . . ."

Sidney Auger's secretary stuck her head in. "Do you want to talk to Bert Sully?"

He turned to Deidre and said, "How much do you want to bet he tells me the pay-or-play deal isn't affected by force majeure?" He nodded to his secretary and switched on the speakerphone.

"Bert, we're doing everything we can. Charlie's on top of the situation in Belgrade. As soon as I hear anything . . ."

"Mr. Auger, can I cut through all of this horseshit?"

In contrast to Sidney's strident voice, Bert Sully's was calm, almost soporific. "We have what you call an irregular situation here. Bobby's been grabbed by a bunch of terrorists due to improper security measures on the part of your studio . . ."

"Bert . . ."

"Would you be kind enough to let me finish what I have to say, Mr. Auger?" There was a long pause for emphasis, then, "Now I didn't call to make your life any more difficult than it already is. I reckon you're up to your neck in it as it is. . . . However, I'd like you to get him the hell back."

"Listen, we want him back safe and sound as much as you do, believe me. . . ."

"I'm not a lawyer, Mr. Auger, but I don't think you need to have passed the bar examination to contemplate the scope of a negligence judgment here."

"It won't come to that. We'll get him back."

"I would certainly hope so."

"We've already beefed up security on the set."

"Where I come from, we call that locking the barn door after the horse's gone." And he hung up softly.

Sidney flicked off the speakerphone. "I hate that son of a bitch. He's got one hand on your jugular and the other in your pocket."

He slumped back down into his chair and muttered, "Can they shoot around him?"

"For a couple of days."

Sidney opened a file on his desk, pulled the budget on *Decker*, scanned it.

"I'm eyeballing we're in for a little more than a million hard currency start-up money. And some of that may be recoverable. The rest is all in dinars. Maybe we should just pull the plug and take the loss."

"Why do that now? Maybe Bobby'll turn up. In the meantime, all we're spending is dinars, and what are you going to do with five million dollars' worth of blocked currency anyway?"

"You got a point." He took a bite of his *tostado grande*, grimaced, then: "It's all dinars and yen. Who gives a fuck, right?"

The Commando for a Free Macedonia made a number of demands over the next few days, but none of them concerned a piece of *Decker*, up-front or back-end. A videotape was delivered to a Belgrade television station of Bobby Mason, sitting on a chair in front of the Macedonian flag, reading the separatists' list of demands. The clip was broadcast all over the world, the lead item in the evening news.

The State Department issued a communiqué deploring terrorism and reaffirming its commitment to fighting it on all fronts. A series of discussions was going on between Washington and Belgrade with regard to options for responding to this "irresponsible and senseless act of lawlessness." On the floor of the House a congressman from Arkansas suggested sending the marines into Macedonia to protect American life and property. A man picketed the Uruguayan mission to the United Nations until he was informed that Bobby Mason was being held hostage in Macedonia and not Montevideo.

At the same time, rentals of Bobby Mason videocassettes soared. Theaters pulled their current releases and showed old movies starring the martial-arts star. Bobby Mason's sweat sock business in Rancho Mirage received a shot in the arm as orders poured in. Postproduction of *Desert Commando*, the recently wrapped BM feature, was accelerated and its release date pushed up.

Through all this, Charlie attempted to keep production moving. He closed the set, not only to satisfy Tricia Jacobi's fears but also to keep reporters out of their hair. The switchboard at the Balkanska had broken down from the overload and Charlie was reduced to making phone calls from the production trailer outside Stage 9.

They shot every interior scene that did not require Bobby Mason. Lionel even managed to find a few more of his scenes that could be given to Nigel without serious disruption to the story. But by the middle of the following week, with no resolution of the hostage situation, they were effectively out of pages.

They would have to shut down. There was nothing else to shoot without Bobby. Lionel was prepared to rewrite the entire script to get rid of Decker. Charlie told him it was senseless. The studio would pull the plug. Without Bobby Mason they didn't have a picture.

After the final day of shooting they all went out to dinner in a restaurant on the banks of the Danube—Charlie, Lionel, Dinak, Wilna, Gubca and Marka Mladosi. They ate *pljeskavica*, washed down with Greek wine, followed by several bottles of *sljivovica*, a potent prune liqueur with a nasty kick. The atmosphere became progressively more maudlin as they gradually realized that this was in fact a wrap party. Toasts were proposed and drunk—in Serbian, Polish, English. Glasses were flung into the Danube. Dinak and Gubca, united at the moment in their common animosity toward Macedonians, sang dirty songs, their arms around each other's shoulders.

This was the first time Lionel had experienced this kind of sentimental outpouring. He sat there, very drunk, tears in his eyes, staring morosely at the dark waters of the Danube as it flowed by briskly.

"It's all over, huh, Charlie?" he mumbled into his *sljivovica*.

"Yeah, I guess so. We don't have a star."

"It happened so fast, like we just got here. I mean, and Dinak and Wilna and everyone are great, really great. . . ."

"It's just a picture, Lionel."

Even as he said the words, Charlie knew they weren't true. It was never just a picture. He knew that and someday so would Lionel. It *was* a goddamn shame. He looked around at what was left of his picture. Dinak was dancing a polka with Wilna. Gubca and Marka were trying to stand a matchbox on four cigarettes. The picture had been put together just like that. A house of cards. Charlie had ridden it as far as it would take him, and he had gotten all the way to principal photography before they pulled the plug on him. How do you cover all the angles? Some political nuts kidnap your star. . . . That's a thousand-to-one shot. Go figure . . .

"Charlie," Lionel said, breaking his train of thought, "let's drink to Disraeli. . . ."

"Which one?"

"Ben. The real one."

They drained their *sljivovica,* tossed the glasses into the river. The waiters immediately replaced them.

"Old Ben, helluva guy . . ."

They closed up the place at two in the morning. The bill was brought ceremoniously to Charlie, but Gubca insisted on paying it. "I charge it to the picture, no? What else do we do with all those dinars? Fucking shame . . ."

In the cab on the way back to the hotel, just before throwing up, Lionel said, "We should've made the other script, Charlie. No one would've been kidnapped making *that* picture."

# 13

Flo Gamish had just finished dinner at home when she got a phone call from a breathless young woman asking if she was in fact *the* Flo Gamish who managed Jeremy Ikon and, *if* she was in fact *that* Flo Gamish, could she hold on for a moment while she put through a phone call from Charles Berns in Belgrade.

Flo Gamish was not sure exactly who Charles Berns was, though the name sounded vaguely familiar, and as she waited for the breathless young woman to put Belgrade through, she racked her Rolodex mind for the connection. All she could think of at the moment was George Burns, and what in God's name would *he* be doing calling her from Yugoslavia?

A soft-spoken man got on the phone, introduced himself. "Flo? It's Charlie Berns in Belgrade."

"How are you, Charlie?" She had no idea whom she was talking to.

"Listen, Flo, I'm calling on something that's just come up over here."

"What's that, Charlie?"

"I've got something terrific for Jeremy."

"Oh, really?"

"I'm sitting here with a script that'd be perfect for him, Flo."

"What kind of script, Charlie?" She still had no idea whom she was talking to.

"It's about Benjamin Disraeli. . . ."

Oh shit! She should never have said anything to Howard Draper. She had only been kidding, making Sunday-morning brunch conversation. Word had apparently made it all the way to Belgrade. . . . The last thing she needed was some low-budget art picture in Yugoslavia. Scale and back-end money. They'd never see a dime. Besides, it was crazy over there. They had just kidnapped Bobby Mason . . . wait a second . . . *that's* who Charlie Berns is. Forget it. . . .

"Okay, Charlie, send me the script and I'll have a look at it."

"There's a bit of a problem, Flo."

"What's that, Charlie?"

"I need an immediate answer."

"Well, that's going to be difficult. He's in Rome at the moment."

"Rome? What's he doing in Rome?"

"He's talking to Antonioni."

"No kidding?"

"Uh-huh."

"That's great, Flo."

"Anyway, Charlie, get me the script and I'll give it a fast read. If I think it's right for him I'll get it to him in Rome. . . ."

"You can fax it to him. I'm sure they've got a fax at the Excelsior. . . ."

"He's not at the Excelsior."

"The paparazzi, right?"

"Right. Jeremy can't walk two steps in Rome without being mobbed. He stays in a little pensione nobody's ever heard of. . . ."

"You know, I stayed at a little place like that a couple years ago. . . . Charming little place. Nah, couldn't be the same one . . ."

"What's that?"

"I was just wondering if it's the same place I used to stay at."

"I doubt it."

"This place was on a little street near . . . a fountain."

"The via Margutta?"

"Who can remember? It was a long time ago. . . . They probably turned it into a Marriott. . . . Anyway, listen, Flo, I appreciate your help on this."

"Any time, Charlie . . ."

Charlie was already several steps ahead of her, feeling the adrenaline begin to flow again.

He was back again in preproduction and dancing as fast as he could.

Charlie and Lionel sat in the rear of a packed Alitalia plane for the forty-five-minute flight from Belgrade to Rome. Lionel was wearing dark glasses, trying to recover from the wrap party. He had gotten about three hours' sleep before his uncle had woken him up to tell him they were going to Rome on the nine o'clock plane.

With them was a copy of Lionel's original script, *Bill and Ben*. They were going to Rome to talk a famous English movie star into accepting the role of Benjamin Disraeli. In the state he was in, it all made very little sense to Lionel. What had happened to Lev Disraeli, aka Decker, and Victoria Halevi and all *those* people?

"That was another picture. We're not making that picture anymore. We're making a new picture."

"How did that happen?"

"Last night, when I got back to the hotel, I couldn't sleep. I kept thinking about what a waste it was to shut down the picture. I started thinking about the dinars locked away in Yugoslavia. Lionel, did you ever think about blocked currency? I mean, theoretically?"

Lionel shook his head. He was incapable of theoretical thought at the moment. All he wanted was for his head to stop throbbing.

"What are these dinars exactly? Are they money? Yes and no.

They're only money if they're used to produce a movie in Yugoslavia. Who do they belong to? The studio? Yes and no. The studio can only use them to produce a movie in Yugoslavia. In a sense, then, unless you're producing a movie in Yugoslavia for the studio, they're not money. They're lying in the bank doing nobody any good. They're not doing the studio any good. They're not doing the cast and crew any good. They're not doing the Yugoslavian economy any good. They're not doing the American balance-of-payments problem any good. They're not doing you and me any good. Are they?"

"No . . ."

"Now if we could come up with a way to unblock the dinars, we'd be doing a service to everyone involved, wouldn't we?"

"Sure . . ."

"We'd be putting people to work, generating profits for the studio, enriching the Yugoslavian economy and . . . bringing to the screen a story that deserves to be told, the life story of a great man. Basically, we'd be doing a service to a lot of people."

Lionel thought about all this for a moment, then said, "Okay. So how are you going to pull it off?"

"The movie business, Lionel, is basically about windows of opportunity. Right now, we have a very small window of opportunity. If we act right away . . ."

Windows of opportunity. Stained-glass windows . . . Uncle Charlie was speaking in metaphors again.

"How are you going to talk Jeremy Ikon into agreeing to star in this picture when you have to pay him with money he can only spend in Yugoslavia?"

"Good question. I happen to know, through reliable rumor, that Jeremy Ikon has always wanted to play Benjamin Disraeli."

"How'd you find that out?"

"His manager to Howard Draper to Norman Hudris to Deidre Hearn to me. That's about as reliable as rumor gets. And secondly, I happen to know that he's always wanted to do a picture with Jacqueline Fortier."

"You've *got* Jacqueline Fortier?"

"Not yet . . ."

This was the point at which Lionel learned a new metaphor. The stone-soup metaphor.

"Let me tell you a story, Lionel. . . ."

Lionel leaned back in his seat, closed his eyes to quiet the headache and learned about stone soup.

"There were these soldiers coming back from war. They were tired, hungry and didn't have a penny to their name. They arrived in a village and asked to be fed, but no one was willing to offer them anything. So what did they do? They found an old copper pot and they filled it with water from the stream. They built a fire and put the pot on the fire to cook. And then they gathered a few stones and put them in the pot. . . . Soon a curious peasant came by and asked what they were doing, and they replied that they were making soup. What kind of soup? asked the peasant. Stone soup, replied the soldiers. The peasant said he had never tasted stone soup. Do you suppose he could have some? Certainly, responded the soldiers, but stone soup was really much better with carrots. The peasant ran home and got a bunch of carrots, and they put them in the soup. Soon a second peasant wandered by. What are you making? Stone soup with carrots. Would you care for some? Yes I would, replied the second peasant. Don't you think some onions would be good with the carrots? By all means, replied the soldiers. And the second peasant ran and got some onions. . . ."

"I get it," said Lionel. "Jeremy Ikon's the stone and Jacqueline Fortier's the carrot."

"For the moment."

"You slip the stone soup through the window of opportunity."

"Exactly."

"Can I ask you another question?"

"Sure."

"Assuming you manage to get Jeremy Ikon and Jacqueline Fortier to agree, how are you going to get the studio to agree to shoot an entirely different picture?"

"They're not going to know about it."

They hit an air pocket over the Adriatic, and Lionel felt his stomach convulse. He reached out and grabbed the paper bag.

In an apartment somewhere on the banks of the Sava, in the old city of Belgrade, Bobby Mason sat on a lumpy bed and contemplated another salami pizza without appetite. Although his kidnappers had been doing their best to make him comfortable, it wasn't easy finding a decent pizza in this city. They had explained to him that they had nothing personal against him or blacks or Americans or even movie stars, for that matter, that his kidnapping was merely convenient. They took him because he would guarantee them the kind of exposure they needed for their cause. He just happened to be in the right place at the right time.

Bobby sat and listened to a recounting of Yugoslavian history, going all the way back to the Battle of Kossovo in 1389. He learned about the fierce nationalistic rivalries, the unification under Tito, the economic problems facing the country. Mostly, however, he learned about the plight of Macedonia, the southernmost and poorest of the republics, being relegated by Belgrade's policies to the role of "nigger of Yugoslavia."

"You pardon the expression," said one of his captors behind his ski mask.

"It's cool, man," Bobby nodded.

They wore ski masks in his presence but were otherwise friendly and considerate. They had gone out and gotten him videocassettes to watch, brought him newspapers to read, played checkers and gin rummy with him.

At first he had thought about fighting his way out of there. There seemed to be only three of them, as far as he could tell, and he hadn't seen a gun anywhere in the apartment. Three fairly skinny dudes without a gun were a surmountable obstacle for a third-degree black belt. He wasn't entirely sure, however, that there wasn't a gun somewhere, or that there weren't more of them around, or where the hell he actually was. For all he knew they could have taken him to Macedonia. Wherever *that* was.

Decker wouldn't have put up with this kind of shit, that was for sure. He would have taken out the whole nest of Macedonian terrorists with one well-placed grenade that he had hidden in his boot. Decker didn't fuck around.

But Bobby Mason was no longer in character. To tell the truth, he wasn't entirely sure he wanted to be Decker anymore. The picture was in the toilet. They'd had to shut down without him. No great loss. He didn't really like the chick. She had one of those big moist mouths that made him nervous. He wasn't looking forward to kissing her. And her jugs weren't that great. He had seen better jugs in Vegas.

The first day of his captivity Bobby had explained to the ski masks about the movie, his stop date, the problems that would be caused by his absence. They said they were sorry but that the fate of Macedonia was more important than a movie.

Maybe they were right. Maybe it was time for Bobby to start paying more attention to the plight of oppressed people. Maybe someone in his position *could* make a difference. What if he developed a script about the history of Macedonia? What if they got all the publicity they wanted in 35mm Technicolor film?

The Macedonians were out of Pepsi. They had brought him a Yugoslavian beer to wash down the salami pizza. It was warm and tasted like piss. He lay back down on the bed and closed his eyes. Far away he could hear car horns honking, a radio playing music. He would try to get some sleep.

Tomorrow he would talk to his captors about doing a picture about the oppression of the Macedonian people. They could do a coproduction through Bobby's company. He could put Macedonia on the fucking map.

"Disraeli? *Benjamin* Disraeli?"

"Right. I've got the script with me, in fact."

"How extraordinary . . ." Jeremy Ikon's voice was uninflected and mellifluous, as if he were reciting lines from a Galsworthy novel instead of talking to a producer on the telephone from his pensione on the via Margutta.

"The writer's with me as well," Charlie said.

"I see, yes . . ."

"Do you suppose we could grab lunch?"

"Lunch?"

"Yes. Today?"

"Today, well, I don't know . . . it *is* Benjamin Disraeli, the prime minister of England under Victoria?"

"Is there any other . . . ?"

They met at a little restaurant in the Trastevere in order to avoid the paparazzi. The place was small and dark and smelled of olive oil. Jeremy Ikon sat in the rear wearing jeans held up by suspenders and a Giovanni Grazziani sweatshirt.

They shook hands and ordered Camparis and soda. Lionel, still nursing his Belgrade hangover, kept his dark glasses on.

"How on earth did you find me anyway?"

"Flo mentioned you were staying at the Frescobaldi, and I thought since we were in Rome, we'd get in touch."

"You know, quite recently, they announced this Disraeli project with Bobby Mason. Of course, it turned out to be some entirely different Disraeli, some anti-terrorist Disraeli. Is he still kidnapped by the Montenegrans, by the way?"

"Actually it's the Macedonians," Lionel pointed out.

"Sorry. You really can't be too careful these days, can you?"

"Well, that's one good thing about making a picture about Ben Disraeli. Nobody's going to take offense."

"I suppose not."

"Except maybe Bill Gladstone, and he's apparently not with us anymore."

Jeremy Ikon smiled dimly. He had that English ability of smiling without moving a muscle in his face. "This is all rather hurried, isn't it? You mentioned starting on the eleventh?"

"I'm afraid so," said Charlie. "We've got money waiting in Belgrade. And then there's Jacqueline Fortier's availability. . . ."

"Jacqueline's doing the picture?" Jeremy's phlegmatic voice perked up.

"We're just about closed on her."

"As whom? His sister Sarah or Mary, his wife?"

"As Queen Victoria."

"Jacqueline as Victoria. Splendid . . . splendid. She's perfect."

"She's dying to work with you."

"Marvelous actress. We were going to do a film together for Polanski last year."

"Really?"

"Yes, unfortunately, the money fell through. Who's going to direct, by the way?"

"We're talking to Milos. . . ."

They spent the rest of the lunch talking about how wonderfully *filmic* the life of Disraeli was, how extraordinary it was that no one had made a picture about him before. Lionel, who had done thorough research for his script, recounted a number of anecdotes about the prime minister's life that even such a confirmed Disraeliphile as Jeremy Ikon had never heard.

By the time they parted, they were on cordial terms. Jeremy had the script under his arm, promised to read it that very afternoon, and phone Charlie in Belgrade that evening.

In the cab on the way back out to the airport, Lionel, who was working on an entirely new hangover, said, "Let me see if I've got this straight. Jeremy's the stone, Jacqueline Fortier's the carrot. So that makes Milos the onion, right?"

Charlie smiled at his young nephew. He was getting very fond of him. As the cabdriver cursed his way through Roman traffic, he leaned back in his seat and contemplated his next move. As soon as he landed he would have to talk to Gubca and Marka Mladosi. While waiting for the casting to firm up, they would have to go ahead and start to build the House of Commons. On spec.

For the past ten minutes Sara Donleavy had been on hold, waiting to get through to Norman Hudris. She wanted to confirm the rumor that he was heading for NBC. It was a story which at the moment was only secondhand gossip from a hustling young GTA agent named Brad Emprin, with whom she had just had breakfast at Le Cornichon, the new quiche place on Sunset.

Brian, her assistant, called from his cubicle, "I've got Charlie Berns for you on one-nine. From Belgrade."

Sara Donleavy knew Charlie Berns from the days when she was hustling stories for a Hollywood tabloid. He was a B-movie producer until he disappeared from the face of the earth. Like everyone else, she had assumed that Charlie Berns was either dead or in Tucson. Then there was the bogus obit. While people were trying to verify his death, he was suddenly resurrected. Now he was the hottest story in town. First the Bobby Mason picture, then the kidnapping. Everyone was trying to get to him, and here he was calling her.

She hung up on Norman Hudris's office and picked up one-nine. "How you doing, Charlie?"

"Pretty good, Sara."

"What's going on in Belgrade?"

"Not a whole lot."

"C'mon, Charlie, you didn't call me up from Yugoslavia to tell me that nothing's going on there, did you?"

"No. I called you up for Jacqueline Fortier's home address."

"I'm listening," she said.

"I'll give you an exclusive as soon as I get back to L.A."

"Charlie, you're not blowing smoke up my ass, are you?"

"Sara, would I blow smoke up your ass?"

"Let's not get into that. Is he still being held?"

"As far as I know. I haven't read the paper this morning."

"Charlie, come on . . ."

"The Macedonians are not negotiating with me."

"Sure . . . so what script are you trying to get to Jacqueline Fortier behind her agent's back?"

"Sara, I promise that as soon as I get back, I'll take you to lunch. Okay?"

"Can you get a table at Spago?"

"Why not?"

Sara reached into her pocketbook, took out the key to the lower desk drawer, where she kept her classified Rolodex. She had addresses and phone numbers in there that people would kill for.

"You know, Charlie, she's living with that Russian gymnast."

"Yeah, I know."

"If I were you, I'd find a part for him. . . ."

Enid Schonblum drove her Honda Civic north on Benedict Canyon through the late-morning haze. Beside her on the front seat were two copies of *Bill and Ben*, one in an envelope addressed to Jacqueline Fortier, the other in an envelope addressed to Nikolai Fenderakov. There was a note attached to the first envelope that said

> Jacqueline, sweet: Do have a fast read of the enclosed. It's rather interesting. And you would be the best Victoria I could think of, bar none. It's high time you gave Meryl a run for her money. Wouldn't it be fun working together at last? And with Milos no less? I'm taking the liberty of sending along another copy for Nikolai. He'd be perfect as Bismarck. Don't you think? Hurry and say yes, and call the producer, Charlie Berns, at the Hotel Balkanska in Belgrade. Do say yes, my dear. It'll be splendid.
>
> Kisses, Jeremy

Enid had received a phone call that morning from her boss in Yugoslavia and been asked to run off two copies of the original script and deliver them in separate envelopes to an address in Benedict Canyon. Then he had asked her to write the note in her most masculine longhand and attach it to one of the envelopes.

"Excuse me. Mr. Berns?"

"Just try to write like a man."

"I'm not sure. I know. How to do it."

"Sure you can, Enid. Just don't make too many loops."

"I'll try. Mr. Berns."

"I appreciate it."

"Would you like. Your phone calls?"

"Uh, not at the moment."

"Your office is ready. For you."

"That's great."

"The carpet. Was installed. Last week. I hope. You like it."

"I'm sure I will. Could you get those scripts delivered as soon as possible?"

Charlie Berns was the most peculiar boss she'd ever worked for. He got a hundred phone calls every day, which, as far as she knew, he didn't return. They kept calling back. Some of them were even abusive with her, accusing her of not giving him the message. He had no home phone. She didn't even know where he lived. He was in Yugoslavia at the moment producing a picture whose star had been kidnapped. And now he wanted her to forge a letter.

It was all none of her business, in any event. She had finished the office renovation on schedule, which had been her major concern. The carpet had turned out to work wonderfully with the furniture and the paintings. The only thing she was not a hundred percent thrilled with was the Regency umbrella stand she had put beside the door to give some visual relief to the empty wall. She suspected that it was in fact a bit precious since people rarely carried umbrellas in Los Angeles.

She pulled the Honda over at the mailbox, whose number was written on the envelopes. She got out and put both envelopes in the box, the one with the note on top, as she had been instructed.

Riding back down toward Sunset she decided that, yes, her instincts were right about the umbrella stand. It didn't work at all. Something else would be better. There was a small English country secretary she had seen that might work better in that spot.

*   *   *

Charlie found Tabor Gubca closing down the production office, putting things in boxes, getting ready to move out. Sitting on the desk, with his *niska drina* expiring beside him in an ashtray, Marka Mladosi was looking through some sketches of swimming-pool fountains that he was preparing to show Tricia Jacobi before she left for Los Angeles.

"Where're you going?" Charlie said.

"To Dubrovnik, lie on beach. It's a wrap, Charlie, no?"

Charlie sat down in the production manager's desk chair. He began, "Gubca, how many dinars do we have left?"

"Ballstadium figure?"

"Yeah."

"Forty-five billion."

"How much is that in dollars?"

"Four and a half million . . . give take hundred grand."

Now came the important question. The pot for the stone soup. He chose his words very carefully. "Gubca, I have to ask you a very delicate question, okay?"

"Shoot, Charlie."

"The dinars. Where are they?"

"What you mean?"

"I mean, where *exactly* are they?"

"In the bank."

"Where's the bank?"

"On Terazije Square . . ."

"What's the name of the bank?"

"Banka Jugoslavija."

"Gubca, who knows about this account besides you and me?"

Gubca and Marka exchanged a look, growing a little concerned with the drift of the conversation. "Charlie, you're not talking pulling job here, no? Bonnie and Clyde?"

"Who has the authority to make withdrawals on that account?"

"You do, Charlie. Producer."

"Anybody else?"

"I can write check up to hundred thousand dinars. Otherwise you countersign. That's deal, no?"

Charlie turned to Marka Mladosi and asked, "Marka, can you find me the English House of Commons a hundred years ago?"

"In Belgrade?"

"Anywhere in Yugoslavia."

"You got photograph?"

"I can get you one."

"Does it have chandeliers?"

"I don't think so."

"Tapestries? Mirrors?"

"I think we're talking mostly wood here."

"Wood? Piece cake, Charlie."

Gubca and Marka exchanged a few rapid-fire sentences in Serbian before Gubca said, "Zagreb. You find anything old in Zagreb. What's going on, Charlie?"

Charlie got up from Gubca's chair, walked to the door, turned around and said, "Listen, guys, I wouldn't wrap the production office just yet, okay?"

"No fooling, Charlie?"

"No fooling, Gubca. See how many of the crew will stay on for the same deal. Say four weeks prep, eight weeks principal photography. Marka, go to the library and get every book you can about nineteenth-century English history and a man named Benjamin Disraeli."

"Who?"

"Disraeli."

"He's Italian, Charlie?"

"No, he's Jewish . . ."

Sidney Auger was getting pissed off. Since Friday he had been leaving telephone messages for Charlie Berns, both at the production office and the hotel, and he had not yet heard back from the producer. True, Sidney was only the *acting* head of the studio, but he was nonetheless the person to whom Charlie Berns reported.

There was still no hard news on the succession at the studio. Rumors were flying all over town about who was going to replace Howard Draper, but the Japanese continued to keep a low profile. None of these rumors, of course, mentioned Sidney Auger. He was just the nuts-and-bolts guy, the schmuck sitting there with his finger in the dike, riding out the storm.

Sidney had officially closed down *Decker* as of the last day of principal photography. The dollar deals on Bobby Mason, Charlie Berns and Tricia Jacobi were suspended in accordance with the force-majeure clauses in their contracts. The dinar deals in Belgrade now had to be closed down as the production was progressively wrapped. That was to be the subject of the conversation between Sidney Auger and Charlie Berns, should it ever take place.

Sidney barked at his secretary, "Get me Charlie Berns's agent on the phone."

Brad Emprin was dropping a Gelusil when Tanya told him that Sidney Auger was calling.

"Who?" Brad asked.

Tanya double-checked the name, repeated it. Brad Emprin gave her the who-the-fuck's-that shrug and said, "Ask what it's about."

"May I ask what this is regarding?" Tanya said sweetly into the phone to Sidney Auger's secretary.

Sidney Auger's secretary put her on hold, buzzed back to Sidney that Brad Emprin's girl wanted to know what this was regarding. Sidney darkened a shade, muttered, "Fuck him . . ." Then he told his girl to tell Brad Emprin's girl that it was regarding Charlie Berns.

"It's regarding Charlie Berns," Tanya called to Brad Emprin, who was chasing the Gelusil with a Perrier.

"Tell him he's not available. He's making a movie in Yugoslavia."

Tanya gave the message to Sidney Auger's girl, who repeated it to Sidney, who grabbed the phone and yelled, "You're damn fucking right he is! He's making a picture for *me!*"

Tanya told Brad Emprin that they apparently had the head of the studio for whom Charlie Berns was making the picture in Yugoslavia on the phone. Brad Emprin lunged for the phone and said quickly, "Sid, I'm really sorry. New girl."

"Where the hell's your client?"

"What's wrong?"

"He's not returning my phone calls."

"Well, gee, he must be out on location. . . ."

"The whole production's on a soundstage, and it's shut down. In case nobody told you."

"Right . . ."

"I've been leaving messages for him for days now, and he hasn't returned any of them."

"Yeah, well, gee, Sid, he must be kind of busy. . . ."

"How can he be busy? We're down. . . . Listen, you get ahold of him somehow and tell him to call me."

"You got it."

"Immediately."

"Sounds good to me." Then a fleeting thought flashed across Brad Emprin's brain. He had another client on that picture in Yugoslavia. . . .

"Listen, Sid, how's Tricia working out?"

"Who?"

"Tricia Jacobi, the girl I put in your picture."

"She's history."

"Huh?"

"Force majeure. Read your contract." And he hung up.

Brad Emprin sat for a moment, his eardrum vibrating from Sidney Auger's growling. Force majeure. Probably some boiler-plate shit in Tricia's deal that he neglected to read. . . . Then, suddenly, the two wires crossed in his mind. *That* picture. The one where Bobby Mason got kidnapped. . . . *That* was the picture he had put Charlie Berns and Tricia Jacobi on.

Boy, talk about your bad breaks. You get a kidnapping and

two bookings go south. Next time someone offered a client a job in one of those Third World countries, he'd pass. Who needed the aggravation?

He picked up the phone and dialed the extension of the agency's legal counsel.

"Walter? It's Brad Emprin. . . . What the fuck is force majeure?"

The bar at the Balkanska resembled a fin-de-siècle high school gymnasium. It was large, overlit, with imitation crystal chandeliers and had a raised stage on one end from which a jazz trio played renditions of old Dave Brubeck standards in Slavic tempos. Velvet bunting hung from the walls in a pathetic attempt to shrink the room and give it a semblance of intimacy. Charlie sat with Dinak and Wilna in a corner drinking what passed for mai tais this side of the Danube.

He was telling them about *Bill and Ben,* Jeremy Ikon, Disraeli. Dinak listened without much enthusiasm. It didn't sound like his type of picture. It sounded like a bunch of actors standing around and jerking off. Talk, talk, talk.

In an effort to interest the director, Charlie related the early sequence where the young Disraeli goes whoring with the British garrison in Malta, depicting a cavalry charge with sabers and muskets that wasn't actually in the script. Dinak's interest perked slightly as Charlie described a low-angle shot capturing the dust and noise of the hooves as they stormed past the camera. But he remained by and large skeptical.

"I don't know, Charlie. It don't sound like my thing. Debates in House of Commons?"

"They're just like battle scenes, except with words instead of bullets. You can do all sorts of interesting dolly shots. What if I gave you two cranes? You can shoot A and B cameras from them."

"Charlie, I don't want to talk to no fucking actors."

"Don't worry about that, Dinak. I'll handle the actors."

"You know what I mean? 'Here's your mark. Action. Cut.' That's it."

"I promise."

"Charlie, I think about it, okay?"

"Okay."

The band went into an approximation of "Take the A Train." Dinak ordered another round of mai tais. Wilna lit another small black cigarette. The concierge came into the bar with a silver tray and delivered some telephone messages. Charlie tipped him two thousand dinars and excused himself.

There was a message to call Jeremy Ikon in Rome, as well as messages from Deidre Hearn, Brad Emprin and Sidney Auger in Los Angeles. He took the stairs up to his room, too impatient to wait for the rickety elevator.

With trepidation he dialed the Pensione Frescobaldi on the via Margutta, asked to be connected to Signor Ikon's room. He tapped his foot nervously on the carpet as he waited for the actor to pick up. It rang several times. No answer. Charlie began to despair. Six, seven, eight times . . . until finally on the tenth ring he heard the actor's phlegmatic baritone.

*"Pronto?"*

"Jeremy? It's Charlie Berns."

"Sorry. I was in the loo. . . . Good of you to ring back."

"Well," Charlie said, apprehension in his voice, "can I call you Ben?"

It seemed to be minutes before Jeremy replied, without greet enthusiasm, "I suppose so."

"Terrific."

"The script needs a bit of a brushing up, of course."

"Lionel'll be more than happy to work with you on any rewrites."

"The whorehouse scene in Malta is a bit much, don't you think?"

"We can always lose it. . . ."

"What about Jacqueline? Is she set?"

"Just about."

"Splendid. Listen, I had rather an interesting idea for Bill."

"What's that?"

"He's not actually the type of actor you would think of in a serious role. He's a bit of a scenery chewer. But, you know, Gladstone was a real windbag. He chewed the scenery to death in the House. . . . I don't even know if he's available actually, but it may be interesting to take a shot at Nigel Bland."

"Nigel Bland?"

"Yes. I know it's a rather odd choice, but I've always thought of him somehow as William Gladstone."

"It's very . . . interesting casting."

"See what Milos thinks."

# 14

Against the advice of her agents, Jacqueline Fortier accepted the role of Victoria Regina in *Ben and Bill*, as the title of the picture now read. It was the only demand that Jeremy Ikon had made in agreeing to play Disraeli, pointing out that the picture was in reality *about* Benjamin Disraeli. William Gladstone, he maintained, was merely an antagonist and not a protagonist. Calling the picture *Bill and Ben* would be like calling *Jules and Jim, Jim and Jules*.

Charlie had the title page of the script retyped. Nigel Bland, as the saying goes, "was already in makeup." He had become fond of Yugoslavia, particularly of the bar at the Balkanska, where he had taught the bartender to mix a drinkable brandy and soda. Besides being thrilled with the opportunity of working with actors of the caliber of Jeremy Ikon and Jacqueline Fortier, he was relieved that there were no love scenes for him to play in this script. He would be spared rolling around on a bed with a nubile American starlet in a body stocking.

Charlie and Lionel double-teamed Dinak, getting him to look at the picture as a technical challenge—creating motion with the camera while the actors remained static. They promised him that he didn't have to worry about the talk. If he took care of the photography, they would take care of the talk. Just pretend, Charlie suggested, you're shooting a silent movie.

Gubca and Marka Mladosi were dispatched to Zagreb to find locations and begin work on the House of Commons. The art director had shown Charlie a photo of the Croatian Guild Hall, a large wooden auditorium that would work for the House of Commons a hundred years ago. By the time Marka Mladosi finished altering and redressing the space, you wouldn't be able to tell the difference, he promised. "You think you hear goddamn 'God Save the Queen,' Charlie."

Charlie even came up with a small role for Tricia Jacobi. She had come to him and asked him if it were true that he was doing another picture in Yugoslavia. Her bags were packed but she really didn't want to go back home just yet.

"It's kind of embarrassing, you know. I told *everybody* that I was starring in this picture."

"It was just bad luck, Tricia."

"Why did Bobby Mason have to go get kidnapped anyway?"

"Politics . . ."

"This was going to be my big break."

"There'll be plenty more."

"Is it true that Jeremy Ikon and Jacqueline Fortier are going to star?"

Charlie nodded.

"Imagine working with them. And Milos. You know what I'd give to work with Milos?"

She stood there in his hotel room, in a halter top and salmon-colored shorts, her eyes growing moist. Charlie made himself look busy hoping she would leave. But Tricia Jacobi wasn't leaving. She had a scene to play, which she had apparently prepared but was having trouble getting into. She kept looking at him, then down at the floor, as if checking her mark and waiting for the director to call *action*.

"Look, I really don't know how to do this," she blurted out finally.

"Do what?"

"I want to be in the picture. You're the producer. . . ."

"Yeah . . ."

"So . . . I'm suppose to fuck you, right?"

"Huh?"

She reached behind her back to unsnap her halter top.

"What . . . are you doing?"

"If you want me to go down on you it's all right. . . ."

She slipped out of her shorts and stood there naked in front of him, teetering slightly on her three-inch heels. It was a mythic moment. In all his years as a producer it had never happened to Charlie. And now, in a hotel room in Belgrade, a starlet was actually volunteering to go down on him. He didn't know whether to laugh or cry. So he offered her a part in the picture.

If she was willing to work for dinars and accept a small role, she could stay on. She ran up to him and hugged him.

"Please put your clothes back on, Tricia."

As she slipped back into her shorts and halter, she babbled, "I am *so* excited. You can't imagine. . . ."

"Look, do me a favor, okay?"

"Anything."

"Don't tell your agent anything about this. This is going to be a Yugoslavian deal, strictly dinars."

"Charlie, I'd pay *you* to be in this movie."

She blew him a kiss and made her exit. He listened to her heels clack down the hallway. Charlie lay down on his bed and closed his eyes. The clattering hooves of the British garrison on Malta came to mind. They would need to be serviced by lusty Maltese whores, wouldn't they?

Kiss me, I'm Maltese.

The story made banner headlines in both *Variety* and *The Reporter*. Norman Hudris was actually sleeping at seven-thirty in the morning when the phone rang. Now that he was no longer a vice president of production, West Coast, he didn't have to get into the office at the crack of dawn. Standards and Practices in Burbank was strictly a ten-to-five job.

"Yeah?" Norman said testily into the phone.

"Did you see the trades?"

It was Cissy Fuchs. They had started talking to each other again on the phone. It was an experiment in limited exposure to determine whether or not they should start seeing each other again. Both their therapists agreed that it was better not to rush into anything.

"No. What?" He sprang immediately awake, fearing the worst.

"They hired Andre Blue."

"Who? For what?"

"The Japanese. For Howard's job."

"No shit . . ."

"He said that he has confidence in the old team. . . ."

"What old team? *I'm* the old team. And I'm not there any-more."

"Maybe he didn't hear about NBC."

"It was announced last week. Front page. There was a fucking picture of me. How could he not hear? Does it say anything about Howard?"

"It says that he's exploring various production offers."

"Right."

"Maybe he has something for you."

"Howard? Are you kidding? He was ready to let me go before the Japs took over. . . . Maybe I should call Andre. What do you think?"

"Why not?"

"He's going to need a production vice president, isn't he?"

"Uh-huh . . ."

"I mean, he *knows* I'm at NBC. So *he* should call *me,* right? I should be the first person he calls, shouldn't I?"

"Sure . . ."

"We go back to the Morris office together. What time is it?"

"Seven-thirty."

"Listen, I've got to get off the phone. Talk to you later."

He hung up and got out of bed, his pulse rate already accelerating. In the bathroom he peed, threw water on his face, flossed meticulously. During his last dental visit the words *irrevocable tissue damage* had been mentioned. He didn't even want to *think* about that.

Still in his underwear, he went back out into the bedroom and mounted the Exercycle. He began to pedal furiously, his mind racing to keep up with his heartbeat. First of all, how would NBC take it? He had just signed a contract with them. It was a bullshit job, sure, but *they* didn't think so. He would talk personally to Brandon. Explain the situation about Howard and the Japs . . .

His main concern, however, was how it would look. Here he resigns a job to "explore other creative avenues," and then a few weeks later he returns to the same job. It was really fairly tacky. He could say that he had always wanted to work with Andre Blue, that this was a rare opportunity for him. Maybe that would fly. . . .

As he passed one mile and headed for two, he checked heartbeat and calories expended on the Exercycle's LED readout. So far, so good. His cardiovascular indicators were looking better. Later that morning, he'd put through a call, congratulate him, suggest lunch that week. They'd go to La Spezia for veal florentine. Norman would pick up the check.

One of the members of the creative team in whom Andre Blue reportedly had confidence, the director of creative affairs, did not hear the news about Howard Draper's replacement immediately. She was on the Air France night flight to Paris, uncomfortably wedged into a seat in the economy section of the airplane, surrounded by Basque Boy Scouts returning from a trip to Disneyland. They had been singing Basque Boy Scout songs nearly nonstop since the plane had taken off, and Deidre Hearn had a bad headache.

She checked her watch. Only nine and a half more hours to

Paris, from where she was to connect to Belgrade. She tried to make some headway with the pile of scripts she had brought with her for the plane but was unable to read more than a few pages without glazing over. It was the usual collection of junk. Moreover, she had no idea why she was even bothering to read scripts since the studio was on hold until the new regime took over anyway.

In the meanwhile Sidney had sent her on the mission of finding Charlie Berns and closing down the production. She was going all the way to Belgrade to exercise the authority of the studio to pull the plug. Every penny counted these days. Even dinars.

Charlie Berns wasn't returning anybody's calls from Los Angeles. Sidney was livid. He couldn't believe it. How could a producer simply drop out of sight? Sidney had tried to get through to the Yugoslavian distributor who supposedly controlled the blocked dinars but was told he was on vacation. The situation had rapidly developed into a mania. He screamed into the phone at the desk clerks at the Hotel Balkanska, who kept swearing they were delivering his messages. He even threatened Charlie's agent, Brad Emprin, with a lawsuit.

And now he had sent a posse out after Charlie Berns. Frankly, Deidre wasn't sure she wanted to find him. The night before she left for Belgrade she had an intense session with Ellen. They had gotten into some heavy stuff.

"Look, Deidre," Ellen had said, "You're almost forty. You're a big girl. It's time you started walking past cliffs without leaping."

Deidre took exception to the image. "Don't you find that a bit dramatic, Ellen?"

"Okay, we'll call it a hill, not a cliff, if you prefer. The thing is, Deidre, one way or the other, you're going to wind up at the bottom in a heap. That's your pattern."

"So what do I do? Keep chugging along on the tracks like the Little Engine That Could?"

"Being facetious isn't going to solve anything."

"I can't help it. I'm living the myth of Sisyphus. In living color."

Ellen looked up from her knitting with a tired sigh.

"No, I mean it. Do you realize that I spend my days in an office reading dreadful scripts with no one to report to at this studio that nobody knows who's running? And tomorrow I'm being sent to Belgrade to find this guy and shut down the production. I feel like Martin Sheen being sent up the Mekong River to bring back Brando, for chrissakes. It's ridiculous. . . ."

"Do you know what I'm hearing?"

"What?"

"This guy apparently isn't just . . . *this guy* to you."

Ellen rocked back and forth gently for a moment before saying, quietly, "Remember the work we did on your relationship with your father?"

"I don't want to talk about *him* anymore."

"I don't see how we can avoid it. . . ."

It had gone downhill from there. Deidre walked out of Ellen's house carrying the weight of her entire childhood on her back. She slept badly that night, buffeted by fragments of unsettling dreams from long ago. The cold, withholding son of a bitch who had so affected her ability to relate to men danced through her psyche with a top hat and cane. It was the goddamn Freudian Follies.

She woke up with a migraine, got into the studio late, spent most of the day listening to Sidney Auger hyperventilate about Charlie Berns, before running home to pack and catch the 10:00 P.M. flight for Paris. And now here she was, sitting Sisyphus-like among the Boy Scouts, somewhere over the North Pole, unaware that a deal had been cut late that day to bring a man in to run the studio who was even more cold and withholding than her father. Andre Blue would make T. William Hearn look like Dick Van Dyke.

The crew had already left for Zagreb. Only Charlie, Lionel, Tricia Jacobi and Nigel Bland remained in the Balkanska, pending new hotel arrangements in the capital of Croatia, 392 kilometers to the

northwest. Tomorrow morning they would all fly up to Zagreb
and check into Le Grand Hotel on the Ulica Strossmayerov.

The sooner they got out of town the better. Charlie knew what
Sidney Auger's phone calls were about. He was out of dollars
except for his American Express card that Sidney would cut off
sooner or later. Fortunately, Jacqueline Fortier had been on her
way to London when she accepted the role, and so Charlie was
able to book both her and Jeremy on JAT with the dinar account.

By tomorrow morning, after a stop at the bank, there should
be no trace of them at all in Belgrade. They would become the
phantom production company. He had forty-five billion dinars,
actors and a script. Now all he needed was eight weeks to shoot
the picture. If he could just get to Zagreb and burn his last bridge
behind him, maybe, just maybe, he would be able to pull this off.

And if he didn't, what's the worst they could do to him? Send
him back to Indy Prod? He'd been there before. And sooner or
later he'd be there again. For a brief moment Charlie had the can
opener in his possession. He wasn't ready to give it back just yet.

It was late, after ten, and Charlie had just finished packing
when there was a knock on his door. It was undoubtedly a
brandy-soaked Nigel Bland with yet another question about
William Gladstone's character. Nigel spent hours with Lionel
talking about Whigs, Tories and the Corn Laws. Charlie considered not answering, pretending he was asleep, but thought better of it. He didn't want a drunk Nigel Bland wandering aimlessly around the hotel at this hour.

He went over to the door, opened it and saw Deidre Hearn
standing there with a Vuitton shoulder bag full of scripts.

He looked at her, sighed, shook his head. They had caught him
only a few miles from the border. Twelve hours later, and they'd
never have found him. He tried to keep his tone neutral, as if he
weren't, in fact, facing a deputy sheriff with a warrant in her
pocket.

"Hi," he said, as casually as possible. "What a surprise."

"Hello, Charlie."

"Is that a gun in your pocket, ma'am, or are you just glad to see me?"

"Can I come in please? I've been flying for days."

He moved aside and let her enter, watched as she sat down on the brocade chair in the corner, pulled her short leather skirt down her thighs and rubbed her temples. "Jesus, do I have a headache. You ever fly with a troop of Basque Boy Scouts?"

Charlie sat down on the edge of the bed, for lack of anyplace else to sit down.

"To what do I owe this pleasure?"

"I think you know, Charlie."

"So is this it? Are you taking me in?"

"Can I have a drink? Something fairly strong."

"I'll do my best. Room service is a little spotty in this place. . . ." He dialed the phone and waited as it rang interminably. For a moment they just stared at each other—Charlie, his ear to the phone waiting for the hall porter to pick up, Deidre continuing to rub her temples. Finally, she shook her head, sighed and said, "Charlie, what the fuck are you trying to pull off?"

Before he could answer—as if he *had* an answer—the hall porter picked up. Charlie asked for a bottle of *sljivovica*. It might be his only chance. Knock her out, slip away under the cover of night . . .

"I mean, you can't just pretend that there's no studio back in Los Angeles. You can't ignore Sidney Auger. He's running the place. What is it you're trying to do anyway? You're down. You have no star. You have no movie. Face it."

"Right . . ."

"We need the negative. For the insurance. You know that. . . ."

He nodded, then, "Have you seen the Danube yet? Do you realize that it's the same river that runs through Vienna?"

"Charlie, please . . ." She looked at him harshly. He avoided her eyes for a moment, was rescued by the hall porter's knock on the door. Room service had never been so prompt. He accepted the bottle of *sljivovica*, said *hvala*, the only word of Serbian he had learned, and gave the man a couple of ten-thousand-dinar bills. Then he went into the bathroom, got a couple of glasses, poured two stiff shots, handed one to Deidre.

"This ought to do something for your headache."

She took a sip, did her best not to react to the explosion of fire inside her throat, and coughed.

"It's made with prunes. Keeps you regular as well. . . ."

She put the glass down, ran her fingers through her hair, then said, "Charlie, do you ever take the tap shoes off? Ever since the first day I met you, when you came into my office with this cocka-mamie script, you've been tap-dancing. Don't you think it's time to level? How about it? For once, how about giving me the *emmis?*"

"I thought you were Catholic."

"It's the trading language of Hollywood, Charlie. Even a nice Catholic girl like me knows what the *emmis* means."

He looked at her, this exhausted woman sitting in his room drinking prune liqueur, jet-lagged to the teeth, her skirt riding unconsciously up her thighs. She had come halfway around the world to ask him for the *emmis*. All things considered, it wasn't an unreasonable request. And yet . . .

Where should he start? Should he start with giving up the ghost and the decision to pull the plug on his own movie, the hose and the doggie door? Was that the question she wanted answered?

There was in this woman something kindred he had sensed from the beginning. He suspected that underneath the Vuitton and the leather skirt was a soul as bemused as his. She had been sent here on a fool's errand and knew it. He gave her credit for understanding the absurdity of the situation, for at least not expecting him to salute.

She was right. After all this tap-dancing, he owed her a quick trip through the *emmis*. It was time he took the tap shoes off, and if he was going to do it for anyone, it would be for Deidre Hearn.

It came out very easily, the whole business. In a series of simple, declarative statements, he laid out the complete scenario for her.

"Deidre, I'm shooting the first script. The one about Benjamin Disraeli and protective tariffs. I'm shooting it in Zagreb. With the blocked dinars. Starring Jeremy Ikon and Jacqueline Fortier. Tomorrow we're clearing out of Belgrade with the money and intend to stay incognito until it's in the can. That's it. The whole *emmis.*"

She took a long hit of *sljivovica* without coughing, merely blinked several times and nodded, as if what he just confessed was entirely accepted behavior. With difficulty, she got up and asked, "Where's the bathroom?"

He pointed to the door in the other part of the suite and watched as she teetered off unsteadily toward the bathroom, dragging the Vuitton shoulder bag. The door closed behind her. He heard the sink water running. She seemed to be in there forever. When she finally emerged, she had retied her hair back and touched up her makeup.

"Can we go out and get something to eat, Charlie? I'm starved."

They sat beside the Danube, at the same restaurant where they had held the wrap party, eating *pljeskavica* and drinking Algerian Burgundy. A band played Strauss waltzes with Serbian passion. Gypsy girls kept coming up to the table and offering single red roses for a thousand dinars. Charlie bought them all.

The night was sultry, cooled by the breeze coming off the river. Deidre ate little, drank a lot, her eyes continually wandering off across the Danube, where somewhere upriver Herr Doktor Freud was undoubtedly shaking his cold, withholding, bony finger at her.

But how often do you find yourself beside the Danube at midnight with a pile of red roses beside you? She gave herself up to the surrealism of the moment. Between the sultry air, the wine and the jet lag, she was no longer exactly sure what time zone she was in. She tried to think what time it was in Los Angeles and whether she shouldn't call Sidney Auger, but it seemed to be an impossible task at the moment.

And so she drifted, listened as Charlie recounted his epiphany about the blocked dinars, his getting to Jeremy Ikon in Rome, Jacqueline Fortier in Benedict Canyon. The details were less interesting to her than the conception. There was something definitely heretical about this man. In the Middle Ages they would have burned him at the stake.

Yes, there was something *dangerous* about Charlie Berns. He didn't fit in Hollywood. He didn't salute the flag. He didn't lunch at the Polo Lounge or return phone calls. And he was about to abscond with the studio's money and make a picture on the lam. It was the most incredible thing she had ever heard, and he sat there talking about it as if it were perfectly normal.

At the moment, however, the ethics of the situation were beyond her. She didn't care. She was getting slowly, pleasantly blitzed on the Burgundy, drifting into dangerous waters. She closed her eyes and saw Ellen sitting in the rocking chair shaking her head with disapproval. Deidre opened them again and saw this madman sitting across the table from her talking to her calmly about his picture.

"I've still got to figure out how to break the news to them that Milos has dropped out. . . ." Charlie was saying. "Dinak doesn't talk to actors. . . ."

"Charlie, do you know how to do the waltz?"

"Huh?"

"You want to dance?"

"Here?"

"We're sitting by the Danube. They're playing 'Tales from the Vienna Woods.' How often in your life is that going to happen?"

Charlie got up and led her to the empty dance floor. They started off slowly, then picked up pace as they accommodated themselves to the slightly less-than-three-quarter tempo. Charlie danced more gracefully than Deidre would have expected from looking at him. There was a lightness to his step that surprised her.

She leaned back in his arms and felt the room begin to turn on her. Light spun precariously off the surface of the chandelier. The air was pregnant with roses. The band played on. . . .

She woke at 5:00 A.M., wide awake and still drunk. Charlie snored away gently beside her in the big soft bed in Room 261 at the Hotel Balkanska. For a moment she had no idea where she was and who this man was beside her. Then it came back to her in a flood—the *sljivovica*, the roses, "Tales from the Vienna Woods. . . ."

Her first instinct was to get dressed and run to a phone booth, call Sidney and tell him to send reinforcements. Maybe there was still time to take him alive, before she was entirely compromised. But as she looked over at this strange, mad and tender man, she knew instinctively that she wasn't going to be the one to take him in. They had sent the wrong person after Charlie Berns.

She got out of bed, gingerly so as not to wake him, found his bathrobe on the floor. She sat by the window, looking down at the Ulica Maršala Tita, just beginning to brighten with the first light of day. She shivered in the early-morning chill, pulled the robe more tightly around her, smelled the now-familiar odor of his body. It had been such a long time since she had breathed the odor of a man. Her insides were jumbled up with hot and cold flashes and that vaguely familiar sense of having been connected to another body. She felt disoriented and serene at the same time. And hungry. Making love always made her ravenous.

She sat there watching the dawn fill up the street, devouring the cocktail peanuts that showed up with the *sljivovica*. In the next few hours she would have to decide what to do. By the time he woke she wanted to have it sorted out. She was already beyond the simple morality of the situation—as if there were a simple morality or, for that matter, a morality of any kind in the picture business.

The studio's dinars were of little concern to her, nor was Sidney Auger's opinion of her. What she had to decide was whether she was ready to turn in her teacup. Was it time to get up and excuse herself from the Mad Hatter's tea party? Bye-bye. Thank you very much.

Charlie Berns might be even madder than the Mad Hatter, but Charlie's madness was inspired. She had no idea whether he was going to be able to pull it off, but in a sense it didn't matter. Running away to Zagreb to film the life of Benjamin Disraeli with blocked dinars! It wasn't Sisyphus. It was Prometheus.

Outside, the Tito Mausoleum turned from gray to orange. It was a light that was very different from the flat light of California. It was a light with texture, with contours and depth. There were secrets to be explored in those depths and contours. There were voyages to take.

It got warmer as the sun illuminated the facade of the Hotel Balkanska. She was still sitting in the chair by the window when Charlie awoke at seven. They looked at each other with the shyness of people who are not used to waking up in the presence of someone else.

They hardly spoke. He ordered breakfast—a large tray of rolls with butter and jam and coffee. It was the best coffee she'd ever tasted. She kept his bathrobe. He sat in his underwear.

When they had finished, he looked at her and said, "Well?"

This time she was the one sitting with the *emmis* in her court. She got up, walked back over to the window, stalling for a moment. She had made the decision before he woke, but she didn't want him necessarily to know that.

She looked at him, sitting in his jockey shorts, a thin ring of middle-age pot belly emerging from the elastic band, unshaven, his hair falling every which way. . . . Prometheus at breakfast.

"What's available on the picture?" she asked.

"How about associate producer?"

"Front titles, separate card?"

"Deal."

"Money?"

"Couple hundred thousand dinars."

They walked into the Jugoslavija Banka on Terazije Square at ten in the morning with two large empty suitcases. Charlie was wearing a *Decker* T-shirt, nondescript gray pants, a CALIFORNIA ANGELS baseball cap and sneakers. He walked over to a teller's window, took a crumpled checkbook from his back pocket, asked for a pen and wrote out a check for forty-five billion dinars.

The bank clerk, a fat woman with too much eye makeup, stared at the check for a long moment, counting and recounting the zeroes. She looked back and forth between Charlie and the check several times, trying to find some association between them.

"Identification, please," she articulated with some difficulty.

Charlie handed his passport to her. Without even looking at it, she turned and walked to the rear of the bank, gave the check and the passport to a man sitting at a cluttered desk. She showed him the check and the passport, nodded her head in Charlie and Deidre's direction. He, too, looked back and forth between the check and Charlie, opened the passport, studied it for a moment, then picked up the phone, dialed a number.

"What are they doing?" Deidre asked.

"Probably finding out if I'm wanted for bad paper."

"Are you?"

"Not yet."

Deidre had noticed the video cameras when they walked in. She should have waited outside in the getaway car. Visions of *Midnight Express* flashed through her mind as the man at the desk in the rear had a long conversation with whomever it was he was talking to.

Finally, he hung up and walked back over to the window, the teller at his side, carrying the check and the passport. He put them back down in front of him and said, "Mr. Berns, you are closing the account?"

Charlie nodded.

"We will need some verification."

"Verification of what?"

"Verification of your authority to close the account."

"There are two authorized signatures on this account. Mine and Tabor Gubca's."

"I see."

"Why don't you pull the signature cards and verify?"

The man said a few words in Serbian, and the teller hurried off to find the signature cards.

"This is a very large withdrawal," the man said, without irony.

"Yes, it is," Charlie responded, with equal gravity.

"Extremely large."

"Extremely."

"You were unhappy with our service?"

"Not at all."

"You understand that we must verify such a large withdrawal."

"Sure."

Having run out of small talk, they stood there avoiding each other's look until the teller returned with the account file. There was the signature card that Charlie had signed when they opened the account to fund the picture. His signature was right above Tabor Gubca's.

The man looked back and forth between the card, the check and the passport, finally nodding resignedly and closing the file. He turned on a computer terminal, typed in the account number, copied on a piece of paper the figure that appeared on the screen, handed it to Charlie: 45,015,779,394 dinars. They were even better off than Tabor had estimated.

"You would like to leave the rest of the money in the bank?"

"No. I want to close the account."

"You are leaving Belgrade?"

"Yes."

"Perhaps we can wire the money to another bank."

"No thanks . . ."

"You understand that it is a great deal of currency, forty-five billion dinars?"

"Yes."

"I will have to telephone to other banks."

"Could you get right on it? I have a plane to catch."

He nodded again and said, almost as a statement of fact, "Movie producer?"

"Right."

Of course. That explained everything. They walked out of the bank an hour and a half later, the two suitcases stuffed with dinars. The driver had to keep his foot on the floor to get them to Surčin Airport to make the flight to Zagreb.

It was too late to check their luggage. Just as well. He wasn't going to put the entire budget of his picture in the belly of a JAT DC3. Charlie had to argue with the stewardess to keep the suitcases, which were too big to go under the seat, in their laps. He wound up promising her an audition for a role in the picture. One Maltese whore more or less wouldn't matter.

He looked over at his new associate producer trying to get comfortable beneath the suitcase in her lap and pushing the hair out of her eyes, a nervous gesture that he already had begun to get used to. They exchanged shy smiles. Across the aisle sat Nigel Bland and Tricia Jacobi. There had barely been time for introductions at the airport. Nigel waved and raised his book of Gladstone's parliamentary speeches, as if toasting their departure for Zagreb. Tricia was reading *The History of Malta* to get into character for her role as camp follower to the 357th Hussars stationed at Valletta.

The plane lifted off the ground and gained altitude, climbing above the monotone northern suburbs of the city. *Arrivederci*, Belgrade. The last bridge was in flames behind him.

# 15

Andre Blue returned Norman Hudris's call three days after the vice president of NBC Standards and Practices, West Coast, had called him. And when he did, he had his secretary put the call through at 1:30 P.M., while Norman was out of the office. A "lunch shot," as this technique was sometimes referred to, was only one step above an unreturned phone call and indicated to the callee that you had little desire to speak to him.

Now that he was at the helm of a major studio, Andre Blue had decided to put some distance between himself and certain old acquaintances. He had made a quantum leap into a new caste, and he would have to be very careful about his contacts with the old one. Besides, he didn't have time to listen to Norman Hudris beg circuitously for his old job back. He was up to his ears in problems.

The Katsubishi people had told him that they didn't expect miracles, that they understood that turning the studio around would take time. But Andre knew that beneath their Zen-like placidity, his new bosses had the meter running. There were cost-control people in New York and Tokyo tapping their feet. The samurai had already begun sharpening their swords.

Besides, the deeper the ship sank, the harder it would be to raise it off the bottom. And at the moment they were sinking fast. The production pipeline was paralyzed, with nothing shooting or in preproduction, and very little of merit in development. The one hope for decent grosses had been shut down in Yugoslavia after the star was kidnapped. And to make matters worse, they were being sued for negligence by the star's manager to the tune of several hundred million.

Nothing had been heard from Bobby Mason's kidnappers for some time. In the first weeks following his abduction it had been a major news event, but the story had gradually dropped off the charts until he became just another hostage being held by some crackpot terrorist group. The picture was already shut down, amortized and written off the third-quarter balance sheet. Or so Andre Blue assumed.

That morning he received a peculiar phone call from Candace De Salvio, the vice president of casting, informing him that a deal memo had just crossed her desk for Jeremy Ikon.

"Jeremy Ikon? Are we doing a picture with Jeremy Ikon?"

"Not that I know of," replied Candace De Salvio.

"For what picture?"

"*Ben and Bill.*"

"Are we doing a picture called *Ben and Bill?*"

"Not that I know of."

"That's strange."

"You want to hear something even stranger? According to the deal memo, Jeremy Ikon is working for scale."

After he hung up with Candace De Salvio, Andre Blue summoned Sidney Auger. The former acting studio head, now once again simply vice president of business affairs, trundled into Andre's office munching on a handful of pretzels.

"Sidney," Andre Blue said, "didn't you shut down the Bobby Mason picture?"

"Weeks ago."

"Have you heard of a project called *Ben and Bill?*"

"The Bobby Mason picture used to be called *Bill and Ben*. That was before it was called *Lev Disraeli: Freedom Fighter*, which was before it was called *Decker*. As far as I know we never had a picture called *Ben and Bill*."

"Somebody put out a deal memo for Jeremy Ikon on a picture called *Ben and Bill*."

"Really?"

"For how much?"

"Three hundred sixty dollars a week."

"Scale? For Jeremy Ikon?"

"You want to look into this please. If we're doing a picture with Jeremy Ikon, I'd like to know about it."

"Okay."

Sidney Auger trundled back out of Andre Blue's office. As soon as he was in the hallway, he muttered "Holy shit" to himself. What the hell was going on? *Ben and Bill?* Jeremy Ikon working for scale? Very strange things were happening.

A week ago he had sent Deidre Hearn to Belgrade to find Charlie Berns and close out the blocked dinar account. He hadn't heard word one from her. Was *everybody* getting kidnapped? Was it some kind of fucking black hole over there?

He was, frankly, reluctant to share this information with his new boss. Things had looked bad enough at the studio when Andre Blue took over. Sidney hadn't wanted to tell him about the renegade producer and the now-missing director of creative affairs. It was fairly embarrassing for an acting studio head to confess to his successor the disappearance of an entire production, let alone the emissary sent to track it down.

Sidney Auger decided to keep a lid on this information for the moment. Sooner or later they would have to turn up. Wouldn't they?

Le Grand Hotel in Zagreb was neither very grand nor very French. It was a small, slightly run-down villa, lost on one of the back streets of the old city, with a certain incongruous charm to go with its principal virtue: It was obscure. There were no paparazzi hanging around to bother Jeremy Ikon or Jacqueline Fortier.

Charlie told his stars that he had chosen it for that reason, and they seemed to be very happy with the choice. The two of them spent their time running scenes and working on their lines with Lionel. Their dedication to the script was impressive. They had an almost Spartan discipline and singleness of purpose as they progressively began to inhabit the skin of Benjamin Disraeli and Victoria Regina. Jeremy began to drink port and limp from the gout that Disraeli was afflicted with in his later years. Jacqueline insisted on wearing a Victorian whalebone corset to get used to the feeling of being strangled at the waist.

Nikolai Fenderakov had taken to wearing a monocle and clicking his heels like Bismarck. He and Nigel Bland became drinking buddies in the small bar on the first floor of Le Grand Hotel, where Nigel would practice his parliamentary speeches to a small but appreciative audience. The hotel help soon became accustomed to this small troop of actors walking around in the skin of their nineteenth-century characters.

Meanwhile Gubca, Marka and the crew worked feverishly to get the sets ready for the start of principal photography. Besides the Croatian Guild Hall, they found locations for Disraeli's country estate in Hughenden, his club in St. James's, suitable cheats for the garrison on Malta and the hunting sequence with the Rothschilds at Gunnersbury. They redressed parts of an old château outside of town to work for Victoria's chambers in Windsor Castle and the Radziwill Palace in Berlin.

Charlie had removed one of the principal stones from the soup pot as delicately as he could. Their first night together in Zagreb he had taken Jeremy, Jacqueline and Nikolai out to dinner at the best restaurant in town. They had drunk several bottles of *Château Haut-Brion* '66, at three million dinars the bottle, before he had Lionel, who was back at the hotel, page him to the telephone as arranged.

"Why am I calling you?" Lionel said on the phone.

"To tell me that Milos has to drop out of the picture."

"Oh. Okay."

"Thanks."

He hung up, walked back to the table, practicing a somber face. But when he got there, he found Jeremy reciting Trollope to the delight of Jacqueline and Nikolai. They were laughing uproariously, at Jeremy's enunciation of one of Planty Palliser's speeches in Parliament, a role he had recently done for the BBC. They were still chuckling when Charlie sat back down at the table and announced, "I've got some bad news."

"What's that?" said Jacqueline.

"That was Milos. From Paris."

"When is he getting here?"

"Well, that's just it. He isn't."

"Isn't he?"

"He's not going to be able to fit us in. He's still in the cutting room."

There was a beat of silence while everybody drained their wineglasses. Then Jeremy said, "Well, bugger him. We shall just have to muddle through without him, won't we?"

Jacqueline and Nikolai agreed, and they went back to mimicking Trollope characters. Charlie ordered another bottle of *Château Haut-Brion* '66. Nothing more was ever said about Milos.

The job of associate producer of *Ben and Bill* turned out to be as amorphous as it was hectic. There was little time for the niceties of job and title distinctions; they were moving the tanks once again toward the Polish border with very little lead time.

Deidre Hearn found herself doing whatever had to be done that neither Charlie nor Lionel had the time to do. Sometimes this meant making location and budget decisions and sometimes this meant typing script revisions. And sometimes she acted as intermediary between Dinak and the actors. The director maintained his vow of silence, refusing to discuss anything with them, spending his time working out shot lists and arguing with the director of photography over lighting.

So Deidre became a sort of associate director as well as associate producer. She patiently took Nigel Bland through the intricacies of the Corn Law Repeal Act of 1872 and the purchase of the Suez Canal shares from the khedive of Egypt. She coached Nikolai Fenderakov on his Prussian accent and his attitude at the signing of the Treaty of Berlin to put an end to the Russo-Turkish War.

And now and then Deidre even ran to fetch sanitary towels for Jacqueline Fortier because no one else was free to do it. With a shoestring budget, Charlie had kept the crew small. *Ben and Bill* was a lean-and-mean operation. Behind the camera, that is. On the screen, he wanted every one of the forty-five billion dinars to show. No expense was spared to give the film as rich a look as possible.

In addition to the talent and ingenuity of Marka Mladosi, Gubca had found a costume designer who had worked with Rossellini in Rome in the forties. Signora Cappella, a tiny, bird-like woman of seventy, worked day and night supervising her people bent over sewing machines making the costumes. The prop master was a Montenegran explosives expert, who had been in the hills with Tito during the war blowing up German troop trains. In order to provide as many n.d. members of Parliament as possible, they had an extra casting director who miraculously managed to find some Anglo Saxon-looking extras on the streets of Zagreb and Belgrade.

There was a tacit sense of complicity among the members of the company. Though nothing was ever explicitly said, the crew and the actors sensed that this was a renegade production. The pace with which things were moving, the absence of fat men in suits with cigars, seemed to indicate that this was a low-profile, no-frills operation.

Deidre eventually broke down and wrote Sidney Auger a postcard, which she had a driver mail from Belgrade. She was too well brought up not to send some news back home, just to let them know that she was alive and well.

Dear Sidney,

Arrived safe and sound in Belgrade. The weather is lovely and the people are friendly. Visited the Tito Mausoleum
and Terazije Square.

> Hope you are well.
> Best Regards, D.

She piled into bed every night after midnight and was up at
six. She had never worked like this in her life. There were no
meetings, no phone calls, no coverage reports. Just work. They
were running to keep up with a moving train, and there was no
time to do anything that wasn't directly related to putting the
script onto film. During the day she barely had time to spend
with Charlie. At night, before collapsing, they would often lie on
the bed sipping a glass of wine to come down from the day's
madness, too tired to talk, watching the late news on television.
The images would flicker on the twelve-inch black-and-white set
provided by the management of Le Grand Hotel, accompanied
by nonstop patter in Croatian. Sometimes they were able to glean
what was happening in the world from the pictures, but mostly
they didn't know and they didn't care. They were making a picture. The outside world did not exist. That is, until one night,
about a week into production . . .

They were lying in bed with their wine watching the news,
nodding out, when suddenly they both bolted awake. There was
a familiar face on the screen. Charlie hurried to turn up the
sound, as if that would have made a difference. The commentator was translating the speaker's remarks into Croatian. Standing
at a platform with microphones, surrounded by reporters, wearing the same jogging suit in which he had been kidnapped from
the Hotel Balkanska six weeks ago, was the star of *Decker*.

The day of Bobby Mason's release began like all the other days of
his captivity. He was woken by a courteous knock on the door,
given a breakfast of fresh fruit and yogurt and a copy of the

*International Herald Tribune.* Then he listened dutifully as one of the ski masks translated another chapter from a German history of Macedonia, after which he was invited to ask questions pertaining to the material covered. Bobby did his best to invent questions, but it was often difficult to follow the text, freely rendered from German into an approximation of English. Certainly not the English that Bobby Mason had learned on the streets of Detroit.

His hosts had seemed vaguely receptive to Bobby's idea of developing a script about the struggle for Macedonian self-determination when he first presented it some time ago. They weren't much on following up, however. Even when Bobby had suggested the possibility that he, himself, might even consider starring in the vehicle, they didn't show much enthusiasm. They just smiled and nodded and went back to discussing Yugoslavian politics.

So the idea had been put on the back burner, and the days passed. Whenever Bobby asked when they were letting him go, they shrugged and said that it was out of their hands. When Bobby asked whose hands it *was* in, they told him it was in Belgrade's hands.

It was obvious to a reader of the *International Herald Tribune*, though, that not only wasn't Belgrade budging in its refusal to negotiate, but the publicity value of the kidnapping had all but disintegrated. It had been weeks since there had been the slightest mention of Bobby Mason, Macedonia or the demands that they had made for his release.

This picture was dying. Bobby explained about the law of diminishing returns as it applied to box office; he explained how you had to pull a release when it showed a sharp decline in grosses. In response, the ski masks told him about the long winter of 1941, when Yugoslavia was crumbling before the Nazi juggernaut, how the guerrillas in Macedonia took to the hills, refusing to submit.

It seemed useless to argue the point. Bobby eventually stopped pursuing it. He spent his time watching old war movies, playing checkers and gin rummy, which he had taught one of his guards. The guy was into him for 387,000 dinars.

Around noon one day a new Macedonian showed up. Bobby heard a loud argument from the next room. Annoyed, he turned the sound up louder on *The Battle of the Bulge*. A few minutes later there was a knock at his door.

"Yo," Bobby called.

The door opened, and the new ski mask entered. He sat down on the chair opposite Bobby's bed and asked him in excellent English if he would be good enough to turn the VCR down. It pissed Bobby off to be interrupted during the part when they made the counteroffensive through the woods, but he did as the man asked.

"How are you feeling?" the ski mask asked.

"Can't complain."

"Has the food been all right?"

"Sure . . ."

"So would you like to go home?"

Bobby nodded quickly, then added, "You know, it's not that I don't appreciate the hospitality, if you know what I mean."

"There doesn't seem to be any point in holding you anymore."

"Yeah, right. That's what I've been trying to say to your friends."

"What are you going to tell the world when they ask you about what happened?"

"Hey, it's cool. No hard feelings."

"What are you going to tell them about the Macedonian people's struggle for cultural integrity?"

"I'm going to tell them all about the dudes up in the hills in 'forty-one in the snow blowing up the SS trains. All that shit."

The ski mask smiled, or so it seemed. It was difficult to tell through the slit in the woolen mask if anything more than the mouth was moving. The man sat there for a while, saying nothing, then finally he got up, went to the door, turned back and asked, "Do you know Diana Ross?"

"Yeah," Bobby lied.

"Nice legs."

"She wraps her gams around you, man, you can kiss your cookies good-bye."

Before they blindfolded him to leave the apartment, they drank a toast to Macedonia and said a few words of farewell. Bobby autographed an Italian movie magazine for the gin-rummy fish and told him not to sweat the 387,000 dinars.

They dropped him off on a side street near the Ethnographic Museum and told him how to get to his hotel. Bobby waved good-bye as the car sped off into traffic, and shielding his eyes from the sun, he slouched off toward Terazije Square.

The press conference that Bobby Mason gave upon his release was broadcast around the world. In addition to commenting on the hospitality of his hosts, he spoke about the legitimate longing for self-determination on the part of the Macedonian people and the cultural genocide being perpetrated by the government in Belgrade. His remarks not only caused diplomatic strain between Washington and Belgrade but also led to inevitable accusations of brainwashing. One newspaper ran the oxymoronic headline STOCKHOLM SYNDROME IN BELGRADE?

Bert Sully heard the news in the barbecue pit of his fifteen-thousand-square-foot spread in Palm Springs. He immediately got on the blower and told his lawyers to add irreparable mental damage to the lawsuit and up the ante another hundred million. When Norman Hudris, having lunch in the commissary in Burbank, was told about the brainwashing theory, he said, "What brain?" The remark, unattributed, spread through town like a brushfire and was being repeated that evening at Spago by Howard Draper, who had returned from his exile on Oahu to take the job of senior vice president of a major talent agency.

In the sunken living room of his penthouse condominium in Century City, Andre Blue watched a rebroadcast of the press conference that night on the eleven o'clock news. Afterward, he sat in the austere gray leather armchair, sipping a glass of chilled Sancerre, thinking. Then, after midnight, he picked up the phone and dialed Sidney Auger's home number.

Sidney had been out like a light bulb since ten. Andre Blue's phone call pulled him from a deep, dreamless oblivion. He fumbled for the phone, muttered, "Hmmn?"

"When's the stop date on Bobby Mason's deal?"

"What?"

"The stop date on Bobby Mason's deal. When is it exactly?"

It took Sidney several seconds before he could even remember who Bobby Mason was. Then his nuts-and-bolts, detail-laden mind took over. He flashed the contract, raced through the clauses, came up with the date.

"The twenty-seventh," he said.

"Tomorrow morning, my office, nine o'clock. I want all departments there." And he hung up.

Sidney had to get out of bed, find the list of home phone numbers and wake up all the department heads.

The meeting in Andre Blue's office the following morning was fully attended. No one dared miss a convocation by the new studio head. They sat around on Howard Draper's old Chippendale couch, sipping coffee from Howard Draper's old Sèvres service and waited until Andre Blue walked in the door at one minute after nine and joined them.

There were no handshakes. Everyone had been forewarned. Andre Blue sat down in Howard Draper's old bentwood rocking chair, careful to maintain the perfect crease in his slacks.

"Good morning, thank you for coming," he began. "I asked you all here this morning to discuss starting *Decker* up again. In Yugoslavia. As soon as possible. Same director, same cast, same crew. I'd like a resubmitted budget from all departments on the cost of doing this. Any questions?"

For a moment no one said a word. The announcement was so startling that it took some time to sink in. The vice presidents looked at one another blankly, wondering if they had heard correctly. It was Candace De Salvio who opened her mouth first.

"We have a stop date on Bobby Mason's deal."

"Yes, I know. It's the twenty-seventh. That's sixteen days from now."

Another brief silence before Candace said, a little tentatively, "But how can we shoot a picture in . . . sixteen days?"

"That's not my concern at the moment. Bobby Mason remains under contract to us, at least until the twenty-seventh. If he refuses to work, he's in breach. . . ."

Moe Lehman, v.p. legal, said, "You *are* aware of the negligence suit his manager's filed against us?"

"Yes, I am."

"Given the nature of the suit, I wouldn't think that he would advise his client to report to work. . . ."

"Refusal to report to work would constitute breach of contract regardless of the merits of the negligence suit, wouldn't it?"

"Well, I suppose from a strictly contractual point of view . . . but they could claim prior breach, effectively voiding the contract. . . ."

"Let them. When you work out your budget, amortize the cost of a breach-of-contract lawsuit that we would eventually write against the picture."

Moe Lehman nodded, made notes on his yellow pad. Candace De Salvio coughed nervously. She was dying for a cigarette, but there were no ashtrays anywhere. Andre Blue did not tolerate smoking around him.

"Andre, we're in the middle of force-majeure settlements with all the actors," she said.

"It would seem to be that the force-majeure element is no longer applicable. We're going back into production. They're under contract with no stop date, aren't they?"

"What about the insurance claim?"

"We modify it to cover the cost of a temporary shutdown instead of a permanent one. . . ."

Sidney Auger sat only half listening to these discussions.

There was a rumbling of dread from his stomach in anticipation of the inevitable questions he would be asked by Andre Blue. He had been hoping at least to be alone with Andre Blue when he finally had to confess that the company had vanished, that there were no more dinars in the bank in Belgrade, and that the only news he had from the director of creative affairs was a postcard describing a visit to the Tito Mausoleum.

When Andre Blue finally turned to him and said, "What do we have left over there in blocked currency, Sidney?" the vice president of business affairs, West Coast, shook his head and whispered, "Nothing."

It was the truth. The Yugoslavian distributor had finally gotten back from vacation and returned Sidney's call. According to him, the producer had closed the account two weeks ago. There wasn't one dinar left. And there was no forwarding address.

"Beg your pardon?" Andre Blue said.

"There are some . . . irregularities over there that I've been wanting to . . . discuss with you . . ."

"What sort of irregularities?"

"Well, we've had some communication problems with Charlie Berns."

Andre Blue just glared at him, silently. Sidney Auger had no choice but to come clean.

"He's disappeared."

"The producer has disappeared?"

Sidney nodded.

"Another kidnapping?"

"Not that we know of . . . I mean, there's been no one claiming to have taken him. No, I think he's merely . . . disappeared."

"Sidney, how does a producer just disappear?"

"I don't know. . . . The thing is, I think he's taken the dinars with him. And the crew. And possibly Nigel Bland and Tricia Jacobi. It seems . . . they're missing too."

"Holy shit," Ken Gayotte, the ad-pub v.p., blurted out, unable to restrain himself. The vice presidents began to babble at one another.

"How long have they been missing?" Andre Blue asked, reducing the babbling to immediate silence.

Sidney shrugged. "A couple of . . . weeks."

Andre Blue looked at him with cold incredulity, rocked a few times, his thin hands locked together in his lap. When he spoke again, it was in a very quiet voice.

"No one in this room is to repeat what they've just heard. I mean it. If the news gets out, I'm going to hold you collectively responsible. Get me your revised budgets by the close of business today. That's all."

The vice presidents rose collectively and headed quickly for the door. Sidney was asked to stay behind. Andre closed the door, walked back to the walnut desk, sat down, stared off toward the window, as Sidney stood in front of him and explained.

"It started out he just wasn't returning my phone calls. I left messages every day at the hotel, I called his agent, threatened to fire him . . ."

"And?"

"He stopped returning his agent's calls."

"Did you try sending him a registered letter with return receipt?"

"By that time he had checked out of the hotel. . . . That was after I sent Deidre Hearn after him."

"Who?"

"Deidre Hearn. She was Norman's girl, been involved with the picture from the beginning."

"What happened to her?"

"She's missing too."

# 16

Twenty kilometers outside of Zagreb, on an estate belonging to a distant descendant of the Habsburgs, the crew of *Ben and Bill* were working feverishly to get the sequence before they lost light. They were on Take 14 of the perilously difficult hunting sequence in which Benjamin Disraeli rides to the hounds with Lionel Rothschild in order to get the wealthy financier to bankroll his purchase of the khedive of Egypt's shares in the Suez Canal venture. Besides the two principal actors, the thirty extras in the hunting party, their horses and dogs, they needed a fox who would run roughly in the direction of the camera.

The team of handlers scurried around getting the horses and dogs back into their initial camera positions, while Dinak screamed obscenities at the Bosnian animal wrangler about his fox. Sitting in his PRODUTTORE chair, Charlie looked anxiously up at the horizon, gauging the movement of the sun. After Take 10 he had tried to get Dinak to simplify the shot, but the director was adamant. There were so few production shots in this picture that when he got his hands on one, he wasn't about to give it up.

Charlie estimated that they had one more take of the wide shot before they'd have to go in and get the coverage of Disraeli and

Rothschild talking turkey as they trotted along. That's where the money was. After all, the entire equilibrium of the nineteenth-century balance of power would be irrevocably affected by Disraeli's gambit to limit French influence in the Middle East. The rest was just a fox hunt.

But to Dinak Hrossovic, a fox hunt was not just a fox hunt. It was an opportunity to capture the sweat of the horses and the homicidal yapping of the dogs in their relentless pursuit of the fox, and he wasn't going to give it up just to film two men sitting on horses and talking.

Earlier he had to be talked out of shooting the dogs actually tearing the fox apart. When he heard that Dinak was even considering that, the animal wrangler threatened to walk off the set and take his horses, dogs and fox with him. Charlie tried to explain to Dinak that even if they could get the animal wrangler to sacrifice his fox, they only had one fox on the location at the moment.

"It's okay, Charlie. I get it in one."

Charlie wound up sending Deidre to dissuade the director and to make peace with the wrangler. She had a calming effect on Dinak, a way of getting him to be sensible when he showed occasional signs of veering toward megalomania.

In the middle of all this activity, Lionel came over with new script pages containing the latest rewrite of the scene that Jeremy Ikon had requested. Charlie scanned them briefly, compared them with the previous draft, asked, "What was wrong with the old lines?"

"He said that Disraeli basically didn't like Rothschild. Rothschild reminded him of his Jewish heritage that he had abandoned. And he felt guilty. Jeremy wanted the guilt to come through in the dialogue. You know, kind of sub rosa."

Charlie looked back at the new lines. He didn't see any guilt, sub rosa or otherwise, but if that's what the star wanted to say, that's what he was going to say, apparently.

Meanwhile the sun continued to sink ineluctably in the west.

Charlie was in the process of turning his chair away from the sun so he would stop staring at it when the second assistant told him there was a call in the production trailer. He got up and walked over to the trailer, set back behind the château's hunting stables.

He picked up the phone. "Hello?"

"Hey, how you doing?" Brad Emprin's nasal California diphthongs came over the wire. Charlie had been counting on never having to hear that voice again. It took him a few moments to recover.

"How did you find me?"

"Charlie, you're not my only client on this picture, remember?"

"Tricia told you?"

"She gave me her hotel number. The hotel put me through to this number. Where *are* you anyway? You still in Yugoslavia?"

"Brad, I don't have time to talk right now. We're losing light . . ."

"Listen, I just got off the blower with Andre Blue. He called me himself. He's furious. He's sending Sid Auger over to take control of the picture."

"What picture?"

"What's that?"

"Does he know I'm shooting a picture?"

"He doesn't know *what* you're doing. That's the problem. . . . Look, call Andre, tell him you're sorry, make nice, maybe we can smooth this thing over. . . ."

"When?"

"Huh?"

"When is Sidney Auger coming here?"

"I don't know. . . . Charlie, listen, you can't go around pissing off the heads of studios. These guys have a lot of clout. . . ."

Charlie hung up before his agent had the chance to finish the thought. He picked up the phone again immediately and called the concierge at Le Grand Hotel. He told him that under no circumstances was he to put through any phone calls from the

United States to the set, nor to give out any information about the whereabouts of the production to anybody. He had the location manager repeat the message in Croatian.

Then he called his office in the producers' building in Culver City.

It had been weeks since Enid Schonblum had heard from her boss, Charlie Berns, who was still presumably in Yugoslavia. The phone calls for him had slowly petered out until only the most desperate agents still bothered calling. She continued dutifully to keep the log, in her small, precise handwriting, and repeated the same litany into the phone. "I'm sorry. He's out. Of the office. Would you. Like to leave. A message."

People inside the studio no longer called. Nobody stopped by. There was no inter-office mail. It was dead quiet on the third floor of the producers' building. Nonetheless, Enid arrived every morning at nine, stayed at her post until six, and took no more than an hour for lunch. And she would continue to do so until somebody told her not to.

When the phone rang at 9:15 on a foggy Wednesday morning, she answered it as she always did, "Charles Berns's office," her pen poised over the log to copy down the name and number of the caller.

"Enid. It's me."

"Oh. Mr. Berns." Enid felt a flutter in her upper chest.

"I have something for you to do."

"Certainly."

"Listen carefully, okay?"

When she hung up the phone with him, Enid got up and went to the ladies' room. She needed to compose herself, even though there was no one in the office, nor would there probably be anybody in the office all day. She was upset. Of all the things that Mr. Berns had asked her to do, this was the most peculiar.

All day long she debated with herself whether loyalty to her employer was more important than decent behavior. He had said that it was extremely important, that he wouldn't ask her to do it if it weren't important. He told her that not only did the success of the picture depend upon it but his future as a producer as well. He added that it shouldn't be very difficult to accomplish. All she had to do was wait until they left, probably around seven, then get in there before the cleaning crew came through and locked up the offices. . . .

At six Enid went out to the Taco Bell across the street from the studio and got a *taco suprema* and a Diet Coke. She returned to the office, ate her dinner, did a new crossword puzzle. At seven she dialed the office extension. The secretary picked up. Enid hung up. At seven-twenty she wandered past the office on the way back from the ladies' room and saw that they were still there.

Enid began to get worried. What if they stayed very late? What if somebody came by and saw that she was still in her office at this hour? Wouldn't that look suspicious? She put the crossword-puzzle book away and took out an old budget, pretended to be working on it.

At eight she tried the phone again. Still there. The cleaning crew could be heard down at the other end of the hall, slowly working their way toward Charles Berns's office. The flutter returned to her upper chest. She felt vaguely dizzy. Perspiration began to trickle from her armpits. She'd have to get the sweater dry-cleaned. It cost $6.50 to get a cashmere sweater dry-cleaned. . . .

The cleaning crew was two offices away when the studio's night switchboard finally picked up the line. She hung up, put the budget away, grabbed her pocketbook, left the office. She took the far stairway down to the second floor so that she wouldn't have to pass the cleaning crew. There had to be no witnesses.

The second-floor hallway was dead quiet. She stood at the door to the stairwell listening for a moment before proceeding down the hall, past Andre Blue's office, Norman Hudris's old office, Deidre Hearn's old office and finally to the office her boss had asked her to infiltrate.

Turning back, she took a last look down the deserted hallway to make sure the coast was clear. She entered the outer office, closed the door behind her, looked around. There were two desks for secretaries. One desk was more cluttered than the other. She tried the cluttered one first, opening the desk calendar and moving quickly through the pages. Nothing.

The second desk didn't have an appointment calendar on it. Her flutter changed into a full-fledged palpitation. She was dripping from the armpits, soaking through the cashmere. She'd wind up having to throw the sweater out.

Opening drawers, she began going through the desk, looking for an appointment calendar. She found nothing. She went back and double-checked the first desk, turning the pages carefully, every few seconds expecting the door to burst open and to be confronted by the studio security police. Up against the wall. Hands on your head . . .

Kneeling, she pulled the trash can out from under the desk. She sifted through the contents, gingerly trying to avoid the half-eaten glazed doughnut and the dirty coffee cups. She tried the other trash can.

There was one more possibility. Her heart all the way down her throat, Enid penetrated the inner office. It was enormous and messy. The desk was full of budgets and pretzel crumbs.

She found the appointment calendar buried under a copy of the trades. Opening it, she went through the pages carefully, scanning them for information.

There was a rush of satisfaction when her eyes finally landed on what she had been looking for. Tomorrow evening at 9:40 P.M. Sidney Auger was taking the red-eye into New York. From there he was connecting to Lufthansa Flight 1119 to Belgrade.

She copied the information on the back of a screening pass,

put it in her pocketbook, left the office. Her heart pounded as she hurried down the hallway to the exit.

She would go straight home, make the phone call, then flush the screening pass down the toilet, destroying the evidence.

Charlie had a talk with Tricia Jacobi about security leaks. Even though she worked only in the whorehouse sequence on Malta, which was not scheduled until the end of the picture, the young actress had been spending most of her time hanging around the set, after a week of character research interviewing working hookers in the bars of Zagreb.

Charlie gave her the *emmis* in so far as the future of *Ben and Bill*, and, *a fortiori*, her role in it, was concerned. She sat on the steps of the prop trailer, head bowed, and listened as Charlie explained what he'd had to do in order to revive production in Yugoslavia after the plug had been pulled in Los Angeles.

"Gee, Charlie, I didn't know. . . ."

"Well, now you know."

"You mean, no one knows we're making this picture?"

"Nobody who's not here making the picture."

"There's not even anything about it in the trades?"

Charlie shook his head. Absently, she rubbed one calf with the toe of the other foot and shook her head disconsolately.

"But I don't understand. . . . I mean, can I put this on my résumé?"

They were interrupted by the property master frantically looking for the double of Disraeli's riding whip. The original had been trampled by Jeremy's horse. Charlie took advantage of the interruption to slip away back to the set.

Whether the picture would be on anybody's résumé depended on a number of factors too remote to calculate at the moment. Charlie hadn't thought that far in advance. Making the picture had become an end in itself. Shot by shot, day by day, slowly, painstakingly. Making a film was a military campaign: It was a long time before you saw the Big Picture. Looking at dailies was like reading battle reports. You had no idea whether you were winning the war or merely holding the line. There were miles of film in the canisters they took away every day. Eventually they would have to splice it all together and see what they had.

And then what? There was postproduction, dubbing, scoring, mixing—all the minutiae entailed in converting the film canisters into a coherent story. He wasn't going to get that done in Yugoslavia for dinars. No, by then, he'd have to have come out of hiding. He'd eventually have to come down from the hills and turn himself in.

But he'd have to come down from the hills *with the film,* and there was one big obstacle in his path.

The small amount of time he had spent with Sidney Auger did not provide a key to the man. He was late forties, early fifties, flabby. He had colorless, thinning hair that inadequately covered the front of his head. He was constantly nibbling on pretzels, potato chips, pistachio nuts, talking with his mouth full. How did you get to him?

Charlie looked absently over the set as he contemplated the question. There was the usual last-minute chaos as they prepared to roll the camera. Dinak was on top of a crane operating the A camera. He screamed down something in the direction of his chair. Wilna got up lethargically and moved over to the camera dolly, looked up at him. They had a conversation in whatever language it was that they actually spoke to each other when they spoke, which wasn't very often. She reached into the pocket of her jeans for a pack of cigarettes, took one out, tossed it up to him on the crane. As she did this, she bent forward slightly to get her balance.

The fading sun outlined the contours of her hard, thin, Polish body, and Charlie suddenly realized what he could plant in Sidney Auger's path in the way of a land mine. What else do you get a pudgy, middle-aged, male studio executive on location?

They had been carrying her on the budget since Amsterdam. It was time she made a contribution to the picture.

* * *

That night, in the bar of Le Grand Hotel, Charlie had a talk with Dinak. He waited until Wilna excused herself to go up to bed before broaching the subject. He began with another quick trip through the *emmis*, bringing the director up-to-date with the latest threat to the completion of *Ben and Bill*.

Dinak was on his fifth or sixth rum and Coke, and as he listened to Charlie, his sad Serbian eyes seemed to cloud over. It was never easy to figure out what Dinak Hrossovic was thinking. Tonight was no exception. He sat there impassively, his large, meaty hands around the glass, a cigarette burning down perilously low in his mouth, as Charlie explained that unless they found a way of side-tracking Sidney Auger, they might not be able to finish the picture.

Dinak grunted, scratched his beard. He drained the rum and Coke, ordered another.

"Who is this son of bitch, Charlie?"

"A studio executive."

"I told you—no studio executive puts foot on my set. I rip his asshole off."

"Hopefully it won't come to that. . . ."

"You want me to have him rubbed out, Charlie?"

"What?"

"I got friends in Belgrade. Cost you ten grand American."

Eliminating Sidney Auger was certainly the most efficient way of getting around him. Dead men don't shut down pictures. It would be the ultimate Hollywood joke. He could throw himself on the mercy of the court. But, Your Honor, he was going to *shut down* my picture. . . .

"Actually, Dinak, I was thinking about something a little less drastic."

"You want, they just break legs."

"Dinak, if we can figure out a way to just . . . divert this guy for a week or so. By then we'll have the picture practically in the can . . ."

"Maybe he get grabbed by Macedonians," Dinak said, chuckling at the thought. It was a hoarse, phlegmy sound, somewhere in between a laugh and a cough. They sat there for a while, the two of them, contemplating the possibility of lightning striking twice.

"I think our best shot is a girl," Charlie said, testing the water.

Dinak nodded, thought for a moment. "We hire whore in Belgrade?"

"Too unreliable."

Dinak thought some more. "The wardrobe assistant, little blonde, nice tits?"

"She's married, Dinak. Her husband picks her up every night on the set."

Dinak stubbed out what was left of the cigarette, lighted another. He kept this one in his mouth too. It looked like a lit fuse. Charlie sat there, waiting him out, hoping he'd come eventually to the same conclusion that Charlie had.

They sat in silence for a couple of minutes. Dinak stared off into space, blinking occasionally as the smoke from his cigarette blew into his eyes. He nodded to himself a few times, as if he were having an internal debate with himself. Then he rubbed his eyes tiredly and said, "What happens when we finish picture, Charlie?"

"We come clean. Show them the rough cut, hope they love it and bankroll the postproduction."

"If they don't love picture?"

"We get a small distributor, buy the film back from the studio, show it at Cannes . . ."

"Cannes?"

"Uh-huh. You could win another Palme d'Or with this picture, Dinak."

"I don't like French. Whores put perfume on their pussy."

"No kidding. I didn't know that. . . ."

"You know where I first meet Wilna, Charlie?"

Charlie shook his head, hoping that the segue was not entirely gratuitous.

"In a massage parlor in Copenhagen. She give me a hand job with baby oil. You never got a hand job like this, Charlie."

"Probably not."

"She use handcuffs."

"Handcuffs?"

"Handcuffs." He nodded. "Handcuffs, rubber gloves and a feather."

Lionel was upstairs in his room working on the nightly rewrite for the next day's work. This time it had been Jacqueline Fortier who had invited him into her trailer to discuss a scene. Between her, Jeremy Ikon and Nigel Bland, Lionel had been busy rewriting since they arrived in Zagreb.

Charlie had explained that this was perfectly normal, especially on a location picture. Having nothing else to do at night, the actors obsessed about the script. He told Lionel to do his best to try to make them happy. Easy for him to say. He was down in the bar every night, while Lionel was slaving away trying to make some sense and coherence out of the notes.

The scene in question was one of the most delicate in the picture. Disraeli goes to offer his resignation to Victoria after losing control of the government to Gladstone in 1880. The queen, miserable at the prospect of having to trade her beloved "Dizzy" for that icy pedant Gladstone, was disconsolate. They both knew this might very well be the last time they could meet to discuss the affairs of the nation, the last of those wonderful tête-à-têtes she so cherished with "the bravest, finest man in England."

Lionel had taken great pains to capture all the repressed passion and ardor between Disraeli and his queen. Everything was understated, beneath the surface, unarticulated. And this scene was to be the consummation of all the other scenes between the two of them. They sat there on the hard, stiff chairs of the queen's privy chamber, in the failing light of a winter dusk, talking about politics in veiled references and double entendres while really talking about their doomed passion for each other. Every word and gesture in the scene had been painfully crafted to capture the sadness of the lovers, separated by the barriers of their stations in life. It was a masterpiece of indirection.

Jacqueline Fortier, however, thought it was a trifle too indirect. She wanted Lionel to make it more explicit.

"Really, Lionel, we need to let the audience know what's going on."

"It's all there," he had argued, "in the gestures and the facial expressions. It's in what's *not* said, in the silences. . . ."

"Yes, of course, but with this director I'm not sure we can count on anything that's not said. Suppose we put just a bit of it in the dialogue, there's a good boy."

For the last two hours he had been sitting there over the pages dreamily avoiding doing the work. He was thinking about Jacqueline Fortier's hands, the way they brushed the hair from her eyes nervously and sculpted the air to refine a thought. She was the most beautiful woman he had ever seen close-up. Sitting in her trailer, he had been only a few feet from her. He could smell her perfume as it mingled with the odor of her long thin cigarettes. It was enough to shatter his concentration and keep him from working. The second assistant director would be around in an hour to collect the pages so that Jacqueline Fortier could see them before she went to sleep.

There was a knock on his door. He got up to answer it, expecting to see the a.d. an hour too early. Instead it was Tricia Jacobi with a script in her hand.

"I hope I'm not disturbing you," she said.

"No, not at all," Lionel replied, a little flustered at the presence of the Maltese whore on his doorstep.

"Do you have a moment to discuss just an itsy-bitsy question?"

"Sure," he said. Jacqueline Fortier could wait for her pages.

Tricia entered, looked around for a place to sit down. Lionel had a small room, with only one chair and a bed. The chair was covered with dirty laundry. Lionel moved quickly to remove the laundry, but Tricia sat down on the bed.

"What's on your mind?" Lionel lit a *niska drino* nonchalantly. He had taken to smoking in Yugoslavia. He offered her one as an afterthought.

"No thanks. I don't smoke. I had one cigarette when I was eleven and nearly died." She laughed. Lionel smiled indulgently. He was cultivating the indulgent smile that William Powell used in *The Thin Man.*

She sat there in her brushed-denim jeans, tied at the waist with a gold chain belt, and crossed her legs. Her hair was tied up in back, her skin flushed from the shower. She looked at him and said all of a sudden, "You are *so* cute."

Lionel wasn't prepared for anything quite so disarming. He did his best to carry on nonchalantly.

"What can I do for you, Tricia?"

"It's this scene in Malta. . . ."

As if it were any other scene. It was her only scene in the picture, and she was making a meal out of it. All she had to do was get humped by Disraeli and utter three lines of dialogue.

"What about it?"

"Well, I've been wondering about the character. You know, where does she come from, what was her life like, why is she doing, you know, what's she's doing . . . ?"

Lionel hadn't the slightest idea. It had never occurred to him when he wrote the scene that the Maltese whore was ever anything more than a Maltese whore. She was a plot device, pure and simple.

But Lionel had been around his Uncle Charlie long enough to know that this was not the kind of answer you gave an actress. He got up and paced in front of her, leaving the *niska drino* in his mouth like Lino Ventura in *Sicilian Vespers.*

"I think she's a deeply conflicted character. I think she's working with some very basic contradictions. I mean, this is a woman who has decided in a weird kind of way to take control of her life. . . ."

Tricia started writing rapidly in her script. Lionel increased the tempo, inventing dimensions to the character of the Maltese whore.

An hour later, when the a.d. knocked on the door, he told him that he was sorry but Jacqueline Fortier would have to get her pages in the morning. Lionel took out, a bottle of *sljivovica* from the mini-bar, poured himself and Tricia a couple of stiff ones.

They sat and drank and talked about Tricia's character and her acting lessons in Canoga Park. The temperature in the room went up several degrees. Eventually the point of the scene began to become apparent to him. Even such a master of indirection as Lionel Travitz-Traven could not help realizing the direction in which the scene was moving. He couldn't believe it. Was this actually going to *happen?* To him? Holy shit.

As far as Tricia Jacobi was concerned, she wasn't about to be turned down again. If the producer wasn't interested, she'd take his nephew, thereby reenacting the old Hollywood joke about the Polish starlet who wanted a part in a movie and fucked the writer. Post facto, no less.

Sidney Auger sat in the first-class cabin of Lufthansa 1119 out of New York, en route to Belgrade via Frankfurt, stuffing his face with cocktail peanuts. He was starving. The red-eye was late coming in. He had to hustle to make his connection, and he didn't have time to grab anything to eat.

Then they sat on the runway for an hour waiting for clearance before finally taking off. As if that weren't enough, they delayed the cocktail service another half-hour because of turbulence. It was beginning to look like he would never eat. He'd had two Beefeater rocks since they opened the bar, and he was starting to fog over. He didn't sleep on the red-eye. Who could sleep on a fucking airplane?

Spread out in front of him was the latest budget on what was being referred to around the studio as "the abortion." It was the third complete budget he had prepared—the first one for starting up, the second one for shutting down, and this last one for starting back up. They might as well just go ahead and shoot the fucking budget.

Andre Blue was out of his mind. There was no way they were going to get Bobby Mason back in Yugoslavia to do anything at all, let alone shoot a picture from which he would be contractually released in two weeks. It was at best a legal maneuver, to counter Bert Sully's lawsuit, and because of it Sidney Auger had to fly halfway around the goddamn world. The blocked dinars were worth more as a tax loss anyway. Who knew when they'd have another opportunity to shoot something in Yugoslavia? Better to write the whole thing off.

As far as Deidre Hearn was concerned, he'd just as soon write her off as well. Sidney had always considered her a flake. Those short skirts with the tight sweaters and the high heels. The gams weren't bad, but she was a little chunky in the hips for his money. Sidney liked them on the thin side, with tight little asses and small firm boobies.

Deidre Hearn would be no great loss for the studio. Whoever was coming in to take Norman's job would wind up bringing in his own girl. Besides, Deidre Hearn had egghead tendencies. Sidney suspected she belonged to one of those fucking reading groups that met once a week to talk about Gertrude Stein. If she disappeared, so much the better. They wouldn't have to offer her severance pay.

Dinner finally arrived. They carved him some well-done roast beef, ladled out a large helping of scalloped potatoes, drowned in gravy. He washed it down with a bottle of wine. Too bad he wasn't going to Paris. He could stay in the George Sank, eat like a king and go out at night and see boobies. But fucking Belgrade. What was there to do in Belgrade? He should get hazard pay for going to Belgrade.

In spite of the three cups of coffee he had with the Bavarian cream pie, Sidney Auger drifted off at last. By the time they

started the movie—*Desert Commando*, starring Bobby Mason—
he was out. He slept like a baby all the way to Frankfurt, with
no idea what was waiting for him in Belgrade.

At Surčin Airport there would be a limo driver with a tight little ass and small firm boobies holding up a sign with AUGER
printed on it. She would be wearing a short leather skirt and carrying an overnight bag containing, among other things, a black
negligee, a jar of baby oil, a pair of handcuffs and a feather.

# 17

And so the tanks continued to roll through Poland, uncontested for the moment. Ineluctably. Miraculously. Film passed through the camera, pages of words were transformed into film as the cast and crew restaged the life of Benjamin Disraeli, William Gladstone, Queen Victoria, Otto von Bismarck and the Maltese whore.

All the dinars wound up on the screen. In spite of his refusal to speak to the actors, Dinak shot striking footage. Thanks to his ingenious use of dollies, cranes and multiple cameras, even Nigel Bland's long perorations attacking the Corn Laws had a certain fluidity. And Marka Mladosi's sets were impeccable, down to the spittoons in the House of Commons.

Every night after the wrap, Charlie sat in the production trailer thankful that they had gotten through one more day. And yet as he began to see light at the end of the tunnel, he became increasingly anxious that someone was going to show up at the last moment and pull the plug. He kept expecting the posse to ride up to the set any minute, guns blazing. . . .

They had heard nothing from Wilna in Belgrade. No news was good news. Sidney Auger was presumably handcuffed to a bed in the Balkanska being titillated to death. It wouldn't be the first time that somebody had made the ultimate sacrifice to get a picture shot.

Charlie sat musing in his PRODUTTORE chair in the grand ballroom of the château outside Zagreb which was doubling for the Radziwill Palace, among other things. They had been working since seven in the morning to prepare for the crucial sequence at the Congress of Berlin where Disraeli and Bismarck conspire to block Russian expansionism in the Balkans.

Marka Mladosi had begged, borrowed and stolen every chandelier within a radius of five hundred kilometers to capture the splendor of the Radziwill Palace. Extras milled around in costumes, smoking cigarettes, waiting to be called. The director of photography fussed with the complex lighting, shouting orders to gaffers on ladders adjusting the arc lamps. The set dresser went around double-checking the table setting, adjusting a spoon or a glass, as the prop master put out the large plates of herring to be served at the banquet.

Nikolai Fenderakov emerged from makeup, script in hand, mumbling his lines to himself in French. According to Lionel, there were historians who believed that the cession of Bosnia-Herzegovina to the Austrians at Berlin was largely a casualty of language. Washing down Baltic herring with aquavit, the two heads of state had wound up negotiating the future of Europe in a language that neither really understood very well.

It was the trickiest scene in the picture, and Charlie was nervous. Lionel had written it with a dry comic touch, which the actors would have to bring off subtly to keep it from being burlesque. If played wrong, it could turn out to be a disaster. All those dinars for extras, costumes, props, winding up on the cutting-room floor.

Tricia Jacobi was doubling as an extra in the scene. Every little bit helped. She came up to Charlie, sashaying in her narrow-waisted evening gown, her buoyant breasts straining at the fabric, and asked him if he knew where Lionel was.

"He's in Jeremy's trailer running lines."

She sashayed off in the direction of the trailer. Charlie hoped she was being gentle with his nephew. Lionel had been walking around for days with a smirk on his face. Charlie had run through the possibilities and come up with Tricia Jacobi as the leading candidate. Sooner or later, he was bound to have his first actress. He could have done worse.

Across the set Deidre Hearn finished adjusting the bustle on the back of Lord Salisbury's mistress's gown, and they were ready to go. The first team was called. The second a.d. went to get Jeremy in his trailer. Deidre moved across the set and sat down in Dinak's chair beside Charlie.

"Here we go," Charlie said.

She smiled, nodded, remembering the fit of hysterics she'd had thinking about Bobby Mason playing this very scene. It seemed like a long time ago, a very long time ago, that a man had walked into her office in Culver City with the most cockamamie idea she had heard in a while. Well, here they were, somewhere in Yugoslavia, about to roll the cameras on the banquet of the Congress of Berlin. The cockamamie idea was now called *Ben and Bill*, and she was the associate producer.

Jeremy Ikon walked onto the set, entirely in character, down to the limp. As they taped his mark on the floor, he looked around him blankly, seeing nothing but the nineteenth century, his head full of French. Bismarck came up beside him, nodded nervously, adjusted his monocle. The ministers lined up six feet behind them, headed by Lord Salisbury for the English and the Crown Prince Friedrich Wilhelm for the Germans.

Dinak hovered over them in the crane, checking the framing. He was going to start on one of the courtiers' sabers, slowly widen to discover Disraeli and his host, then travel with them as they entered the banquet hall and took their places at the head of the table. He shouted some last-minute instructions, lit a cigarette, gave way to the operator.

The clackboard moved in front of the camera. "Two ninety-seven Beta, Take One." He banged the sticks.

The first a.d. lifted his megaphone and called, "Background action." Eighty extras began to mill along precisely defined tape marks, silently mouthing conversations.

Dinak sat on the crane, surveying the battlefield, his finger on the trigger. It was a moment he cherished, a moment of omnipotence. Everyone was waiting for him.

He looked down toward his star and said almost reluctantly, in his garbled Serbian accent, "Action, Jeremy. . . ."

The boom man hurried after them like an eavesdropper, stepping lightly in his bare feet.

"*Je suis comblé, Excellence, de la chaleur de votre accueil,*" said Benjamin Disraeli.

"*Je vous en prie, Monsieur le Premier Ministre,*" responded Otto von Bismarck.

Charlie reached over and took Deidre's hand. They sat there, both of them, caught up in the magic of the moment. It was, indeed, amazing it ever got done.

Andre Blue had been with the lawyers for hours. And he was developing a headache. One of those dull, low-grade attacks that aspirin wouldn't touch. Bobby Mason's suit against the studio and the studio's countersuit against him had all the earmarks of becoming one of those endless litigations that go on for years, outliving the issues of contention as well as the people involved.

He disliked lawyers. They were nitpickers and temporizers. Everything they said was qualified in conditional clauses. Andre Blue liked clear, concise answers to clear, concise questions. And he wasn't getting any.

So when his secretary interrupted to tell him that Sidney Auger was on the line from Belgrade, he seized the opportunity to dismiss the lawyers. They got up and shuffled out, taking their contracts and deal memos with them.

Andre Blue switched the box on and went over to Howard Draper's rocking chair, for which he had developed a great fondness.

"Yes, Sidney . . ." he said.

It had been nearly a week since Sidney Auger had gotten off the plane in Belgrade. His voice sounded weak, far-off.

"How you doing?"

"I was expecting to hear from you days ago."

"I haven't been feeling well."

"Beg your pardon?"

"I came down with the flu on the plane. I've been on my back for days."

Andre Blue sighed, inaudible on the speakerphone. He crossed his hands in front of him, said, "I'm sorry to hear that. Have you found Charlie Berns?"

"Sort of."

"What does *sort of* mean?"

"Well, I think they're making a picture. . . ."

"What?"

"I'm not sure about this, but I snuck out of the hotel. . . . You see, they sent this limo driver to meet my flight . . . and with the flu, and the doctor doesn't want me to leave the hotel room. . . ."

"How can they be making a picture? What picture?"

"I don't know exactly. I found the distributor, who sent me to a film lab, where I found film with the studio's name on it."

"There's film in a lab in Belgrade with our name on it?"

"Uh-huh."

Andre rocked back and forth several times to try to calm the throbbing in his temples. "What is the name of this . . . picture they're shooting?"

"According to what's written on the film cans, it's called *Ben and Bill*."

It took Andre Blue a few seconds to make the connection. Candace De Salvio. The deal memo . . .

"Let me ask you something, Sidney, is it possible that Jeremy Ikon is in this . . . picture?"

"Gee, I don't know. I mean, it didn't say anything on the film cans about who was starring in it. . . ."

"Do you remember a conversation you and I had several weeks ago? The deal memo for Jeremy Ikon? I asked you to look into it? Did you?"

"Did I what?"

"Look into it."

"Sort of . . ."

"You didn't do anything, did you?"

Sidney remained silent. Andre took out a Daniel Hechter handkerchief from his jacket pocket, mopped up some perspiration that had begun to collect on his lower lip. Carefully refolding the handkerchief, he put it back in his pocket. His voice was measured and even, as it always was when he was furious.

"Sidney, listen very carefully. This is what I want you to do. Go to the film lab and seize the film. Then find them wherever they are and shut them down."

"Right."

"If you have to, walk right up to the cable and actually pull the plug. Understand?"

"Right."

"Don't come back until you've shut them down."

"Right . . ."

Andre Blue got up, walked across Howard Draper's deep-pile rug and switched off the box, cutting Sidney Auger adrift in Belgrade. He buzzed his secretary, asked her to bring him a V-8 juice.

He returned to the rocking chair, sat and rocked. The V-8 juice arrived, in a thick goblet with two Evian ice cubes, the way he liked it.

"Get me Flo Gamish," he told his secretary.

He would get to the bottom of this. One way or another. The secretary went out to find Flo Gamish's number and dial it. While she was doing this, Andre Blue had a very disquieting thought. Wouldn't it seem odd for the head of a studio to call a star's personal manager to ask if she knew anything about a picture the studio was supposedly making? "Excuse me, Flo, but where is it again that we're shooting this film? And who exactly is in it? And what is it about again?"

There was no way he could make that phone call. The story would be all over town by tomorrow morning. It would get to Tokyo and back before the sun rose.

When the secretary buzzed that she had Flo Gamish on the line, Andre said, "Tell her I'll have to get back."

He got up and walked over to the window. For a while he stood there mesmerized by the rotation of the lawn sprinklers. Unconsciously, he began shaking his head in the same slow rhythm as the sprinklers.

It was ridiculous. It was absurd. It was preposterous. How could he be making a movie and not know about it?

Having died and gone to heaven, Sidney Auger now began to see the chariots of hell gaining on him in the rearview mirror. The wages of sin were collecting around his soul, having already settled like radioactive fallout on his beleaguered body. During the past week he had indulged in activities which he hadn't even imagined in the most febrile recesses of his fantasies. He had tasted a smorgasbord of exotic pleasures of the type he thought reserved for brothels in Marrakech. And now he was suffering from indigestion.

He was too old for this kind of shit. Enough was enough. The silent Polish girl with the small firm boobies and the little tight ass had run him through the wringer. There was nothing left. He could barely walk, and now he had to saddle up the horses again and go after the renegades.

He struggled out of bed and stood under the shower, soaking, as the water got progressively colder. Fucking Belgrade. They wouldn't have run out of hot water in the George Sank. He got out, shaved, put on a pair of J. C. Penny slacks and a Ban-Lon shirt. He packed quickly, wanting to be gone by the time she got back.

Should he leave a note? "Dear Polack, thanks for the memories"? He decided against it, went downstairs and checked out of the Balkanska. *Arriverderci,* Bimbo. There was a Holiday Inn in the phone book. There at least they would have hot water. And maybe he could get a decent fucking breakfast.

He checked into the Holiday Inn, went down to the coffee shop, had two eggs over easy with an approximation of bacon and felt a great deal better. He considered his next move.

Okay, first of all go get the film. Take possession of the picture in the name of the studio. Then he would find out where they were actually shooting and disconnect the cable.

The lab was in a seamy suburb of Belgrade on the other side of the river. Sidney told the cabbie to wait for him, went inside, found the same dipshit he had spoken to when he was here the first time.

"I'd like all the film canisters to date on *Ben and Bill,* please."

The dipshit looked up at him blankly.

"I'm seizing the film. All of it." Sidney assumed an attitude of authority, squaring his stooped shoulders and looking the man in the eye.

"Begging your pardon?"

"Look, I am the vice president of business affairs, West Coast, of the studio which owns that negative. And I want it."

Sidney took one of his business cards, put it down on the counter. The dipshit looked at it, got up, shuffled inside. After a moment, he came back out again with a man wearing a crumpled suit without a tie and smoking one of those smelly cigarettes.

"What is it that you want?" the guy asked.

"*Ben and Bill,* all the reels that you have in the vault. I have a taxi outside."

"Why do you want them?"

"Listen, that's not your problem. This is official studio business."

The dipshit and the suit exchanged a look. Then the suit said, "I have to make a telephone call."

"Who you calling?"

"Tabor Gubca."

"Listen, I don't know who this Taborgubka is, but I don't think he outranks me."

"Tabor Gubca is the man I make deal with. So I call him."

And the suit went back inside, leaving Sidney alone again with the dipshit. Sidney decided to try his luck with this oafish-looking man in a DALLAS COWBOYS T-shirt.

"So how's the shoot been going?"

The dipshit said nothing.

"Nice weather they've been having here in Belgrade. Good weather for shooting here in Belgrade."

Nothing. Not even a shrug. He gave up and waited for the suit to come back out. The man was gone for a long time. Sidney could hear a conversation in Serbian from somewhere down the hall. Finally, the suit came back out and said, "I am sorry. Tabor Gubca tells me that I cannot give you the film."

"Who the fuck is this Taborgubka anyway? I was on the phone with Andre Blue last night, the head of the whole goddamn studio, and he told me to get the film. If you don't believe me, we'll call him. Right now."

"I am sorry, but the only person who may remove the film is Tabor Gubca," the suit pronounced. "Now please leave."

The guy was a good six feet, six one. He had a boxer's build and a nasty complexion. Even if Sidney hadn't been out of shape and completely depleted by the Polish bimbo, this one wouldn't go half a round.

"Okay. You guys are in for one fucking big lawsuit. We're talking possession of stolen property, refusal to render stolen property, breach . . . just for openers. See you in court." And with that, he exited as litigiously as he could.

Back in the cab, he sat for a moment trying to make a decision. The police? Interpol? "Excuse me, sir, but I'd like to report a missing film company. . . ."

It'd never fly. No, there was only one way to handle this situation. He fumed to the cabbie and said, "How'd you like to make some hard currency?"

When the cabdriver looked back at him blankly, Sidney reached into his wallet, took out a couple of Franklins and waved them at the driver.

"It has been an honor to serve England, sir," said the Maltese whore, as she let the cover drop just a bit to reveal one of her perfect boobies.

"Indeed," replied Benjamin Disraeli, starting to close his breeches. And in doing this, he tore the button off. "Bloody fucking button!" he yelled.

"Cut," yelled Dinak from the top of the crane.

"Reload," said the first a.d.

"Shit," said Charlie on his PRODUTTORE chair. They had done eleven takes and still didn't have the scene. Jeremy Ikon lit a cigarette, came over to Charlie.

"I think we have a problem here."

"What's the problem?"

"Every time she says, 'It's been an honor to serve England,' I hear in my head, 'It's been an honor to *service* England,' and I start to laugh and lose the thread. It's the pun, you see. It's a very unfortunate play on words. Do you suppose we can have a rewrite?"

Charlie looked for Lionel, found him standing purposefully between Tricia Jacobi, whose boobies were being retouched by the makeup lady, and the camera. Since she had gotten rid of the body stocking, Tricia Jacobi was perfectly relaxed walking around without anything on at all. Her immodesty drove Lionel to fits of jealousy, and between takes he placed himself in what he imagined to be the eye line of the voyeurs on the set.

He beckoned for his nephew, and Lionel tore himself away from his post and walked over to his uncle's chair, flashed Jeremy a sour look.

"Jeremy wants a new line from Tricia here," Charlie said.

"What's wrong with the old line?"

"There's a pun . . . an honor to serve England sounds to Jeremy like an honor to *service* England. . . ."

"It's intentional."

"Really?" Jeremy Ikon raised an eyebrow imperceptibly.

"That's right. You see, this screenplay functions on more than one level. The pun gives it an ironic dimension."

"Well, my dear boy, irony or no, we have to *deliver* the dialogue, now don't we?"

Lionel rocked back and forth on his feet for a moment, digging in. Charlie saw it coming, the inevitable explosion. Here they were, the end in sight, the battle almost concluded, and tempers were starting to fray. Lionel had been building up to this for some time. For months he had been rewriting endlessly for everybody in the picture. He was getting sick and tired of running around taking dictation.

"Look," he said petulantly, "it's Tricia's line, not his. If *she* wants it changed, I'll change it."

Jeremy took a last drag on his cigarette, stamped it out with his boot, in a gesture that said clearly, "Who does this little prick think he is?" Lionel folded his arms in front of him in a position of defiance. They were clearly at an impasse.

"I'll be in my trailer," the actor said pointedly, and withdrew.

As Jeremy Ikon limped toward his trailer, Lionel muttered through his teeth, "I hate him. He's a pompous asshole. And I'm not changing the line. Period."

Charlie sighed. One more brushfire to put out. If they could just get out of the tunnel, into the daylight. If they could just get this scene and wrap the thirty-five extras in their tunics, scarlet coats and cavalry swords, not to mention their horses . . .

"Lionel, it's just a line."

"No, it's not just a line. It's a dimension. Besides, I'm tired of him and his goddamn notes. Why can't he just say the lines?"

"Because he's an actor, Lionel."

"Aren't actors supposed to work for producers?"

On the set, they were ready to go again. Charlie would have to make this quick. He leaned back in his chair for a moment, adopted his best avuncular tone, "Lionel, let me explain something to you."

Lionel began to see the big pot with the water and the stone heating up to a boil.

"Look around you," Charlie continued. "What do you see? A hundred people hanging around this set. They've all stopped working and started waiting. While they're waiting, unfortunately, they don't stop getting paid. Money continues to flow. Imagine a water faucet turned on full force with no bucket to capture the water."

Lionel looked around him, observed the small army of people waiting for Jeremy Ikon. He tried to imagine them as flowing water from a faucet.

"What are all these people waiting *for*? They're waiting for Jeremy Ikon to come out of his trailer so that they can film him saying his lines. . . . Now how do we get him to come out of his trailer to say his lines? We give him lines that he's *willing* to say. . . . We put a bucket underneath the faucet. . . ."

They were so close to the end. They just had to carry the baton across the finish line. This was no time to lose control.

Charlie went on talking, expanding on his bucket-and-faucet metaphor, all the time listening in the distance for the sound of hoofbeats.

Parked outside the film lab in the taxi, watching the door, Sidney Auger felt like a private dick in a B movie. He didn't have much of a choice. This was his only legitimate lead. Sooner or later, they'd drop off the previous day's film and return to the set. With Sidney Auger on their tail.

Business at the lab was slow. Hours passed without anybody arriving or leaving. The driver was dozing in the front. Sidney made himself as comfortable as he could in the small backseat and tried not to drop off in the torpid heat.

Then late in the afternoon, a familiar sight pulled him out of his daze. She got out of a cab and entered the lab, her perfect little ass encased in a pair of tight jeans. Jesus. *Cherchez la bimbo.* The plot was definitely thickening.

At moments during the days and nights of silent bliss he had spent with the Polish bimbo, Sidney had reflected on the fortuitousness of the limo service sending a girl to pick him up at Surčin with a valise full of gadgets. But since no one else knew when his plane was arriving, there was no other explanation for the stroke of good fortune. God was being kind to a middle-aged man. He was giving Sidney one more party before he packed it in.

He had tried communicating with her several times, but all she did was shake her head and murmur, "Polska." He didn't pursue the point. Nationality seemed irrelevant at the time. Now her arrival at the film lab presented a completely new possibility. Could this once again be the Big Guy playing with his head, or was the whole thing a setup?

Could those fuckers have actually done it? Could they have sent her to waylay him, those pricks out there making a movie with his dinars? Jesus. Mata Hari in rubber gloves . . .

Sidney woke up the driver and put him on alert. Draping another Franklin over the seat to keep the man interested, Sidney kept his eyes glued on the door through which the Polish bimbo had entered the lab. Follow the broad. She'd lead him right to the main cable.

An hour later a battered Peugeot station wagon pulled up in front of the lab. A guy got out, entered the lab. He made three trips, each time carrying film canisters. The next time he came out the Polish bimbo was with him.

"Start the motor," Sidney said to the cabdriver.

When the man hesitated, Sidney slipped the Franklin into his shirt pocket. The girl got in the Peugeot beside the driver.

Sidney uttered a phrase he had always dreamed of uttering. "Follow that car," he said, his voice hoarse with excitement.

\* \* \*

The idea of holding the wrap party on the Maltese-whorehouse set was Marka Mladosi's idea. It seemed foolish to move to some restaurant in town when they had a nineteenth-century brothel already rigged and lit. Gubca had hired a rock band from Sarajevo, that was, according to him, the hottest group in the Balkans. Charlie had authorized him to pull out all the stops, and it promised to be a terrific wrap party.

That is, if they ever wrapped. The last few scenes dragged on interminably. As soon as Charlie patched up the squabble between Lionel and Jeremy Ikon and they were able to resume shooting, one of their generators went down. Then Tricia Jacobi lost a contact lens. By the time they got her spare pair from the hotel, planes started flying over the set at regular intervals. Somebody figured out that they were in the approach path to Zagreb Airport. Unfortunately, it was too late to fire the location manager.

The sun had long ago sunk in the west. Inside the brothel, the lights flickered and crackled. Every time the generator coughed Charlie's stomach twisted a notch. There was no tomorrow. Gubca had told him that morning they were out of dinars. There was just enough for the last day and the wrap party. Word had gotten around the set that they were running low on funds, and the extras had demanded to be paid daily. The 357th Hussars were keeping a close eye on the clock.

What if the British-garrison extras walked? He needed them for the last shot, a wide angle of Disraeli leaving the brothel to rejoin his comrades waiting outside. This was a crucial moment in the film, the moment when the hero decides to forsake a life of frivolity and devote himself to politics and the future of England. Dinak had designed the shot to start wide on the EXTERIOR BROTHEL NIGHT, capturing the restlessness of the soldiers and horses milling around, slowly tighten as Disraeli emerges from the whorehouse, to register the look of resolution on his face as he turns away from the insouciance of youth to take on the responsibilities of manhood. Then he would mount his horse, take one last look behind him at the Maltese whore standing in the door-

way, and ride off to meet his destiny. The shot depicted the turning point in the young Disraeli's life, the symbolic representation
of his movement from young, shiftless parvenu to the man who
would dominate English politics for nearly forty years.

If they didn't get the shot, they'd have to find some trick in the
cutting room to make the transition with the next scene—
Disraeli, his wild oats sown, back in England addressing a political meeting in Sussex. At the moment, they were stuck inside on
a series of cutaway shots of soldiers cavorting in the hallways,
drunkenly swearing, singing and carrying off the girls. Dinak
wanted them to swear and sing in English, to give the production
track texture and avoid the artificiality of the dubbing stage, and
he had Lionel furiously trying to come up with appropriate
nineteenth-century British military argot to be pronounced by
the Croatian extras.

Charlie finally intervened. He took Dinak and Lionel aside
and explained that they were going to go into Gold Time soon,
that the dialogue could be added later, that the money shot was
the exterior.

"You want authentic film, Charlie?"

"Dinak, do you think anybody really knows how British soldiers swore in whorehouses on Malta in the eighteen thirties?"

Dinak looked at him, crushed. Lionel protested, "It's texture,
Charlie."

Charlie looked at his watch, said, "Maybe, but in a few hours
we're out of dinars, and unless you want to lose thirty-five extras,
you better blow the inside off and start lighting the exterior."

Dinak grabbed one more shot of a drunken soldier mounting
a girl and firing his musket while shouting, in a Croatian accent,
"Long live Saint George and England."

Then he went outside to supervise the lighting of the martini
shot.

Sidney Auger sped through the night in the backseat of a 1971
Fiat taxicab. The driver had to hold his foot down on the floor in

order to keep the taillights of the Peugeot in sight. Sidney kept asking him where they were going, and the driver shrugged. After they passed signs for Kuzmin and Bos. Saac, wherever the fuck *they* were, the driver said they were going toward Zagreb.

"How far is that?"

The driver shrugged, held up three fingers.

"Three what?" Sidney asked.

The driver pointed to his watch.

"Three hours?"

The driver shrugged again. For all Sidney knew he could have meant three days or three weeks. It was all ridiculous anyway. Here he was in a taxi with bad springs, going 150 kilometers an hour, however fast *that* was, chasing a Polish bimbo through the night to track down a phantom production company.

They were on some sort of highway with no speed limit and very little traffic. Miles went by without passing another car. He had no idea where they were. Somewhere in Yugoslavia. Sidney wondered what the *Variety* obit would be if the taxi blew a tire. SIDNEY F. AUGER KILLED ON LOCATION IN YUGOSLAVIA. Would the studio take out a full-page ad? "We mourn the passing, in the line of duty, of Sid Auger, a thorough pro and a hell of a nice guy. . . ."

Andre Blue wouldn't spend the money for a full-page ad. There was no longer a picture to write the expense off against. Did he realize what Sidney was going through just to try to save the studio some blocked dinars? Andre Blue didn't give a shit. No, Andre Blue wouldn't take out an ad. By the end of the week he'd have him replaced with one of those young new bottom-line business affairs guys. Sidney would be history, the cost of his trip to Yugoslavia amortized into the studio's general overhead budget, buried somewhere in the gardening and parking-lot expenses.

Sidney leaned back in the seat and closed his eyes. He began not to care whether he bought it or not in this taxi with bad tires somewhere between Belgrade and Zagreb. What the hell? He'd had a pretty good run. And he'd gone out with a bang. Jesus. The

Polish bimbo. It was too fucking unbelievable to think of what had happened in that hotel room. At his age he was taking his life in his hands carrying on like that.

Then a thought occurred to him. Maybe *that's* what they were counting on. Maybe they expected him to buy it in Belgrade. . . . Maybe they were in league with Andre Blue. Both sides working together. This whole thing was an enormous wild-goose chase to get rid of Sidney Auger and not have to pay off his out deal. . . .

Sidney fell asleep calculating just how much the studio would have saved if he had died under morally turpitudinous conditions, handcuffed to a bed in a hotel room in Belgrade, thereby nullifying his contract and sparing them the expense of settling out his deal.

They were lit and ready to go. The extras were in position. The horses were on their marks. The track was laid, the dolly grips ready to move. The d.p. took a last light reading. The operator verified the focus. The second had blocked off the area to traffic. The sound man looked up at the dark sky for airplanes. The makeup girl gave Jeremy a final dab of pancake on his nose. Tricia stood on her mark, wrapped in a shawl. . . .

Charlie crossed his fingers and prayed. The shot was planned to be done in one complex camera move. A push in, hold on Disraeli as he looks back toward the Maltese whore, then pan with him as he mounts his horse, and widen as he rides off into his future.

This was it. The martini shot. Charlie needed it in one take. It would take half an hour to reset, and he didn't have an extra half-hour at this point. He looked over at Dinak, up on the crane, about to swallow his cigarette.

"Well, Dinak, what do you say?"

Dinak looked back at him with that mad glint in his eye and nodded. There was nothing else to do but shoot it. Here we go. Knock down the first domino. He motioned for the first a.d. to ready the background action. The clackboard moved in front of the camera. . . .

It was the longest sixty seconds of Charlie Berns's producing career. He held his breath as the grips pushed the camera carefully along the track, as the extras mounted their horses, as Jeremy exited the brothel, melancholy and resolution in the nuances of his performance, as Tricia emerged in her shawl, the portrait of Disraeli's dying youth, of all that is mysterious to the Anglo-Saxon soul . . .

Charlie didn't come up for air until the horses rode off out of frame and Dinak whispered *cut* to the operator. It was a miracle. They'd got it in one. It was over. The picture was in the can.

Charlie turned and embraced Deidre. They were both too exhausted and overwhelmed to speak. He held her tight, relishing the moment, heard Dinak ask the operator if they'd gotten it, heard the operator answer that they had, waited for the traditional announcement that the war was over. It came like a bugle call of retreat over a smoldering battlefield.

"It's a wrap," the first a.d. called.

Cheers went up on the set. Then Charlie and Deidre heard a vaguely familiar voice bellow from across the set, "You're damn fucking right it's a wrap."

They turned and saw Sidney Auger making his way toward them. The vice president of business affairs, West Coast, climbed through the cables, stepped over the horse shit and past the Hussars removing their tunics and lighting cigarettes. He walked right up to Charlie and Deidre.

"I'm shutting you down," he announced.

"That was the martini," Charlie said.

"Huh?"

"It's in the can." They stood there for a moment, not knowing where to go from here. Finally, Deidre said, "You might as well come to the wrap party, Sidney. It's already paid for."

At three o'clock that morning Charlie and Deidre lay in bed in his room at Le Grand Hotel. The wrap party was still going on at the Maltese-whorehouse set, as far as they knew. They had slipped away before it got too rowdy. It had been a great success, the *sljivovica* flowing copiously as the cast and crew of *Ben and Bill* consumed the remaining dinars in an orgy of exhausted sentimentality.

Sometime during the evening, a *sljivovica*-soaked Lionel announced with tears in his eyes that he loved everybody on the crew and then proposed to Tricia Jacobi. She said that she had to talk to her therapist about it but it sounded like a good idea. Dinak and Wilna had their reunion in sight of Sidney Auger, who wound up being consoled with one of the available Maltese whores. After a few strained moments at the beginning of the party, Sidney had wound up resigning himself to the fait accompli and entering into the spirit of the evening. After all, a wrap party was a wrap party, even among renegades. What the fuck else was there to do at night in Zagreb?

He and Deidre downed a couple of *sljivovicas* while he brought her up-to-date on life at the studio under Andre Blue.

"If I were you, I wouldn't bother coming back," he told her. "He's going to clean house anyway."

"You think so?"

"Yeah. We're all history. In six months there won't be a straight guy in the whole fucking studio. I've got feelers out at Paramount."

Jeremy Ikon proposed a toast to Ben Disraeli. Everyone drank to the health of the late prime minister. Then Nigel Bland gave a thundering rendition of William Gladstone's farewell speech to Parliament. There wasn't a dry eye in the house.

Later, lying in bed, Deidre and Charlie held hands, staring up at the ornate ceiling of the room at Le Grand Hotel, feeling that peculiar emptiness that comes upon the completion of a picture. There remained a great deal to be done, of course—the editing, dubbing, scoring, the fine-tuning of *Ben and Bill* all had to be done somewhere, somehow. But for the moment they were both too exhausted to contemplate anything beyond the miracle of the picture being wrapped. The film was in the can. That was enough.

Charlie Berns faced a very uncertain future. He faced excommunication from the church of Hollywood, not to mention possible felony charges for absconding with a film company and forty-five billion dinars. They could throw the book at him. They could take his can opener away and banish him to Indy Prod forever.

But Charlie Berns had been there already. He had weathered it once and he'd weather it again. Like Scarlett O'Hara he would worry about it all tomorrow. Now he lay exhausted on his bed, overwhelmed with the realization that he had pulled it off. In the face of enormous odds, he had actually shot the picture. He had managed to slip the stone soup through the window of opportunity only moments before it slammed shut on him. . . .

His accomplice lay beside him, as exhausted as he was. For her part, Deidre Hearn, an accessory to the felony and a fellow heretic, had as many unknowns facing her as Charlie Berns had. She had no idea what she was going to do after tonight. The one thing she did know was that she wasn't going back to writing coverage for lunatics. She was checking out of the Mad Hatter's tea party once and for all.

Skidding on two wheels, her life had nonetheless turned a corner. She was heading out into terra incognita, with only a machete to hack away at the underbrush. From here on in she would travel light and keep her eyes open.

She turned toward Charlie Berns, looked at him with amusement and tenderness. If there was a place to begin, it was here with this completely inappropriate man lying beside her. There were questions yet to be answered, things to be said that they hadn't had time to say during the madness of the preceding weeks. In a sense, they hardly knew each other.

The best place to start was at the beginning. She leaned over and put her hand against his cheek. And smiled. He smiled back.

"Charlie," she began, her voice hesitant, "how come there's a tree in your swimming pool?"

# 18

April Fool's Day. The Santa Anas had come in unseasonably and sucked the basin dry, leaving dead leaves and coughing in their wake. The whole town was suffering from a dull sinus headache. A low-grade anxiety buzz floated around like radiation—ubiquitous, inescapable. Psychiatrists were beeped at lunch. The emergency room at Cedars-Sinai was full of imaginary heart-attack victims. There was a run on Valium at prescription counters. . . .

The mercury hit 94 at City Hall, 98 in Toluca Lake. Trim fuel-injected engines gasped for oxygen, clogging the freeways, breaking down inconveniently at major intersections. Tow trucks and drug dealers roamed like predators, freelancing on a cash-only basis. The entire city was strangling in gridlock and jangled nerves.

No business of consequence was transacted that day. The clocks stood still in the glass offices of Century City, Burbank and Hollywood. Phone calls remained unanswered, deals unconsummated. By three in the afternoon all battle stations were deserted. Nobody was home. It was a ghost town.

By five, the limousines began to head east, moving through

unfamiliar territory, streets full of open windows and Spanish grocery stores. It was no-man's-land down here, and the drivers kept the doors bolted. In spite of the glacial air conditioning in the limos, the passengers sat perspiring in their rented Yves Saint Laurent tuxedos, their Nina Ricci knockdown dresses, pill vials of all sorts hidden away in pockets among lipsticks, Kleenex, chewing gum. . . .

Brad Emprin braked and pulled the 325i into Figueroa, no longer even hearing the *galump*. He was sandwiched in between two limos, one of which contained Howard Draper and his wife, and he was hoping not to be noticed. He had decided to self-park the BMW, which would not only save him the three bills for the limo but enable him to make a quick getaway afterward. Now he was wondering whether a successful agent should be going to the Awards in his own car. What if Howard Draper had seen him?

Even if Howard Draper had seen Brad Emprin, he wouldn't necessarily have connected him with the résumé on his desk of the young man who wanted to leave GTA and come over to his shop. Howard was deep into his second Chivas and trying to tune out the incessant chatter of Winnie, beside him in her $7,800 Emilio Cardenza original.

"Jesus, I hope we're not going to be next to some lug. Last year Arnold Schwarzenegger hogged the entire armrest."

"It's not his fault, Winnie. He has big arms."

That was the extent of the conversation between Howard Draper and his wife en route to the Shrine Auditorium.

Several blocks behind them, in a less expensive limo without a bar, Norman Hudris and Cissy Fuchs looked out at the incomprehensible graffiti on the buildings. They had been seeing each other regularly for months and were about to try living together on an experimental basis.

"You know who I'm having lunch with next week?" Cissy said. "Lionel Traven."

"Who's Lionel Traven?"

"Who's Lionel Traven? He's the kid who wrote Charlie Berns's picture. Everyone in town's after him. He's up to seven-fifty a pop now."

"No kidding," Norman said without interest. Since he had moved over to television, he had lost touch with events in the feature-film world. He was isolated, exiled in Burbank blue-penciling dirty words for television movies. Andre Blue never managed to take his phone calls. To make matters worse, he had hired a thirty-two-year-old former agent to take Norman's job.

It looked to Norman Hudris as if he was going to be on Elba for a while.

"This kid's got some sort of script about a crop duster in Nebraska. Everyone in town is bidding on it. . . ." Cissy said, fishing out a breath mint from her purse and placing it on the edge of her tongue like a communion wafer.

The kid, Lionel Traven, née Travitz, downshifted the jet-black Carrera, revved and watched the tach hit 4500 rpm. Beside him Tricia Jacobi sat lusciously in her Côte d'Azur frock with lace décolletage and minijupe that revealed large stretches of her tanned thighs. This was her first Academy Award ceremony, and she was thrilled, even though her part in the picture was minuscule. She was in the picture, her name on the credits, and tonight she would be seen on the arm of a hot young writer.

Lionel had moved out of Charlie's house and taken a small place at the beach. It was only twelve-five a month and had a view of Catalina. He had abandoned the buses for the Porsche and the Selectric for a Toshiba laptop. He spent every day having lunch with a different agent or producer, basking in the glow of instant fame.

He and Tricia were blissfully in love. They had decided to postpone marriage until Neptune was no longer square to Sagittarius and Tricia's astrologer gave them the green light. Meanwhile he wrote scenes for her to take to her acting class and was working on an idea of a biopic of Marie Antoinette in which she would star and Dinak would direct. One of the agents he had lunch with last week said he could package it in ten minutes.

The previous month Lionel Traven had been featured in *Los Angeles* magazine in their "People on the Move" column. Because of it he had to get an unlisted phone number. He already had a manager, a taxman, a car phone, a fax, an exercise coach, a personal-fulfillment counselor, a cocker spaniel named Orson, a share in a medical building in Panorama City and $267,500 in the bank.

In the same ice-blue limo that, as part of his deal, took him home every night from the studio, Andre Blue sat sipping a glass of chilled Saumur and wondering how he was going to follow this act. Some people in town were saying that he had stepped in dog shit and come out smelling sweet. Perhaps. But he had had, nonetheless, the acumen to recognize that *Dizzy and Will*, the new title for the picture that had been shot behind his back with blocked dinars in Zagreb, was an Academy Award nominee. As soon as the lights went up on the first assemblage of film, he sensed that the slow-moving but epic saga could be just the type of film to be considered for the Big One. It was grand and ponderous, an old-fashioned type of movie. Jeremy Ikon and Jacqueline Fortier were magnificent. Nigel Bland gave the performance of his career. The dialogue was literate; the photography sweeping; the production elegant. Andre Blue suspected that in this era of fatuous nostalgia, this was just the type of turkey to win the blue ribbon.

And so instead of prosecuting Charlie Berns for breach of contract and grand theft, or even taking the postproduction away from him and the Yugoslavian maniac who shot the picture, he signed them both to overall deals. Now he was trying to figure out how to ride this wave should they wind up with their name in the envelope.

Since Disraeli dies at the end, a sequel was out of the question. Gladstone goes on for another ten years leading England, but Nigel Bland couldn't carry a picture. There was, however, the girl in the whorehouse in Malta. She had a special quality about her. In two months she'd have a pile of scripts on her night table and offers of a million plus to read them.

Andre Blue would have to act fast. Win or lose, tomorrow he would get his new director of creative affairs to find a script for her. He'd call Alan tonight at his apartment, after the awards. . . .

Almost the last limousine to fight its way through the traffic in front of the Shrine Auditorium contained Alan's old boss, Deidre Hearn, and the producer of *Dizzy and Will*, Charlie Berns. They were late because Charlie's rented tux was missing buttons and Deidre had to do a last-minute sewing job.

The two of them sat there, shell-shocked, still not quite believing that all this was actually happening. The postproduction had been as hectic as the production. Charlie, Deidre and Dinak worked around the clock to get it ready for a week's run in December to qualify for the awards. That was the quid pro quo that Andre Blue exacted in return for giving them back the picture they had originally stolen from him.

They managed to deliver a two-hour-and-forty-minute cut from the thousands of feet of film that Dinak had shot. The print was shipped four days before the picture opened. Charlie and Deidre didn't even attend the premiere. They went to Dubrovnik to lie on the beach and drink *sljivovica*. Lionel sent them the reviews. Vicenzo Di Rimisci called *Dizzy and Will* "a tour de force of filmicity." *Variety* said it was "art-house fodder." Box office was lukewarm.

On February 28, when the awards nominations were announced, only Andre Blue wasn't surprised. He had already prepared a publicity campaign. He was quoted as saying that the nomination speaks for the "creative partnership between studios and filmmakers. This is the type of collaboration we can all be proud of."

But at 5:15 on April Fool's Day, as his limo inched toward the Shrine Auditorium, Charlie wasn't thinking about creative collaboration. He was concerned that the button that Deidre Hearn had sewn on his cummerbund wouldn't hold. What was he going to do if he had to give a speech?

He turned to Deidre and said, "What if I have to go up there?"

"Keep your stomach sucked in and don't forget to thank the Macedonians."

Flashbulbs exploded as Charlie and Deidre got out of the limo in front of the Shrine. Reporters and photographers closed in on them.

"This can't be for us," Deidre whispered.

"It's not," Charlie said. "Turn around."

Deidre looked over her shoulder to see Bobby Mason getting out of his pink stretch limo, accompanied by his manager Bert Sully and a new group of bodyguards.

"Hey, how you doing?" Bobby waved as he made for the entrance in his silk tux. He was intercepted by the television people and asked if he was still thinking of shooting his next picture in Thessaloniki.

"Whatever I can do for the cause of freedom, you know what I mean?"

Then he threw up his right hand in a variation of the old black-power salute and said, "Long live a free Macedonia."

Inside the lobby Charlie and Deidre ran into Sidney Auger, there with Candace De Salvio, who was wearing a black sheath dress with rear décolletage down to her coccyx. They exchanged pro forma hugs and Sidney said with a wink, "Break a leg. We're only picking up the limo if you win."

The ceremonies began at six o'clock Pacific standard time, beamed around the world by satellite. In his small house outside of Belgrade, Tabor Gubca sat up in the middle of the night watching with his wife and kids. Jeremy Ikon, miffed at being bypassed by the Academy, was asleep in the Pensione Frescobaldi on the via Margutta in Rome. In his flat in Kensington, Nigel Bland sipped brandy in bed and tried to stay awake. Jacqueline Fortier and Nikolai Fenderakov watched on the patio of her house in

Benedict Canyon. Enid Schonblum sat in the kitchenette of her studio apartment on Sweetzer Avenue in West Hollywood watching her twelve-inch black-and-white portable. And in a bar on Alvarado, Madison Kearney drank tequila straight and blearily stared at the Lakers game on the TV, trying to remember what a three-second violation was.

Charlie sat with Deidre in the fifth row center, attempting to stay alert and not get caught yawning each time the camera panned the orchestra. It was one of the crueler ordeals he had endured in his life. He just wanted it to be over.

It dragged on for hours. Dance numbers and acceptance speeches followed one another endlessly. They sat in that over-heated fishbowl and waited for people to open envelopes and proclaim the names of those to be crowned. The collective anxiety was overwhelming. If you lit a match, the entire place would go up.

And the winner is . . . squeals of surprise . . . hugs and kisses . . . buttoning the tux jacket . . . the walk up to the stage . . . the girl with the statue . . . the glaring lights . . . the speech buried in the wrong pocket . . .

"I'd like to thank Herbie and Stan and Marcia. . . ." One after another they marched up and claimed their prize, babbled inanities into the microphone to be rebroadcast around the world.

Charlie sat watching with horror. Jesus, what if he actually won? He hadn't considered this possibility when he took the masking tape off the windows and put the tap shoes on again. All he had wanted to do was to make a picture. Now here he was, fifth-row orchestra, sweating profusely in a rented tux, faced with the possibility of having to address the world. He had absolutely nothing to say to the world. He was a complete blank.

By the time the starlet in the sequined gown opened the envelope and announced that the best picture of the year was *Dizzy and Will*, Charlie was nearly catatonic. Deidre squeezed his hand, kissed him lightly on the cheek.

He got up in a daze, groped his way to the end of the row, past the applauding people, past Sidney Auger and Candace De Salvio, past Andre Blue, who had a supercilious smirk on his face. Charlie managed to get into the aisle and orient himself in the glare of the lights.

As he reached to button his tux jacket, he felt the cummerbund go. His worst fears were realized. He was now exposed to the world, buttonless on planetary TV.

Somehow he made it up to the podium, following the retreating cameraman in the general direction of the stage, where the starlet waited for him with a statue. He walked like Napoleon, a hand tucked into his tux jacket firmly on his abdomen, holding his cummerbund closed.

On stage he found himself kissing the starlet, whom he had never met before, as he accepted the statue from her. He turned slowly and looked down at the audience, saw the television cameras devouring him from every angle. He tried to find a point of reference somewhere in that mass of applauding tuxedos. He searched for Deidre Hearn and couldn't find her.

The applause died down. Suddenly it was dead quiet in the Shrine Auditorium. He stood there frozen, unable to make his mouth move, unable to make anything move. He'd had it. He was finished. They would have to come and carry him off, take him away through the back door.

What rescued Charlie Berns was the vision of Benjamin Disraeli. He saw him standing in front of the House of Commons, frail with age, gout-ridden, delivering his famous farewell speech. "England is the taper burning in my night. . . ." If old Ben could shuffle in his condition, the least Charlie could do was give it a try.

He cleared his throat, removed the hand clutching his cummerbund and started to speak.

"It has been a lifelong dream of mine to make a movie about Benjamin Disraeli. . . ."